Everything We Lost

Also by Valerie Geary

Crooked River

Everything We Lost

VALERIE GEARY

wm

WILLIAM MORROW

An Imprint of HarperCollinsPublishers

P.S.™ is a trademark of HarperCollins Publishers.

HarperCollins books may be purchased for educational, business, or sales promotional use. For information, please email the Special Markets Department at SPsales@harpercollins.com.

FIRST EDITION

Designed by Diahann Sturge & Leydiana Rodriguez

Library of Congress Cataloging-in-Publication Data

Names: Geary, Valerie, author.
Title: Everything we lost : a novel / Valerie Geary.
Description: First edition. | New York : William Morrow, [2017]
Identifiers: LCCN 2016049209 | ISBN 9780062566423 (paperback)
Subjects: LCSH: Psychological fiction. | BISAC: FICTION / Suspense. | FICTION
    / Contemporary Women. | FICTION / Coming of Age. | GSAFD: Mystery fiction.
Classification: LCC PS3607.E354 E94 2017 | DDC 813/.6—dc23 LC record available at
    https://lccn.loc.gov/2016049209

ISBN 978-0-06-256642-3

17 18 19 20 21   LSC   10 9 8 7 6 5 4 3 2 1

For you, Dad, with love

Everything We Lost

1

Lucy Durant stood on the roof of her father's house with her toes close to the edge and peered down into a gaping black hole. It was almost midnight, the sky moonless, the front lawn drowned in shadows. Gravity nudged her shoulders forward. How easy it would be to let go, to tip and spin into oblivion. How high up was she? Twenty feet? Thirty? High enough for bones to shatter, though the darkness below was so concentrated it seemed that if she fell, she would fall and fall forever and never hit the ground.

A swell of laughter rose from inside the house. Glasses clinked. Jazz music filtered through the open attic window behind her. Four hours in and the engagement party showed no signs of being anywhere close to winding down. No one noticed her slip away. No one noticed her before that either, as she stood in the corner of the living room staring at her shoes. All the focus was on Robert and Marnie's happily-ever-after. Which was fine with her, or should have been, and might have been, if they had picked any other day but this one. The fifth of December—ten years to the day that her brother went missing.

She had asked Robert to change the date. Any other Saturday, she'd pleaded, but Marnie insisted on the fifth. Marnie and Robert met five months ago on the fifth of July at 5:55 P.M. when the elevator they were riding in stalled between the fifth and sixth floors. They were stuck inside for fifty-five minutes before the fire department came and got them out. The number painted on the fire truck waiting outside the building was fifty-five. It was fate, Marnie liked to say. Her lucky number had always been five, and if that wasn't a sign, she didn't know what was. The universe brought her and Robert together, and now she wanted her fairytale ending, and whatever Marnie wanted, Marnie got.

"We've never made a big deal of it before," Robert had said to Lucy when she brought up the potential awkwardness of an engagement party overlapping their unofficial day of mourning.

It was true. In years past, December fifth came and went without ceremony. Robert never brought it up, and a few times Lucy didn't even realize what day it was until after it was already over and she was left with halfhearted guilt that she'd forgotten something so important. But there were other years when she was plagued with a dark inertia in the days leading up to and following the fifth of December. Years when she didn't see the point of even getting out of bed. Ten years was a long time to miss someone and yet the hollow ache in her belly never seemed to lessen.

After her father refused to change the date of the party, Lucy tried to distract herself with preparations. She sent out invitations, helped decorate the house, and even offered to pick up Marnie's five-tiered, eight-hundred-dollar engagement cake from the bakery the morning of the grand event. What happened next wasn't her fault.

A street preacher had set up his pulpit a few steps from the bakery entrance. He stood barefoot on a five-gallon paint bucket that bulged and started to crack under his shifting weight. The sheet wrapped toga-like around his body was pink daisies on a white background, dirty and stained along the bottom where the hem dragged. Eyes wild and darting, he spread his lips and bared crooked yellow teeth at a small crowd of curious onlookers. His coal-colored hair was unwashed, long and knotted down to his shoulders. White crumbs from some prior meal caught in the tangles of his thick beard. He smelled sour from too much sun, overripe and festering. Beckoning with fingers curling and uncurling, he said, "We are a part of something bigger than anything your small minds can even begin to imagine."

Lucy paused on the outskirts of the crowd to watch. She'd stopped looking for her brother in the faces of strangers years ago, but this street preacher was about the right age, midtwenties, and though she never saw Nolan with a beard, she imagined it would look something like this, unkempt and curling at the ends. She studied him for a moment, noting the stooped shoulders and lanky arms, the familiar cadence of his voice, the fury and ache of a broken mind, a man-child suffering delusions of grandeur.

"I have been given a gift," the street preacher said with a stoner's smile. "To see the connections." He fluttered his fingers away from his body, his hand a bird taking flight. "I know what is coming, and I am here to prepare the way."

Then he turned his cold blue gaze on Lucy. His eyes like

iced-over lakes, bottomless and ringed in dark indigo. Nothing like Nolan's, which were baked-earth and warm.

The street preacher winked at her and in a singsong voice said, "You and you and you and me. The sun and the moon and the stars are free."

Someone threw a handful of coins into a can at the man's feet. The clanging sound jolted Lucy from her daze. She turned away from the preacher, embarrassed to have thought him anything like her brother, and went into the bakery where she paid for the cake without looking at it. Her hands shook a little as she carried the cake to her car. She drove fast, hoping speed might unravel the guilt knot forming in her throat. The street preacher was not her brother, but if he had been, Lucy wasn't sure she would have said or done anything different. She would have walked by in the exact same way, pretending she didn't recognize him, one among hundreds of vagrants in Los Angeles County looking for a quick handout. She still would have lowered her gaze and left him behind.

When she got home, Lucy delivered the cake to the kitchen. Marnie opened the lid and peered inside. She gasped, clutching one hand to her chest. "Oh, Lucy," but her voice was not that of a woman delighted by a perfect engagement cake. Rather, she sounded quite despondent.

"What did you do?" Robert peered into the cake box.

The lilac fondant was cracked straight down the middle. The tiers had slumped and shifted, exposing decadent chocolate cake and glistening raspberry filling. Lucy tried to push the cake back together, smooth the frosting with a butter knife, but another crack appeared, and then another, narrow fault lines spreading ruin.

She tried to explain. "There was this street preacher and

this crowd, they were blocking the sidewalk. I had to push to get through."

She didn't mention anything about the man reminding her of Nolan because her father had made it clear that today was Marnie's day, and there would be no talk of what happened ten years ago, nothing depressing, nothing unsavory, nothing upsetting, end of story.

Marnie sighed and when she looked at the cake a second time, tears gathered on her lashes.

"We could cut it up before the guests get here," Lucy suggested. "Arrange each piece on a plate with those pretty little purple flowers from the garden. What are those called?"

"Pansies." Robert picked up the cake box.

"Right, pansies." Lucy smiled at Marnie, but received nothing in return. "It's a little unconventional, but I doubt anyone will even notice, or if they do, they certainly won't care once they start eating. I'm sure the cake still tastes good. It's just a little cosmetic damage, that's all. I'm sure it's still delicious."

As she spoke, Robert carried the entire cake across the kitchen and dumped it in the trash.

Lucy started to protest, but Robert held up a hand to silence her. "I refuse to serve this mess to my guests."

"Robert . . ." Marnie started, but he silenced her too.

"I'll call Donna. She'll be able to find us something."

Donna was the woman catering the event. She was good at her job, the best, and expensive, but Lucy didn't know how even she would manage this minor miracle of finding such a high-quality cake at the last minute. Robert wasn't going to bother Lucy with the details, though. He shooed her out of the kitchen like she was a child. "I think you've helped enough for one day. Why don't you make yourself scarce until the party starts? And try not to screw anything else up tonight, okay? Do you think you can do that?"

She would certainly try.

Lucy stayed in her room until the first guests arrived a little after eight. Then she wandered downstairs. A table near the front door quickly filled with expensive bottles of wine and flawlessly wrapped gifts. On a smaller table in the center of the room was an exact replica of the cake Lucy had ruined. She went over to see if it was real, but a tall woman wearing a tuxedo shooed her away. Marnie swirled from person to person, a shimmering rainbow of lilac and blue, her elegant dress hugging tight to her curves, her hair done up in a regal twist, her three-carat diamond engagement ring polished and dazzling, her smile even brighter. She kissed cheeks and giggled and charmed and swept Robert and everyone else up in her youth and gaiety. She had been a ballerina once, or so she claimed, and she moved like one now, with grace and a complete awareness that the whole room was watching her.

Everyone but Lucy dressed like they were attending a red carpet event. Long, flowing gowns and sparkling jewels, neatly fitted suits, ties, and polished shoes. Lucy was out of place in black skinny jeans and a baggy navy blue knit top, her russet-colored hair pulled into a nothing-fancy ponytail. But at least she was comfortable. This had been Robert's one concession, a way to ease whatever small amount of guilt he felt for scheduling his engagement party on December fifth: Lucy could wear whatever she wanted. She might have disappeared against the wallpaper, a Prussian blue floral pattern, had it not been for her neon pink and green running shoes, which clashed with everything. Marnie made a face when she saw them, but said nothing.

It was ridiculous, this superstition of Lucy's, this refusal to wear anything else on her feet. No flats, no sandals, absolutely no stilettos. Even slippers or going barefoot for long periods of time made her uncomfortable. She knew it was stupid, with no basis in reality, but she still did it, comforted by the tight laces and cushioned heels, knowing that if all other modes of transportation failed, at least she'd have on the right shoes. At least she could run like hell.

Lucy tucked herself in a corner and watched the house fill with people she didn't know. She recognized a few of Robert's business associates, but couldn't remember their names. They didn't bother to reintroduce themselves; they didn't even notice her. Robert had told her to invite a few of her friends. He'd said it as if she had so many to choose from. She talked to the barista at the coffee shop down the street sometimes, about books and the weather and the woman who came in every day and ordered nothing but foam, but an invitation to her father's engagement party seemed too friendly, too personal for someone who only talked to her because she was hoping for a bigger tip. There were people in her running group, but they, too, were little more than casual acquaintances with running in common and little else. So maybe she was antisocial. So maybe she liked it this way. By distancing herself, she didn't have to talk about personal things, nor was she barraged with the inevitable questions about family and siblings and what she was like when she was a kid. She never had to explain.

The volume of the party increased as more people arrived and then started in on their second and third drinks. Chandeliers threw gold prisms onto freshly waxed oak floors. Someone wondered loudly enough for everyone else to hear, how it was possible for such a beautiful young woman to be marrying such an ugly old man. Someone else answered that money had a way of making anyone handsome. Robert and Marnie laughed with the rest of the room. Then she squeezed him around the waist, looked into his eyes, and said, "I guess love makes you crazy. Because that's what this feels like. Crazy, out of my mind, out of this world, love."

The room heaved one great, affectionate sigh. Robert dipped Marnie in his arms and kissed her like they were teenagers again, young, in love, not caring who watched. A wolf whistle, a toast, the party swirled on.

It was too much for Lucy. The music, the glitter, the sequined bodies and made-up faces, the smell of alcohol on everyone's breath, Marnie's little speech. After the day she'd had, seeing her father with Marnie like this, the two of them happy, living in the present, unconcerned with the past, it cracked open some part of her and she had to escape. She needed fresh air. She carried a tumbler of ginger ale up the stairs two at a time to her attic bedroom and then crawled out the dormer window onto the gently sloped roof where she could finally be alone.

Lucy doubted any of her father's friends knew very much about Nolan, doubted how much even Marnie knew. Robert was a self-made man, a rich man, who made his money buying, selling, and investing in tech companies, who lived in a nice house in a nice neighborhood, who owned a second house in Aspen, who drove a Mercedes or sometimes a Porsche, who still had all his hair and rugged good looks and was about to marry a former ballerina half his age. From the outside, his life was perfect. It was no wonder he kept his shame of a son to himself. Lucy was embarrassment enough. Twenty-four years old, still living with her father, working as his part-time secretary, no college education, no boyfriend, no prospects.

Despite the late hour, the sky above her was a wash of murky sienna, a purée of marine fog and city lights that blotted out most of the stars. Planets like Venus and Mars, as well as a few of the closest, brightest stars were still visible, though they, too, were watery and pale and hard to see. She used to know these handfuls of dots by name, and others that weren't visible here, too dim to break through the pollution blanketing Los Angeles. As a girl, she'd lived in a place much darker than this, and on warm summer nights she and her brother would lie on their backs for hours tracing constellations with their fingertips. Too much time had passed since then, and she'd made no effort to remember. Their names, their stories lost to her now.

Across the street, the neighbor's motion-sensor lights snapped on, illuminating a closed garage door and empty driveway. Lucy scanned the street and sidewalk and the narrow alley between the neighbor's house and the one next door, but didn't see anything that might have triggered the lights. A minute later, the lights snapped off again, returning the driveway to darkness.

She took a sip of ginger ale, then swirled the ice so it clinked against the sides of the glass, regretting now not taking the flute of champagne her father had offered earlier. She was careful about avoiding alcohol, afraid of how it changed her, the ways it muddled her brain and made her too much like her mother, but today was a day she wouldn't mind forgetting. It wouldn't be so bad to wake up tomorrow with no memory of this party and Marnie's ruined cake, or of the madman who looked too much like her brother. It wouldn't be so bad to drown out the words playing on repeat in her head, pulsing to the rhythm of the music below: *ten years today, ten years today, ten years today.*

She was about to climb back inside, go downstairs, find something fiery and strong to mix with her soda, toast to forgetting, and chug, when the power cut out. A loud pop and then the whole block went dark. Up and down the street, the neighbors' porch lights turned off simultaneously, their houses descending into shadows. The music downstairs stopped, and the guests let out gasps of surprise.

Blackouts weren't unusual, especially during hot summers when everyone ran air conditioners at full blast, but it was December and temperatures had been average, if a bit cooler than normal. There had been no squealing tires, no metallic crunch, no indication anyone ran into a power pole either. From her vantage point, Lucy could see over the rooftops to the surrounding neighborhoods where lights still blazed. Only this street, a string of houses to the left and right of her father's, was shrouded in darkness.

The power wasn't out for long. Enough for a few bewildered blinks, and then another pop sounded and the streetlamps flickered and hummed to life again. The porch lights flared bright all at once. The music downstairs exploded. Saxophones and trumpets picked up right where they'd left off. The guests cheered, a sweeping crescendo followed by clinking glasses and heady laughter.

Lucy tried to laugh it off, too, but something caught her attention at the end of the driveway near a row of hedges separating their lawn from the sidewalk. Something crouched in a sliver of deep dark where the streetlights didn't reach. Maybe not, maybe her eyes were playing tricks on her. Then the shadow moved. It shuffled forward a little and then retreated, as if it sensed her watching. A raccoon. It was just a raccoon. What else could it be? But even as she thought it, another part of her brain screamed that it was too big to be a raccoon. Much too big.

She stared at the shadow, waiting for it to move again, willing it to shuffle into the light so she could see its black-rimmed eyes and fur-covered face, confirming its raccoon-ness, but the shadow stayed low, all features concealed. The longer she watched, the more she began to doubt herself. There was nothing there. A blacker shred of night and that was all. Her mind running wild because her father was getting remarried, and today was December fifth, and she'd run into that street preacher who had reminded her, and her brain was finding patterns, making shapes, turning emptiness to substance, filling the world with monsters.

Lucy hurled her tumbler toward whatever-the-hell thing, real or imagined, was hiding in the bushes. The throw fell short. The glass struck the concrete driveway dead center with an explosive crack and splintered to a million tiny pieces, the shards below more visible than the stars above.

2

The well-worn path wove through chaparral and oak. Lucy ran with her arms loose and her head up, taking long strides, devouring the distance. The sun was high enough to make her squint and hot enough to make her sweat, but she didn't slow down inside the shady patches. She pushed her legs harder. Somewhere in the distance a creek burbled. She flew past an old man and his Jack Russell terrier. The dog yapped and whipped around to bite her heels, but he wasn't quick enough. Two miles down. Another three to go before she turned around or even thought about slowing her pace.

She was trying to outrun the dark thread threatening to stitch its way up her spine and into her brain in the shape of a migraine, the last thing she needed right now. She pushed faster, harder, until there were only her shoes hitting the dirt, only her chest aching, only the motion, the blur of trees in her peripheral vision.

Two days before her eighteenth birthday, Lucy thought she saw Nolan in Seattle. Robert had dragged her up to the University of Washington for a campus tour even though he knew she wanted to take a year off to consider her choices before committing. Robert scoffed at her. Of course she was going to college. No child of his was going to become part of the uneducated moocher class. Besides, she'd been offered a track and field scholarship, and there was no way she could turn that down. She didn't bother telling him that she already had.

They were on a walking tour of the campus when she heard a familiar laugh. Loose and free and round and full, boisterous, like the person laughing didn't care who heard. She tracked the sound to a dark-haired boy standing in front of the library talking to a girl with curly brown hair and black-framed glasses. The boy was tall and lanky and he kept pushing his hair out of his eyes. The girl said something, and the boy tilted his head back to laugh again, inviting the whole world to join him. And in that moment, it seemed so perfectly simple: Nolan was alive. He had a new life now. In Seattle. He was a student at UW. He had a girlfriend who made him laugh.

This would have been enough for Lucy, if it had in fact been him. She wouldn't have needed any kind of explanation or reason or promise to reconnect when the time was right. She wouldn't have needed anything but this knowledge that he was alive somewhere. Alive and happy. But the boy glanced in her direction, and the illusion crumbled. His face was too round, his nose too snubbed. His forehead heart-shaped, his chin feminine and soft, his lips too full, his eyes pale. Lucy excused herself from the tour and raced to the nearest bathroom to throw up. She told her father it was food poisoning, that she'd eaten some bad potato salad. They flew home a day early, neither of them saying a single word the almost three hours it took to get to Los Angeles.

Halfway through the flight, the plane passed over the Sierra

Nevada mountains and floated for a while above a flat, tan expanse that from so high up looked completely empty of life, though she knew it wasn't. Lucy stared down at this once familiar terrain that now resembled the lonely surface of Mars. She imagined her brother somewhere below them, wandering circles through the dunes and scrub for years and years, battling sun and storms, digging for water, catching raindrops, chewing leaves, eating ants and grubs, trying to find his way out. Then her mind drifted back to the boy standing in front of the library, how hopeful she'd been, how desperate. It was then she decided to stop looking for Nolan everywhere she went. If he was out there somewhere, and she wasn't convinced he was, but *if* he was, wherever he was, whatever he was doing, if he wanted to, he could find her easily. During the six years that followed, she stayed in the same place. She didn't travel, barely even left the ten-mile radius around her father's house. Now all that was about to change.

Early this morning, Robert had called her into his office. She thought he wanted to talk about the cake, apologize maybe, but when she sat down in the high-backed, antique chair that Marnie had picked up at an estate sale, he started in on the same lecture he gave Lucy every year around this same time. "You know, when I was your age, I was married, with a mortgage, and had already been promoted to senior accounts manager. I was thinking about starting my own business, starting a family. I had plans."

"I have plans," Lucy said.

"Well, I'd love to hear them." Robert laced his hands together across his broad chest and rocked back in his oversized leather office chair. His mahogany desk took up half the room, but somehow he didn't look small behind it. The opposite, actually: the desk a dollhouse size and her father a giant.

She knew what he was thinking. Here she was, twenty-four, in the prime of her life. She should be out on her own by now, doing whatever it was other twenty-four-year-olds did. Traveling the world, sleeping with older men, working entry-level jobs in Fortune 500 companies, cozying up to her boss, building her résumé, going to bars and clubs and underground rock concerts, meeting new people, dancing, drinking, experiencing life. All Robert wanted for her was what any father wanted for his daughter. Opportunities. Money enough not to worry. Love that lasts. He wanted her to be happy. What he didn't seem to understand, what no one did, was how easy it was for a person to get stuck. There were so many dead ends in life, so many wrong turns and missteps and she found it all so paralyzing. It was safer to stay put. You couldn't get lost if you didn't go anywhere.

He kept a large bronze statue on the corner of his desk. A bald eagle with wings spread wide, talons clasped tight around a skinny log. Lucy stared at it instead of her father when she asked, "Have you spoken to Detective Mueller recently?"

Robert reached over and made a small adjustment to the statue, straightening the base so it was flush to the edge of the desk. "You know how this works. If they have any new information, they'll call."

"But we could call first, couldn't we?" She knew it was a waste of time. The detective would tell them the same thing he'd been telling them from the beginning. Without new leads, new evidence, new witnesses, they were at a dead end and there was nothing more to be done but wait. Sometimes missing persons cases found resolution years later. Sometimes they never did. It all appeared to hinge on luck and good timing.

"I didn't call you in here to talk about your brother." Robert leaned his elbows on his desk. His gaze narrowed as he studied her, trying to figure out where he'd gone wrong, how he ended up with such a failure of a child, two failures, if he counted Nolan, though Lucy knew he never did.

"We only want what's best for you, Luce," he said.

"We" being he and Marnie. As if her opinion counted, as if at twenty-nine, Marnie had lived so much more life than Lucy. As if five years made a difference when it came to having your shit figured out.

"Maybe I should have pushed you harder," he said. "But I know how difficult it's been for you, and I wanted to give you time to grieve, to try and figure things out on your own. I think I've done that. I think I've given you more than enough time. And now that Marnie and I are getting married, well, she just thinks . . ." Robert folded his hands together on the desk. "We both think it's the right time."

Lucy struggled to understand. The right time for what? She shuddered at the thought of a pregnant Marnie waddling around the house, of having to pretend to care about a new sibling who would never even come close to replacing the one she'd lost.

"You can stay through the end of the month, of course," Robert said. "Spend Christmas with us. And we'll help you with a security deposit, first month's rent if you need it. Consider it a housewarming gift."

They were kicking her out. She had seen this coming, was surprised it hadn't happened sooner, like after she dropped out of college her freshman year, but still her eyes blurred with tears that she quickly blinked away. She wasn't ready. She would never be ready.

"You should also start thinking about a new job." At least he looked sorry about this part. "A full-time position. Something that can offer you a bigger paycheck, better benefits. You can still work part-time with me, of course, if you need the extra money, but I think it will do you some good to get out there and see how the rest of the world works."

What else could she do? She agreed to his plan, gave him the compliant smile he wanted, then left the office, laced up her running shoes, and headed for the nature park at the end of the street.

For ten years Robert had sheltered her from the tangled memories of her past and the public's relentless curiosity. He had allowed her to hide from a history she didn't understand anymore, if she'd ever understood it in the first place. Ten years ducking and avoiding and doing what she could to not think about Nolan and the night he disappeared. Ten years hoping someone else would come up with answers. But no one had. They were no closer to finding out what happened to Nolan than the day he went missing, and her hope was a desperate and useless thing, a thorny vine bleeding her heart dry.

Lucy reached the end of the trail. She turned and ran back the way she'd come. Her freshman year of high school she'd joined the track and field team to impress a boy, a boy she thought she would love forever. She placed in a few events, but was never a star like Patrick. None of them were. He was born running, and always came in first, minutes ahead of the others during practice and competitions. The rest of them breaking their bodies to try and keep up. When she left Bishop, she lost touch with everyone, including Patrick, but the running stayed with her. Her only love now.

It was strange how some memories from that time were so clear, while others were blurry and could not be trusted, obscured by time and distance, or missing completely. Take the day Nolan went missing, for example. She could recall quite clearly what time she woke that morning, what she ate for breakfast, when she left the house. But what happened later that night, who she talked to, what she did, how she got home—there were several empty hours, as if someone had taken an eraser to her brain and scrubbed it clean. She remembered what she told people she remembered, after he was already gone and there were questions needing answers, but they were things she made up at the spur of the moment because saying she didn't know, that she couldn't remember, felt too much like an admission. Of what, she wasn't certain, but saying something seemed better at the time than saying nothing. She doubted that remembering the truth about what happened that night would make any difference or bring him back to her, but sometimes she wondered, *What if it does?*

There were a few things she knew with certainty, facts established apart from herself. Witnesses, evidence, concrete things that other people could turn over and discuss and confirm, saying, *Yes, it happened like this.*

On December 5, 1999, sixteen-year-old Nolan Durant left home with his wallet and a backpack filled with clothes, food, his toothbrush, and several hundred dollars in cash. He never returned. The missing person's report was officially filed with the Inyo County Sheriff's Department four days later on December 9, 1999, once it became clear to the boy's mother that he was not with his father or with friends or camping out in the desert by himself. An alert went out to all relevant agencies and media outlets. A few days later, Mr. Stuart Tomlinson, a neighbor of the Durants, came forward and told the investigating officer that he heard yelling around midnight on December 5, 1999, and when he went to see what was going on, he witnessed Nolan shoving someone into his pickup and then speeding away from the house. He was unable to offer any specifics about the person Nolan supposedly left with that night because of poor lighting and bad angles. He was certain of only two things: Nolan drove off in his pickup around midnight, and he was not alone.

Perhaps there should have been a rush at this point to uncover more leads before the trail went cold. Perhaps if Nolan had been a girl instead of a boy, or six instead of sixteen, things might have gone differently. As it happened, the sheriff's department, which was already short-staffed because of the holidays, suddenly found themselves inundated with panicked calls about Y2K and potential grid shutdowns, and Nolan's case waited in limbo until a research scientist working at Owens Valley Radio Observatory called almost three weeks later to report an abandoned vehicle near their property. A navy blue 1989 GMC Sierra. The exact make and model Nolan was last seen driving. It didn't take long for police to run the plates and identify him as the registered owner.

The pickup was parked on the shoulder of Leighton Road less than one hundred yards from the telescopes. The doors were shut, but unlocked. The windows rolled up. The gas tank a quarter full. The keys were in the ignition, but there was no sign of Nolan's backpack, his wallet, or the money, which led the police to believe he left town of his own volition. There was something else found inside the vehicle that the public never heard about. An officer had come to Lucy and her mother's house the next day carrying a black marble composition notebook in a plastic evidence bag. When he asked if they recognized it, Sandra started crying uncontrollably, and Lucy was forced to answer in her mother's place. It was Nolan's casebook, a journal he carried with him everywhere so he could take meticulous notes about supposed UFO sightings and things he called "Strange Happenings." The officer put on a pair of gloves to remove the notebook from the bag and turned to the last entry. Lucy couldn't remember the exact wording, but it was something about how the world was unraveling, how he couldn't tell what was real anymore. The only line she remembered was the last one, where he'd pressed down hard enough for the paper to tear. *I'm sorry.*

No one except Lucy and her parents and the investigating officers had ever read his last entry. The media didn't know about it, but it was still a matter of police record, evidence filed away with the rest, stuck in a box and forgotten on some basement shelf.

After Nolan's pickup was discovered, there were a few searches of the area around the observatory, but nothing of interest was found. There was a powerful storm the night he went missing and several smaller ones in the days following. The police said that whatever evidence there might have been once—footprints, tire tracks, remains—was likely washed away. Posters went up around town, asking for tips, and for a while, people were interested. They speculated and came to their own conclusions. Some said suicide. Some said he joined a cult. Some suspected a drug deal gone wrong, or a gang hit. Maybe he'd been put into witness protection. Most certainly he was dead. A psychic wanted a thousand bucks to deliver a message from Nolan's tormented spirit. Then a tip came in, someone swearing they saw him alive and well in Reno. None of it was true, or all of it was, depending on who you asked. No one knew anything, really, and speculating can only last so long before people start to get bored. Especially when there's no body, no evidence of any heinous crime or any kind of crime at all. And especially with a kid like Nolan who had always been a bit of an outcast.

The media moved on to other stories. Then someone started tagging the posters, drawing flying saucers around the edges and giving Nolan antennae and a ray gun. After that, the posters were torn down and thrown away. Finally, the police shrugged their shoulders and said that given the evidence to date, Nolan was most likely a runaway. Most likely, he would come home on his own whenever he felt like it. Or maybe he never would, but that was his choice, too. They began to focus their manpower and resources on other cases. Then at the end of January, a pretty, blond mother of two went missing, and the public, the police, the whole rest of the world, forgot about Nolan completely. Robert was satisfied with the Inyo County sheriff's investigation and conclusion, and stopped calling the house every day to check in. But Sandra refused to accept the theory that Nolan had left without telling anyone. He was a good boy who loved his family. She tried to keep the public's interest by hiring a private investigator and paying someone to set up a web page. But she also stopped sleeping and started drinking heavily, and by February, she was no longer fit to be anyone's mother. By March, Lucy was living in Los Angeles with her father, and trying her best to put the worst day of her life behind her.

Those were the "facts." The things Lucy didn't have to remember because they were in the case file and the newspapers
and on the Internet where anyone could find them. And the
rest of it? The missing hours of that day, the things she couldn't
remember, the memories that remained elusive and fickle,
slippery at the back of her mind, the fleeting moments, images
that felt more like dreams than reality? These were the reasons
she ran.

3

Lucy's cell phone chirped from across the room. She ignored it and continued pulling shirts and blouses off hangers and tossing them into three piles. Keep, Goodwill, Garbage. She was amazed at how easy it was to accumulate so much stuff without even trying. She could take it all with her, rent a truck, fill it with everything she owned, cram whatever she could fit into a studio apartment, and put the rest in storage. But that seemed like a lot of effort for things that were so easily replaceable. Her cell phone chirped again, and then started to ring. She grabbed it off the bed. Another number she didn't recognize. She'd lost count of how many calls she'd gotten so far this morning. She sent this new caller to voice mail and went back to sorting clothes.

Christmas had come and gone, a quiet affair with the three of them exchanging gifts early in the morning before Robert and Marnie drove to San Diego for the weekend to celebrate with her parents. Lucy had spent most of that time by herself, curled up on the couch watching old movies and eating caramel popcorn. Now she found herself with less than a week left to finish packing and find a nice place she could afford, which every minute seemed a little more impossible. She wondered what Robert would do if she refused to leave, if January rolled around and he found her still sleeping in her attic bedroom, all her clothes still hanging in the closet. What *could* he do?

Her phone rang again, the number blocked. This was getting ridiculous. She ignored the call, but a few seconds later the ringtone went off for the thousandth time, another blocked number, or the same one, it was impossible to tell.

This time she answered. "What?"

The caller seemed shocked either by her harsh tone or that he was finally speaking to a real person. He stammered a few seconds before spitting out his name. "I'm Kevin Handler with the *San Francisco Chronicle*. I'm trying to reach Lucy Durant?"

"Wrong number." Lucy hung up.

Sometimes this happened around the anniversary of her brother's disappearance. A reporter would want to write a follow-up piece, a "Where Are They Now?" kind of deal, and they would call to interview her for this paper or that blog, or tape her for some *48 Hours* special on missing children. Usually, though, the calls came a few months before the actual anniversary, and in the past, there had never been so many. They were also never this persistent. Lucy didn't give interviews, to anyone, even when they offered her money. Most of the time all she had to say was "No, thank you," and they left her alone. Maybe this year was different because it was the tenth anniversary. A decade gone. Maybe there was something special about that.

The phone rang. Again. How these people got her number,

she never knew. She kept a low profile online. She had a Twitter account, but she didn't use her real name and mostly followed celebrities and news outlets. She stayed away from Facebook entirely. They found her anyway, and Lucy sometimes wondered why they didn't put their energies and resources to better use. Like finding her brother, for instance.

She listened to the first of ten new voice mails.

"Lucy, this is Jupitar Pilar. I'm with *Specter Magazine* and I was hoping you might be able to answer a few questions about the UFO your brother saw the night before he went missing. Call me anytime at—"

Lucy deleted the message and then listened to the rest. Though they were calling from different publications, ranging from the more serious news outlets like *The Oregonian* to the bizarre pseudo news journals like *Conspiracy USA*, they were all asking about the same thing: the UFO Nolan saw the night before he went missing. There was even a message from a producer at Coast to Coast AM radio who wanted to schedule an interview about her close encounters. "I'm sure you know how things like this can run in the family," the chipper woman said. "We'd love to get your take. Why you think they took your brother, but left you behind?"

Lucy deleted all ten voice mails without taking down a single name or number. She'd received a few calls from UFO freaks over the years, though most of the time they sent emails. They were usually men, and she imagined them fat and hunkered down in front of computers in dank basements, their faces covered in acne and Cheetos dust. Most of the time they wrote to her about their own encounters, as if they thought she cared. Sometimes they wrote wanting information about Nolan, or offering ridiculous theories about what might have happened to him. She never replied to any of them, never thought to take them seriously. Who would?

The phone buzzed in her hand. She flinched, but didn't answer. After five rings the phone went silent, and Lucy released the breath she'd been holding. A few seconds later, the phone chirped, letting her know she'd received a text. Surprisingly, no one had thought to try this before. The message was brief. Care to comment? This was followed by a link. There was no name included, no information about who had sent the text other than the phone number. She clicked on the link out of reflex more than anything else. If she'd been thinking at all she would have deleted the text as soon as it arrived.

The link took her to an article published a week earlier in *Strange Quarterly*, an online magazine for all things supernatural and unexplained. The headline read in bold:

PHOTOGRAPHS TAKEN BY MISSING BISHOP BOY PROOF OF EXTRATERRESTRIAL ENCOUNTER

Lucy scanned the article, the words running together, until she got to the photograph halfway down the page. It was dark, a night shot, and the object centered against the black background was blurry and out of focus. A glowing blue orb, a corona of light spreading around a blazing hot center. It could have been anything—a passing car, a streetlamp, the moon— but Lucy knew exactly what it was and with growing dread she scrolled back to the top of the article to read from the beginning.

The writer, a man named Wyatt Riggs, said he'd been contacted by Sandra Durant one year earlier, claiming she had proof her son was abducted by aliens. After many subsequent interviews and further research, they decided it was finally time to make Sandra's evidence public. She claimed the photographs were taken by Nolan exactly one night before he disappeared and that he'd dropped them off at Walgreens the following morning to be developed, but vanished before he had a chance to retrieve them. Walgreens contacted Sandra a few days later to pick them up. She brought them to the police, but the police determined them irrelevant to the investigation and so she took them home and put them in a box in the closet where they stayed for nine years until, she said, her eyes were finally opened to the truth.

The article then rehashed the details surrounding Nolan's disappearance, the facts as they were—everything the local paper printed ten years ago. One paragraph described how the photos were examined by several experts and determined not to be doctored or Photoshopped in any way, that they did indeed appear authentic. The final paragraph clarified that Sandra was coming forward now, all these years later, because she was ready for the world to know what really happened on the night of December 5, 1999. She was tired of government cover-ups, disinformation, and police collusion. Nolan's story, the real one, deserved to be told. The photographs, she said, were proof of an alien encounter, and there was a high probability that the craft captured on film during this initial encounter was the same craft that abducted Nolan the following night.

An email address and an appeal to the public for any information related to Nolan's disappearance or recent UFO activity was listed at the end of the article along with a color photograph of a man and a woman standing close together. The man was tall with short black hair slicked back from a high, strong forehead. He had thick eyebrows, broody and stern. He stared down the camera, his expression serious. Lucy guessed he was in his mid to late thirties. He looked like a man who knew things, a man people trusted. The woman was older and several inches shorter. Her dyed blond hair styled in a shoulder-length, no-fuss bob. She clutched an envelope with the Walgreens logo printed on it. The caption read: *Sandra Durant with world-renowned ufologist and paranormal investigator Wyatt Riggs.*

Lucy made the image bigger. She stared at her mother's face, the crooked tilt of her mouth, the one-sided dimple that was really a chicken pox scar, the blue-green eyes so bright people always asked if she wore contacts. She'd gained weight. Her clothes were disheveled. There were dark circles under her eyes and wrinkles that Lucy didn't remember from before.

She scrolled back to the image of the glowing blue orb. *Photograph of UFO sighted outside Durant residence on December 4, 1999.* She didn't even realize Nolan had taken any photographs that night, but here it was, blasted across the Internet for the whole world to see and being held up as proof of a theory that was completely insane. In the months before he went missing, Nolan's behavior had become increasingly disturbed, his conversations turning more and more to UFOs and close encounters, but they'd all dismissed him—Lucy, her parents—no one believed he was being contacted by beings from another planet. He was making it up, or he was sick, but none of what he said was happening was actually true. It couldn't be.

Quickly, Lucy ran a search for her brother's name. Several articles had been posted in the last twenty-four hours, all referencing the original *Strange Quarterly* article. The story wasn't exactly going viral, but it was getting enough attention to make her uncomfortable.

She went downstairs to the living room, where Robert and Marnie, returned from San Diego this morning, relaxed with post-dinner glasses of wine. Soft music played on the stereo. Robert reclined in an overstuffed chair, a Theodore Roosevelt biography spread open in his lap. Marnie perched on the edge of a floral print couch and flipped through a stack of interior design books. Neither of them looked up when Lucy entered the room.

She held the phone out to her father. "Have you seen this?"

Robert's eyes narrowed as he read the headline. Then he took the phone from Lucy and skimmed the rest of the article.

"Unbelievable," he said when he finished, giving the phone back to Lucy.

"Did you know about the photographs?" Lucy asked. "Did you know she was going to do this?"

He sighed. "Of course not. I haven't spoken to Sandra in years."

"Can you call her for me? Tell her not to do stuff like this anymore? These reporters keep calling—" As if to prove her point, the phone started ringing. She turned it off completely and slipped it into her back pocket.

"Your mother stopped listening to me a long time ago." His eyes drifted back to the book in his lap. He turned a page, his way of letting her know this conversation was over.

Back in her bedroom, Lucy threw herself down onto the bed, across from the disarray of clothes waiting to be sorted. When viewed separately, the events of the past few weeks— first the street preacher, then getting kicked out of her father's house, now her mother's supposed new evidence—were of little consequence, really nothing more than coincidence. Except Lucy couldn't stop thinking of something Nolan had said to her a long time ago: *One strange event is an anomaly, two is a fluke, three is a pattern and we should probably start paying attention.* She took a deep breath and reminded herself that toward the end, Nolan believed a lot of things that didn't make sense. Weird things happened, and there didn't have to be a connection. None of this had to mean anything.

The article, the sudden increased attention, this anxiety boiling in the pit of her stomach—it would all die down eventually. It had before. She just had to wait it out. Something else would happen. Another more interesting article would go viral, and the name "Nolan Durant" would again be forgotten. Like a meteorite streaking across the heavens. One minute all glory and splendor. The next, gone. Burned down to nothing, swallowed up by the black, eternal sky.

CLASSIFIED: TOP SECRET
INQUIRY AND EVIDENCE
UFOs and Other Extraterrestrial Phenomenon
FIELD INVESTIGATOR:
Nolan R. Durant

CASEBOOK ENTRY #1

SIGHTING:
The Buttermilk Lights

DATE: July 15, 1999

LONGITUDE/LATITUDE: 37.329170 W, 118.577170 N

SYNOPSIS: At approximately 20:00 hours, I observed lights moving erratically in the sky from the North to Southwest. The lights moved quickly at first and then slowed as they approached, hovering for several seconds directly overhead before moving out of sight behind the Sierra Nevada. No engine sounds detected.

OBJECT DESCRIPTION: 6 disc-shaped lights, orange around the edges and bright white in the center, first noticed out of the North traveling Southwest approximately 45° off the horizon. Discs were evenly spaced and maintained a 2x3 formation. Diameter of each disc estimated to be 20 feet.

OTHER WITNESS STATEMENTS: Several potential witnesses fled the scene before I had a chance to interview them. The two who stayed behind are both minors, Patrick Tyndale (age 17) and Lucy Durant (age 14), and are proving to be anxious, hostile, and contradictory.

WEATHER INFORMATION: 75°F, winds from the S at 7mph, clear skies, sunset at 20:14.

LOCATION DESCRIPTION: California, Owens Valley, West of Bishop, Eastern Sierra Nevada foothills, off Buttermilk Road in Buttermilk Country, an area popular with climbers. Closest landmark: Grandpa Peabody Boulder. Valley area population is less than 20,000. It should be noted that Owens Valley has an extensive history of reported UFO activity. Possible hot spot.

PHYSICAL EVIDENCE: None collected.

CONCLUSION: Visual evidence suggests encounter with extraterrestrial craft, but more earthly explanations do exist and given the reluctance of witnesses to come forward with the truth, I am forced to mark this sighting as Undetermined.

Before leaving the house, Nolan wasn't feeling optimistic about a sighting, but he prepared anyway. He gathered everything Wyatt said a good investigator might need and stuffed it into his backpack: casebook, three pens, a tape recorder, binoculars, a compass, a retractable tape measure, plastic bags for taking samples, rubber gloves, a pocketknife, and a camera, which technically belonged to his mother, though he hadn't seen her use it since before the divorce. It was a Nikon 35mm point-and-shoot. Easy to use. Easy to develop. Lucy carried a bottle of water.

"What are we looking for again?" She scanned the ground, turning over rocks with the toe of her hiking boots.

Nolan pointed at the pale violet turned indigo sky. "Lights, shapes, silhouettes, reflections. Anything out of the ordinary."

"UFOs . . ." She sounded skeptical.

"You don't have to come." He readjusted the straps of his backpack and kept walking, following the narrow footpath leading from their house on Skyline Road through the boulder lands to their favorite stargazing spot, a wide, flat rock on a hill that overlooked all of Owens Valley.

They used to come to this rock all the time, hunting meteorites in the surrounding scrub until dusk when they would stretch out on their backs on the sun-warmed stone to watch daylight fade and the stars blink on. Sometimes they brought Nolan's telescope; other times they took turns telling stories about Starman and Asteroid Girl, an intergalactic superhero duo, who flew their spaceship into uncharted territories making contact with other life-forms and saving the universe, one troubled planet at a time. Until their mother called them home for dinner.

He thought it would be nice having Lucy with him today, like old times. If he witnessed a UFO, she'd be there to corroborate, but if he saw nothing, at least he'd have her good company. But there was a tension between them now that hadn't existed before, a strained silence he didn't know how to navigate. They were spending less time together this summer than in past summers. Nolan had a job now, working for minimum wage as a courtesy clerk at Bishop's Grocery where he gathered carts from the parking lot, bagged groceries, helped old ladies to their cars, swept floors. Grunt work, basically, whatever his boss asked him to do. And lately, any free time he had he spent with Wyatt and the UFO Encounters Group,

either at meetings or out hunting UFOs. Lucy seemed less than
enthusiastic, even a bit confused, about this increased interest
in a hobby that before had been little more than a game of
make-believe.

He'd invited her to a meeting once, hoping it might help
her understand him better, what he was doing and why it mattered, but she'd curled her lips in disgust. "You don't really
believe in that stuff, do you? I mean, *really*, really?"

He'd shrugged. "So what if I do?"

Nolan first became aware of the group after someone posted
a flyer to the community message board outside the grocery store break room. The flyer was half-hidden behind one
offering guitar lessons, but the neon-green sheet and bold let-
tering caught his attention.

....

WE ARE NOT ALONE!!!

Have you ever experienced any of the following?
- **Insomnia**
- **Feelings of panic**
- **Feelings of being watched**
- **Inexplicable marks, scars, or cuts on your body**
- **Waking up in a different part of the house or
  wearing different clothes**
- **Missing time**
- **A sense of recognition and camaraderie with
  someone you've never met before**
- **Sighting strange lights or objects in the sky
  above your house**

- Feelings of paralysis, inability to move your arms and legs
- Unexplained pains in any part of your body
- Night terrors

You may be one of the millions of people being contacted by beings from another dimension.

YES, ALIENS!
THEY'RE HERE!

Your friends and family might think you're crazy. The government is definitely lying to you. But do not fear! There are others like you! Others who have had similar experiences, people who are questioning the current state of "reality." We can help you understand what's happening. We can offer peace.

UFO ENCOUNTERS GROUP, EASTERN SIERRA CHAPTER: Join us every Saturday starting at 7 P.M. in the basement of the Bishop Senior Citizen Center, 74 Adams Street. Coffee and cookies provided.

THE TRUTH IS OUT THERE!!

A flutter of recognition tickled his throat, and he found himself unpinning the flyer from the board, folding it in thirds, and stuffing it in his pocket.

For the next few days, he carried it with him everywhere, taking it out sometimes to read it again, folding it and unfolding it so often that the creases softened the paper and it tore a little. He tried to tell himself it was simple coincidence how many things he had in common with people who'd been contacted—the many sleepless nights, the panic he sometimes felt stepping outside his front door, the way his skin tingled for no reason, how often strangers stared at him in passing, the peculiar lights he saw when he was ten, the time he woke up in the middle of the night to find himself curled up on the couch fully dressed, with both shoes on, laces tied, but no memory of how he'd gotten there. He tried, like his mother taught him, to find a more reasonable explanation and had convinced himself that it was probably just stress-related, probably hormones, the misery of puberty, and given a few more years, his life, his brain, his body would return to normal, or some version of normal anyway. He was passing through the living room on his way to the kitchen to throw out the flyer when his attention caught on the morning news program his mother was watching on television.

"The woman claims the lights hovered above her swimming pool for several minutes before flying away," the reporter said.

Nolan stopped midstride and stared at the screen. The reporter, a blond woman wearing too much makeup, shoved her microphone into a young man's face. The man stood remarkably still as his name flashed on the bottom of the screen: *Wyatt Riggs, Ufologist.* He stared into the camera with such intensity, Nolan took a step back.

There was no humor in Wyatt Riggs's voice when he spoke. "Based on the statement and the photographic evidence provided, we can conclude that this was most likely an earth light, a rare but natural, and very terrestrial, phenomenon. They're known in some places as ghost lights or spook lights, and seem to occur in areas experiencing seismic activity or tectonic stress."

"So not a flying saucer from outer space?" The reporter smiled at him.

"No. At least . . . not this time." Wyatt smiled into the camera, and Nolan found himself smiling back, feeling like he was being let in on a remarkable secret.

His mother muttered something about poppycock and nonsense, and then changed the channel.

Nolan retreated to the den where they kept the family computer and searched for information about Wyatt Riggs online. A graduate of Bishop Union High School, class of '91, more recently he'd been registered at Cerro Coso Community College, though Nolan couldn't find any information about what he was studying or if he still attended. More notably, Wyatt appeared to be a rising star in the paranormal community, especially concerning UFOs. He had written several articles for *UFO Monthly* and a handful of other paranormal magazines. He had also spoken at a few regional UFO festivals. His main topics of discussion appeared to be the future of UFO studies, how to bring legitimacy to the community, and pressing prominent astronomers and planetary scientists to give more time, money, and serious consideration to the UFO and abduction phenomenon. One article quoted him saying, "How can we expect to find answers if we refuse to look?" And in an obscure notation at the bottom of another, Nolan found this: *Wyatt runs a UFO Encounters Group that meets every Saturday at the Bishop Senior Center and is open to the public.*

Nolan took the flyer from his pocket and unfolded it. It seemed like more than simple coincidence then, rather a strange sort of fate nudging him in a new direction. Or perhaps this was the direction he was always meant to take; it was only now becoming clear to him. He attended his first UFO Encounters meeting the very next Saturday.

His introduction to Wyatt was brief, perfunctory. A quick flash of teeth, a softening around the eyes, "Happy to have you joining us today," and then the rest of the group gathered, taking their seats in a circle of chairs. Nolan sat next to an older woman with gold bangles around her wrists and steel-colored hair who introduced herself as Gabriella.

They started off sharing stories. *Experiences.* That's what Wyatt called them.

"Who has an *experience* they'd like to share with the group?" he asked after they were all seated.

Gabriella raised her hand and spoke about an extraterrestrial being named Chrysler who had been visiting her since she was a child. "He's come to me two nights in a row this week. He says change is on the horizon, but seems unable or unwilling to provide me with any other details."

Another woman named Tilly talked about a book she was reading about extraterrestrial encounters and abductions written by a Harvard professor and Pulitzer Prize winner, a man trying to shake up the scientific community from the inside. A man named Jim said he believed his niece was being abducted. She kept waking in the middle of the night screaming and had started to wet the bed. Nolan listened to all of this, feeling both bewildered and relieved. He stared at his palm, the skin still tingling from Wyatt's firm handshake.

For as long as he could remember, he'd been curious about extraterrestrials. He liked thinking about life on other planets, about all the things that might be going on in the far reaches of the universe, imagining how there might be something bigger and more expansive than this small, sad, lonely planet

Earth. He loved the movies *E.T.* and *Close Encounters of the Third Kind,* had seen both several times, had kept watching them, even after the boys who used to be his friends moved on to scarier ones, horror flicks like *Invasion of the Body Snatchers* and *Alien.* He read any kind of alien or UFO book he could find at the library—fiction, nonfiction, it didn't matter. He had a shelf in his bedroom dedicated to his favorites: *Communion* by Whitley Strieber, *Missing Time* by Budd Hopkins, and Arthur C. Clarke's novel *Childhood's End.* All three books came from his uncle Toby, his father's brother, a man no one talked about anymore. The books arrived in the mail a few months before Nolan's tenth birthday, around the time his parents were finalizing their divorce. There was no return address on the package, only a postmark from Juneau and a hastily scribbled note tucked inside: *Trust no one.*

Nolan didn't know what to think of the note, but he devoured the books, wondering at the extraordinary events Strieber and the people in Hopkins's book had experienced, wondering at their certainty and wanting to absorb it somehow. It was the same with this group, each person speaking with confidence and conviction about mysteries and miracles, which Nolan always had trouble describing. But now, here he was, in a room full of people of varying ages and all different backgrounds, and though Nolan was new to the group and the youngest in attendance, no one talked down to him or looked at him strangely. No one called him a freak or a weirdo or told him to grow up, and it seemed like finally he had found a safe place filled with people like him, people who gazed at stars and believed impossible things.

Then it was his turn. All eyes on him, and Wyatt leaned slightly forward in his chair, singling him out, as if there were no more important person in the room at this moment. "And what about you, Nolan? Do you have something you'd like to share?"

"Well, there was this one time . . ." he started. "But it was probably nothing . . ."

He told them anyway about the lights he saw when he was ten, a few days after his dad packed up the rest of his stuff and moved to Los Angeles. Nolan and Lucy were rambling together in the boulder lands behind their house when they saw a cluster of glowing orange orbs, small and far away, moving like yo-yos along infinite lengths of string. It was a faded memory, easily explained away as lightning or helicopters passing, and so when Wyatt began peppering him with questions about relative size and distance and speed, Nolan stumbled over the answers.

Wyatt sat back in his chair with a disappointed sigh. "If you want people to take you seriously, Nolan, then you must take yourself, and the things you experience, seriously. You must pay attention to the details. Specificity is important. Things that can be measured. All of the rest is anecdotal. A nice story to tell at parties but hardly worth holding up as evidence."

Nolan hung his head, disappointed in himself too. Then Gabriella told Wyatt to go easy, it wasn't like they taught UFO Investigation 101 in school.

That's when Wyatt suggested Nolan start keeping a case-book. "If we aren't writing down Sightings and Strange Happenings when they happen, then we might forget they even happened in the first place and then no one will ever believe us. We have to get our facts straight. We have to be meticulous and systematic. The public wants proof. They need it. They're demanding science, so we're going to give them science. Nonbelievers look at people like us and assume one of two things. Either we're crazy or we're starved for attention. We must be extra vigilant and work overtime to prove them wrong."

The next day Nolan bought an unassuming black marble composition book, and for the past few weeks, he'd been carrying it with him everywhere, ready to write down any encounter, any sighting or suspicious activity, anything that might be proof of extraterrestrial visitations. He looked for patterns. He paid close attention. He scanned the skies as often as possible, but so far he'd seen nothing worth writing about, nothing very interesting at all.

Laughter ricocheted off the huge boulders scattered across the mesa leading up to the rock. Lucy hesitated, glancing behind her in the direction of the house, but Nolan kept walking, coming over a small rise to find a group of teenagers sprawled across the rock—*his* rock—lounging, drinking beers, passing around clove cigarettes. He recognized most of them from school, Patrick Tyndale and Grant Highbringer, Megan and Natasha and a girl he thought was named Laura. The rest he'd never seen before. The group fell silent when Nolan approached. Lucy stayed a few steps behind, her boots scuffing the dirt.

He'd been friends with Patrick and Grant until eighth grade when he'd gotten sick, really sick, and had to miss several weeks of school. During his absence, something changed, he didn't know how or why, but when he finally returned, his friends were no longer his friends. They avoided him at lunch, teased him in the hallways, passed mean notes behind his back in class. They called him Space Case and Alien Lover and Little Green Freak. It sucked. The worst part was Patrick—his best friend, ex–best friend now. He'd tried several times to find out what he'd done wrong and how he could fix it, but each time Patrick told him to get lost, and stay lost.

Nolan fixed his gaze on his old friend now. "What are you doing here?"

He knew this was Nolan's sacred space. Nolan was the one who'd brought him here when they were still friends, showed him the trail, the incredible view, the way the stars appeared like magic when the sun went down. This place had been sacred for him once too.

"Free country." Patrick tipped a beer to his lips, finishing it in one swig, then tossed the empty can off the edge of the rock. It clanked against loose stones and tumbled down a slight hill. Glancing at Nolan's backpack and the binoculars around his neck, he asked, "Trying to make contact with your little green friends again?"

The other kids laughed. Someone flicked a cigarette butt at Nolan. It struck his chest before falling into the dirt. The ember flared, and he stomped it out with his shoe before it could spark a flame in the surrounding dry brush. He turned to Lucy. "Let's go."

Patrick hopped off the rock. "You don't have to go, Lucy. Not if you don't want to. You can stay, hang out with the big kids."

His hand lingered on her arm and he bent to whisper something in her ear. Lucy blushed, but Nolan no longer paid them any attention. He turned his eyes to the charcoal sky. The stars had yet to make an entrance, but Mars flickered on, tinted red, and there was Jupiter too, a brilliant diamond in a bed of coal. He scanned the horizon, then arched his neck to search the sky directly above him. A glorious spread of night, thick as black-berry jam, he could easily lose himself in its sweetness.

It happened fast. Suddenly. Nolan didn't even have time to grab the camera from his backpack. Six orange lights appeared, a wavering brightness against the dark sky.

Nolan grabbed hold of Lucy's arm and pointed. "Do you see that?"

She looked up, but the lights were already gone.

"They were right over there. See where that juniper bush is? Hovering right there." He walked a few steps in that direction, pulling Lucy with him, but she dragged her feet and squirmed against his grip.

"Knock it off, Nolan," she said in a low voice, her eyes darting to Patrick.

"Did you see them?" Nolan asked again, louder, this time directing his question to everyone, not just Lucy.

No one responded.

"There were lights? Six of them?" He stared at the place where the lights had been, willing them to reappear.

"Lights." Patrick squinted up at the sky. "Like that one?" He pointed at Jupiter.

"Nolan, let me go." Lucy twisted her arm to break free of him.

Nolan tightened his grip. He blinked, and a star appeared, and then another. "Please, tell me you saw them," he said to the group still clustered on the rock. He searched their half-drunk faces. "Someone, one of you, must have seen them! They were right there, for God's sake. Right there!" He jabbed the air with his free hand.

"Nolan . . ." Lucy pleaded through clenched teeth. "Stop."

"Let her go, man." Patrick grabbed Nolan's shoulder.

Nolan shrugged him off, keeping his grip tight around Lucy's wrist. "Don't pretend you didn't see them. I can't be the only one who—"

"Nolan, there weren't any lights." Lucy grabbed his fingers and tried to peel them back. "Stop it. No one saw anything."

With a final tug, she wrenched from his grasp and stumbled a few steps backward. Patrick caught her around the waist, steadying her again.

"What's your problem?" He glared at Nolan. "You high or something?"

Nolan was having trouble catching his breath. This wasn't like the first time, when it was just him and Lucy, when the lights were small and blurred by distance, when they could have been anything, a figment of his imagination even. This time was different. The lights he'd seen not even a minute ago, they'd been right on top of him, right there, huge and bright and clear enough that anyone within a ten-mile radius should have seen them. Lucy, Patrick, Grant, everyone else, they'd been standing, sitting, right here. They must have seen the flash. It would have been impossible not to.

He slipped his backpack off his shoulder and rummaged for his tape recorder, then pressed Record and spoke into the microphone, "This is, um, Nolan Durant. It's, um, it's Thursday? I think? July 15, 1999, and it's, um, about eight o'clock at night, and I'm here with several witnesses to a major light phenomenon that took place in the Buttermilk Rocks area near Grandpa Peabody Boulder about five miles east of 33 Skyline Road."

He couldn't talk fast enough. Words tumbled one over another.

Patrick stared at Nolan with a bewildered look, and asked Lucy, "What's up with your brother?"

She shook her head and backed away, massaging her wrist.

The other kids were rising now, calling to Patrick, "Let's get out of here. Space Case is killing our buzz." They climbed off the rock and headed toward a trail that led to a public parking lot at the bottom of the hill. One by one they disappeared into the dark until it was only Lucy and Patrick and Nolan. Nolan shoved the microphone into Lucy's face and said, "Please state and spell your full name for the record."

Lucy ducked away from him and started running home. She was fast, halfway down the hill and picking up speed before Nolan called after her, "Lucy, wait!"

She didn't slow, didn't look over her shoulder. She was a streak, a blur, and then gone.

"Nice going, freak." Patrick shoved his shoulder into Nolan as he took off, sprinting to catch up with Lucy.

Nolan stopped the recorder and raised his face to the sky again. He watched another minute as more stars emerged from the black folds of night, then he hoisted his backpack onto his shoulders and walked home.

All the lights inside the house were on. Nolan watched Lucy and Patrick through the sliding glass door. They sat side by side on the living room couch. Neither one noticed Nolan there, on the other side of the glass, looking in. He watched from the shadows. He watched as Lucy leaned into Patrick, her mouse-brown hair falling over her face. He watched Patrick rub his hand in circles across her back. He watched, and his stomach knotted.

He didn't like seeing them together like this. His pudgy-cheeked little sister who danced around the house in sock feet to Britney Spears music, and still slept with a night-light and her favorite raggedy blue teddy bear, Mr. Snuffles; his sister who didn't look so pudgy-cheeked anymore in her cutoff jean shorts and spaghetti strap tank top, her suddenly long limbs summer bronze, her lips pink and pouting like the girls in Nolan's class. His baby sister. His ex–best friend, who didn't know the meaning of the word loyalty, who thought love was for suckers and screenplays. Patrick had been like a second brother to Lucy once, but that was a long time ago. Nolan didn't know what was going on with them now. Whatever it was, he didn't like it.

He slid the door open and came inside. Lucy and Patrick leaped away from each other, suddenly self-conscious, color rising in their cheeks. Lucy stared at her lap.

"What happened out there, man?" Patrick cracked his knuckles. "You went a little nuts."

Nolan ignored him and sat down in the chair across from Lucy. She scooted as far back against the couch as she could, glaring with eyes rimmed red and glistening.

Last week, yesterday even, Nolan would have been able to tell what she was thinking simply by a shifting eyebrow or a twitching lip, but her face was closed off to him now, unreadable. She pulled a strand of hair into her mouth and sucked on it, something she hadn't done since kindergarten. He noticed a bruise forming on her wrist, the edges bright red, the mark of his thumb still visible. He hadn't meant to hurt her. He only wanted her to admit she'd seen the lights too. She'd been standing right there with him and he'd pointed his finger straight at them and how could she have not seen?

"We need to talk about what just happened," Nolan said to her.

Patrick said, "Yes, we do," and Nolan shot him an angry look.

"Why are you still here?"

Patrick rested his hand on Lucy's knee. "Do you want me to go?"

Lucy shook her head.

Nolan sighed and dug into his backpack for the tape recorder again. He set it on the coffee table and pressed Record. He pulled out his casebook, too, spreading the pages open on his lap and shifting his attention back to Lucy. "Let's try this again, okay? I need you to tell me, in your own words, what you saw tonight."

Lucy didn't answer right away. She and Patrick exchanged a look before she finally said, "I saw you freaking out over nothing."

Nolan took a deep breath, working to keep his voice even and confident. This was his first time questioning a witness, but according to Wyatt, confidence was key to keeping the conversation going. If a witness sensed you had any doubts, she might turn hostile and shut down. There was a delicacy to uncovering the truth; there was an art. He realized his earlier misstep, trying to question everyone at once, assuming they would cooperate. Interviews worked best when they were one-on-one, when a witness did not have to fear reprisal or humiliation, when they could speak from the heart without worrying what others might think.

"Did you see the lights?" he asked gently. "They were only there for a second, but you looked right at them."

"There was nothing out there," Lucy insisted.

"You don't have to be afraid. You can tell me." He reached for her, but she pulled away.

"Man, there was nothing," Patrick said.

Nolan realized then his second mistake. He'd left the two

of them alone long enough they were able to agree on a cover story, some other explanation for the incredible thing they had all witnessed tonight. Wyatt had talked about this before at meetings, how the human mind is notoriously unreliable when it comes to accurately remembering events and how it's best to take a person's statement as soon after an encounter as possible, before the witness has a chance to reconsider or talk themselves out of the truth. He rubbed his temples, wishing Wyatt was here with him now, so he could get it right, because the more Lucy and Patrick argued against him, the more he questioned what it was he actually saw. Already the clear image he had of those six orange lights hovering, then moving away, moving unlike any man-made craft he'd seen before, already the certainty was fading.

Patrick rested his elbows on his knees and clasped his hands together. "Let's say there was something. What makes you think it was a flying saucer? Maybe it was an airplane."

"I saw six lights," he said. "Orange. Airplanes use red, green, and white."

"Okay, so maybe it was something else," Patrick said. "Maybe military."

"I know what I saw." Even as he said it, his doubt grew.

A reasonable explanation for everything, his mother liked to repeat. If she were here now, that's what she'd say to him, praising his vivid imagination, but wondering if maybe he shouldn't put it to a more useful purpose. You're sixteen now, she'd taken to lecturing him. Practically an adult. Time to start acting like one. That's why she'd started working the graveyard shift at the hospital, because it paid more, but also because she believed her children were old enough and responsible enough now to take care of themselves.

Nolan shut off the tape recorder and closed his casebook. He looked at Patrick when he said, "You're right, maybe it was military. Or a weather balloon or something."

Patrick nodded. "Yeah, man, or that thing, what do you call it? Ball lightning? Some kind of electrical storm. Exploding ions or some shit." He seemed giddy with the possibility.

Lucy scowled at her hands, her silence echoing her earlier denial.

Nolan didn't tell them about the four other sightings that had occurred in the past month near that same area. He didn't tell them there were other people, adults with normal jobs and normal families, one was even a city councilman, who had seen similar lights, orange orbs dancing low on the horizon. They wouldn't have believed him anyway.

"Occam's Razor, am I right?" Patrick grinned with pride over his cleverness.

He rose from the couch, unfolding to his full height of six feet, as tall as Nolan. Growing up, they'd seemed to have growth spurts at the same time. Their mothers joked about them eating from the same box of Wheaties, but where Nolan was lanky and all sharp bones, Patrick was broad-shouldered and muscled. He had always been stronger and more handsome, too, more popular with girls, more athletic, a better test taker, better it seemed at everything, except the one thing he really wanted to be good at: drawing and writing comic books. He didn't have Nolan's imagination or skill with ink and paper. He couldn't tell a good story if his life depended on it. All he ever did was copy other people's ideas.

Nolan had tried to help him, back when they were still friends, tried to explain the hero's journey, how characters need an arc, need to change, but for whatever reason, it never clicked for Patrick. He would just get frustrated and tear his drafts to pieces. Once he'd torn up a collection of Nolan's panels, pages he'd been working on for over a year, a story he was particularly proud of, and one he'd planned on giving to Lucy for her birthday. Shortly after that, Patrick stopped drawing altogether and stopped talking to Nolan, too, and as far as Nolan knew, he never started up again, his ambitions turning to track and field, and to becoming a star athlete and scholar, becoming whatever his parents wanted him to be. They had been inseparable once, more brothers than best friends. Now Nolan hardly recognized the half-grown man standing in front of him.

"Are you going to be okay?" Patrick brushed his fingers lightly down Lucy's arm.

She tucked her wrist against her body and offered him a half smile. "I'll be fine. Thanks."

"Don't let this guy get under your skin," Patrick said, as if Nolan wasn't sitting right there listening. "If you need anything, anything at all."

Lucy nodded.

"It was good running into you, Lucy Durant." Patrick said her name as if it were something to savor. Then his gaze narrowed on Nolan. "If you ever decide to rejoin us here on planet Earth, let me know." With that, he showed himself out the front door.

When they were alone again, Nolan inched forward on the edge of his chair. "Lucy," he said. "Those lights—".

She stood up quickly. "If I saw them, I would tell you."

Before he had a chance to respond, she stormed to her bedroom, slamming the door behind her.

Nolan sighed and sank back against the cushions. His gaze

shifted to the sliding glass door where his reflection wavered against a backdrop of night. He tried to visualize again what he had seen in the boulder lands not even an hour ago, but he wasn't sure anymore, not exactly, and he wanted to be sure, the way Wyatt and Gabriella and the other group members were sure. They didn't need proof to believe, so he shouldn't need proof either. Except he did. He grabbed his camera and went out to the backyard where he lay down in the middle of the grass and waited for his eyes to adjust to the darkness. He had read somewhere that extraterrestrials communicated telepathically and so, with the camera clutched in his hands, shutter open, lens aimed at the stars, he sent his thoughts to the universe, asking Them to reappear, to give him another, better sign. Give him something tangible and undeniable.

He waited over four hours watching the sky, but the extra-terrestrials were either too far out of telepathic range or They were ignoring him, or it was like Lucy and Patrick said, and They were never there in the first place. The stars stayed in their places, and the only thing that appeared above him was a circling, swooping bat.

4

The year 2010 rolled in with little fanfare. When midnight struck, Lucy was finishing up some last-minute packing. In the distance, fireworks exploded. A car drove past honking. Downstairs Marnie began to sing "Auld Lang Syne" loudly and off-key. Robert's baritone laugh tripped along in harmony. Lucy paused in the middle of stuffing socks into a duffel bag and turned toward the window, but there was nothing to see, a distorted reflection, a see-through version of herself standing in the middle of an empty room.

Interest in the *Strange Quarterly* article and Nolan's disappearance hadn't dwindled as fast as she thought it would. The article was still making the rounds online two weeks later, and now the photograph of the supposed UFO was showing up in conspiracy forums where they discussed Lucy in the comments. Everyone wanted to know where she was now. Why wasn't she coming forward? What did she know about that night? Had she told the police the truth? Could anyone believe a word she said? Mostly she ignored the things they wrote about her, but some nights when she couldn't sleep, she'd skim the articles with a nervous pulse, her eyes slowing to a stop whenever she came across her name.

Lucy's been given plenty of opportunities to come forward and tell her side of the story, but she remains silent? WHAT IS SHE HIDING?

She was a little girl when it happened—give her a break.

Fourteen is old enough. She's definitely hiding something. Little slut probably did it.

Even her mother thinks she's guilty.

She never felt the urge to respond. These strangers seemed to be talking about some other girl named Lucy, not her, not the person she was now.

Reporters continued to hound her, too, though after the first week the people calling were mostly from tabloids, small zines, and blogs no one had ever heard of. She deleted every message and didn't return any calls. She even changed her phone number, but then they started calling the house. It was only after Robert threatened to sue for harassment that the calls finally stopped.

Downstairs a champagne cork popped. Marnie laughed. Neither she nor Robert called Lucy to come and join them, so she went back to stuffing socks in her duffel bag. In years past, this transition from old year to new had always felt like the beginning of something. Today it felt like an end. It was after one o'clock when she finally crawled into bed. Downstairs Marnie was singing again, low and soft, a song unrecognizable.

The next morning, Lucy loaded suitcases and boxes, her whole life as it was, in the trunk of her car. Marnie and Robert were still in bed when she left, sleeping off champagne hangovers. She left them a note saying she'd call when she got settled, she'd have them over for dinner, then she drove fifteen

minutes to the three-story gated complex that was to be her
new home. She'd signed a six-month lease on a studio apartment. First month's rent was paid, thanks to her father. All she
needed were the keys.

She parked on the street and sat with the engine idling,
waiting for the landlord to arrive. She should feel good about
this. New apartment, new job opportunities. Thanks to her
father's business connections, interviews were pretty much
guaranteed. All she had to do was send in her résumé. Her whole
life moving in a new direction, she had no reason to feel anything other than optimistic, and yet a dull, throbbing ache was
starting up at the base of her skull. *Thud-thud-thud*, like someone
trying to break in. Everything's going to be fine, she tried to
convince herself. This was what she needed. A fresh start. Only
it wasn't, not really.

She couldn't stop thinking about the article, how certain
her mother seemed, even though she was so absolutely wrong.
All of them—the reporters, the online forums, that Wyatt
Riggs person with his faux professorial demeanor—they had
it all wrong. They were wrong about the orb in the pictures,
they were wrong about Nolan, and they were wrong about
her. If she'd had Sandra's phone number, she would have called
right then and set the record straight. But then maybe it was
better that she didn't, because what she needed to say needed
to be said in person. She didn't give herself time to think about
the details or the logistics or how it had been over nine years
since she last spoke to her mother and maybe Lucy was the last
person Sandra wanted to hear from right now. She didn't think
about what she would tell her father or what she was going to
do about the apartment, her already-paid-for apartment, her
landlord on his way with the key. She was well aware of how

quickly days turned to weeks, to months, to years, how easy it was to slip into a routine and put off important things for so long they ceased to be important anymore. If she didn't do this now, she never would.

She turned her car around and drove east out of Los Angeles, east over the Sierra Nevada mountains, east to the house where she grew up at the end of Skyline Road. Home. And yet, not home. Not anymore.

It was dark when she got there, and the single-story ranch looked black, though she remembered it painted moss green, trimmed in white. None of the lights inside the house were on, only the porch light, which illuminated brass numbers screwed into the wall and a dried-up Christmas wreath hanging crooked from a nail on the front door. Beige slippers lay like two dead birds on a worn and tattered welcome mat. The orange honeysuckle she and Nolan planted fifteen years ago for Mother's Day was overgrown now, snaking shadows up the side of the house and clawing at the gutters.

The last time Lucy was on that porch, she had a suitcase in one hand and was wiping tears from her eyes with the other. Sandra tilted in the doorway behind her taking large swigs from a half-empty bottle of vodka and screaming, "Fine! If that's what you want. Go! Get out of here! I can't stand the sight of you anyway!" The last time she was here, she vowed to never return.

She stared out the windshield at the ragged mountains she'd just crossed, trying to work up the courage to finish the journey. All she had to do was get out of the car. *You've made it this far. What are a few more steps?* A few steps, a thousand miles, ten years, a lifetime.

She threw open the driver-side door and hurried up the

driveway before she could change her mind. At the last second she swerved and slipped around the side of the house and through the unlocked gate into the backyard where the moon, full and bright, cast the world in a glittering silver net. Patio furniture was stacked against one side of the house. Drapes hung across the sliding glass back door, but no light filtered through. It was close to ten, late enough Sandra was probably asleep, or passed out drunk on the living room floor.

Lucy crept across the backyard and stopped in front of another gate along the back edge of their property line that once allowed access to acres of public land beyond, but which was padlocked shut now. She gave the lock a hard tug. It didn't budge.

When they were kids, she and Nolan came in and out of this gate whenever they pleased. Like wild things, they ran across the land on the other side of the fence. Kicking up dust, turning over stones, chasing jackrabbits and tumbleweeds, climbing boulders as big as semitrucks, staying out until after dark to watch Venus rise. She had flickers of memories from those early years, images that flashed and darted away before she could examine them too closely.

She was seven, carrying a bright red bucket, trailing behind Nolan, who led her deeper and deeper into the strewn boulder field, explaining how meteorites would be smoother than regular rocks. "They might look like metal or charcoal. If you aren't sure, ask me." Now a little older, lying on their backs on a flat and sun-warmed rock, seeing her first meteor streak across the starry dome. Now a different time, a different summer, she didn't know how old they were, they found something in the brush. A rabbit? A lizard? A mouse? The animal kept changing shape in her memory, and then she was seven again, carrying a bright red bucket and trying to keep up with Nolan's long strides.

She had only one clear memory of something that happened on the other side of the fence. It was July, the summer before she entered high school, and hot. Sticky pavement hot. Burning metal hot. Melting to a puddle hot. The kind of hot that can make a person see things that aren't really there.

Sandra had just left for work, and Lucy was watching television by herself when Nolan came into the living room carrying a backpack on his shoulders and binoculars around his neck. He stopped at the back door and asked if she wanted to come along. Nothing good was playing on TV, and she had no better offers, so she laced up her boots and followed him out the gate into the boulder lands. She didn't see what the big deal was, why Nolan was suddenly so obsessed with UFOs. Growing up, he'd been interested in aliens and sci-fi movies, and she played along with his backyard games, but he'd become so serious of late, everything done in earnest. It was obvious he wasn't playing anymore, that he seemed to really believe in all this alien contact nonsense, and that's what Lucy didn't understand. Wasn't he getting too old to believe in something so absurd? UFOs were the kind of fad a person should grow out of eventually, except Nolan only seemed to be sinking deeper into the fantasy.

Lucy heard the other kids before she saw them. She almost turned around and went home, and looking back she wished she had, but at the time Nolan kept going, and so did she.

The only person in the group she recognized was Patrick. He used to come over to the house all the time when they were younger, but then something happened between him and Nolan, something Nolan refused to talk about, and he didn't come over anymore after that. The last time Lucy saw Patrick was a few months ago at a track and field meet. She'd hidden behind the bleachers to watch him run. He'd grown taller since then, and his blond hair was thicker, cut short along the sides and long on top. He was drinking a beer and being obnoxious and Lucy might have died of embarrassment except he didn't even see her. Then Nolan said, "Lucy, let's go," and Patrick's gaze was drawn to her for the first time in a long time. His eyes moved up and down the length of her, and it was as if he was seeing something new, someone other than the little girl he used to know, his best friend's tagalong baby sister, who liked to play with Barbies and was addicted to purple Nerds and laughed so hard once she peed her pants.

He said, "You don't have to go, Lucy."

He said, "You can stay."

He leaned close to her and whispered, "Since when did you get so beautiful?"

And then he smiled. A rush of heat spread through her body. Patrick's smile was everything. Even as a little girl, she would run circles around him, doing floppy cartwheels and telling silly knock-knock jokes that she plagiarized from a library book, trying to get his attention, trying to get his dimple-cheeked Prince Charming smile. She had it now. For one fleeting, perfect moment. Until Nolan ruined everything.

He grabbed her wrist, clamping down hard. "Do you see that?"

In the seconds before she looked up, she believed she would see something. She *wanted* to see something. But the sky was empty. A dark expanse, purple twilight melting the edges and nothing more. Nothing at all.

"They were right over there." He started to drag her away from Patrick and he wouldn't let go, even though she fought him.

She couldn't believe he was doing this, embarrassing her like this in front of these older kids, in front of Patrick. It wasn't funny, and she asked him to stop, but he kept going on and on about the lights, how they'd been right there, right there! But no one else saw them. Because there were no lights to begin with. He was just making it up to humiliate her or he was pissed that someone other than him was using his stupid star-gazing rock. She broke free of him and thought that would be it, but then he pulled out his tape recorder and the other kids stared at him like he was a pod person or an axe murderer or something worse, and they looked at her like that too, like she was crazy by association. He shoved the recorder in her face, and that was all she could take. She left him and Patrick then, turned and sprinted back to the house.

It surprised her when Patrick showed up a few minutes later at the back door. He knocked and made silly faces against the glass. She let him inside and they sat down on the couch together.

"Are you okay?" he asked.

She didn't want to cry in front of him so instead she started talking about the weather, how hot it was this year compared to last, and then seeing the bored expression on his face, she changed the subject to the new *Star Wars* movie. Patrick wouldn't stop talking then. He said the movie was a shit storm of awfulness compared to the original trilogy, and then he told her about the BMW his parents bought him last month for his sixteenth birthday. "You want to go for a ride sometime?" She said yes, she'd like that. Then he asked her about starting high school. "Are you nervous?" She was, a little, but tried not to show it. He told her to come find him on the first day. He'd show her around, introduce her to people. He'd make sure no one gave her any shit. As they talked, Patrick moved closer to her. Their knees touched. He smelled spicy, a hint of cloves or something like that, something delicious. Then he started rubbing her back, and she tried to think of something cute and clever to say, but all her brain could come up with was, he's touching me, he's touching me, he's *actually* touching me.

She wanted it to go on forever. Patrick's hand on her back. Patrick beside her. Patrick coming to her defense, making sure she was going to be okay. She'd liked him for a long time before this, a little-girl crush she never expected to blossom into anything interesting, and yet Patrick was here, looking back at her with the bluest blue eyes she had ever seen, eyes that made her feel finally real. They might have kissed right then if Nolan hadn't come stumbling through the back door. When Patrick pulled away from her, Lucy felt herself disappear again.

That day in July, that blistering-hot day. That was when it all started to fall apart.

Lucy stepped back from the locked gate and her eyes swung to where the Milky Way pinwheeled, stars exploding from its center. She had forgotten what it was like out here. How bright the stars, how they seemed to go on forever. The weight of the universe, the vastness of it, the eternity, so much space, too much. It settled on her chest, a crushing pressure under this too-thick blanket of night. She couldn't catch her breath. Her heart beat too fast. She was unraveling, coming undone and starting to drift. She would fly up to the stars and disappear among them and no one would come looking for her. No one even knew she was here. She was a speck. A speck among specks. A single tiny thread in the infinite fabric of the cosmos. She didn't matter. Sandra didn't matter. Neither did her father. The reporters, this place, Patrick, what happened to Nolan, her memories—compared to the expansive sky, none of it mattered. Only it *did* matter; it mattered to her.

She squeezed her eyes shut until the spinning sensation stopped, then she turned to go back to the front of the house where she would ring the doorbell like a normal person, and then what? She hadn't thought that far ahead. What would she say to Sandra? What could she possibly say after nine years of silence? Hi, Mom. Mom was too familiar. Just hi. Hi, I know it's been a while, but I was hoping . . . Hoping what, exactly? For an apology? To be invited in for a cup of tea and a nice cozy chat? For a chance to explain?

Words seemed impossible tonight. But maybe she'd feel differently if she came back in the morning, after a good night's sleep and a strong cup of coffee, maybe in daylight when there weren't so many shadows to contend with, and so many stars looking on.

She made it halfway across the backyard when a security light snapped on. She froze in place, blinking against the white-hot brilliance.

A man called out to her from the direction of the sliding glass door. "Who's out there?"

Lucy raised her arm to block the light. The man who stepped onto the back patio was dressed only in boxer briefs and a white tank top, but he was big, over six feet tall, and had a wooden baseball bat propped on one shoulder, both hands gripping the handle, ready to swing.

"I was looking for Sandra Durant?" Lucy called to him, trying to sound as nonthreatening as possible.

"No one here by that name." His voice was a low growl.

"She's about fifty? Short blond hair. Sandra? Durant?"

"I said there's no one here by that name. Now get the hell off my property or I'm calling the cops."

Lucy moved slow and sideways toward the open gate that led into the front yard, keeping the man and his bat in her sight line until she was through. Then she shut the gate behind her and broke into a trot, hurrying down the driveway to her car. She pulled a U-turn and sped away from the house where she grew up, the house that apparently now belonged to strangers.

She drove in circles awhile. Bishop hadn't changed much in the years she'd been away. Semitrucks and cars passing through to someplace else still clogged the main highway through the center of town. Even at this late hour, the sidewalks were crowded with tourists who used Bishop as their kicking-off point for backpacking and climbing trips. To the west, the Sierra Nevada mountains loomed. The White Mountains and the Inyos rolled to the east. Owens Valley was trapped in between. To the north, a thin, winding highway climbed, then disappeared into even more mountains. To the south, the land flattened but was no more welcoming. The lush river basin surrounding Bishop too quickly gave way to barren desert scrub and Death Valley beyond. There was no easy way out of this place.

The light ahead changed from green to yellow. Lucy slowed the car to a stop and glanced over at a dark-haired boy collecting abandoned shopping carts from the parking lot of Bishop's Grocery. His head was lowered, his shoulders hunched as he strained to push the weight of the carts. It couldn't be Nolan, it wasn't possible, but even so Lucy wanted to see the boy's face. It suddenly seemed the most important thing in the world. She started to roll down the passenger window. A car behind her honked. The boy looked up. Not a boy, a man twice her age, with a stiff mustache and a wad of chewing tobacco tucked inside his cheek. The man turned his head to one side and spat. The car behind her honked a second time. The light had been green for a while. Lucy pressed down on the gas.

The headache from earlier today was returning, hammering its way into her skull. She stopped at the next motel she came to and rented a room for the night, charging it all on her credit card. She grabbed a pair of pajamas, her toothbrush, and her laptop from the boxes in the trunk, but left everything else packed away.

In the motel room, she took two ibuprofen and then ran a search for Sandra Durant in the White Pages. She didn't find anything useful. Not even the old address on Skyline Road. Sandra's name was all over the Internet, in articles about Nolan's disappearance and in UFO forums, but no one seemed to care about her physical whereabouts. Either that or she deliberately went to great lengths to keep the information private. Lucy searched for over an hour and found nothing about where Sandra was currently living or how she could be reached. She looked up the Skyline Road house on a real estate website and discovered it went into foreclosure eight years ago and was purchased by the new owners shortly after that.

Though Lucy always imagined her mother dying in that house waiting for Nolan's return, she wasn't surprised by the foreclosure. Two months after Nolan went missing, Sandra lost her job at the hospital. She'd gone to work drunk and nearly killed a patient with the wrong dose of medication. Lucy left

Bishop shortly after that, but even when she'd been living with her mother, even with child support checks coming in, and alimony, and the hospital paycheck, they were always short on cash. Without the paycheck, without the child support, Lucy didn't know how Sandra would have been able to keep up with the bills.

She pulled up the *Strange Quarterly* article again and scrolled down to the photograph of Sandra and Wyatt. They stood in front of a nondescript gray brick building with no business or street signs, no mailbox numbers, no notable landmarks or details, no clues of any kind that would help Lucy determine where the picture was taken. Her eyes caught on the email address at the end of the article. She typed fast and then hit Send, the email disappearing off her screen before she had a chance to change her mind.

> Dear Mr. Riggs,
>   My name is Lucy Durant. I'm in town for a few days and was hoping to speak with my mother, but I'm having trouble tracking her down. I think you might be able to help me?

She only had to wait a few minutes for his reply.

> Can you meet at Riley's Bar in an hour?

5

Riley's was quiet for a Friday night. At the bar, an older man sipped a pint, his eyes fixed on a television hanging in the corner. Footage of a college football game flickered across the screen. A couple sat whispering together in a dimly lit booth on the other side of the room. The man would say something and the woman would laugh and toss her hair so it draped across his arm. Someone was playing pool in the back. Balls clattered across the table. The bartender had his back to the whole place and was drying tumblers with a towel. Lucy had never been inside this particular bar, so maybe it was always this empty, or maybe everyone who normally came out drinking on a night like this had stayed home to sleep off their New Year's Eve hangovers. Whatever the reason, she was glad for the near-empty room; this reunion was going to be awkward enough without a crowd of strangers listening in.

Lucy arrived a few minutes early, but Wyatt was already waiting for her at a booth near the front door. He looked exactly like his picture. Same slicked-back hair and stern expression. Same stiff posture. He recognized her as soon as she walked in and rose to greet her, reaching to shake her hand. "You have no idea how thrilled I was to get your message. It's an honor. Truly."

"Where is she?" Lucy's eyes darted toward the restroom near the back of the restaurant.

"Sandra?" He shook his head. "She's not coming."

Lucy tensed, and as if he sensed her pulling away, he rushed on, adding, "I asked her. But she thought it might be better if you and I talked first. Just the two of us."

He gestured for Lucy to sit down.

She stayed standing. "She doesn't want to see me."

"No, it's not . . . she's just . . . she's nervous, I think. She isn't sure if she can trust you."

Lucy bit down on her bottom lip. This wasn't how she'd imagined it. She'd come all this way and Sandra couldn't be bothered, had sent this man, this stranger to deal with her instead. It hurt, a paper-cut slice to her heart, but maybe it was what she deserved.

"Let me buy you a drink." Wyatt gestured toward the bar.

"I don't drink."

"A club soda, then?"

There was something about the way he tugged at the sleeves of his shirt, trying to pull the cuffs down around his knuckles, that made him appear vulnerable, something kind in his eyes, and Lucy felt herself softening toward him, being drawn in despite her misgivings. She slid into the booth. "Club soda is fine."

"With lemon?"

"If they have it." She didn't care either way.

He went to the bar and returned a few minutes later with two tumblers of club soda, lemon slices bobbing like yellow boats between the ice cubes and fizz. He slid one of the glasses across the table to her. She wrapped her hands around it and waited for him to speak first. He sipped his drink. When he smiled, dimples creased his cheeks and wrinkles formed on the bridge of his nose. All the hard angles of his face diminished, making him look younger, and Lucy liked him better for it.

"So how do you know my mother?" she asked, finally breaking the silence. "I mean, how did you meet?"

"She contacted me through my website about a year and a half ago," he said. "She was having trouble sleeping, holding down a job, not getting much of anything done besides drinking and falling apart. She went online trying to find answers and found her way to me. We exchanged emails for a few months. She was reluctant to share her real identity at first, which is completely understandable considering the circumstances, but once she did, I asked her if we could meet in person." He leaned his elbows on the table. "I knew your brother from before."

This made her sit up straighter and look at him more closely. She tried to recall his face ten years younger, tried to put Nolan and him together in the same room, but her memory was coming up blank. She thought she'd known all of Nolan's friends; there weren't very many to keep track of, especially in those last few months.

Wyatt seemed to understand because he shook his head. "I don't think you and I ever met. He was a member of a group I ran . . . still run, actually . . . a group for people who are interested in studying extraterrestrial phenomena and discussing what it means for humanity's future."

Lucy lifted the glass to her lips. The club soda was so cold it made her teeth ache and burned her throat going down.

Nolan had invited her to go to a UFO Encounters meeting once, when they were still getting along. He'd shown her the flyer. She thought it was a joke.

"Sandra came to me for help," Wyatt continued. "She'd been through something incredible, an experience that her previous knowledge and limited vocabulary could not explain. I was able to help her understand what had happened to her. And now she's putting her energy into much more productive endeavors."

"Like what?" Lucy did nothing to hide the cynicism in her voice. She twirled the melting ice in her glass. A fresh set of bubbles burst to the surface.

"Well, she has a job, for one thing, working full-time as a waitress at the casino." Wyatt leaned over the table. "And she's helping me now, too. We're working together to try and find out what really happened to your brother that night in the desert."

This was not the kind of conversation she wanted to be having. Not in so public a place with a stranger who somehow seemed to know more about her own family than she did. Not anywhere with anyone actually. Yet this was why she'd come. To set the record straight. Or try anyway.

"So do you think he was abducted by aliens, too?" she asked, her tone flat and noncommittal.

"It's where the evidence seems to be pointing us at this time."

"And what evidence is that again?"

"Have you seen the pictures?" He started to reach into a messenger bag sitting on the bench next to him, but Lucy gestured for him not to bother.

"I saw them," she said. "That's why I'm here, actually. That article . . . It should have never been published. Sandra shouldn't have given you permission to use those pictures."

He seemed intrigued by this. "Why not?"

"It's irresponsible," she answered. "It's going to slow the investigation and damage what little reputation my brother has left."

"Your brother cared more about the truth than his reputation. He would want us pursuing whatever avenues are available. Besides, the so-called investigation is at a standstill anyway. I don't see how the article is going to slow it down any more than that. In fact, it might even speed things up a bit, get things moving again."

"In the wrong direction."

He fell back against the vinyl seat, a stunned expression on his face.

"You don't believe." It wasn't a question.

"I never have," she said, and then, "I'm sorry to disappoint you."

"Sandra never told me. I was working under the assumption . . ." But then he shook his head like whatever he'd been about to say no longer mattered.

Lucy wasn't surprised Sandra hadn't told him. Sandra probably didn't know. She stopped paying close attention to her children, and Lucy especially, after her divorce. One day in middle school, after a particularly disgusting cafeteria lunch, Lucy decided to stop eating meat. She came home and told her mother she was a vegetarian now and Sandra said, "That's nice, dear," then two hours later served her a ham and cheese sandwich for dinner. When Lucy wiggled the ham from between the bread slices and set it to one side of her plate, Sandra stared at her in surprise. "Since when did you stop eating meat?" Later, Nolan and Lucy had laughed about it in her bedroom, mimicking their mother's startled sparrow voice and comically overwrought facial expressions.

"Look," Lucy said to Wyatt, who studied her intently. "I just, I need to speak with Sandra. Can you help me or not?"

Wyatt rubbed his hand across his cheek, and the hem of his long-sleeved shirt inched up, revealing a dark sliver of ink on his right wrist. Lucy gestured to see the tattoo. Wyatt pushed the sleeve up to his elbow and held out his arm for her to see. She leaned over the table, twisting for a better look. Inked on the soft underside of his forearm, about an inch up from his wrist, was a stereotypical alien face no bigger than the circumference of a silver dollar. It was outlined in black, the skin inside shaded a rich blue-gray. Just a head, no body. Bulging cranium, narrow chin, a tiny mouth, huge and hollow eyes that gave it an otherworldly and shell-shocked expression. Eyes that sent shivers up Lucy's spine and made her stomach turn. She sat back in her seat. Air released from the cushions in a huff.

"What do you think?" He turned his arm to admire it now, and the corners of his mouth curved up, his chin lifting with pride.

Lucy hesitated a moment and then reached for her purse, talking as she dug around for enough loose change to pay for her club soda. "You know what's funny is that you seem like a reasonable man. Sane even."

"I'm as sane as you are," he said.

"So you must be doing all of this . . ." She dropped the change onto the table and gestured to his tattoo. "For what? Money? Attention?"

He tugged his sleeve down and drew his arms close to his body. "Why is it that one belief held by the majority of a population is accepted as normal, no matter how strange its tenets? While another belief shared by the minority is considered to be delusional and dangerous?"

The questions were rhetorical. He gave her no time to answer before continuing, "Christians can't prove the existence of guardian angels. Psychics can't prove the existence of ghosts. But no one cares about that, do they? No one tries to lock those people away in mental institutions or stuff them full of clozapine. No one laughs at the pope, no one points fingers at him, crying narcissism and greed. No one called Mother Teresa a liar."

He reached into his bag and pulled out a pen. Then grabbed a napkin from the holder and began scribbling on it. "Everyone on this planet wants answers, Lucy, to who we are and why we're here and what the hell it all means. For some of us that meaning comes from the stars, and from the extraterrestrial life-forms you are so quick to dismiss. Maybe you don't believe, and that's fine, but it doesn't mean those of us who do are crazy."

He shoved the napkin at her. He'd drawn a map and directions to some place in Bishop.

"My house," he said, sliding out of the booth. "Sandra's staying there with me for a while. She has the day off tomorrow."

Before Lucy could say anything—argue, defend herself, apologize—Wyatt was gone.

She stared at the map for a few seconds, then slipped it into her purse and started to get up. A man approached the table, his small mouth spreading in a grin, exposing crooked teeth that made him look just this side of lecherous. His beady, dark

eyes, long rat nose, and shaggy auburn hair were all too familiar, and Lucy crossed her arms tightly over her chest, a reflex
from freshman year of high school when she'd spent far too
much time trying to dodge Adam Paulson's horrible, groping
ape hands.

He laughed when he reached her, a startling and obnoxious
sound, like a drunk donkey. "I almost didn't believe it. I was
back there playing pool and I said to myself, 'Goddamn it, Self,
but if that pretty lady doesn't look a helluva lot like lovely little
Lucy Durant.'"

She cringed at the nickname he'd given her the first day
they met. He didn't seem to notice her discomfort and kept
right on talking, his lips flapping whiskey-loose. "But then I
thought, nuh-uh, can't be, no way in hell she'd come back to
this shithole town. But just in case, I walk over to get a closer
look and what do you know, but I was right! It *is* lovely little
Lucy Durant! Not so little anymore, though." His eyes roamed
over what parts of her were visible above the table, then he
winked.

"Adam . . . ?" She pretended to have a hard time coming up
with his name. "Adam Paulson, right?"

"You got me." He snapped his thumbs back so they were
pointing at his chest, then in a single swift motion, slapped his
palms down flat on the table, shaking the whole thing and
sloshing soda over the edges of Wyatt's and Lucy's abandoned
glasses. "Fuck's sake, babe, how long has it been? Seven? Eight
years?"

"Almost ten." She forced a smile, hoping she looked more
relaxed than she felt. Her cheeks ached from trying. Her heart
a mad hornet trapped inside her chest.

"Is that right? Ten years? I'll be damned, but time does fly like a motherfucker." He tilted his head back and squinted at the ceiling like he was trying to think of something important that had slipped his mind. Then he returned his attention to her. "There a reunion going on nobody told me about? You think I would have heard about something like that on Facebook."

Lucy had never liked Adam. She'd only put up with him because he was friends with Patrick. Though, how Patrick could stand him, Lucy never understood. One time she asked Patrick about it, why they let a loser like Adam hang around. "He's not a loser any more than the rest of us," Patrick had said. "You just don't know the whole story." Then he told her that Adam lived with his grandmother because in first grade his dad tried to kill someone, a business partner supposedly, and was serving life in prison, and his mom was fucked up on meth all the time and once tried to pimp Adam out to her dealer, who, as it turned out, drew the line at child molestation and ended up calling social services.

"So what? You feel sorry for him?" Lucy pressed. "That's the reason you let him hang on like a leech?"

Patrick made a face. "Baby," he said, and she preened under his attention. "Baby, Adam's the one who scores us weed and booze and those little pills you like so much. You don't really want him to stop hanging out with us, do you?"

She didn't care about the booze or the drugs. She only drank to keep up with Patrick and his friends, to prove herself worthy. And she only used because Patrick wanted her to. He paid her more attention when she was wasted. He liked her better high. At the time, she liked herself better too, but now it was only one of a long list of things, along with putting up with Adam Paulson's bullshit, that she'd done for Patrick and later regretted.

"No reunion," she said, answering Adam's question. "Not that I know of. I mean, I'm not on Facebook so maybe there is but no one told me about it either."

She laughed, but he didn't join in.

She mumbled something about just being in town for a couple of days to do some sightseeing, which was a stupid response. She could have thought of something better; she wished she had. Adam raised his eyebrows. With one finger, he pushed at the half-full glass of club soda in front of him, bumping it across the table closer to her.

"That guy you were with just now," he said. "Isn't he that UFO nut job, what's his name? I see his face all over the news, talking bullshit about little green men and flying saucers like they actually exist. You're not going all Looney Tunes on us like your brother now, are you? I didn't think crazy was contagious."

He leaned way back in the seat and made a cross with his fingers. Then he chuckled to himself and lowered his hands to the table again.

The ibuprofen she'd taken two hours ago had worn off, and her headache was working itself into a full-blown electrical storm now. She could almost hear her brain crackling as it shot lightning bolts through her temples. She massaged her forehead.

"Speaking of your brother . . ." Adam started to say, then stopped and gestured to the bartender. "I need another drink. You want one?"

"No, thanks, I really should be going." She started to slide out of the bench. "It was good to see you again—"

"Sit down, Lucy." His voice was taut and high-wire thin.

Something about it made her think he wasn't nearly as drunk as he was acting. She sat back down.

Adam leaned his elbows on the table and pressed his face close to hers. "What are you doing here? I mean, what are you *really* doing? Not sightseeing. That's bullshit."

She swallowed hard, trying to push down the lump building in her throat. She had nothing to say to him, and her skull felt like it was going to crack wide open, or she was going to throw up, or both, and she needed to get the hell out of here. So what was she doing still sitting, listening to this asshole's blathering nonsense, why was she having so much trouble getting her legs to obey?

"I guess it doesn't matter why you're here," he said. "As long as you're not thinking about doing something stupid. You're not thinking about doing something stupid, are you, Lucy?" When she didn't answer, he smiled again. "No, I didn't think you were, because you're a good girl. Lovely little Lucy. Isn't that right?"

She pressed her lips between her teeth, clamping down against a rising wave of nausea.

The bartender was beside their table now, waiting to take their drink order.

Adam smiled up at him. "Scotch on the rocks, for me. And whatever the lovely little Lucy wants."

She shook her head and then finally managed to command her knees to straighten, her legs to push up. She lurched to her feet and, clasping her purse to her chest, stumbled toward the front door. Adam's mocking voice chased after her. "Was it something I said?"

She burst outside and gulped in a pint of cool night air. Just before the door swung shut behind her, she heard Adam call out, "I'll tell Patrick you said hello."

Three blocks stretched between Riley's and her motel room. Lucy hurried along the sidewalk, every step expecting to hear Adam coming up behind her. The traffic on Line Street was lighter than when she'd walked to the bar a half hour earlier. Fewer people roamed the sidewalks. Shops and restaurants were closed, their windows shuttered and dark. She snuck glances over her shoulder, certain he would follow, but the bar door stayed closed.

Feeling returned to her fingers and toes and slowly into her limbs, even as her headache raged on. Not a headache, a migraine. A thousand tiny hammers beating a thousand tiny nails into the delicate flesh of her brain. She hadn't experienced one so intense in years. Usually painkillers were enough to dull the pain to a slightly uncomfortable but innocuous pulse. Running helped too. The last time she remembered having a headache this bad was the morning after Nolan disappeared.

Her hands shook. She fumbled with the motel key card, dropping it once on the ground before finally slipping it into the lock and getting the green light. In the bathroom, she sank to her knees and bent her head over the toilet. She dry-heaved twice, and then sat there with her head resting on her arms for another ten minutes until the nausea passed and the pain faded to a slightly more manageable roar. Then she got to her feet again, rummaged in her purse for ibuprofen, filled a glass with water, and swallowed two pills. She found her way to the bed in the dark and collapsed on top of it without bothering to climb under the blankets.

CASEBOOK ENTRY #2

SIGHTING:
OVRO Disc Landing

DATE: August 12, 1999

LONGITUDE/LATITUDE: 37.231453 W, 118.282702 N

SYNOPSIS: At 22:44 hours I observed a craft approaching Owens Valley Radio Observatory from the SE out of White Mountains. Approach was steady with no apparent change in elevation or speed. Craft arrived at 22:46 and hovered above telescopes for 43 secs before touching down briefly on the N side of antenna. Craft was on the ground <30 secs before taking off again and moving NNW toward Sierras. Craft moved out of sight at 22:52.

OBJECT DESCRIPTION: 6 disc-shaped lights similar to what I saw at Buttermilk Rocks, only these lights varied orange to green and maintained triangle formation. No engine sounds detected. Wind gusted during touchdown and again at liftoff. Based on my location S of antenna, approximately 100 yards from touchdown location, I estimate width of the craft to be 450 ft—nearly the equivalent of two 747s parked end to end. Too dark to see much of the mechanical or physical structure of craft. Lights rotated counterclockwise on landing and takeoff.

OTHER WITNESS STATEMENTS: One possible witness to event. Seconds after the craft flew out of sight, I saw a shadow moving in the scrub near the telescopes. However, I was unable to make contact. I called out, but there was no response. Shadow appeared humanoid in shape and walked upright. I attempted to get closer, but area is restricted, and the shadow moved quickly, vanishing into the night before I had a chance to capture any further details.

WEATHER INFORMATION: 78°F; winds from SSE at 13 mph; clear skies; New Moon

LOCATION DESCRIPTION: California, Owens Valley, 6 miles SSE of Big Pine, Leighton Road, near Owens River. Owens Valley Radio Observatory is a university-operated research facility currently studying blazars, cosmic microwave background, and star formation. It should also be noted that there are rumors of a top-secret, underground military testing facility near this location, though at this time I have no evidence to confirm this.

PHYSICAL EVIDENCE: None. Craft moved away before I could secure photographs. Unable to inspect touchdown location due to restricted access.

CONCLUSION: Certainly the most remarkable sighting to date. Size and behavior of craft suggests it is neither natural phenomena nor weather related. No man-made craft that I know of maneuvers like this. Most likely extraterrestrial in origin.

The girl appeared out of nowhere.

One second, Nolan sat alone in his pickup staring into the empty alleyway behind Bishop's Grocery, distracted with thoughts of what he'd witnessed not even twenty-four hours earlier at the observatory, wondering what it could possibly mean. The next, a figure materialized from the shadows, a piece of night breaking off and coming to life, approaching with tentative steps and a cautious look on her full moon face.

She wore a hodgepodge of vintage clothes. Green corduroy bell-bottoms and a fringed leather vest overtop a billowing red blouse. Pearls and puka shells hung around her neck. She'd braided feathers into a thick strand of her hair, the rest of which swept loose and long to her waist, dark and shimmering burgundy under the glow of a nearby bar sign. She strode across the parking lot in heavy-duty hiking boots that were scuffed and covered in dust. The plum-colored backpack she carried over one shoulder was crammed full and near bursting at the seams. When she reached him, she swung it around to access the front pocket, and his gaze caught on an orange and silver shimmering patch stitched to the front. Saturn. Sixth planet from the Sun. A gas giant with a radius nine times that of Earth and an atmosphere mostly made of hydrogen and helium. Seven spectacular, visible rings of dust and ice. Fifty-three known moons, including Titan. Incapable of life as we know it.

She pulled a map from the pocket and waved it at him. Her voice drifted through the cracked open driver's window like a soft ribbon coiling over his skin, making him think of distant places, starlight, and yearning.

"I'm a little turned around. Can you help?"

The lights were on inside the store, but the place was empty, the doors locked up for the night, the alarm set. Carol, the store's manager and Nolan's boss, had gone home. They'd walked to the parking lot together not even fifteen minutes ago. Nolan, too, would have been almost home by now, except all day he'd been plagued by a strange sort of inertia.

He'd lain in bed that morning staring at the ceiling, trying and failing to lift his heavy limbs, until his mother burst in around noon, threatening to sell his truck if he didn't get up right this instant and take out the trash like she'd asked him to do two days ago. After that, he'd wandered aimlessly through the house for a while before coming to a stop in front of the sliding glass door. The back gate was open, even though he remembered closing it. Lucy came into the room a few minutes later, but walked right back out when she saw him.

They'd barely said two words to each other since the Buttermilk Rocks incident. She left the house as often as she could to avoid him, going who knew where and doing who knew what with her friends. He asked her once when she thought she'd be back. She told him it was none of his business, and maybe it wasn't, but he worried about her sneaking out after their mother left for work, staying out past curfew, and he should probably bring all of this to their mother's attention at some point, but he had bigger things to deal with at the moment.

Last night he'd witnessed a miracle. A craft almost certainly of extraterrestrial origin had touched down right in front of him, and he was struggling to understand how something so significant could have happened to him. A nobody, a doubter. Why not Wyatt? Or Gabriella? Why not any number of other, more prepared, more qualified people? And only a month after his sighting at Buttermilk Rocks. It seemed a remarkable bit of good fortune, but then a quiet whisper started up in the back of his mind, growing louder as the day wore into night. What if it wasn't luck at all? What if They had chosen that place, that moment? What if They had chosen him? Maybe it was the same craft that he'd seen—or thought he'd seen—at Buttermilk Rocks. Maybe They had in fact tried to reach out to him that day in July and since that first attempt failed, tried a second time last night.

Wyatt had a saying, one he repeated to the group often: One strange event is an anomaly, two is a fluke, three is a pattern. Nolan hadn't understood it at first, but he was beginning to. Three strange events had meaning on a grander scale. Three strange events were likely connected in some way. Three strange events meant someone somewhere was trying to get your attention.

The girl waited, still holding up the map and smiling hopefully, looking at him with such beautiful and peculiar eyes. Flecked with gold, they were molten, shifting copper to amber to brown to amber and back to copper again. They seemed to search the very depths of him. He experienced a moment of déjà vu, convinced he'd seen eyes like hers before, but he struggled to remember where. Then it came to him: he'd drawn these very same eyes just last week.

He was working on a comic about a warrior princess from the distant planet Aurelia, who comes to Earth with orders to destroy this tiny, messed-up place before it wreaks havoc on neighboring star systems, but winds up falling for an earthling boy instead. The star-crossed lovers find themselves in a race against time to save Earth and their newly budding love before other Aurelian warriors carry out the orders the princess could not. He had drawn the princess with long dark hair and copper eyes. Copper eyes that could melt glass and the coldest of hearts. He had drawn the princess and now she stood in front of him, flesh and blood and waiting. Her smile started to slip, but he didn't know what to do or say. He stared at her like an idiot. His mouth went dry. Sweat trickled down his back. He couldn't think straight. He couldn't get his brain working right. He lost all feeling in his hands.

This wasn't possible, she wasn't real, she couldn't be—

"I'm trying to get to the ocean?" The girl, the very real girl, unfolded the map. She turned it one way and then the other. "The Pacific? Santa Monica?" She lifted her gaze and scowled at their immediate surroundings, then at the mountains edging the horizon, then back at the map. "Clearly, I took a wrong turn somewhere."

She laughed, and the sound shocked energy through Nolan's veins, returning him to himself. He got out of the pickup, leaving the door open so the dome light stayed on, took the map from the girl, and spread it over the hood. It was a standard California road map, the creases soft from use. One corner was stained with what looked like coffee.

Nolan dropped his finger down on a greenish-colored area a little over halfway down the length of the map near the Nevada state line south of Lake Tahoe. "You're here. This is Bishop." He moved his finger, following Highway 395 south to the 14 and then west to a broad expanse of blue on the opposite side. "That's the ocean." He tapped a city on the edge where land met water. "Santa Monica."

The girl leaned close to him, squinting to read the map. She smelled faintly of coconut. Her hair brushed his arm, and he shivered. It was only a coincidence that she looked so much like his warrior princess, and yet, Nolan didn't believe in coincidence. Not anymore. Not since meeting Wyatt and the others. But if it wasn't coincidence, then what did it mean? He wasn't sure. He had an idea, but it was just as ridiculous as her being here now, leaning close enough for him to breathe her in, close enough to touch.

When she finally pulled away, Nolan experienced an ache in his chest, unlike anything he'd ever felt before. Worse than the time when he was five and his favorite toy was reduced to tattered stuffing and bits of thread in the washing machine. Poor Owley had to be thrown out; Nolan cried for days. Worse, too, than how he'd felt after the death of their second-grade class guinea pig, Petunia, for whom he'd stayed up all night writing a eulogy and decorating a shoebox coffin. Worse even than when his father left. Nolan didn't know this girl's name, but she felt familiar to him; already she was important.

She refolded the map and returned it to the front pocket of her backpack.

"I'm Nolan." He pressed his fingers to his chest, introducing himself and hoping she would do the same.

She ran her eyes up and down the length of him, as if trying to decide something. Her fingers tapped her backpack. A song, a beat, a message. She stopped drumming and said, "You're not a creep, are you? You don't look like a creep."

His mom said he looked like a young Keanu Reeves, but less tormented. After he grew his hair out last year, his sister said he looked like a sheepdog. Nolan thought he looked normal and boring, like any other sixteen-going-on-seventeen-year-old boy who was fighting acne and still growing into his loose skin and too-long bones. He smoothed his fingers over his hair, worried that it was doing that thing it sometimes did if he sweat too much, flipping and curling at impossible angles, making him look less like a sheepdog and more like an electrocuted poodle.

The girl watched him closely. Those eyes.

He dropped his hand to his side. "I'm not a creep."

"Yeah, I didn't think so."

He worried about her then, how she could so easily trust someone she just met. But wasn't this the reason for all of Earth's turmoil? Because humans were all too eager to rush to suspicion, to shoot first and ask questions later? Because no one trusted anyone anymore, no one allowed themselves to be vulnerable? Earth would be better off with more people like her, people who were brave. Fifteen minutes in her presence, and he already felt different, felt himself changing. He wondered what might happen if they spent an entire day together.

The girl, who still hadn't said her name, asked, "Do you know if there's a bus station around here? Like a Greyhound or something?"

There were local buses, but these were notoriously unreliable. He'd seen people waiting outside the grocery store for hours and hours for a bus that never came. "I don't know of any Greyhound stations," he said. "Your best bet would probably be Reno or Lancaster, but they're both three hours away by car so . . ."

She thanked him and started walking into the night. His heart tugged after her, whatever thread that brought them together not yet ready to be severed.

"Wait!" he called out.

She stopped and came back to him.

"What are you going to do?"

She shrugged. "Stand on the side of the highway, I guess, stick out my thumb, and wait for someone to pick me up."

"You can't do that." The very idea horrified him.

"Why not?" She seemed intrigued that he should care so much.

After all, they'd only just met. After all, he knew nothing about her. But he wanted to. He wanted to know everything.

"It's not safe," he said.

"It's all right. I know what I'm doing." She started to walk away again.

He grabbed her elbow and then, feeling her arm tense up, immediately released her. She cinched her arms close to her body and brushed at the spot where his hand had been. She stared at him, the gleam in her eyes like a dare. She was a foot shorter and probably forty pounds lighter than him, but he had this thought that if she wanted to, she could flip him on his back with a simple flick of her wrist.

"I didn't mean to startle you." He softened his tone. "It's just, it's the middle of the night. The highway's dark. Cars aren't going to be able to see you. They'll be speeding."

"What do you suggest then?" She crossed her arms defiantly.

"Wait until morning."

"And what do I do in the meantime?" she asked with a hint of frustration. "Sleep on a park bench? Under a bridge, maybe?"

Don't leave my side, he almost said, but stopped himself, realizing how stupid that would sound, how strange. He wanted to convince her to stay another day or two, not scare her off.

"There's this motel." Heat spread through his cheeks as he said it. "The Creekside Lodge. It's clean, safe. I know the woman who runs it. I can probably get you a discount."

She thought about it a moment, then shook her head. "I barely have enough money to pay for a bus ticket."

"I'll drive you to Santa Monica." He blurted the words without thinking, startling himself as well as the girl. He rushed on, improvising his plan as he did so. "I mean, I couldn't drive you until Sunday because I have to work tomorrow, so I guess that's two nights, but I could pay for one, or even both, and—" He stopped. She was staring at him like he'd lost his mind. He was talking too fast, sounding too desperate. He took a breath before continuing, slowing himself down. "I'm sorry. That's weird. It's too much, I know . . . it's just . . . I kind of believe that there's no such thing as coincidence, that things in life don't just happen by accident. Crazy, right? But hear me out. What if . . . I mean, maybe our paths crossed for a reason, you know? What if . . . ?" But he was too embarrassed to finish the thought.

He stared at his shoes. The left had come untied. Quietly, he said, "It's okay if you've changed your mind and think I'm a creep now. I'd understand completely if you did."

He waited to hear the girl moving away from him, her footsteps growing faint. Instead, she laughed, a tender sound, and her fingers brushed his arm. He looked up. Her eyes were bright, edged in starlight and secrets.

"I believe in destiny too." She walked around to the passenger side and climbed into the cab.

They stopped by an ATM on the way to Creekside Lodge. Every week, Nolan deposited half his paycheck into an account he opened a year ago with fifty dollars his father sent for his birthday. The rest he used to pay for gas, clothes, comic books, art supplies, and sometimes groceries. He had almost seven hundred dollars in his account, which he called his Rainy Day Fund, and lately, he'd been thinking of doing something special with the money, like taking Lucy and his mom to Disneyland or paying for ski lessons at Mammoth. He wasn't sure how much Gabriella would charge him for two nights at the Creekside, but he withdrew two hundred dollars, thinking that would be plenty and he'd still have money left over for a trip with Lucy and his mom later. If the Creekside turned out to be more expensive than that, he could always come back for more. He handed the money to the girl with the copper eyes, who still hadn't told him her name.

"It's too much," she said, but took the money anyway, slipping it into her backpack.

At that moment, a patrol car drove into the bank parking lot. It wasn't running lights or sirens, and anyway, they weren't doing anything wrong, but the girl froze a second and then shrank down in the passenger seat, putting up a hand to block her face. Her eyes tracked the cop car as it circled the lot. She relaxed again only after it turned a corner and drove away. Then she laughed nervously. "Sorry, old habits."

Nolan didn't ask her to explain.

When they arrived at the Creekside, they found Gabriella working the front desk. Her hair was piled on the top of her head. Three pencils stuck out from the knot. She smiled when Nolan came through the door. "Well, what a lovely surprise! And to what do I owe this visit, my dear boy?"

"My friend . . ." He gestured to the girl who hesitated at the door, suddenly shy. "She's in town for a few days."

Gabriella waved her hands, motioning him to say no more. "Of course, of course. Any friend of yours is a friend of mine." She turned and frowned at the wall of empty hooks behind her, then clucked in dismay and turned back to Nolan. "I'm sorry, dear." She gestured outside to the No Vacancy sign glowing venomous red. "It's the busy season, otherwise you know I would gladly—" She stopped midsentence, her eyes narrowing thoughtfully, then she smiled again.

"You can stay with me," she said, speaking directly to the girl. "I have a guest room. You'd have your own private bathroom, too."

"Oh, we couldn't ask you to do that," Nolan protested.

"You didn't ask." She winked at them both.

"We can pay you," Nolan said.

"Nonsense." Gabriella rummaged under the counter until she found a set of keys. She took one off the ring and pressed it into Nolan's hand, squeezing gently before letting go. "This is what we do, we take care of each other. This is how we heal the world."

Then to the girl, she said, "Please, make yourself right at home. I'm working late tonight, so don't wait up. Oh, and there's cheesecake in the fridge."

"Thank you." She was clearly baffled by Gabriella's generosity. "That's . . . thank you."

"All I ask is that you remember kindness, and pass it along when you can," Gabriella said.

The office door opened and a balding man entered, rolling a suitcase behind him. Gabriella shooed Nolan and the girl away from the counter with a reassuring smile and then turned her full attention to the man. "Welcome to Creekside Lodge. Do you have a reservation with us this evening?"

The girl waited until they were back inside the pickup before asking, "How do you know her?"

Nolan hesitated and then said, "We're part of this group. It's kind of like a church." Or what he thought a church might be like, since he'd never actually set foot inside one. "We meet once a week in the basement of the senior center and we talk and . . ." He drifted to silence, not sure how to explain it in a way that wouldn't make him sound completely nuts.

"And you take care of each other," she added.

"Yeah, something like that."

"It sounds nice." There was a wistfulness to her voice, a longing.

"Maybe you can come with me sometime."

The smile she gave him was cluttered with sadness. She turned and stared out the window, her gaze distant, stretching toward the mountains. "Maybe."

They were silent the rest of the way to Gabriella's house. Questions tangled on the tip of Nolan's tongue. There were so many things he wanted to ask her, so much to discover, but every time he started to speak, something stopped him. She would sigh or shift in her seat or clear her throat or twirl a section of hair around her finger. She kept her head turned away from him. Halfway to Gabriella's she leaned over and turned on the radio.

"Do you mind?"

He shook his head, even though the oldies station she stopped on wasn't coming in very clear and the static made his teeth hurt.

They arrived at Gabriella's around eleven thirty. Nolan shut off the radio. "This is it."

The house itself wasn't much to look at, a single-story bungalow in need of new windows and paint, but the front garden was magic. Sunflowers craned their long necks toward the stars. Jasmine climbed along the white picket fence. Glass globes of varying colors spun from the spreading branches of a maple tree. Tiny white lights danced inside the glass like fairies.

"So tomorrow I can come by after work, if you want," Nolan said. "We could get something to eat, I don't know, and have you heard of the Perseids? It's this incredible meteor shower and it's happening right now, it's at its peak."

"Yes," the girl said. "Yes, I think I'd like that very much. All of it." Then she reached into her backpack and took out the two hundred dollars he'd given her. She started to hand it to him, but he pushed it away.

"You keep it."

She bit down on her lip and stared at the money, trying to decide. Finally, she curled her fingers around the bills. "Okay, but I'm buying dinner."

He smiled. "Deal."

She opened the door and slid out of the pickup.

"Hey." He leaned across the seat. "You never told me your name."

For a moment he thought she wasn't going to tell him, then she did. The whole way home Nolan repeated it to himself, shaping his lips around the contours of each letter: Celeste. Like the heavens, the stars in the sky, like a meteorite cratered in his soul.

After his shift ended Saturday night, Nolan found Celeste waiting for him in the parking lot, sitting on the lowered tailgate of his pickup, swinging her feet in the air. A picnic basket sat atop a folded blanket beside her. She smiled as he approached and patted the wicker lid. "Gabriella let me borrow these. I thought we could have a picnic under the stars."

"You read my mind," Nolan said.

She laughed, and he wanted to capture the sound so he could listen to it anytime he wanted. She hopped off the tailgate. "You know of a good place to go?"

"I know the perfect place."

He took the basket and blanket from her and loaded them into the small cab space behind the driver's seat. The entire drive to the Buttermilks, he couldn't stop grinning.

Instead of taking the path from the house on Skyline, Nolan parked in the public lot on the north side, and he and Celeste hiked up the main trail toward the flat rock. He doubted Lucy was home, but he didn't want to risk running into her and having her ask questions about Celeste.

Watching the Perseids was a thing they'd done together as a family every August since their father left. It had been their mother's idea. "We need a new tradition, something with just the three of us." They drove out to the desert and pitched a tent, which they rarely slept in. Instead, they would spread their sleeping bags by a small fire, eat hot dogs and s'mores, tell stories, and look through Nolan's telescope until the fire died to coals. Then they would stretch out on their sleeping bags and spend the rest of the night oohing and aahing over small bursts of light, meteors streaking like match flames across the dark sky, a flash and then gone. Nolan looked forward to the trip every year, had been looking forward to it this year too, but Sandra was working graveyard at the hospital now and couldn't get the time off. She'd told Lucy and Nolan they could go without her, but Lucy had mumbled something about how once you've seen one meteor, you've seen them all, and shuffled to her room. They hadn't talked about it again.

The weather tonight was perfect for stargazing. Clear skies, not a single cloud, and warm too. Warm enough Nolan wasn't worried about Celeste getting cold in her purple paisley short-sleeved shirt and billowing gray pants, but he grabbed a sweatshirt from his pickup just in case.

As they hiked, they made small talk. Favorite colors: his

was blue, hers was rainbow—even after he argued that wasn't one color, but many. Favorite foods: he liked bacon cheese-burgers, she was partial to calamari and caramel pecan ice cream, though not at the same time. Favorite television shows: his was *X-Files*, hers was *Bewitched*. Favorite animal: they both loved blue whales. When they ran out of silly questions to ask each other, Celeste told him how Gabriella woke early that morning and made blueberry pancakes. "They were crisp on the outside, but fluffy in the middle. They were perfect. I can't figure out how she made them that way."

"I've never had her pancakes," Nolan said.

"Next time I'll invite you." She smiled at him, and though he tried to push it down, a thread of hope began to inch its way into his heart.

They reached the rock after a moderate, twenty-minute climb. The last section of trail was also the steepest and when they reached the top, Celeste leaned against a boulder, panting a little, trying to catch her breath. "Where are you taking me?"

Nolan pointed to the expansive view of Owens Valley behind her. She turned, and her breath left her a moment, her whole body going very still. Then she sighed and said, "It's . . . a dreamscape."

He had never thought of it like that, but once she said it, he couldn't see it any other way. From this high up and this far away, all of Owens Valley shimmered. The tiny buildings seemed made of spun sugar. The thin highway a licorice road. The Inyo Mountains rolled on the horizon, purple gumdrops against a Kool-Aid sky. In this moment, seeing it new, through Celeste's eyes, it seemed too beautiful, too perfect, to be real.

Nolan spread the blanket over the flat rock and climbed on top of it, then stretched out his hand to help Celeste up with the picnic basket. The rock was wide enough for both of them to sit comfortably side by side and stretch out their legs with room for the picnic basket between them.

Celeste opened the lid and pulled out two plastic-wrapped sandwiches. She handed one to Nolan and unwrapped the second for herself. "Fluffernutters. It's the only thing I know how to make."

She took a bite. Marshmallow fluff and peanut butter squished from between the two pieces of bread onto her cheek. She wiped it off and then stuck her thumb in her mouth, sucking the sticky concoction clean, laughing as she did. "I know," she said. "It's such a little kid thing to eat."

"I'm sure it's delicious."

"You've never had one?" She seemed surprised.

Nolan shook his head. He'd never even heard of fluffernutters before. He unwrapped his sandwich and bit into it. His teeth ached from the shock of sweet, and he wanted to spit it out, but the way she looked at him, so eager for his approval, he could do nothing but swallow and take another bite.

"It's like a candy sandwich," he said, trying to make it sound like a good thing.

She smiled, nodding, but there was sadness in her voice when she told him, "My mom used to make them for me."

"She doesn't anymore?"

A brief pause, a quick frown. "She's dead. She died a long time ago." And then she brushed it away, as if it were nothing, as if she were telling him about a pet goldfish. Her smile returned, though a little dimmer now, and the excitement in her voice sounded more strained than before when she asked him, "So, Nolan, tell me your life story. Start at the beginning and leave nothing out."

He wanted to go back to what she'd said about her mom, he wanted her to feel comfortable enough to confide in him, to share with him things she had never shared with anyone, but he could tell by the look on her face and the tension across her shoulders that she wasn't ready for that. *Don't ask*, her body language told him. *Move on*. So he did.

"It's not very exciting." He squinted into the distance. "I was born here. I've lived in the same house my whole life and have never left the state. I have a sister, just one. She's younger and better-looking."

Celeste laughed, a full and melodic sound like before, and Nolan felt his chest puff up a little knowing he had this effect on her, that he could bring her back from sadness.

"I work at Bishop's Grocery," he continued. "But you already knew that. I hate school, but get pretty good grades. My mom's a nurse. She works a lot. I don't know what my dad does anymore, but he used to run some kind of software company. They're divorced. He lives in LA now. I don't see him very often."

"Oh, that's . . . I'm sorry." She sounded like she meant it, too.

"It's okay," he said. "They split up when I was little. And anyway he's kind of an asshole."

He didn't tell her that sometimes he sat in what used to be his father's favorite leather recliner and whispered to the cushions about his day, or that he kept a half-spent cigar in a box at the top of his closet so he would never forget the way his father smelled. He didn't tell her either that sometimes he woke in the middle of the night in a panic, feeling too much and all at once, overwhelmed by his own irrelevance. Abandoned, unlovable. In those dark moments, he was the loneliest person on the planet, in the whole universe, convinced that there had never been—would never be—any creature as lonely as him.

He didn't tell her any of this, but she seemed to know because she reached over and covered his hand with hers, giving a gentle squeeze. She had freckles, a splash near the base of her thumb in the shape of the constellation Cassiopeia. Nolan stared at them and wished for her to never let go. But she did, and it took him a moment to gather himself before he spoke again.

"Anyway, when I'm not at school or work, I'm out here with my telescope, trying to find something that no one's ever seen before."

"Like a new planet?"

"Yeah, or a star, or . . ." He hesitated, wondering if he should tell her what he was really searching for.

Before he had a chance, she changed the subject. "I wanted to be an astronaut when I was little."

"But not anymore?"

She touched her stomach. "Motion sickness. I can't even ride in the backseat of a car without wanting to puke."

"So what do you want to do now?" He balled up the plastic wrap from his sandwich and tucked it back inside the picnic basket.

"First, I want to see the Pacific Ocean. Have you been?"

He shook his head, and her mouth popped open in surprise. "But you live so close!"

"It's like a five-hour drive," he said. "On a good day."

"Well, that's closer than I've ever been." She laughed.

He shrugged, not wanting to talk about it anymore, not wanting to remember that hot summer day five years ago, the beach outing his dad planned for them, a father-and-son trip, how Nolan waited all morning at the bottom of the driveway with an overnight bag and a boogie board Patrick let him borrow, how his mother came out of the house around eleven to tell him Robert called, something had come up and he wasn't going to make it. She told Nolan to come inside for lunch, but he refused. Instead, he sat on the curb, the bag and the board next to him, and stared down the empty road as the sun blazed hotter and hotter. Sometime in the middle of the afternoon, Lucy appeared beside him with a ham and cheese sandwich, a glass of ice water, and his favorite baseball cap. She put the cap on his head and set the rest on the curb, then stood for a while with her arms crossed, glaring at the road. Then she sighed and kicked a rock. "Who cares about the stupid beach anyway? It's crowded and you get sand everywhere, and the ocean's full of poisonous jellyfish and toxic waste and I wouldn't be there so it's probably good that you're not going because you'd be bored to death. We'll go together when we're older and can drive ourselves." She was trying to make him feel better, but it only made him feel worse, his stomach knotting, tears burning his eyes. "Did I ask your opinion?" he'd snapped at her, and when she still didn't leave: "Don't you have Barbie dolls to play with or something?" She'd gone away then, storming off in a huff and leaving him to cry alone.

Nolan didn't like thinking about that day, and the ocean could go drown itself for all he cared. What was a single, tiny ocean compared to an entire universe?

"And after that?" he asked Celeste. "After you see the Pacific? What then?"

"Hollywood," she said, a dreaminess settling on her face. "I want to be an actress."

Right after she said this, she tensed and dropped her gaze,

like she regretted telling him. She didn't say anything for a while and neither did he, and finally she raised her eyes to his again. "You didn't laugh."

He smiled. "Why would I do that?"

"Everyone else I've ever told laughed."

This time he was the one reaching for her hand, and he didn't let go.

For a second, neither of them moved except to breathe. He stared into her copper eyes and saw his reflection there in miniature. He wondered if her eyes were special, if that's why he could see himself, or if she, too, saw her reflection in his eyes, his dull brown, undeniably plain and human eyes. He leaned a little closer. Celeste blinked, breaking the enchantment, and lifted her face toward the sky. "I've never seen so many before."

The sun had set while they ate their sandwiches, and the sky above them was dark now, the moon barely a sliver, which made the stars stand out, many and bright. A canvas of white and blue and yellow twinkling lights, more than anyone could possibly hope to count, and these were only the stars they could see. There were even more that were too dim or distant to be visible with the naked eye. An impossible number of stars made more beautiful with her beside him. The longer he looked, the more he saw. They seemed to leap to the foreground, blasting like trumpets, making his head spin. He had never seen so many either. All the stars in the universe had come out for them. For her.

Nolan traced her profile with his gaze, chasing starlight along the soft curve of her neck. He had a sudden yearning to take his finger and brush her hair back, press his mouth to the hidden spot behind her ear, feel her skin on his lips, discover what she tasted like.

"What are we looking at?" she asked. "I mean, is there anything special up there? Anything interesting?"

He pointed toward a pinpoint of light no brighter than any of the others. "That's the Orion Nebula. It's 1,344 light-years from Earth. Give or take."

Even if they'd been looking through his telescope, it wouldn't have looked like much, but he'd seen pictures of it online, amazing images filled with light and color and stars emerging from voluminous clouds of cosmic dust. Beauty enough to soften even the hardest soul.

"It's not a star, not technically," he said. "It's a whole bunch of them. A stellar nursery."

As they watched, even now, new stars were forming, new worlds born.

He pointed to a different bright splinter. "That's Jupiter, the largest planet in our solar system." He moved his finger over an inch. "And that bright spot there is the Andromeda Galaxy. Which is a spiral galaxy like the Milky Way, and the farthest interstellar object that can be seen with the naked eye."

She looked where he pointed. Every part of him was tuned to her, aware of her body in relation to his, of her heat, her pulse, the quiet rustling of her hair against her shirt, her hand still wrapped up in his, anchoring him to Earth. He felt her fingers individually—thumb, pointer, middle, ring, pinky—each with its own distinct weight, and he was reluctant to move, for fear she might slip away. But he continued to point out interesting things in the sky, constellations, Cygnus and Orion and Gemini with its twin stars, Castor and Pollux. He told their stories, and then she asked about the dark space in between.

"What about those shapes? How come they don't have names?"

"We can name them if you want," he answered.

She lay back then, pulling him down onto the blanket with her, and keeping their fingers intertwined, she lifted their hands together and traced shapes in the air, outlining a spot in the sky near Pegasus where no stars were visible. "This right here . . . Perdita. The lost girl."

She lowered their arms back to the blanket. Distant voices from some other part of the Buttermilks reached them, but they stayed far off, not coming any closer, and after a while, Nolan barely noticed. He was too focused on listening to Celeste breathe, the stars dimming with each inhale, swelling brighter each exhale.

They were two alone under a nothing moon and dazzling stars, and there was no better time to ask her all the things he'd been holding back. Where had she come from? Why was she here? What did she want with him? He turned toward her with the words on the tip of his tongue, only to find that she was turning toward him, rising up on her elbows, moving closer.

He'd kissed a girl only once before. In fifth grade. Molly Condell, on the bus ride home from a field trip. Patrick had dared him, and he'd done it, and Molly's lips had felt like gummy fish, dry and sweet from her strawberry lip gloss. She'd shoved him away after a few seconds and wiped her hand across her mouth, squealing, "Gross!" Her girlfriends laughed. Patrick laughed hardest of all.

Nolan almost backed away from Celeste then, thinking of how humiliated he'd been after, but she hovered, waiting, and he recognized want in her eyes, a question only he could answer. He cupped her face with one hand, pulling her down to him. Their lips touched.

He closed his eyes and they spun together, up from Earth,

out through the atmosphere, rising above the Milky Way Galaxy, looking down as it grew smaller and smaller, feeling the pull of the whole universe inside him. A humming started in the back of his mind, quietly at first, like a room full of people talking, and then louder, louder, turning to a vibrating thrum, an electric current coursing through him to her, or her to him, he couldn't tell. Did it matter? The thrum turned to a song, a haunting and vaguely familiar melody. The stars, the stars were singing, and Celeste was the reason why. All loneliness, all worry, all fear, forgotten. The stars, her lips: the antidotes, the only splendors that mattered now.

Sunday morning arrived too soon. Nolan couldn't let Celeste go. They were just getting to know each other, just getting started. But neither could he force her to stay. He picked her up from Gabriella's at nine o'clock and, by nine fifteen, they were headed south toward Lancaster, flying it seemed. Celeste clutched her backpack in her lap. She had the window rolled down, her hair a tornado, and the radio tuned to the same oldies station as before, the volume cranked high, static crackling. Between the noise and the smell of her coconut shampoo, Nolan was having trouble thinking straight.

They were almost to Big Pine now, and panic set in. If he didn't think of something soon, it would be too late to suggest turning around, and then it was only a matter of hours before they were in Santa Monica and Celeste was getting out of the pickup, swinging her backpack over her shoulders, saying good-bye, walking into the sunset, lost to him forever. The best idea he'd come up with so far was to run his pickup off the road. He imagined losing control, slamming into a fence post, one or both of them getting seriously injured—so, not the best idea. He tried to think of something else, but the music made it impossible.

Without warning, Celeste switched off the radio. She bent forward, squinting and pressing her face close to the windshield, then gasped and said, "Stop! Stop the car! Pull over!"

Nolan slammed on the brakes. Tires squealed. Celeste lurched in her seat, the seat belt tightening across her chest. Her backpack fell off her lap and into the foot well. Nolan steered onto the highway shoulder and stopped. He had been so consumed with trying to come up with a plan to get Celeste to change her mind and stay in Bishop, that he hadn't even realized how close they were to the observatory.

A few miles ahead, three massive radio telescopes rose from the valley floor. Some people called them the Big Ears, but Nolan thought they looked more like umbrellas turned inside out by a great gust of wind. Ears, umbrellas, however else they might appear, one thing not in question was their imposing stature. They were the tallest man-made objects for miles in any direction, giants with skinny bodies and oversized heads, bright white faces always pointed toward the sky. He knew it was only an optical illusion, but sometimes when he saw the telescopes from a distance, they appeared taller even than the mountains.

"What are those?" Celeste asked, her voice a mix of fear and wonder.

"Telescopes," he answered. "It's a radio observatory. We can get closer to them if you want."

She nodded, keeping her wide eyes fixed on the telescopes as he steered back onto the highway toward Leighton Drive, a single-lane road leading to the observatory. He snuck glances out of the corner of his eye, trying to gauge Celeste's reaction.

Was she simply impressed with their size, curious about these strange-looking machines pointed at the sky? Or was it something else? Recognition, maybe, or déjà vu.

Only three nights ago, Nolan saw what he believed to be an extraterrestrial craft touch down at this very spot. Two nights ago, he met Celeste. And now, they were here together, and she was leaning as far forward as she could, her hands pressed against the dashboard, her fingernails pale from the force of her grip. A muscle in her jaw twitched.

Nolan parked in the scrub in front of a large Authorized Personnel Only sign. Fifty yards past this stood one of the three telescopes. The other two were set up farther away, though still close enough to be intimidating. Celeste got out of the pickup, and Nolan did too, following her to a flimsy-looking barbed wire fence meant to dissuade people from trespassing. If they drove through the gate and another half mile down Leighton Drive, they'd come to the observatory itself, a squat beige building that all but disappeared into the desert landscape.

Nolan had been there once, when he was younger, with his mother and father and a dozen other people he didn't know, for a public tour of the facility. Lucy had been a toddler still, barely old enough to walk. Nolan didn't remember much about the trip except the way his father treated the astrophysicist leading the tour. Like he was some kind of superhuman genius who made the Earth spin and the stars appear.

Celeste stopped a few steps from the fence and tilted her head back to take in the full height of the closest telescope. "What are they for?"

"They're listening to the universe," Nolan said. "I like to think of them as eavesdropping on the stars." When she didn't say anything, he added, "It's similar to studying stars with an optical telescope, only instead of gathering light waves, these telescopes gather radio waves. Every object in interstellar space emits different wavelengths and these telescopes gather that information. It all gets focused into the antenna, and then the receiver converts them to electrical signals and then those signals get turned into data that astronomers and other scientists can sort through and interpret to develop new theories or confirm old ones about the universe and our place in it."

She lowered her gaze to his, and for a second he couldn't breathe. Then she blinked, releasing him, and walked back to the pickup. She swung the tailgate open and climbed onto it. He came and sat beside her.

They were quiet a moment, then Celeste asked, "What do you think your place in the universe is, Nolan?"

The question surprised him, and he didn't know quite what to say.

"I mean, why do you think you're here?" she clarified.

"Here . . ."

"On Earth," she said. "In Bishop. At this particular point in time. Why here? Why now? Why you?"

"I . . ." He paused, scratching at a fleck of blue paint peeling off the tailgate. "I guess I've never really thought about it. No, I have. Thought about it, I mean, but I haven't come up with any good answers."

She sighed and took his hand, interlacing her fingers with his. "Yeah, me neither. Before I met you, I thought I was destined to be alone. I thought that in order to be safe, to be free, to be . . . myself . . . I had to keep moving."

In the distance, cars passed on the highway, some traveling north, some traveling south, all traveling on without her.

She smiled like she was remembering something nice, something she hadn't remembered in a long time. "I had this feeling about you, you know. The night we met." Her fingers traced her collarbone like she was searching for a necklace that was no longer there. "Do you ever get that? Like a buzzing under your skin? Intuition, I guess it's called. Like . . . you just know things? About a person? Or a place?" She looked back up at the telescopes. "I got that when I saw these. A feeling like we were supposed to stop here. I don't know why, I don't know what it means, but I got that same feeling with you, too. Like you were the person I was supposed to find, the one person in the whole world who would be able to help me." Before he could respond, she rushed on, "Tell me a secret. Something you've never told anyone else before."

He chewed on the inside of his cheek for a moment, contemplating. There were so many things he could say, so many late-night thoughts about loneliness and belonging, about his parents, his father especially, how he always felt like he was disappointing them, never able to live up to their expectations, about Lucy, about how afraid he was of disappointing her too, all these things he'd never wanted to share with anyone until now, until her. Finally, he said, "I think I was born on the wrong planet."

He held his breath, waiting for her to laugh and let go of his hand, but she didn't. She squeezed tighter.

"What do you mean?"

He tried to explain. "Sometimes when I'm at school or at work, surrounded by so many people, all the cars, the lights, the buildings, everyone talking and rushing to get places, I start to feel dizzy, confused. I don't know. I feel lost. But then, I look up at the stars. And it feels like home."

She didn't say anything.

"It's stupid, I know."

"It's not." She lifted her face to the sky even though there was nothing to see but empty blue and a blinding sun. "I've had days like that, too. Days when I feel like I don't belong here, when I'm surrounded by people who don't see me, not the real me."

He wanted to hold her and whisper that he saw her, that from the very first time they met, he knew how special she was, how rare. He wanted to kiss her again, too, but he wasn't sure if she wanted the same.

She lowered her gaze and caught him staring, but she didn't pull away. She smiled softly and rubbed her thumb across the back of his hand. "Tell me what you're thinking about right now."

"The rule of three."

Her thumb stilled, and her eyes narrowed slightly. He could tell she didn't understand, that it wasn't what she'd been expecting him to say, so he explained, "If you have one extraordinary thing happen to you, you can consider it an anomaly. If two extraordinary things happen, then you might be able to brush it off as coincidence. But three things, and that's a pattern. It has meaning and so you should pay attention."

"Has something extraordinary happened?" she asked.

"The night before I met you, I saw something out here. Lights." He wasn't nervous at all telling her, the way he would have been if he were talking to his mom, or Lucy, or even Wyatt, who believed the same as Nolan. He didn't have to try and impress her, he didn't have to be anyone other than himself. "They touched down for a few seconds by that telescope. I think it might have been . . . well, I don't know what exactly, but it was definitely extraordinary."

"So an anomaly, then?"

He shook his head. "A month ago I saw similar lights hovering over the boulders behind my house."

"Like UFOs?" It didn't sound like she was making fun of him, but he hesitated anyway, and she added, "I saw a ghost once."

He waited for her to elaborate, but she didn't.

"The lights flew," he said. "And I have yet to identify them, so technically, yes, Unidentified Flying Objects."

She laughed, but in a way that made him feel expansive, rather than belittled. Then she asked, "Was there a third thing?"

He traced the freckles on her hand. "You."

This time she kissed him, and it was even better than the first time, deep and sweet, their bodies humming in harmony, and he never wanted it to end.

She pulled away, but only for a second, long enough to whisper, "What if I stayed?"

6

Lucy woke early, when the rose-colored dawn seeped through the motel room's thin curtains and flared across her face. She lay in bed watching the light creep up the wall and set the room ablaze. Her migraine was gone, but she still felt a little shaky. Yesterday had been a long day. A lot of hours behind the wheel, a lot of disappointing conversations, far too much of Adam fucking Paulson—she shuddered thinking about him—also she didn't remember eating anything after breakfast. Most likely the headache was a consequence of all those things combined. A stress headache, a hunger headache, and nothing more to worry about.

She rolled out of bed, ate a granola bar from the vending machine, then changed into her running gear and headed out for an easy two miles. She stuck to the main streets, choosing neighborhoods with lots of houses, and as she ran, she tried to work out what she was going to say to Sandra. The trouble was deciding where to start. There were just so many things that needed saying, ten years' worth of words. More than that even, because really they'd stopped talking about important things long before Nolan went missing. But first, before any-thing else, Lucy had to come clean about the photographs. She had to tell Sandra, and now Wyatt too, she supposed, the truth about what she'd done.

Back at the motel, Lucy showered and changed into the same clothes from yesterday, jeans, a red T-shirt, and black hoodie. She blew her hair dry, then slipped back into her run-ning shoes.

Her father called while she was in the shower. She listened to his short message. "It's me. Just wanted to find out if you're settling into your new apartment all right." Then deleted it. The landlord called yesterday after she was already an hour outside of Los Angeles. She told him there was a slight change of plans. She had a few personal matters to attend to before she could officially move in, and since she'd already paid the first month's rent, she asked if he would just hold the apartment for her, assuring him that she still wanted the place, apologizing for any inconvenience, and promising he could keep her secu-rity if she wasn't moved in by the end of the month, which she would be, she assured him again. The landlord told her she had until the fifteenth to pick up the key. Otherwise, he would rent the place out to someone else *and* keep her money. At some point Lucy would have to tell Robert where she was and what she was doing, but not yet. He wanted her to grow up and start handling life on her own. That was his whole reason for kick-ing her out of the house. So here she was, doing just that, or trying anyway.

On her way out to the car, Lucy stopped by the front office to pay for another night's stay. Then she drove north, follow-ing Wyatt's map until she came to a no-name dirt road distin-guished by a wooden post stuck in the ground with an antelope skull perched on top. Another half mile and the road ended in front of a double-wide trailer. A few yards from that was a small airplane hangar. The siding was new and shining. A row of small windows ran along the top, winking in the sunlight. A large satellite dish, set up in the space between the two buildings, pointed southeast at a sharp angle from the horizon.

Lucy pulled up next to a motorcycle and a blue sedan, but didn't get out of the car. Earlier she'd been so certain she was doing the right thing, but now that she was here, her mind flooded with excuses of why she should leave. Sandra wasn't going to believe her anyway. Maybe Sandra wasn't even here. Maybe Wyatt had lied in order to lure her out to this isolated location where no one could hear her scream. Now she was just being ridiculous. She drummed her fingers on the steering wheel and stared into the distance where clouds threw down blue shadows over a row of golden-fleeced and rolling hills. The light was in a constant state of flux, goldenrod to ochre to burnt sienna to gray and then a flash of brilliant yellow as the clouds cleared for a brief moment before scudding in again and turning the landscape violet. Anyone else might have sighed at the beauty of it, snapped a picture or two. Lucy looked at those mountains and their shifting light, and saw only duplicity.

Before she could come to any decision, one of the hangar doors opened, and Wyatt stepped out. He walked toward her, raising his hand to wave. A large black dog trotted at his side. Lucy got out and met them halfway.

"Any trouble finding the place?" he asked.

She shook her head, her gaze moving past him to the open hangar door.

The dog bumped against her leg. His mouth hung open in a sloppy grin, his tail wagging his whole body side to side. He was a German shepherd covered in thick black fur, all black, night black, with pointed ears, sharp teeth, strong haunches, paws as big as pancakes, and muscles that rippled with even the slightest motion.

"This is Kepler," Wyatt said. "Kepler, this is Lucy."

The dog wagged harder.

"Technically, he belongs to Sandra," Wyatt explained, reaching to scratch between his ears. "But some days I think he fancies himself the whole world's dog."

Kepler grinned at Lucy and then reached a long, pink tongue to lick the back of her hand. She laughed, and then she and Wyatt started to speak at the same time.

"About last night, I shouldn't have—"

"I'm sorry I stormed off—"

They both stopped midsentence. Wyatt smiled. His hair wasn't slicked back today. It was loose and tumbling. He looked casual, relaxed, more like a person and less like a pundit, and Lucy thought that if this had been the man she met at the bar the night before, things might have gone quite differently.

"I think we can agree we both started off on the wrong foot," he said. "Let's just call it water under the bridge and start over fresh, okay?"

She nodded and then asked, "Does she know I'm here?"

He scratched the top of Kepler's head again. "We've been waiting for you."

She followed Wyatt and the dog into the hangar, which was far more cavernous than it appeared from the outside. The front half was set up like a living area with a couch, a television, and a small kitchen, while the back half appeared to be both a workshop and office space. There was no clear division between the two sections. Various tools, machinery, and kitchen appliances cluttered workbenches along three walls. An engine hung from the ceiling by a heavy chain. Along another wall were filing cabinets and a corner desk where Sandra sat working at a computer, her back to the door. Lucy recognized the shape of her shoulders, the hunched-over way she'd always sat at a desk, hunting and pecking the letters with two fingers.

Kepler went over and nudged her leg. Sandra patted his head, but kept working. Wyatt cleared his throat, his eyes darting between Lucy and Sandra, then he turned away from both of them and went to a row of cabinets, taking a kettle from one and filling it with water out of an industrial sink. He poured the water into a coffeemaker and then busied himself scooping grounds into the filter and finding cups and sugar.

Lucy stood frozen near the door, all the words she'd practiced earlier evaporating like so much steam. What do you say to someone you haven't seen in over nine years? What do you say to a mother who hates you? This was a conversation that should have taken place years ago when it would have made a difference. The silence stretched to breaking, and Lucy was about to turn and go because what the hell was she thinking coming here anyway? There were not enough words in the English language to fix all that was broken between them. Then Wyatt called across the room, "Sandra, come have a cup of coffee with us."

Sandra didn't move for a long minute, then she sighed and pushed back from the desk, and Lucy had to remind herself to breathe as her mother came closer. Sandra stopped in front of Lucy with her arms crossed over her chest. She'd gained weight. Her cheeks were puffy and round, and there was very little definition now between her chin and neck. The clothes she wore were loose and baggy, all that extra fabric adding pounds. Lucy wondered if she had changed as much in Sandra's eyes as Sandra had changed in hers. Was there anything familiar? Any trace of that bubble-cheeked, pigtailed, happy little girl Lucy used to be? Or was she completely unrecognizable now? Only a shell of her former self. She had grown up, which was more than Nolan ever had a chance to do, and maybe that's what Sandra was seeing now: all the things her son would never be.

"Does she have a device?" Sandra asked.

Nothing about her voice had changed, her words still clipped short and no-nonsense; the sound of it still made Lucy shrink a little on the inside.

As far back as she could remember, Lucy had never known how to talk to her mother. They spoke, it seemed, in two different languages, and every conversation that didn't include Nolan acting as mediator ended with someone, usually Lucy, breaking down in tears. Lucy spent much of her childhood feeling invisible in her mother's presence, or on the worst days, inferior. She wasn't artistic or clever like Nolan. She wasn't sick or bleeding like the patients who came into the hospital. There was nothing very special about her at all. For years, she tried to be noticed. She was a good girl and followed all the rules and fought for her good grades, even did all the extra credit problems or made up her own if there weren't any, and helped out other kids who were struggling, and her teachers said she was a joy to have in class, a special little girl indeed, but her mother, distracted as she was with the divorce and then her work and her wine and later Nolan, could only see the things Lucy got wrong. How she didn't sort the laundry right. How she stayed up too late watching television and because of this sometimes missed the bus the next morning. How she got an A on her spelling test instead of an A+. Nothing Lucy did, it seemed, was ever good enough for Sandra.

"Does she have a device?" Sandra asked again, and though she stared at Lucy, her question was clearly directed at Wyatt.

He lifted his eyebrows, giving Sandra a bemused look. "Do you really think that's necessary?"

"That's how they track us," she countered. "You know that. They're listening to every word we say right now."

"Who is?" Lucy asked and then pressed her fingers to her lips, horrified that these were her first words to her mother after all this time, that her tone betrayed what she was thinking. *This is nuts. You are nuts.*

"The NSA," Sandra said. "The FBI. The police even. They're all listening."

Lucy stared, trying to figure out if Sandra was drunk. Her eyes were bright, her hands steady, her words clear. There were no empty bottles lying around, no stench of booze on her breath. She looked sober enough. Though that didn't mean much. For many years after the divorce, Sandra was a highly functional drunk. If confronted, she denied it. A glass of wine after work, what's the big deal? she always argued. And that was fine for a while, but then she started to work graveyard and "after work" was seven in the morning and the glass of wine was her breakfast. She was sober again by the time her next shift started and except for a few times when she'd fallen asleep and forgotten about Nolan and Lucy, who then had to fend for themselves at dinner—taking money from her wallet and ordering a pizza, or eating cold cereal and toast in front of the television—except for those few times, Lucy hardly even noticed. It was only after Nolan went missing that Sandra replaced wine with vodka, and the liquor seemed to mix differently with her pain, turning her angry and mean.

Speaking to Wyatt again, Sandra said, "I'd feel more comfortable if she left it in the car."

Wyatt looked at Lucy and shrugged. "It's up to you."

Sandra had always been a very rational-minded woman. She used to tell Lucy and Nolan that there was a reasonable explanation for everything, and if something sounded impossible, it probably was, and to question everything twice. She drilled the scientific method into their brains the way other mothers drilled the alphabet. When she found out about the UFO Encounters Group, she forbade Nolan from attending, and even as he ignored her and collapsed deeper into his delusions, she fought to bring him back. She fought, and she lost. And maybe that was when the old Sandra, the reasonable-explanation-for-everything Sandra, took a step back and allowed this new, my-son-was-abducted-by-aliens-and-the-government-is-listening-to-every-word-we-say Sandra to take over.

Lucy took her cell phone out of her purse and gave it a little shake. "Is this what you're talking about?"

Sandra made a face. Wyatt nodded. She had already come this far, hadn't she? She went back to her car and left the phone in the glove box. When she reentered the hangar, Sandra and Wyatt stood close together, talking in low voices. They stopped when she came in.

"Want one?" Wyatt held up a cup of coffee.

Lucy took it and sat down on a folding chair next to the minifridge.

"Thank you for humoring me." Sandra smiled stiffly, taking her own cup and sitting on a spread of rumpled blankets covering the couch. A suitcase lay open at her feet. Clothes spilled out of it onto the floor.

Wyatt perched himself on another folding chair near Lucy. With a heavy sigh and jangling tags, Kepler sank onto the rug in the center of their clumsy circle. He laid his head on his paws and shifted his keen black eyes between the three of them. Lucy hoped Wyatt would speak first and break the building tension, but he seemed wholly focused on his coffee, taking long, thoughtful sips and then staring into the cup as if he might be able to discern their future in the swirls of cream.

Lucy tested the coffee, but it was too hot for her to drink. She held the cup in her lap. Someone had to say something. The silence was starting to feel oppressive. "I went by the house looking for you."

"I haven't lived there in a long time," Sandra said.

Lucy waited for her to continue and fill in the missing years, but she didn't, and the silence rushed in again, expanding and making it hard to breathe.

What happened to everything she left at the house on Skyline Road? Lucy wondered. The twin bed pushed up against the wall, covered in a hot-pink comforter she received as a present for her thirteenth birthday. The wooden nightstand painted robin's-egg blue and riddled with stickers. The stack of Boxcar Children books she kept on the bottom shelf. The matching dresser. The oval mirror that hung on the wall above it. Her clunky boom box that sat on top surrounded by meteorites and other interesting rocks she and Nolan had collected together. The posters of her favorite track stars Jackie Joyner-Kersee and Steve Prefontaine taped to her closet doors. She didn't take any of it with her to her father's house. She'd asked him to buy her all new things, and he had. He'd given her a whole new life. But where were her old things now? Boxed up and collecting dust in some storage unit? Rotting in a landfill? She scanned the hangar, glancing over the filing cabinets and several small cardboard boxes scattered throughout the shop. Nothing looked big enough to hold all she'd left behind.

Sandra's voice cut into her thoughts. "Have you shown her the pictures?"

"She saw the article," he said.

This was it, an opening. No more excuses. Lucy took a breath to confess what she should have confessed ten years ago, but Sandra was getting to her feet now, setting her coffee on the table, and rushing across the hangar to her desk.

"You need to see the originals to get the full effect." She rifled through a stack of papers and returned carrying an envelope printed with a Walgreens logo. She held it out for Lucy to take.

Lucy set down her coffee first, then shook the pictures from the envelope and flipped through them slowly, stalling for time. Each one was a variation of the image she'd seen on *Strange Quarterly*'s website. A blue orb against a midnight background, spikes of bright light shooting from its center. Lucy didn't understand how anyone in their right mind could see this and conclude they were looking at something extraterrestrial. To her it was an obvious hoax, one she would recognize even if she hadn't helped build the stupid thing.

They'd spent three days in Patrick's parents' garage putting it together. Patrick and Adam did most of the labor, attaching a frame to a remote control helicopter and then adding special lights. Lucy stood by and instructed them on how it should look. Another girl, Megan, was there too, but Lucy didn't remember her doing much of anything besides smoking clove cigarettes and flirting with Patrick. They waited until after midnight, then drove to the house on Skyline Road and parked at the bottom of the driveway near the mailbox. Lucy pointed out which window was Nolan's. Adam and Patrick chucked small rocks, *click, click, click*, against the glass. Then they ran back to the car and started up the helicopter. A marvel of swirling lights, it reeked of half-burned fuel. They flew it up and down and side to side for several minutes, chugging down a whole case of Pabst between the four of them, but Nolan never came out of the house. They thought it was a bust, that Nolan had either slept through the whole thing or recognized it for what it was: nothing. A joke. Bored kids playing stupid games. They didn't think Nolan would take it seriously; they didn't think anyone would.

Lucy passed the photographs back to Sandra.

"We believe this UFO might be the same one that took Nolan." There was no irony in Sandra's voice when she said this, no shade of sarcasm nor hint of a laugh.

"It's fake." Lucy looked at Wyatt when she said this because if she looked at her mother, she would lose her nerve.

Sandra inhaled sharply, but Wyatt held up his hand for her to stay quiet.

"We've had several experts look at the film," he said. "It hasn't been manipulated in any way."

"No, that's not what I mean." Lucy twisted her fingers together in her lap. "What's in the picture, that light . . . it's not a UFO."

She was going to explain further, except Sandra waved the photographs in her face again. "What else could it possibly be?"

Lucy shook her head, her mouth opening and closing, the words refusing to come out.

"I knew this was going to be a waste of time." Sandra stuffed the pictures back in the envelope.

"What happened to you?" Lucy asked, surprised by her own voice and the defiance she felt simmering beneath her rib cage.

Sandra's jaw tightened, but she said nothing. She clutched the envelope to her chest.

"You used to hate this stuff," Lucy said. "I remember you saying that people who believed in anything supernatural were either creeps, psychos, or liars. You wanted to take Nolan to see a specialist. Don't you remember that? You said there was something wrong with his brain."

Sandra's nostrils flared. "I just didn't understand what was happening, that's all. I chose not to see what your brother saw all along. What he tried to show us."

"And what was that exactly?" They were getting off track, but Lucy couldn't help herself. After all, it was Sandra who'd taught her to question absurd claims such as these.

"That there's more to this universe than our small planet, more to life than what our limited human brains can show us," Sandra answered. "Your brother . . . he was . . . he *is* very special. We think that's the reason They took him and why They haven't returned him to us yet. His brain, his mind, it's different from most, and They recognized that. They saw his potential in a way we couldn't and so They took him from us."

"Like as punishment?" It sounded so ridiculous. Lucy had a hard time suppressing her laughter.

"Maybe, but doubtful. We're not that important to Them." Sandra raised her shoulders a little higher, and, with a completely straight face, said, "More likely They wanted to study him and find out if his gifts could be used for the betterment of the universe."

A single laugh escaped Lucy's lips. "You do realize how nuts that sounds, don't you?"

She didn't intend for the words to come out so cruel and jagged, but being here, listening to this, she was beginning to feel like she was losing hold of reality, and when she went looking for something solid to grab on to, she found anger.

"Lucy . . ." Wyatt's voice a warning.

"If you have a better explanation, we'd love to hear it." Sandra spread a hand in the air, gesturing for her to give them something, anything.

Both of them watched her, waiting. Even Kepler, his big eyes blinking up at her. All of them with such high expectations and naked hope. She could think of any number of other explanations for what had happened to Nolan—he committed suicide, he got lost and died of exposure, he was kidnapped by a pedophile—but refused to say them out loud. They were all too awful. She didn't want any of them to be true, and some superstitious part of her feared speaking them into existence. So she gave the only explanation she could live with.

"He ran away."

"Bullshit," Sandra said. "That's bullshit and you know it as well as I do."

Lucy flinched and stared at the floor.

Then Sandra turned her anger on Wyatt. "She's as close-minded and myopic as the rest of them. I should have never agreed to letting her come here. She doesn't want to help us. She's the same as she's always been and nothing has changed and we're no closer to bringing him home than if she hadn't come at all." She sank onto the couch again and buried her face in her hands.

Wyatt looked at Lucy, a question in his eyes, a plea for her to wait and give this more time. But Lucy was halfway to the door already. Ten steps more and she would be gone from this place, back in her car and driving west to LA, back to the half-life she'd cobbled together from the fucked-up pieces of this one. She'd tried. Maybe she hadn't given her best effort, but at least she'd made one, which was more than her mother could say.

Outside, the sky was blue glass. Shredded wisps of clouds hung above the mountains. A breeze swayed the yellow grass and cooled her too-hot skin. She stopped next to her car and hugged her arms around her chest, focusing on the feel of the earth beneath her, how solid, how still. Even though she knew there was nothing still about this planet, all of them spinning together, a thousand miles an hour, it was a wonder they hadn't spun to oblivion eons ago. The worst part of this whole thing was that Sandra was right: Lucy didn't want to help. Not if helping meant relinquishing her hold on reality.

The hangar door opened. Wyatt came and stood beside her. For a while they said nothing, simply stood elbow to elbow and stared up at the endless blue.

"You know," Wyatt said. "That actually went better than I thought it would."

"What the hell am I even doing here?" Lucy asked, not expecting him to answer, but then he reached into his pocket and handed her a folded piece of paper. "What's this?"

She unfolded it and scanned her eyes down a list of names, all of which she recognized.

Detective Harold Mueller
Stuart Tomlinson
Robert Durant
Patrick Tyndale

Her own name was scribbled at the bottom, but then crossed out.

"This is a list of people who refuse to talk to me about Nolan's disappearance." Wyatt reached into his other pocket, this time pulling out his wallet. He showed her a laminated badge that resembled a driver's license with his picture and name, only instead of State of California across the top, it read *UFO ENCOUNTERS: Senior Field Investigator.*

"These are the only credentials I have." He slipped the wallet back into his pocket. "So, you can probably guess how seriously the people on that list take me. I leave messages that never get returned. I send emails that go straight into trash folders. I try to meet with them in person and they laugh in my face, call me freak or nut job or psycho, and then walk away. I've been trying for months and getting nowhere."

"But you think I'll have better luck." She refolded the paper, sliding her fingers across the seams.

"You're his sister. You're family. Added bonus, you're a nonbeliever. They'll talk to you."

She stared at the folded square, turned it over in her hands.

"I think the article was just an excuse," he said.

"What do you mean?"

"I think you want to know what happened to Nolan that night just as badly as the rest of us. Otherwise why bother making the trip out here? I think you *do* want to help." Wyatt reached over and tapped the paper twice. "This is where you start."

7

Lucy called the county sheriff's office from her car. The woman who answered told her Detective Mueller retired from the force four weeks ago. "Is there a specific case you're calling about? Because if so, it's probably been reassigned and I can put you through to that detective."

"It's a missing person's case," Lucy said. "Nolan Durant?"

The woman didn't recognize the name and had to look it up on her computer. After a few seconds humming and mumbling to herself, she finally found it. "This one's been assigned to Detective Williams. I can transfer you to his voice mail."

"I'll just get his number from you, if that's okay."

Lucy added the new detective's information to the bottom of Wyatt's list and then drove to Mueller's last known address, which Wyatt had given to her earlier along with the advice to ask open-ended questions and let people talk as long as they want. It sounded like the flimsiest kind of detective work. She had no training in this kind of thing, no idea what she should be listening for. "You'll know," Wyatt had said. "When you're onto something, you'll feel it here." He'd tapped his fingers against his chest. Besides, he'd told her, she couldn't do any worse than the shit job that had already been done.

It was almost two in the afternoon when Lucy knocked on Harold Mueller's door. An older woman answered, holding a paintbrush in one hand. Her auburn hair was pulled back in a neat ponytail. Bright splotches of paint stained her coveralls. Her mouth curved up in a warm, but questioning smile. "Can I help you?"

"Does Harold Mueller live here?" Lucy asked.

The woman nodded, her brow furrowing a little. "That's my husband."

"I'm Lucy Durant," she started to explain, but the woman recognized her name.

"Come in." She swung open the door and stepped back. "Harry's in the backyard."

She led Lucy through the house to a set of French doors that opened onto a large brick patio. A man in rubber waders and a green flannel shirt stood in the middle of the lawn with his back to the house. He whipped a beautiful redwood fishing rod back and forth, over his shoulder and then out in front of him toward a fence that encircled the yard, casting an invisible fly into an invisible river. Harry's wife nodded for Lucy to go ahead and then left her on the patio to make her own introduction.

Lucy remembered Harold Mueller as a clownish man, red-faced and fumbling, on the downhill side of middle-aged, plump and always reeking of cheap coffee. She had a clear image of him standing in the doorway the morning after Sandra called the police. Brushing crumbs from the front of his wrinkled suit jacket, frowning at a mustard-brown stain on his tie. His right shoe was untied. When he introduced himself as the primary detective assigned to Nolan's case, shaking Sandra's hand first and then Lucy's, his palm had been slick and sticky with something—grease or sweat or melted sugar, all three maybe. It was that moment, taking her hand from his and wiping the stickiness off on her pants, that Lucy realized she was never going to see her brother again.

Lucy stepped onto the lawn. "Detective Mueller?"

Without looking at her, he said, "Not anymore, I'm not. Harry will do just fine." He continued to cast, the tip of the rod cracking whip-like through the air.

"I don't know if you remember me . . ." she started to say.

His eyes flicked over her and then returned to the invisible river. "I retired a few weeks ago."

"Yes, I heard."

"If you want to talk about your brother's case, you're going to have to call the office, make an appointment with whichever poor son of a bitch it's been reassigned to."

She put her hands in the pockets of her jacket and watched him cast for a few minutes. He was skinnier now, though his cheeks were still flushed red. Sweat beaded along his receding hairline and dampened the collar of his shirt. He squinted into the distance, his fingers and arms going through the motions, choreographed perfectly with the movement of the rod. Lucy had never been fly-fishing, but she knew there was a delicacy to it, techniques that took time and patience to master.

She broke the silence. "Where do you fish?"

He glanced at her warily, a scowl tugging his mouth.

When a few minutes passed and he still hadn't given her any answer, she said, "My brother and I used to hike out to

McGee Creek. We had these dinky little kid rods, you know, the plastic kind with the big reels. Mine was pink. His was blue. They weren't good for much except catching leaves. But we tried anyway."

For hours, they'd dabbled their bait in the shallow pools near the shore. For hours, their lines hung slack. They sat on a log with their bare feet dangling right above the glittering surface. Stretch and you could swipe a toe through the clear water and send ripples into the rushing center current. The sun beat down warm on their necks, the lap and gurgle of the creek harmonized with the trill and twitter of unseen birds. Those hours, those useless, nothing hours, were as close to perfection as Lucy could remember now.

There was only one time she could recall when they pulled a fish to shore, though not with either of their dinky excuses for rods. It was a lazy summer day, interchangeable with all the other lazy days that summer. Lucy was about to start fifth grade, Nolan was going into seventh. Patrick had come over to show off a real rod he'd gotten for his birthday from one of his dad's many rich business associates. They passed it around a while, oohing and aahing, sliding their fingers along the slick graphite, toying with the heavy-duty reel, spinning the knob. Then they decided to take it to the creek. They raided the pantry for marshmallows since Patrick hadn't brought worms and none of them wanted to waste time digging.

At the creek, they settled down on a flat rock half-submerged in water. Patrick went first, snagging a bit of marshmallow on the end of the hook and casting the line downriver far out into the center current. "You'll have more luck casting upriver and letting the bait drift down," Nolan tried to explain, pointing toward a deep pool shaded by an overhanging tree. "Try that spot over there."

Patrick waved his words away with authority. "I know what I'm doing."

After about twenty minutes, with Patrick flicking the rod back and forth, skipping the increasingly soggy and disintegrating marshmallow across the tiny rapids, but catching nothing, Nolan stretched out his hand. "Let me try."

With some hesitation, Patrick gave him the rod. "You better not break it."

Nolan removed what was left of the old marshmallow and flicked it into the creek before reaching into the bag for a new one. Then he turned to one of the deepest pools running along the bank, a pool he'd pointed out to Lucy on more than one occasion, telling her that the biggest monsters probably hid there, but they would never know for sure because there was no safe way to get close and their poles were too short to cast so far. But Patrick's rod could reach. Nolan flung his arm back and then forward with strength Lucy didn't know he had. The marshmallow soared through the air and then landed with a plop right in the middle of the pool. Ripples spread across the surface. The marshmallow and hook sank into the murky depths. All three of them stretched forward, watching the line closely for any twitch or tug.

It happened fast. The line tightened. Nolan let out a single shout and whipped the rod back hard. The fish on the end fought, dragging the line in zigzags across the pool and then darting into the center of the stream. Patrick jumped up and down, shouting at Nolan to give him the rod. "You're going to lose him!"

But Nolan's hands were steady, his expression one of intense concentration. He played that fish, reeling him in a little and letting him out again, until the beast began to tire. A few minutes passed, though it felt like more, and then Lucy saw the first flash of silver near the surface. A flick of tail in the air, a splash, then the fish dove back into the deep. Nolan was laughing now, enjoying the fight, but Patrick was impatient, pacing the edge of the rock, tugging at his hair, saying, "Come on, come on. Reel him in already."

When Nolan finally did, Lucy was surprised at the size of the fish. It was much smaller than she thought it would be for the kind of fight it gave. No bigger than a foot, its scales were shimmering gold and speckled black. Nolan pulled it out of the water and flopped it onto the rock. It snapped its tail a few times, still fighting. Its mouth opened and closed, its gills working uselessly. If it stayed out of the water longer than a minute, it would die.

"It's just a baby," Lucy said.

"We'll throw it back." Nolan squatted down and worked the hook from its mouth.

He started to curve his hand around the fish, readying to lower it back into the creek, when Patrick shoved him out of the way. Placing one hand over the fish to keep it still, Patrick pulled out his pocketknife and stabbed the fish in the head. Lucy cried out, horrified. Nolan tried to shove Patrick aside, but it was too late. The fish stopped moving. Its eyes clouded over. A thread of blood slid down the golden scales, turning them the color of rust.

"What did you do that for?" Nolan shouted at Patrick.

"My rod." Patrick shrugged. "My fish."

It was their last time fishing together, the last time at McGee Creek. When they got home that day, Nolan took both his and

Lucy's rods from the shed, broke them in half across his knee, and tossed the pieces in the garbage. They hadn't talked it over—they didn't have to—Lucy would have done the same if Nolan hadn't done it first.

"I haven't fished McGee in years," Harry muttered, more to himself than actual conversation. "Used to be a good hole for browns and rainbows up there."

He made one final cast into the invisible river, then drew the rod close to his body and turned to face her. His expression was hard to read. The creases deepened around his eyes and his lips puckered together, as if he was thinking over what to say, trying to find the words that would make her leave. Then he let out a long sigh and his face relaxed.

"What can I do for you, then, Lucy?" His voice softened around her name.

He'd used the same tone with her ten years ago when he took her statement. She and her mother had sat across from him at the table, his pudgy fingers fumbling to open a small notepad, his hands trembling a bit as he pressed a pencil nub to the paper, promising Lucy she wasn't in any trouble. Information was all he needed, anything that might help them figure out where to start looking for her brother. She had struggled with what to say to him back then, and she struggled again now.

"I want to know whatever you can tell me about Nolan's case," she finally said. "What evidence you collected, who you interviewed, any suspects you had, leads you followed."

His expression hardened again.

"I was so young when Nolan went missing," she tried again. "I don't remember much about what happened in the days after and no one in my family will talk about it. I was hoping you might be able to help me put some of the pieces together. So I can understand and maybe get some closure."

Harry tapped his finger against his fishing pole as he studied her. "See now," he said. "That was the biggest problem with your brother's case. We didn't have all the pieces."

"Anything you can remember would be helpful," she said. "I just want to know what happened to him. I just want some answers."

"Afraid I can't help you with that."

"The case file? Your notes?"

He shook his head. "All of that stayed with the department. It's all in a box in the basement somewhere. And I imagine that's where it will stay. Unless new evidence is found or a witness comes forward or . . ." He paused and a muscle in his jaw clenched. "We never found a body. For all we know your brother could be going by a new name now, working at a Denny's in Texas or mixing margaritas in Cabo."

"Do you really believe that?"

"It's more likely than some of the other stories going around these days." He gave her a knowing look and then continued, "I saw the article. Someone sent it to me in the mail. Anonymously, like they were doing me a favor." He laughed, a bitter sound, and shook his head. "From the very beginning your mother was a challenge. Always questioning the way I ran things. Questioning the department. She had this habit of calling my captain every morning to see if there'd been any overnight developments. But even all that was better than the way she started acting after those pictures turned up."

Several weeks into the investigation, Lucy had come home from school to find all the curtains drawn and her mother sitting cross-legged in her bathrobe in the middle of the living room with the lights off, nursing a half-empty bottle of vodka. Photographs lay scattered on the floor around her. Lucy turned on a lamp in the corner, and Sandra shrank from it.

"Turn it off!"

Lucy did as she was told and then stood in the dark waiting for her eyes to adjust. On the handful of occasions when their mother went overboard with the wine—drinking two bottles instead of just one glass—Nolan had always been the one who handled it. Talking softly to her, he would take Sandra by the arm and guide her to the bedroom where he tucked her under the covers. Then he would sit and watch old romantic comedies with her until she fell asleep. Lucy took a shuffling step forward, reaching out to touch her mother's shoulder, but Sandra flinched away from her. She bent over the photographs, studying them and muttering to herself as she sipped from the vodka bottle.

"Mom?" Lucy kept her voice soft, the way Nolan always did.

Sandra blinked and looked up at Lucy in surprise, as though she only now realized she was no longer alone. Then she gestured to the photographs, which, at the time, looked to Lucy like nothing. Black, underexposed shots of the moon, maybe, nothing important. Nothing worth getting so worked up over. She had not recognized them for what they were, but even if she had, she wouldn't have said anything. She'd been so scared then. Of her mother, of Patrick and of Adam, of herself. Scared that someone would find out what she'd done.

"I brought them these," Sandra said in a hushed, conspiratorial voice, sloppy with booze. "I showed them and they said it's nothing. It's not related, has nothing to do with your brother. That's what they said. But I think they're lying. I can see it in their faces. Sons of bitches. They know what this is and for some reason they're not telling me. Why? What are they hiding?"

Detective Mueller told them from the beginning that there would be things he couldn't talk about, questions he couldn't answer while the investigation was actively being worked.

"They're doing the best they can," Lucy said.

Sandra's whole body went stiff. "So you're taking their side now?"

Before Lucy could protest, Sandra scooped up the photographs and shoved them into an envelope. "I'm going back down there. They have to listen to me. I will make them listen." She gulped more vodka, some of it spilling onto the front of her shirt. "They can't ignore evidence."

She tripped on her way to the bedroom to change. The bottle fell from her hand and landed with a splintering crack on the floor. She cried out. Lucy ran to help her. Glass shards lay scattered at her feet. She lifted her right foot. Blood dripped from a deep gash along the sole. Lucy reached to steady her and help her into the bathroom to clean the wound, but Sandra pushed her away, hard enough that Lucy banged her head against the wall.

"You're lying to me, too," Sandra said, oblivious to the tears welling in Lucy's eyes. "I can tell."

Panic rose in Lucy's chest. She expected Sandra to confront her then about the things she'd told Detective Mueller, all her many half-truths, but instead Sandra mumbled something incomprehensible and limped to her bedroom, slamming the door behind her, leaving Lucy standing alone and panting for a breath that wasn't choked by fear. A few seconds passed and then came a quiet sobbing from Sandra's bedroom, a sound that crept into the shadow places and pressed into the cracks in the walls and floorboards, the cracks in Lucy's heart. She retreated to her bedroom, dragged a high-backed wooden desk chair to the door, and shoved the top bar under the knob. Then she scrambled onto her bed and pushed herself back into the corner as far as she could go, curling her knees to her chest.

She had never seen her mother so unhinged and erratic. Before Nolan disappeared, whenever Sandra drank too much she fell asleep. She was useless, but never mean, never violent. Her behavior that night was something new and terrifying, and the next morning, early, before sunrise, Lucy slipped from her bedroom, crept to the kitchen, and called her father. "Please come get me," she'd said. "It's not safe here anymore." He didn't come for her right away. He said it was more complicated than that. There were custody agreements and court orders. He had to talk to Sandra first. He told her to sit tight, to be patient with her mother who was going through a lot right now, but he came for her eventually, after several long phone calls with his lawyer and several shorter ones with Sandra.

Her last day at the house, as Lucy packed her single suitcase with clothes, Sandra sat on her bed drinking straight from a new bottle of vodka and alternating between sobbing and screaming. With one breath she begged Lucy to stay, with the next she called her a traitor and accused Lucy of lying about Nolan, lying to get her way, lying and abandoning her own mother, the woman who'd given birth to her, who'd raised and loved her more than her son of a bitch father ever could. Lucy packed quickly and silently, and when she left, she had felt nothing but relief. She didn't have any idea until now what those photographs had been, or where they'd come from, or why they'd been so important to Sandra, how far they'd sent her spinning over the edge.

"For a while your mother wouldn't give up on those photo-graphs," Harry continued. "She insisted they were important to the case, that they were evidence of . . . of something. At first we took them seriously. We had a specialist take a look. We *wanted* them to be something, our smoking gun. But then she began to throw around words like flying saucers and alien ab-ductions and government cover-ups and, well . . ." He scowled into the middle distance, silent for a while.

Lucy waited him out.

"Your mother made my life hell for a long, long time." He returned his gaze to Lucy. "She turned an already shitty case into a full-blown shit storm. And we lost so much traction because of her behavior, too, because of her drunken claims of UFOs and police collusion. No one took her seriously after she started spouting that nonsense. No one in the department wanted to work with her. Whatever leads, whatever momen-tum we had, were lost. She fell apart on us, and then the case fell apart too."

His grip tightened around the fishing pole. "Your brother's case was the biggest disaster of my career. I lost a promotion because of it and was turned into a laughingstock. The other guys started calling me Agent Mulder and clipping articles from those trashy magazines to hang above my desk. 'Woman Gives Birth to Two-Headed Alien,' that kind of bullshit. If I could go back, I would do a lot of things differently, starting out with not taking the case in the first place."

"You did the best you could, given the circumstances." It wasn't true, he could have done more, but Lucy said it anyway, to soothe his wounded pride.

He nodded and his tone softened again. "I appreciate you're wanting some kind of closure, but I've worked enough cases in

my lifetime to know there's no such thing. It's a myth perpetu-
ated by psychiatrists and greeting card companies. Finding out
what happened to your brother that night will only break your
heart even more than it's already broken."

He leaned in close to her then and she caught a whiff of
stale coffee beneath a thick cloud of sunscreen. "Look, I get it.
I have a big brother. I know how it is. You idolize him. You
think he can do no wrong. But trust me when I tell you that
Nolan was a troubled kid headed nowhere fast. When it comes
to the people we love, we don't always see clearly. We don't always know what's really going on in their lives. Or we choose
not to see. But maybe that's okay, you know? Maybe it's a kind
of self-preservation."

He smiled at her, but there was a sadness in his eyes, and
something like relief. "You know, Lucy, it's okay if you want to
tell yourself that he ran off with that girlfriend of his and they
lived happily ever after. It's okay to let it go with that and move
on with your own life. No one will think any less of you."

He tipped his head toward the house. "Let me walk you
out."

Back in her car, Lucy considered how different this Harold Mueller was from the man with the badge and fumbling
hands, who had come to their house with so many questions
and frightened her into saying something, anything, just so he
would go away again.

Sandra had held Lucy's hand through the entire interview,
rubbing her thumb across her skin with enough force to leave
a small bruise. Lucy told Detective Mueller the truth, or what
she thought was the truth. Mostly. "I went out with Patrick
after Mom left for work. Around seven. We went to the Burger
Barn and then we just drove around for a little while. I got

bored and he dropped me off at the house. I went to my bedroom and put on headphones and fell asleep. I didn't see Nolan at all that night."

She told him she hadn't heard anything either, or noticed anything unusual until the next morning when Nolan didn't come to breakfast and then she just assumed he'd woken early and left the house already because his pickup wasn't in the driveway. He was upset about being expelled from school and about being sent away to live with their father; he was upset about a lot of things, but he'd been especially worried about this girl, Celeste. This was Lucy's excuse for why she waited so long to mention Nolan's absence. She thought he'd gone over to Celeste's house and stayed there. She wanted to believe that's what happened anyway. For two days she kept her mouth shut, and only on the third day, when Sandra asked if she'd spoken to Nolan recently, did Lucy admit that she hadn't seen him since Friday.

She kept the rest of the story to herself. How before they went to Burger Barn, Patrick stopped by his house and they raided his parents' liquor cabinet. How she drank so much that large chunks of the night were lost to her now, swallowed up in a tidal wave of booze. How she couldn't remember exactly what time she got home, or *how* she got home.

She'd been confused and scared and fourteen, and lying to Detective Mueller and her mother seemed better than telling them the whole truth about how she didn't really remember much of anything except the harsh taste of liquor burning down her tongue and a knot in the pit of her stomach. Had Patrick dropped her off? Had she walked? Did she call a cab? She had no idea. She remembered being out with friends and then the next thing she remembered after that was waking up in her own bed with sunlight streaming through the window, and she was wearing the same clothes from the night before, only they were covered in dust and her jeans were ripped, dried blood caking her knees. When she woke, she had a pounding headache and a bitter taste in her mouth. When she woke, she raced to the bathroom and puked up the watery contents of her stomach. When she woke, Nolan was gone and she didn't know where, but it seemed in her best interests to keep her mouth shut about the drinking and all the things she didn't remember. It seemed a good idea to simply pretend she'd been home. Her memories grew no clearer with time. They weren't like marbles carried in her pockets, whole and solid objects to be taken out whenever she needed them, turned over and over and never changing shape.

So many times in the past ten years, Lucy had thought about the night Nolan went missing and the days leading up to it. She'd gone over and over it in her head, lost sleep wondering, but it hadn't made any difference. What she could remember was always less than what she couldn't, and even if she told the truth, it wouldn't be enough to bring him home. Away from Bishop, it had been easier. Ten years spent acting as if it didn't matter, as if her missing brother and her missing memories had nothing to do with each other. Ten years in denial. Ten years wasted. Harold Mueller was wrong. There were worse things in life than a broken heart.

CASEBOOK ENTRY #3

STRANGE HAPPENING:
Dead Birds

DATE: September 13, 1999

LONGITUDE/LATITUDE: 37.363084 W, 118.39929 N

SYNOPSIS: Discovered two dead birds in the bed of my pickup at 15:00. They were arranged chest up, wings spread as if they fell midflight. Wings intact. Unclear how long birds had been lying there prior to my arrival as my pickup was left unattended from 12:35 to 15:00.

OBJECT DESCRIPTION: Both birds are brown in color, small—possibly house sparrows. No apparent injuries. No aircraft of any kind spotted in the vicinity at time of discovery.

OTHER WITNESS STATEMENTS: None have come forward, though student parking lot was crowded at time of discovery. Experienced strong sensation that I was being watched, but could not find anyone in my vicinity who was paying specific attention or behaving in an overtly suspicious manner.

WEATHER INFORMATION: 64°F; winds from W at 9 mph; mostly cloudy; light rain early in the day, but no electrical storms or high winds.

LOCATION DESCRIPTION: Bishop Union High School student parking lot, NE corner of campus at W Pine and N Fowler St, Bishop, California. Pickup was parked in first row, 10 spaces from the left.

PHYSICAL EVIDENCE: I received a small shock opening the tailgate. Residual static from UFO?

CONCLUSION: Pending autopsy results. Will bring birds to County Health Dept. to be tested for possible cause of death.

Nolan told the UFO Encounters Group about the dead birds at the next meeting. At first he wasn't going to. Birds died every day for various reasons. They flew into car windows, or were eaten by cats. Whole flocks struck by lightning or a fast-spreading disease, birds falling down dead in a great tumble of feathers and beaks. He heard about it on the news sometimes: 150 starlings dead in Boaz, Alabama; over 1,000 snow geese dead in Sandpoint, Idaho; 300 waxwings dead in Eustis, Maine. Once, a bird flew hard into the glass of his closed bedroom window and didn't get up again. He buried it under a bush in the front yard.

Dead birds were common, but the ones in his truck bed were so oddly placed and perfectly intact—just the two of them, side by side, their wingtips touching—that his mind went straight to Celeste, who had met him for lunch earlier that day, how perfectly her hand fit in his. Standing in the parking lot, Nolan had felt the hairs on the back of his neck pop and his skin tingle, the air electric, though the skies were clear for as far as he could see, and though he hadn't seen an extraterrestrial craft prior to or immediately after finding the birds, it seemed a very real possibility that one had come and gone, generating some kind of sonic boom or electromagnetic pulse that brought these two down. He'd spent a few minutes searching the rest of the parking lot, but found no other birds fallen, no flocks or feathered evidence. He'd sealed the two birds into Ziploc bags with every intention of leaving them with the county health department to determine cause of death, but the receptionist sent him and the birds away with a look of disgust, and he had no choice but to take them home and stick them in the back of the freezer under a Butterball turkey until he could connect with someone in the department who had more authority to order the kind of test he needed.

Five days later in the windowless basement of the senior center, Nolan tried to explain to the group why he believed the birds were evidence of an encounter.

"Maybe someone's just messing with you?" Tilly suggested, picking at the skin around her fingernails. "Kids were always doing shit like that when I was a teenager."

He supposed it was possible, but who would do such a thing? Who would kill innocent birds just to mess with him? He didn't really have friends at school, though neither did he have enemies. None that he knew of anyway. For a fleeting second he thought of Patrick, but this seemed too heinous a prank, even for him. Especially considering Nolan had done nothing to deserve it. They hadn't spoken since the Buttermilk Rocks incident. They had only one class together this year, AP History, and Patrick always ducked into the classroom right as the bell sounded, and darted out again when they were dismissed. He didn't linger, hoping to talk; he hardly even looked in Nolan's direction.

"What about the two sightings I had over the summer?"

Nolan told the group about the lights immediately after the sightings took place. There was a flurry of initial excitement, but this faded after a few weeks when there ceased to be any further developments.

"You think they're connected to these birds somehow?" Jim asked.

"It's possible." Nolan looked across the circle at Wyatt, wanting him to weigh in, but Wyatt seemed content to sit and listen, to let them work it out on their own.

I don't have all the answers, he was always saying, though he was the most knowledgeable of the group, a smart and focused man, a man who, with a different kind of ambition, could have become a doctor or started his own business or traveled the world, but who instead chose to work part-time fixing motor-cycles and restoring engines, who lived in a run-down double-wide on a dusty piece of scrub-covered property passed down from his great-grandfather to his grandfather to his father, and finally to him, a man who lived frugally, simply, so he would have more time to pursue his greatest passion: proving the existence of extraterrestrial life here on Earth. If anyone knew how the dead birds were connected to Nolan's earlier sightings, it would be Wyatt. But Wyatt just sat there, his lips turned down slightly in a thoughtful way, his arms crossed over his chest, one finger tapping silently against his elbow.

Nolan had a theory of his own. One he hadn't shared with the group yet, with *anyone*, because it seemed so outrageous. He wasn't even convinced of it himself.

Celeste had been at the school a few hours before he found the birds. She'd taken a job as a waitress at Jake's Family Res-taurant a few days after she decided to stay in Bishop permanently. Gabriella was friends with the owner, who owed her a favor, and after a short fifteen-minute interview, Celeste walked out with an apron, a brand-new white polo shirt, and a name tag to pin on her chest. Starting out, she'd mostly worked the breakfast shift, even though the tips were lower, but more recently she'd been picking up lunch and dinner shifts, and since school started Nolan was seeing her much less often. But she had Mondays off, and on that Monday, she'd dropped by the school to surprise him with burgers and fries from the Burger Barn. They'd eaten together in his pickup, listening to music and talking about the book he was supposed to be reading for English, *Lord of the Flies*. Celeste had never read it; she'd skipped that class, she said, skipped all of them, actually, and got her GED instead. School was a waste of time, she said, the whole world her classroom.

They'd made out awhile before she left, and Nolan was five minutes late to his next class, which meant he spent the rest of that period in the library serving detention. His first tardy, and the end of his perfect attendance record.

The birds weren't in the truck bed during lunch. He would have noticed them. So sometime between Celeste's departure and the end of the school day, this terrible thing had happened to those two unlucky birds. A flying saucer had appeared in the vicinity, and the birds flew into its path or it flew into theirs. Either way, Nolan believed the flying saucer was there because of Celeste, but he couldn't tell the group any of this because Gabriella was sitting next to him, and Celeste was still living in Gabriella's guest bedroom. They saw each other every day. They talked. They were becoming friends. Gabriella cared for Celeste as if Celeste were her granddaughter, and Nolan didn't want any of that to change. He didn't want Gabriella to treat Celeste any differently just because she was, or probably was, or maybe was, one of Them.

Wyatt shifted in his chair. Everyone, including Nolan, turned to look at him.

"The birds are still in your possession?" he asked.

Nolan nodded. "They're in a safe place."

"Good," Wyatt said. "Then I suggest tabling this topic until we have more information. Speculation will only get us so far."

With that, the group began discussing a ufology conference being held in Denver at the end of the month, a conference Nolan wasn't attending because he had school and because Wyatt hadn't invited him. He tuned out their voices, trying to picture Celeste's face instead, the color of her eyes, the way they flickered and shone when she saw him. He tried to picture her lips, her perfect and kissable lips. But her face was a blank, a shadowy, shapeless form in his mind that could have been anyone. It bothered him that he couldn't picture her when they were apart, that he had to flip through his comic book drawings to be reminded of her features, that they had to be apart at all.

It had been Celeste's choice to stay with Gabriella. Nolan had suggested she move in with him and his family instead, but she'd quickly dismissed the idea. She was comfortable with Gabriella and besides, she said, it was good to spend time apart. Absence makes the heart grow fonder and all that other bullshit. Nolan disagreed. The longer he went without seeing her, the more he wondered if maybe he was mistaken and the connection he thought they had was no connection at all, rather something he'd imagined, his brain misfiring. In her absence, she ceased to be extraordinary, and if she wasn't extraordinary, then neither was he, and so what was the point of any of this? A meaningless life, another cog in the machine. He needed her to be extraordinary; he needed all this to mean something.

The meeting ended, and the group dispersed, some gathering to make small talk around the coffeepot and a box of donuts, others leaving out the front door, eager to return to their regular lives. Wyatt hung around chatting a few minutes before he finally said his good-byes and left. Nolan followed him out to the parking lot.

"Is everything all right?" Wyatt asked when Nolan appeared at his side. "You seemed a little distracted during the meeting. Things okay at home?"

"Yeah, everything's fine." Nolan dug around in his pockets.

Wyatt stopped beside his car, a two-door clunker sedan. "School's fine? Kids aren't bothering you, are they?"

"Yeah, yeah, it's all great." Nolan found the folded-up piece of paper he'd been looking for. He took it from his back pocket, unfolded it, and smoothed out the edges. "There's someone I think you should meet."

"Oh yeah?" Wyatt looked curiously at the paper, but Nolan held it close to his chest, not quite ready to share. "And who's that?"

"Remember the craft that touched down near the observatory?"

Wyatt nodded with a hint of impatience.

"The next night this girl . . ." Nolan hesitated. To call her simply a girl felt wrong. "She found me. And there's something about her. Something different. Special. I've been working on this theory—"

"Slow down there, kid." Wyatt laid his hand gently on Nolan's shoulder. "I'm having trouble following you. This girl—"

"No, she's not . . . she's . . . more than that. More than just a girl." He held the creased piece of paper out for Wyatt to see.

It was a photocopy of one of his comic book pages. A black and white sketch of his Aurelian warrior princess standing on the edge of a windy cliff, her fists set strongly on her hips, her hair blowing behind her, a dark cape. Her eyes, the only chips of color he'd added to the page, copper and sparkling, staring into the distance. Her eyes alert, victorious.

"You drew this?" Wyatt lifted the page closer to his face. "I didn't know you were so talented with this kind of stuff. How come you've never said anything?"

Nolan jabbed his finger into the page. "It's her."

"What?" Wyatt's brow furrowed.

"The . . . the one who found me the night after the observatory sighting." He jabbed the paper again. "It's her."

Wyatt started to laugh, but seeing Nolan's very serious expression, stopped. "I'm sorry. I don't understand."

"Celeste," Nolan said, taking the paper back from Wyatt and refolding it.

"Your friend who's staying with Gabriella?"

Nolan nodded. "I think she might be a—I think she might be one of Them, a Visitor."

"Hold on a second . . ."

"I'm not a hundred percent sure."

"I should think not."

"But it makes sense." Nolan began listing things off on his fingers. Two UFO sightings in two months, her unique fashion choices, how she carried everything she owned in a backpack with a patch of Saturn stitched on the front pocket, her strange and elusive behavior, how she was hitchhiking across the country, how no one seemed to miss her.

"And this." Nolan rattled the folded comic book page in the air. "She looks exactly like I imagined she'd look."

"So let me make sure I'm understanding you. You're saying that because she looks similar to this picture you drew, she's some sort of extraterrestrial." He sounded skeptical.

"No," Nolan said, then shaking his head, "or yes. I don't know."

He was certain of two things: he'd asked the stars for proof and shortly after that, Celeste walked into his life.

"Have you told anyone else about this yet?" Wyatt asked.

"No, of course not." Nolan stuffed the comic book page into his pocket. "I wanted to talk to you first."

"Good, that's good, Nolan. And has she said anything to you about being . . . different?"

"Not in so many words." But there had been moments when she'd hinted at something before backing away again or changing the subject entirely.

Wyatt rubbed the bridge of his nose, closed his eyes a moment. When he reopened them, Nolan could tell a plan was forming.

"Okay," Wyatt said, speaking faster now, the way he did when he was working up to something important. "Okay, this could be huge, you know that, right?"

Nolan nodded eagerly.

"But it could be nothing, a false assumption. Wishful thinking."

"It's not," Nolan protested.

"I hope that's the case, Nolan, I do, but we still have to go about this carefully. We have to work slowly, methodically, make sure we explore every angle. Do you understand what I'm saying?"

"We can't get ahead of ourselves."

"Exactly." Wyatt smiled. "We take our time. We do this right."

Nolan felt himself relax again. Wyatt was an expert. He knew what he was doing. If there was a discovery to make, if this was the paradigm shift the world needed, he would find it and Nolan would be with him when he did. And if Celeste turned out to be normal, terrestrial, human in every usual way, then that would be okay, too. They would be okay. He'd make sure of it.

Nolan and Wyatt met in the parking lot of Jake's the next afternoon at a quarter to three. Nolan parked his pickup down the street so when Celeste arrived for her shift, she wouldn't see it and come looking for him. Then he climbed into Wyatt's sedan, which was parked in the first row nearest the restaurant with a good view of the picture windows stretching across the front.

"Okay," Wyatt said. "Let's go over the plan again."

"So we go in," Nolan started, but Wyatt cut him off.

"*I* go in. You stay here."

"But—"

"We talked about this." Wyatt sighed. "At best, you'll be a distraction. At worst, you'll give us away. I need to meet her first by myself. I need to get a feel for her without you prejudicing the conversation."

"I wouldn't prejudice anything." Nolan was hurt that Wyatt would think him so unprofessional. "I'd simply introduce you to her and then you can ask her whatever you want. You'll hardly even notice me."

"You've spent so much time with her already, and if she's

what you think she is, she can probably read your thoughts." Wyatt took the keys from the ignition and put them in his pocket. "I need to have this first conversation with her alone. That's just the way it has to be."

"Fine." Nolan slouched low in his seat. "*You* go in. I wait here."

A few minutes passed and then Nolan broke the silence. "What are you going to ask her?"

Wyatt shook his head. "I don't know yet."

Nolan scowled out the windshield. He'd imagined this whole thing going differently. He'd imagined being with Wyatt every step of the way, a sidekick, not a bystander.

Celeste came around the corner then. She wore the same green corduroys and hiking boots as the night they first met, but her top was the nearly brand-new white polo required for work. Her hair was tied back in a sloppy bun. A springy tress had come loose and curled down the length of her neck, bobbing as she walked. She smiled a little to herself. The backpack she carried with her everywhere, even now, seemed to weigh nothing. Nolan wondered what was inside it, if she kept mementos of their time together, receipts and movie ticket stubs, dried wildflowers he'd plucked from the side of the road, weeds really, dandelions and poppies, prettier for their tenacity to live in such an arid climate. He carried mementos of her around in his casebook: sketches of her face, a notation of all the places they'd been together, every conversation they'd had, all the ways she surprised him.

"That's her," Nolan said to Wyatt.

They watched her enter the restaurant. Then Wyatt opened the driver-side door and got out. He paused before closing it and leaned his head in again. "Stay put."

Like a dog. Like a kid who would only get in the way.

The door slammed shut. Nolan glared at the back of Wyatt's head until he disappeared inside the restaurant. It wasn't fair. She'd come to Nolan first. He should be the one in there asking the questions, not Wyatt. But what if he was wrong? What if she laughed at him? Or worse. What if she left?

After a minute, Wyatt reappeared on the other side of the large glass windows. He sat down at a table and looked at a menu. Nolan leaned forward. The restaurant windows weren't tinted, and so he could make out most of what was happening as long as it happened close to the glass; anything beyond that was invisible to him, hidden by shadows.

A few seconds after Wyatt sat down, Celeste appeared. She smiled and said something to him, the typical niceties, Nolan assumed. *How are you today, sir? Yes, lovely weather we're having. May I get you started with something to drink?* Wyatt said something in return, laying down his menu and placing one hand on top of it. Celeste laughed at whatever it was Wyatt said, and something in Nolan's chest pinched. He rubbed his knuckles across his breastbone until the pain passed. A few minutes went by. And then five more. And then ten. Celeste was still at Wyatt's table, still talking. She hadn't taken out an order pad, wasn't writing anything down. She looked relaxed, her hands moving freely, her smile warm and open. Whatever Wyatt was saying to her, she appeared to be very much engaged.

Nolan drummed his fingers against his knees. This shouldn't be taking so long; first impressions only, in and then out. It made sense for Wyatt to order coffee or orange juice or something so as not to arouse suspicion, but that didn't seem to be what was happening here. Celeste leaned in a little closer to Wyatt, as if she was about to whisper in his ear.

Knuckles rapped on the car window, breaking Nolan's concentration.

Patrick peered at him through the glass and, in a too-loud voice that made Nolan cringe and slide down low in his seat, said, "Hey, Space Case, what the hell are you doing out here?" He leaned back, inspecting Wyatt's sedan. "Whose car is this?"

Nolan rolled down the window so Patrick would stop shouting. "What do you want?"

He darted a glance at the clones flanking Patrick on either side. Adam Paulson, a mean kid Nolan had never liked, and Grant, who nodded at Nolan, silent and unsmiling.

"We're just going to grab something to eat," Patrick said, gesturing to the restaurant. "Saw you sitting out here like some creepy little perv."

Adam laughed, a hideous blast like an air horn, and nudged Patrick in the ribs. Patrick shot him a hard look, and Adam went quiet again.

Three girls waited in the parking lot slightly behind the boys. Nolan recognized Megan and Natasha immediately, junior girls who were both on the track team with Patrick and who had probably both slept with him at least once, maybe more, depending on which rumor you believed. But it took him a second, and a few blinks, to realize that the other girl was Lucy. She was sandwiched between Megan and Natasha and wearing jean shorts that barely covered her butt and a shirt that looked more like a bandana. The older girls passed a cigarette, paying very little attention to Nolan, but Lucy stared bug-eyed, her cheeks flaming red. He stared back, whatever words he should be saying to her now dried up on his tongue.

"She's pretty, isn't she?" Patrick asked, and for a second, Nolan thought he was talking about Lucy. Then he realized

Patrick was staring at the restaurant, through the picture windows where Celeste still stood beside Wyatt's table.

"Her name's Celeste," Patrick said, and Nolan's stomach recoiled at the sound of her name on his lips. "Celeste," he said again. "It's like porno for your tongue."

Both Adam and Grant laughed this time, and Patrick joined them without much enthusiasm. He said, "She's from the East Coast. She wants to be an actress." It was clear from the way he said it that he was making fun of her. "Maybe you would know some of this already if you actually went inside and talked to her instead of sitting out here like some kind of a chickenshit Peeping Tom."

Without thinking about what he was doing, Nolan listed off all the things he knew about Celeste. "Her favorite color is rainbow. Her favorite flavor of ice cream is caramel pecan. She loves *Bewitched* and hates daytime talk shows. She doesn't have any siblings and her parents are dead. She smells like coconut and kisses like a thunderstorm."

"Damn," Adam said.

Patrick glared at him and then narrowed his gaze on Nolan. "Lucy," he said, without looking at her. "Did you know your brother has a girlfriend?"

Since school started, they hadn't seen much of each other. Nolan gave her a ride every morning, but she insisted on listening to the radio and always took off to find her friends as soon as he parked. Since she was a freshman, their schedules were completely different and they rarely passed each other in the halls. She had signed up for the track team too, and stayed after school most days to practice, or when there wasn't practice, she got a ride home from someone else. Nolan had been busy too. Busy at the grocery store, busy with Celeste, busy trying to keep up with the homework that kept piling up no matter how much studying he did. There'd been no opportunity for him to tell Lucy about Celeste, but even if there had been, he wasn't sure it would have made a difference.

Lucy blinked, then shrugged and said, "He only wishes he does."

She gestured for Megan to pass her the cigarette. As she raised the cancer stick to lips that were stained a rich scarlet color their mother would hate, she stared at Nolan, daring him to try and stop her. She inhaled deeply, blew a puff of smoke in the direction of Wyatt's car, then passed the cigarette back to Megan.

The smoke reached Nolan through the open window, the acrid stench of it filling his nose, and it was as though a glass dome lowered around him, trapping him in a place where sounds were distant and distorted, where lips moved, but the words made no sense, where bodies appeared malleable and trembling, as if he might be able to push his hand straight through flesh to the other side, their eyes turned to wormholes that led to far-off galaxies. Then, as quickly as it had left, sound rushed back in, loud and startling. Their bodies solidified again, their atoms returning to the right frequency.

Patrick tapped on the car roof. Nolan didn't know how long he'd been trying to get his attention. "Earth to Nolan, Earth to Nolan."

"What?" he barked out, annoyed at the distraction, at the fact that Patrick was even here right now, that he knew who Celeste was, that he was letting Lucy smoke like she was old enough, like she could handle it, annoyed, too, that he couldn't see what was going on inside the restaurant anymore.

"Easy, Romeo." Patrick took a step back from the car and

pointed in Celeste's direction. "I was just going to ask if you wanted me to tell her you said hi?"

He didn't wait for Nolan's response, simply turned and walked toward Jake's. The others followed, Megan dropping the cigarette onto the pavement at the last second, letting the ember burn out on its own.

Nolan started to go after them, but through the restaurant window, he saw Wyatt rise from the booth and make his way toward the front door. Celeste was nowhere to be seen.

When Wyatt returned to the car, he said, "You were right to come to me first. We need to keep this theory to ourselves until we know for sure. The last thing I need is for this to turn into another Bower/Chorley crop circle hoax."

He was referring to two men who had recently admitted responsibility for hundreds of crop circles that mysteriously appeared in the English countryside during the '70s and '80s, crop circles that were once thought to be UFO landing pads and had been held up as proof of extraterrestrial life. The men had used rope and planks of wood and fooled everyone. But this wasn't the same thing, not even close. Nolan didn't want fame or glory or his name written in the history books as the man who discovered the first extraterrestrial life-form. He didn't want anyone to know about Celeste at all, was even regretting telling Wyatt. Celeste was special, and for now she was his and no one else's, and all he wanted to do was keep it that way, keep her safe.

"What are you going to do now? I mean, now that you've talked to her? What did you find out? What did she tell you?" Nolan knew his voice sounded strange, strained and high-pitched, aggravated from his encounter with Patrick, from thinking about him talking to Celeste, charming her with his ocean-blue eyes and deceptively earnest smile.

Wyatt didn't seem to notice. "She's certainly very mysterious." He rubbed his knuckles and stared in the direction of the restaurant. "There's definitely something about her, something . . . I don't really know what."

He twisted in his seat to face Nolan. "Okay, here's what we're going to do. Things are a little hectic for me right now because of the ufology conference next week, but after that, my schedule clears up and I'll start digging around, doing some research, seeing what I can find out about her. I need to rule out a few things before we can say definitively one way or the other. She might just be eccentric, you know? She might just be running from a checkered past."

"The birds," Nolan said. "The lights—"

"I know," Wyatt interrupted. "But look, it could all be a coincidence."

"You said there's no such thing."

"Sometimes there is."

Nolan was starting to get a headache. None of this made very much sense, and he wanted to be left alone to think it through. No, he wanted to be with Celeste. He glanced at the restaurant window. Patrick and his friends had taken the booth Wyatt vacated. Patrick saw Nolan watching and waved.

Nolan inhaled slowly, exhaled, inhaled, five times like this, counting his breaths, the way the doctor he'd seen after his parents' divorce taught him to do. When his mind felt calm again, his heart no longer racing, he returned his attention to Wyatt. "And what should I do while you're gone?"

"Watch her," Wyatt said. "Keep her close, take notes. If she is one of Them, I suspect we'll know it soon enough."

Nolan nodded, readily agreeing to this plan.

"But keep your theories to yourself," Wyatt added. "Don't

tell anyone else what you told me, okay? We don't want this to go public until we know for sure. And absolutely under no circumstances are you to tell *her* about any of this. If she's one of Them we don't want her to know we know, but if she's not one of Them, if she's terrestrial, well, that wouldn't be good either, okay?"

Inside the restaurant, Celeste appeared beside the booth where Patrick and his friends sat. Nolan watched her face carefully for signs of distress, but saw none.

"Nolan?" Wyatt touched his arm.

He snapped back to attention, blinking at Wyatt, trying to figure out what he'd missed.

"Yeah, okay," he said. "Tell no one."

Wyatt looked like he wanted to say something else, something important, but then he gave a quick shake of his head and asked, "Do you want me to drive you back to your truck?"

"No, I'm fine walking." Nolan got out of the sedan, and Wyatt drove away.

Nolan stood in the parking lot, shivering even though it was warm and the sun was still high, high enough to cast a reflection on the restaurant glass, making everything inside waver like a mirage. Patrick said something to Celeste, and she laughed like she meant it. She smiled at him the way she smiled at Nolan. She tucked the loose tendril of her raven hair behind her ear and leaned closer, and Patrick leaned closer too, and Nolan thought he saw their hands brush. He couldn't be sure, maybe they hadn't, but imagining it was enough for him to experience a frightening and overwhelming urge to run inside, clamp his hand over her mouth so no one could hear her voice or see her smile, cover her eyes so no one else could be captivated, and drag her away to some locked and windowless room for which there was only one key kept on a chain around his neck. He stuffed his hands deep into his pockets and, after a while, walked away.

A month passed, and then another week, and Nolan still hadn't heard from Wyatt. He tried not to worry. According to Gabriella and the other group members, Wyatt had done this before, slipped away for weeks at a time to work on something no one else knew anything about, dropping off the grid, making it impossible for anyone to reach him, even in an emergency. He'll be back, they said, whenever he's done working on whatever it is he's working on. He always comes back. The difference this time was that Nolan knew exactly what kind of project Wyatt was working on, and how dangerous it was.

He couldn't help but wonder if Wyatt had been asking the wrong people the wrong questions, if government agents had heard about what he was looking for and tracked him down and if even now he was being tortured for information, even now revealing Celeste's whereabouts. Nolan stayed awake sometimes imagining it, losing her. The two of them walking down the street, when suddenly they'd be surrounded by black SUVs. Doors slamming. Men dressed all in black, gesturing with automatic rifles, forcing them apart, shoving Celeste into one of the cars, tires squealing as they drove away, leaving Nolan behind.

He spent as much time with her as he could, knowing he was the only one who could keep her safe, but she had work and he had work, and school too, and they were apart far more often than together. He struggled to pay attention in his classes. He watched the clock and doodled in the margins of his notebooks—flying saucers and Grays of assorted sizes, new adventures with his Aurelian warrior princess. There was a pop quiz in his English class. He left half the answers blank. Between classes he moved through the halls like a ghost: unseen, unnoticed. At the grocery store he had to be told two or three times what he was supposed to be doing, and sometimes even then he walked away from a task, like unpacking boxes or gathering carts, before it was finished. He called the restaurant often, checking on Celeste, pretending he missed her and nothing more. He did miss her, that was true. He would miss her even more if she disappeared.

A few days before Halloween Nolan picked Celeste up from the restaurant. They had plans to rent a movie and watch it at Gabriella's place. Gabriella was working all night at the motel, and Celeste had been hinting to Nolan about a hot and heavy make-out session, maybe they'd even go all the way, but he kept her at a distance. He hardly noticed when her hand slid high up on his leg, almost to his crotch.

Wyatt should have been back by now with answers, and the longer he was away, the more Nolan's mind felt like an earthquake, uncertain and trembling, a crack forming through the center of the thing, this theory of his, a once-solid notion, each day splitting wider. Despite many hours spent with Celeste and careful scrutiny over the past month, he had discovered very little in the way of incontrovertible proof. She was doing a fantastic job of playing ordinary. Or maybe she wasn't playing. Maybe she was nothing more than a girl like any other girl, a citizen of planet Earth, born in the usual way and bound by the laws of gravity and time.

"Hey." Celeste's voice pulled him from his circling thoughts. "If you don't want to do this, we don't have to."

She took her hand from his leg, her arms folded now across her chest, her body slightly angled away from him.

"No, it's not, I do," Nolan stammered. "It's just, I'm not feeling, it's something with my stomach, something I ate, I think."

This wasn't the first time he'd lied to her since Wyatt went away, and he didn't like it. Celeste never believed him either.

She glared at him for a moment and then her face softened again and she returned her hand to his leg. "Rain check, okay?"

He nodded.

"Just drop me off at Gabriella's and then go home and get some rest." She squeezed his knee. "Chicken soup."

He cast her a sideways glance.

"That's what you're supposed to eat when you're sick, right?"

He could just ask her, come right out and say, *Are you from outer space?* Or something a little less childish, but still, he could ask her.

"What?" She touched her hair and then her face. "Do I have something in my teeth?"

"No, I was just . . ." He shook his head and returned his attention to the road. "Nothing. Yes, chicken soup. I think we have some in the pantry."

She smiled and laid her head back on the seat.

Wyatt had warned him to say nothing to her about his theory, but Wyatt didn't know Celeste the way Nolan did. He'd met Celeste once. One conversation, and a short one at that. And anyway, Wyatt wasn't even here. He'd been gone over a month. How much longer did he expect Nolan to wait? This wasn't the right time, not this night, this moment, but soon.

They reached Gabriella's, and Celeste hesitated, saying, "I could come over and make it for you. The soup, I mean."

Nolan leaned over and kissed her on the cheek. "Thanks, but I think I can manage."

She seemed disappointed, but tried to hide it with another smile, another squeeze of his knee before letting go. She got out and walked to the front door. Like always, he stayed, idling at the curb, until he was certain she had her key and could get inside. Tonight, though, instead of blowing him a kiss and slipping through the door, she turned and jogged back to him, her eyes bright and wide.

He rolled down the window so he could hear her.

"I almost forgot! You know Patrick, right? From school?"

When Nolan didn't respond, she added more timidly, "He said you guys were friends."

"What about him?"

"He invited us to a party at Ship Rock," she said. "Well, he invited me, but now I'm inviting you. Sounds like it could be fun. What do you think?"

Nolan thought it was a terrible idea. He'd heard how quickly Patrick's parties descended into chaos—Spin the Bottle turning into Seven Minutes in Heaven turning into a drunk girl losing her virginity in the back of a Honda Accord—but he didn't tell her any of that. "If you really want to go . . ."

"Only if you're there with me."

He should have told her no. He should have suggested something, anything else, but she was looking at him with those beautiful, mysterious eyes of hers, smiling like he was the only person in the universe who mattered, and he wanted to matter. He wanted to matter to *her*.

Ship Rock was a large outcrop located several miles down a single dirt track in an isolated section of the Tablelands, a barren landscape a few miles north of Bishop. As the name implied, it rose like an ocean liner from the flat desert floor, a hulking, dark giant among shrubs and dust and empty space. Nolan parked next to a small group of cars near the base of the promontory. "I guess this is it."

A flashlight bobbed in the distance, moving toward the bluff. Celeste flipped down the visor and fussed with her hair for a few seconds, then snapped the visor closed again, opened the door, and got out. A clamor of voices and laughter echoed across the expanse. Nolan hesitated inside the cab.

"Are you sure you want to do this?" he asked Celeste, who leaned against the open door and peered in at him expectantly. "I have my telescope in the back. We could drive out to the observatory instead, just you and me . . ."

He let his words trail off, knowing she'd already made up her mind.

"Just try." She came around to his side, grabbed his hand, and pulled him out of the cab. "I'll be with you the whole time. Give it at least a half hour. After that, if you're still not having a good time, we can leave."

The moon was a waning half, but bright enough for them to pick their way to the bluff without a flashlight. They walked around the outcrop, out of sight from the main road, where the party was already under way. Smoke and flames writhed from a towering inferno of stacked wooden pallets, spitting hot embers at the stars. Light reflected off a high stone cliff, illuminating a horseshoe-shaped cove where a dozen or so kids from school scattered in groups, guzzling cans of beer and chain-smoking cigarettes. Girls gyrated their hips to the music in their heads while boys watched with their mouths half-open, lust smeared over their faces. Everyone's skin tinted orange. A pallet split in two, exploding a cloud of flame and sparks into the night, and a shout rose, dying again as the embers vanished to ash.

Nolan hesitated at the edge of this chaos, feeling like an astronaut, the first of his kind, about to touch down on a strange and alien planet. He didn't belong here and yet here he was, and this was his mission, to take one small step, and there was no going back now, not with Celeste tugging his arm, pulling him forward into the light. People turned to look at them. Conversations fell silent. For a second, only the fire made sound: a hiss, a scream, the loud pop of water evaporating in intense heat.

Then someone muttered, "Who invited the freak?"

A few people laughed.

Then someone else said, "The aliens have landed."

And another person in a singsong voice, "They're here . . ."

Everyone laughed now. Nolan took a step back, retreating toward the shadows, but Celeste's hand found his and held him steady.

He knew it was a bad idea coming here; he tried to talk her out of it earlier when he picked her up from Gabriella's, but she said they were too isolated, that it wasn't healthy to be just the two of them all the time, they needed more social interaction, more time with other people. But did other people have to be *these* people? He'd known most of *these* people since elementary school, and they weren't all that interesting. They had been interesting once. Before middle school turned them into monotonous zombies. He remembered how much fun they had in elementary school. He and Patrick imagining whole worlds for the other kids to get lost in. One time they were an intrepid team of space explorers transported to the planet Zork to collect unique specimens of rocks and sedi-

ment. They scooped dirt and pebbles and playground saw-
dust into empty Tic Tac boxes. Another time they were on
a planet with no gravity and had to walk taking giant, slow
steps. One false move and you'd float to your death in deep
space, which, to the untrained eye, looked nearly identical to
a metal slide.

He'd had friends once, and it had been nice. But then his dad
left. And then he got sick and had to leave school for a while.
And somewhere in that span of time his friends turned into
strangers who wanted nothing to do with him, who seemed
to be on another plane of existence entirely. Or maybe it was
Nolan who changed, Nolan who floated untethered in another
universe. Either way, he felt out of place among *these* people,
these once friends. Their concerns—celebrity gossip, fashion
trends, who did what to whom at such and such a party—all of
it so trivial and fleeting.

"It's okay," Celeste whispered into his ear. "I won't leave
your side."

He scanned the scattered groups of people, looking for
someone they might be able to talk to, someone who wasn't a
complete idiot. Like Kevin, his lab partner in chemistry who
had memorized the periodic table in sixth grade because he
was bored, or Jenny, the girl he sat next to in English who read
philosophy books under her desk when the teacher was lecturing. He doubted either of them were invited.

His eyes skipped over a trio of girls standing off to one side
of the fire pit, then skipped back. He blinked, hoping it was a
trick of light and he wasn't really seeing Lucy standing with a
beer in one hand, her once-brown hair now bleached white-
blond with the ends dyed bright pink, her twiggy frame somehow boasting curves, squeezed into a too-tight, sparkling blue

tube top he'd never seen before. He took a step closer. She laughed at something one of the other girls said and gulped from the beer can.

"What is it?" Celeste asked.

"Lucy's here." He'd told Celeste about his sister, but had never formally introduced her.

"Where?"

He pointed. "The one in the middle."

When Celeste spotted her, she said, "I'm sure she's fine. She's with her friends."

Natasha and Megan were not Lucy's friends. The girls Lucy hung out with were all her age, quiet and shy, and one of them had asthma, and another was always talking about spiders. Lucy was supposed to be with them tonight. That's what she'd told Sandra earlier that afternoon, that she was going to a sleepover at one of the girls' houses, and they were going to rent *Hocus Pocus* and carve pumpkins. But now that Nolan thought about it, he hadn't seen Lucy with any of those girls in a while, not since school started at least.

"Let's go find Patrick." Celeste tugged Nolan's hand, but he didn't follow her lead.

Lucy was better than this, than all these clones who talked the same and dressed the same and acted the same. He marched over to her, dragging Celeste with him. Lucy made a face when she saw them coming and exchanged eye rolls with the other girls.

"Go back to your mother ship, Space Case," Natasha said. "No one wants you here."

Nolan ignored her and gave his full attention to Lucy. Firelight flickered over her bare and goose-bumped shoulders and arms.

"You're going to catch a cold." He removed his windbreaker and held it out to her.

When she didn't reach for it, he tried to swing the jacket over her shoulders. She pushed him away, sloshing beer on the ground in the process.

"Go 'way, Nolan." Her words sloppy and drunk.

"How much have you had?" He used the same calm, but authoritative tone that he used with their mother whenever she started to slur her words and sway. It worked on Sandra every time. A look of shame would creep into her eyes and she would set down whatever bottle of wine she was working on and make herself a cup of tea instead. She would apologize, and kiss Nolan's forehead, and thank him for looking out for her. *I'd be a mess without you*, she'd say.

But Lucy took it as a challenge.

"I'm just getting started." She lifted the can to her mouth and chugged.

Nolan snatched it away from her.

"Hey!" Lucy lunged, but he held the can over his head, out of her reach.

It was almost empty. Six other empty cans littered the sand around the girls' feet. A cooler rested nearby, the lid lifting and shutting in a steady rhythm, hands reaching, grabbing cans, snapping them open with a hiss.

"I'm taking you home." Nolan poured the rest of Lucy's beer out in the sand.

"I'm not going anywhere with you." She took a step back, stumbling a little.

"You're drunk," he said, reaching for her.

Natasha and Megan leaned into each other, giggling. One of them belched and the laughter got louder.

"God's sake, Nolan," Lucy whisper-hissed. "Can't you try and be normal for once? Just be cool, okay? I don't need you looking after me. I can take care of myself."

"Clearly." He glared at the older girls. "They're drunk too. Who's driving?"

Lucy gave him a pleading look, but he remained unmoved. Being embarrassed by your older brother was better than crashing into a pole and dying on the side of the road somewhere.

For a second, he thought he'd won. Lucy's false toughness was cracking. She would surrender and let him drive her home. Then her attention was drawn to something over his shoulder, and she tensed up again, then began to fuss, tugging on her shirt, running her fingers through her hair, dabbing at the corners of her pink and glittery mouth.

"Starlight, you made it!"

Nolan flinched at the loudness of Patrick's voice, the way it echoed off the rocky outcrop. He emerged uninvited and suddenly from the shadows, wrapped his arm around Celeste's shoulders, pressed his mouth close to her ear, and said something no one else could hear. Celeste gave Nolan a helpless look and tried to shrug him off, but Patrick hooked his arm tighter, pulling her closer to him. He was clearly drunk, swaying, struggling to stay in one place, and didn't seem to notice Lucy and the other girls or even Nolan standing close by, watching as he slurred something about a kiss, just one little, itty-bitty, teensy-weensy kiss. He pushed his lips toward Celeste, who reared away from him, telling him to knock it off. Even then, he wouldn't let her go. Nolan had to grab hold of his arm and physically pull him off.

"What the hell, Spaceman?" He shoved Nolan back. "You

lost? You put the wrong coordinates into your spaceship or something?"

He laughed at his own joke and then lunged for Celeste again, trying to swing his arm back around her shoulders. He missed and sloshed beer down the front of her shirt.

"Shit." Patrick laughed and slurped at a trickle running down his wrist. "Sorry, babe. Let me get that for you." He reached for her chest.

"It's fine." She pushed him away. "I've got it." She moved closer to Nolan and brushed at the damp stains spreading across her shirt.

"It was an accident." Patrick's gaze narrowed on Nolan a moment before returning to Celeste. He gave her a sloppy grin and puppy dog eyes. "Don't hold it against me, unless the 'it' is your body." He slid up close to her again.

It was the cheesiest line Nolan had ever heard and he wondered how that kind of stupidity worked on other girls. Celeste certainly wasn't impressed. She pressed close to Nolan's side and slipped her hand into his.

"Maybe you should slow down." Nolan gestured to the beer in Patrick's hand. "You're acting like an idiot."

"Yeah, well, maybe you should catch up, Spaceman, because you're acting like a prick." He gulped down the rest of his beer and tossed the can away, then stumbled toward a nearby cooler, returning with two unopened cans, one of which he shoved at Nolan like he was offering it to him. Before Nolan had a chance to respond, Patrick yanked the beer away.

"Sorry, Spaceman. You're going to have to get your own. Or wait . . . do aliens even drink beer? Or doesn't it make them explode? I read that somewhere, I think. No, never mind, I'm thinking of seagulls and Alka-Seltzer. Yeah, that's it, right? Oh shit. Who fucking cares?" He cracked open one of the cans and drank deeply, then held the second, unopened can out to Celeste. "Come on, let's get out of here before we catch some kind of space disease. Little green man mumps or some shit."

"I'm here with Nolan." Her grip on his arm tightened.

Patrick stared at her, confused. Some dark emotion passed across his face and then he shrugged. "Whatever. Your loss." He gulped down one beer and then the other, then crushed both cans and dropped them into the sand at Nolan's feet. To Celeste he said, "When you get tired of hanging out with this loser, you know where to find me."

He stumbled away from them to the other side of the fire where Grant and Adam sat on coolers, taking shots from a large glass bottle.

"You were right," Celeste said. "This party blows. Let's get out of here."

Nolan turned to where Lucy had been standing earlier, because if they were leaving, he was taking Lucy with them, but she and the other girls had slipped away sometime during his confrontation with Patrick. He spun around, scanning the cove, thought he saw three girls moving in the darkness toward the bluff, and called out Lucy's name. No answer.

"They're probably halfway home by now," Celeste said, trying to pull him back to where the pickup was parked.

But he couldn't leave without knowing for sure. He moved toward the outcrop, scanning the faces of everyone he passed, but none of them were Lucy. Celeste stuck close to him. When they reached the base of the cliff, they discovered a narrow path zigzagging up the face of the plateau. They climbed in silence to the top.

"It doesn't look like anyone's up here." Celeste peered over the edge of the cliff at the bonfire.

Nolan left her and walked across the plateau to the opposite side where Owens Valley unfolded to the south, a quilt made of black and orange squares. Bishop and Big Pine sparkled neon in the distance. The mountains to the east were dark and gentle slopes, like a giant woman sleeping on her side. He couldn't tell where the Inyos ended and the White Mountains began. To the west, the jagged crags of the Sierras, like a row of sharp teeth gnashing the stars. Another narrow path wound down this side of the bluff, and Nolan followed it with his eyes, looking for signs that Lucy and her friends had come this way. They must have. They weren't at the party anymore, nor anywhere on top of this plateau. He scanned the Tablelands, as far as he could see, but there was no movement in the darkness, no sister-shaped silhouettes against the scrub.

Celeste came up behind him and slipped her hand into his again. "She'll be okay."

"You don't know that."

She stared up at him, moonlight pooling silver in her copper eyes, and Nolan felt himself relaxing, falling into her gaze. Her lips didn't move, but a voice that wasn't his own whispered through his mind, *Nothing bad will happen to her.* And he believed it.

"It's pretty up here. Quiet too." Celeste led him to a place in the middle where the ground was soft and free of stones and pokey shrubs. They sat down, shoulders touching. Voices and laughter from the party barely reached them up here; they might have been ten thousand feet in the air, sitting on a starry throne.

"You shouldn't let Patrick talk to you the way he did down

there," Celeste said, cradling Nolan's hand in her lap. "All that 'Spaceman,' 'loser' bullshit? Does he always say stuff like that?"

"Sometimes, yeah," Nolan said. "But not always, I mean, he can be nice. He can . . ." He trailed off, not entirely sure why he was trying to defend Patrick's behavior, except that at one point, not so long ago, they had been best friends.

Not so long ago, Patrick had been shy and funny and his feet had been too big for his body and he was always tripping, but ended up making a joke out of it, stumbling around like Charlie Chaplin and purposely bumping into walls to get a laugh out of Nolan. The Patrick before he grew into his feet and found out how fast he could run, the Patrick before the girls and the booze and the need to look cool, that old Patrick bought Nolan comic books with his allowance and set aside all his green M&Ms because he knew Nolan liked them best. That old Patrick had drawn passable monsters and villains to fight Nolan's superheroes; you couldn't have one without the other. He had stared up at the sky, too, the two of them lying awake on sleeping bags in the backyard, counting distant points of light and making up stories about the man on the moon, arguing until dawn about whether or not warp drives and transporters would ever be invented, and which superhero had the best sidekick, and what really happened to a person after he died. Nolan thought there was probably some of the old Patrick left over, hiding somewhere inside the new Patrick, but that he'd been pushed so far down, buried under all the rest, it would be nearly impossible to draw him out again.

"Well, I think he's a jerk," Celeste said. "And the next time he talks to you like that, you should . . . I don't know, you should do something."

He laughed. "What, like punch him in the face?"

"Yeah." She nodded vigorously. "Yeah, and if you don't do it, then I will."

He liked that she wanted to stand up for him, but he was supposed to be taking care of her, not the other way around. He wrapped his arms around her waist and gently laid her back on the ground. She touched his cheek with her fingertips.

"It's just, he's wrong, you know. About you." Her eyes flashed. "You believe in something big, something incredible. That doesn't make you a loser. If anything, it makes you interesting. More interesting than small-minded idiots like Patrick."

They hadn't talked much about Nolan's belief in UFOs and extraterrestrial contact, but she lived with Gabriella, and she knew about the Encounters group, and they had spent enough time stargazing together and contemplating life's bigger questions that he didn't have to come right out and say it. She knew and she was still here, bringing her lips to his, her tongue slipping into his mouth.

She let out a soft moan as his hands slipped under her shirt, as he ran his fingers across her impossibly smooth, too-perfect skin. She tasted tropical, familiar and yet new somehow, and he wanted this to last, he wanted her hands to continue their exploratory trek down his abdomen to the button of his jeans and lower still. He wanted to feel her arch against him, breathe and sigh his name, but he wasn't sure what the rules were for this kind of thing, if there were any to begin with. He worried about diseases, about toxic skin, or a virus that his human immune system would be unable to handle. Then again, they'd already been in close contact, skin to skin, lip to lip, tongue to tongue; they'd shared spit and nothing terrible had happened. But there were too many factors, too many unknowns, and they should talk about it first, he should make sure this was what she wanted, and what he wanted too, that they knew exactly what this next step would mean for their future, and for the future of humanity.

He pulled back from her slightly so he could look into her eyes. She smiled at him expectantly, her breath, her pulse, fluttering her throat. Then she threaded her fingers through his hair and stretched to kiss him again.

"Celeste, wait."

She sank back onto the ground, pouting a little.

"There's something I need to ask you."

But before he could get the words out, a panicked shout reached them from the valley below. "Cops!"

Nolan squinted through the darkness toward the path they'd come up, but there wasn't much to see. Shrubs in the dark, a cliff dropping off into nothing. He was going to stay, hide up here until the chaos died down, but Celeste pushed him away, rolling out from under him and leaping to her feet. She said nothing as she bolted, running to the edge of the bluff. Nolan scrambled to his feet and ran after her. A commotion, shouting and a confusion of voices, swelled up from the bonfire. Below them, groups splintered. People fled the light for the shadows. A few kicked sand over the fire and poured out their beers, trying to extinguish the flames. Then they, too, took off running.

Celeste was a gray wraith, light and swift, bounding down the zigzag path and leaping over rocks, defying gravity. She didn't check to see if Nolan was following, and she didn't wait for him when she reached the bottom. She vanished into the shadows with the others.

He tried to catch up to her, slamming down the path, but his shoes came untied and he kept tripping and he was so heavy and clumsy, bound by the rules of physics. Once he fell so hard his ankle popped and pain flared and then as quickly dulled. He could put weight on it and walk, so he knew it wasn't broken, but it still hurt, and slowed him down. When he made it to the bottom of the bluff, the bonfire was out and everyone who had been at the party was gone. Everyone but Nolan. Engines revved in the distance, speakers thumped, tires puffed and hissed through soft dirt as they made their escape, leaving him behind.

Alone in the dark, and the moon had fled, too, darting behind a swollen cloud. Nolan set off again at a slow, defeated limp. He didn't blame Celeste for taking off the way she did, only himself for not having the foresight to double-knot his laces. If she'd hesitated, looked back, waited, if she'd slowed down at all, he would have shouted at her to go.

Several people in the Encounters group, including Gabriella, had warned him before about the police, how some were good and just doing their job, but how a few were crooked, paid by the government to act as goons and spies, showing up uninvited on a contactee's doorstep and threatening to arrest them without cause, searching and seizing property without warrants. Just a week ago, in fact, Nolan had read an article about a man who'd been arrested for having child pornography on his computer not twenty-four hours after appearing on the *Today Show* to talk about his experiences. His wife tried to argue that the whole thing was a setup, the pornography planted by the cops who were under orders from a top-secret government agency, after her husband refused to stay silent about the miraculous things he'd seen. But no one listened. The man was still sitting in jail, awaiting his joke of a trial.

Nolan's was the only vehicle left parked on the side of the road. A patrol car had pulled up behind it. Headlights and a blinding spotlight shone into the cab and stretched long, strange shadows across the desert. A uniformed officer walked a slow circle around the pickup. He spoke into his radio, then turned when he heard footsteps approaching and pointed a flashlight beam into Nolan's eyes. His other hand went for his gun.

Nolan stopped walking and raised his hands above his head.

"Is this your truck?" the officer asked.

Nolan nodded, too afraid to speak. For an instant, he worried that Celeste had waited for him, but he didn't see her lurking anywhere and hoped she'd hitched a ride from someone else. As long as she wasn't here, as long as this cop didn't learn of her existence, she'd be safe.

The officer lowered the flashlight to Nolan's chest. He was a silhouette behind the beam, a dark and anonymous blob. His voice was gruff and void of emotion. "Go ahead and come on over. Put your hands flat on the hood for me."

Nolan hesitated. He thought about running, but the officer had a Taser on his belt. And a gun. The best thing to do was play along, do as he was told, do whatever the officer asked, and get this over with as fast as he could. He hadn't been drinking or doing anything illegal that he knew of, and if he didn't give the officer a reason to arrest him, he didn't see any reason why he shouldn't be driving home within the half hour, driving to find Celeste.

He did as he was told. The spotlight on the patrol car shone into his face. He lowered his head, stared down at his fingers spread wide, and tried not to panic.

The officer reeked of leather and some kind of spiced aftershave. Metal rattled on his belt. "You got a name, kid?"

"Nolan Durant." His voice trembled without his permission.

"Carrying any weapons, Nolan? Anything sharp?"

"No, sir."

The officer roughly patted down Nolan's arms and chest, his hips and the backs of his legs. He took Nolan's keys from his pants pocket and tossed them onto the hood, out of reach. "Do you have your driver's license with you?"

"It's in the truck. In the glove box."

The officer's radio crackled and squawked. Nolan flinched. The officer muttered something to the dispatcher on the other end and then raised his voice again. "You want to tell me what you're doing out here tonight, Nolan?"

"Stargazing." It was the truth. Mostly.

"All by yourself?"

Nolan thought of Celeste, her lips soft and warm, her body fitting so perfectly with his, how quickly and beautifully she came to life under the stars, how quickly she'd disappeared.

"Yes, sir," he answered, swallowing around a hard knot forming in his throat. "Just me."

The officer leaned in close, first grabbing Nolan's right arm, then his left, then pulling both hands behind Nolan's back. He tried to look over his shoulder, but his arms twisted too tight, and any position other than looking straight ahead caused pain. Handcuffs bit into his wrists.

"What's going on? Am I under arrest?" Nolan couldn't keep his voice from sounding panicked; he didn't even try. "I didn't do anything."

The officer turned Nolan so his back pressed against the grill. The handcuffs were tight, and Nolan's fingertips tingled from lack of blood, but he was too scared to complain.

The officer turned off his flashlight. He was younger than Nolan expected, probably no older than thirty, black and clean-shaven, his dark hair trimmed close to his scalp. Stitched in white thread across his shirt pocket was his last name: Williams. There was an intensity to his gaze, and Nolan really started to worry then, afraid the man would be able to work a confession from him without Nolan saying a single word. He would see Celeste reflected in Nolan's eyes, smell her on his skin, penetrate his thoughts and find her there too.

"Have you had anything to drink tonight, Nolan?" Officer Williams asked.

"No, sir." He shook his head.

"Drugs?"

"No."

"Do you deal?"

"What? No, of course not."

"And this is your vehicle? This one here?" He pointed the butt of his flashlight at Nolan's pickup.

"Yes," Nolan said, wanting to get to the point, to get through this next part as fast as possible so the handcuffs could come off and he could get the hell out of here. "Yes. The registration's in the glove box. With my name on it. And there's an insurance card too."

Officer Williams stared at Nolan, his expression unreadable.

"Go ahead." Nolan gestured with his elbow to the keys on the hood, frantic for the man's eyes to be off of him now. "Have a look."

Officer Williams grabbed the keys and unlocked the driver-side door. He ducked his upper body into the cab. Nolan craned his neck, trying to see what the man was doing, but he couldn't get turned around and the angle was bad, the spotlight on the patrol car keeping him from seeing anything properly. A few minutes later, Officer Williams straightened and held up something for Nolan to see. A clear, plastic sandwich bag, twisted at the top and knotted, inside which were a dozen or more white pills that looked like tiny aspirin tablets.

"What is that?" Nolan asked.

For the first time that night, Officer Williams's expression changed. His mouth twisted into a smirk, and he shook his head like he was disappointed. He balled up the bag in his fist, shut the door, and returned to where Nolan stood. "I'm placing you under arrest for possession of an illegal substance."

"Wait." He struggled against the handcuffs. "That's not mine. Please, listen, you have to believe me. I've never seen that bag before. That wasn't in my truck when I parked. That wasn't . . . I don't even know what those pills are. Someone else must have put them there."

Ignoring his protests, Officer Williams took Nolan by the elbow and guided him to the patrol car.

8

Lucy spent the rest of Saturday night in her motel room, watching reruns of *Law & Order* and eating potato chips and a Snickers bar from the vending machine, the only dinner she could afford since she had to pay for another night's stay. She wasn't sure how much longer she could live off her credit card. A few more days, maybe, before the balance snowballed into a burden. She thought about calling her father and asking to borrow more money, but she could imagine his response. Most likely he would demand she come home. Most likely he would want the money he gave her for the apartment returned immediately. And there was no chance in hell he'd even consider financing her dead-end quest. At one point, during a commercial break, Lucy opened her laptop and a Word document and tried to re-create from memory a timeline of what she remembered from the night Nolan went missing, but this proved more frustrating than useful, white space swallowing the page, the cursor mocking her with its incessant blinking.

Sunday morning, after a restless night's sleep, she called Detective Williams. He was surprised to hear from her, but told her to come down to the station before eleven; he was catching up on some paperwork and would be more than happy to try and answer whatever questions she had. Lucy showered and dressed, then drove thirty miles south to the Inyo County sheriff's office in Independence.

On her way there, she had to pass by Owens Valley Radio Observatory, and though the actual site was some distance from the highway, the telescopes were visible from the road. She tried not to look at them, but they were impossible to ignore. So tall, so regal, their wide, white faces tilted at a sharp angle, reflecting the sun. When she was a little girl, she'd imagined herself working there someday, side by side with Nolan, scanning the skies for mysteries. Now this place only served as a reminder of everything she'd lost.

Detective Williams met Lucy at the front desk. He looked young for a detective, midthirties or a little older, and was dressed casually in dark jeans and a gray polo shirt. Stitched onto the front of his shirt beneath the left collar was a small sheriff's star that matched the Inyo County seal. Other than that, there was nothing about him to indicate he was law enforcement. No handcuffs, no badge, no gun.

After a quick handshake, he escorted Lucy into the main office. Most of the desks were vacant of people, though cluttered with papers and coffee mugs, as if the occupants had simply stepped away for a moment. Across the room a uniformed officer worked at a computer. Somewhere a phone rang. Tacked to a bulletin board were sketches and photographs of wanted men and women, their half-dead eyes staring out across the room. On another board were the faces of children. Girls and boys of varying ages and ethnicities, all of them smiling and happy, their innocence not yet shattered. These pictures had been taken at school or on vacation, when they were safe with their families, during a period of time when their future was bright—before they went missing. Lucy scanned the posters for Nolan, but none of the faces were his.

"After you called, I pulled up your brother's file." Detective Williams gestured for her to take a seat in a plastic chair beside his desk. "I remember him."

"You do?" Lucy didn't think she would have forgotten Detective Williams. In this area, a black man in a uniform was something memorable. Plus, he was handsome, and projected the kind of seriousness that she would have latched onto if he'd been an active part of the initial investigation. As far as she could remember, this was the first time they'd ever met.

"Yes." Detective Williams leaned back in his chair. "I arrested him for possession a couple months before he went missing."

Lucy's hands curled in her lap. The party at Ship Rock. She hadn't thought about that night in years. It was her first high school party, and she'd lied to her mother about where she was going, mumbling something about a sleepover with the small group of girls she'd been hanging out with since elementary school. But those girls had stopped talking to Lucy over the summer, or she had stopped talking to them. She couldn't remember who stopped talking first, but it was because of Patrick and the others, because her old friends didn't like her new friends and her new friends thought her old friends were babies. Lucy was the only freshman to be invited to Ship Rock. She couldn't *not* go.

Megan and Natasha had picked her up at the end of her driveway a few hours before the party started. They went to the mall first because, according to Megan, Lucy's billowy white skirt and red flannel top made her look like a Raggedy Ann doll, and according to Natasha no one wore cowboy boots anymore and braids were out, too—"You're fourteen, for God's sake, not four." They gave her a makeover, cutting her hair straight across at her shoulders, then stripping the brown out with bleach until her hair was white-blond and straw-crisp, finally dipping the ends in a bowl of pink dye. They wouldn't let her see until they'd washed her hair, blown it dry, and flat-ironed it straight. Only then did they turn her toward the mirror. An unfamiliar woman with rock star hair stared back at her, eyes lined thick black and smoky, her lips smeared the color of burst-open cherries. She looked like the kind of woman who had sex for fun. Lucy smiled, and the woman smoldered. Lucy touched her cheek. The woman did too, a gesture of longing. Megan and Natasha stood behind her, inspecting their work.

"Patrick's going to flip," said Natasha.

"He won't be able to keep his dirty paws to himself," said Megan.

They laughed a twin laugh, their matching chestnut hair spilling waterfalls around their cream and perfect shoulders. They'd found out about Lucy's crush a few weeks ago after practice when she'd accidentally dumped out the contents of her backpack onto the locker room floor. They were helping to gather her things when Megan held up a folder with Patrick's name scribbled on the front and surrounded by hearts. "I think someone's in loooo-ve." They didn't tease her about it, though. Neither did they run and blab to Patrick. Instead, like older sisters, they took her under their exquisite wings, promising to turn her from ugly duckling into graceful swan. Lucy touched her hair again, wishing they had dyed it to match theirs, wishing it had the same shine and sleekness and depth. She lifted a piece to her nose, grimacing at the chemical scent of bleach. Natasha and Megan smelled like gardenias. They spun her around again and held up clothes against her scarecrow frame, finally deciding on a tube top and jeans that hugged her in such a way as to create the illusion of curves. Natasha wolf-whistled. Megan shimmied her hips. They told her Patrick would have to pay attention to her now. They told her he would be falling all over himself, drooling like a Labrador puppy.

But when they got to the party, Patrick took one look at Lucy and, with his nose screwed up like he was smelling someone's dirty sock, asked, "What did you do to your hair?"

She drank then, can after can of lukewarm, fizzing beer, until her stomach swam and her ears buzzed and the crushing pressure on her chest dissipated. She was as light as a bird, as air, a feather. She felt nothing, was nothing, and fuck Patrick and his stupid perfect hair and his stupid perfect lips. She was a goddess with rock star pink hair. She was the sun, burning hot and setting the world on fire. When she walked, the earth rose up to meet her. Fairies streaked by, hissing ribbons of red and yellow. She reached to catch them, but someone jerked her back, laughing, screaming, "You fucking pyro!" and she realized the fairies were flames. Then she was twirling between Natasha and Megan, or they twirled around her. She told them to stand still, she was trying to count the stars. They laughed, champagne bubbles popping, and handed her another beer.

Then her brother and his stupid secret girlfriend. Out of nowhere. Both of them suddenly in front of her, and Nolan wagging his finger, scolding her like she was some fucking idiot toddler who'd colored permanent marker rainbows on the wall, scolding her like she was their mother. She tried to get him to leave her alone. Didn't he understand what it was like? Couldn't he see he was embarrassing her? Hadn't he been fourteen once, dying to be older and popular? But Nolan wasn't normal, had never been normal. He didn't care about fitting in. He didn't see the point. She didn't think it could get any worse, but it did. Patrick stumbled over to them, and at first Lucy thought he was coming to get her, but then he put his arm around Celeste. Falling all over himself for Celeste, drooling over Celeste. He didn't see Lucy at all.

Nolan was distracted then. He turned his back for a second, and Lucy fled into the dark with Natasha and Megan pulling her along, calling him a freak, a nutcracker, a dildo dodo dipshit. "How do you even stand living with him?" one said, it was too dark to see which. The other, their voices were almost identical, screeched, "If he were my brother, I'd fucking kill myself."

They raced up the side of a cliff to the moon. Lucy leaped to grab hold of it. She wanted to swing, to perch, to hang like a trapeze artist upside down, wearing the night sky as her cape, the stars as diamonds woven into the fabric. She leaped and stumbled and fell to her knees in the dirt. Not light enough, goddess enough, to defy gravity. She bet Celeste could, though, catch the moon, pull down the stars, make the whole universe orbit around her perfect, mysterious brilliance. Lucy's stomach heaved and she puked. Most of it splattered on the ground, but some of it dribbled down her chin onto her shirt, and more caught in her hair. It smelled bad. She backed away from the puddle, but the smell followed her, was her. She puked again and then reached her hand up for help. Natasha, Megan . . . anyone? But they had abandoned her, and she was alone with the moon, who laughed at her now, leering over her shoulder. The night-sky cape strangling her, the stars turned to glass.

She pulled herself up and, on unsteady feet, walked to the edge of the cliff. She looked down expecting to see the bonfire, but instead saw Megan's car driving away, taillights red in the dark, a steady thump of bass stretching the distance. Her stomach knotted. The plateau was spinning now, too fast. She sat in the dirt with her back against a rock and held her head between her knees waiting for the feeling to pass.

Voices climbed up the side of the cliff. One was her brother. She started to stand, relieved that he hadn't forgotten about her, that he was climbing up this steep plateau to make sure she was all right, and she wasn't all right. She would tell him that. She would apologize and let him take her home and tuck her into bed and then she would tell him he was the best brother in the whole wide universe. But then she recognized the voice of the other person, Celeste, and so she slumped back down behind the rock, staying hidden in the deep night shadows.

She didn't want them to see her like this, alone and covered in her own vomit. She didn't want to hear Nolan say I told you so, or see the smug better-than-you smirk on Celeste's stupid, perfect, porcelain moon face. She would wait for them to leave and then she would go and find Patrick and then whatever happened after that would be up to him.

Lucy peered around the rock to see how much longer she would have to wait. Celeste and Nolan were lying on their backs now, looking up at the stars, and Lucy's disdain for Celeste deepened. Stargazing was something she and Nolan did together, what they had always done together, and now this girl from nowhere, who had stolen her brother's time and attention and more recently Patrick's heart, now this bitch was stealing the stars from her, too.

They stopped talking and started to kiss. Their faces mashed, their hands fumbling, their bodies bucking. Lucy turned away from them and glared at the sky. She should be the one kissing someone tonight. Nolan wasn't even supposed to be at this party; he hadn't been invited. It wasn't fair. It wasn't fucking fair. Well, she didn't have to just sit here and watch it happen, did she? Patrick was probably still at the party, alone and feeling betrayed like her. Drunk and looking for comfort.

Lucy crept to the opposite edge of the plateau from where she'd come up, quietly, quietly, to another path that Megan and Natasha had taken down to the car. She slid her feet along the ground, knowing that a misstep would take her straight off the side. Humpty-Dumpty style, all the king's horses and all the king's men, but somehow she reached the bottom of the cliff without falling once.

What happened next was chaos. Blue and red lights flickered in the distance. Then people were shouting, running, coming out from behind the outcrop, diving into their cars, peeling out in the dust. Lucy didn't know what to do. She froze as people streamed around her, and then Patrick grabbed her hand, saying something, saying, "—get the fuck out of here! Come with me!" She raced with him to his car, almost there, when all of a sudden, he stopped. She ran into him. He took something from his pocket and threw it into the open window of a pickup that looked vaguely familiar, and for that brief instant—his arm flying out, his fingers opening—time slowed as her mind tried to catch up with her eyes, but then they were moving again and whatever Patrick had done was not as important as getting the hell out of there before the cops showed up. Lucy got into Patrick's car and as she did, she thought she saw Celeste scrambling into the next car over. Nolan wasn't with her, or maybe he was; Lucy didn't know. And she didn't fucking care. He could take care of himself. She was with Patrick, and he was holding her hand.

There were many ways to go, the land flat, so many off-road tracks splintering in all directions. The blue and red lights came from the park entrance, along the main road. It was easy to drive in any other direction and disappear. There were other exits to the east. Patrick pressed on the gas. The world turned to gold dust. Lucy rolled down her window and howled.

She should have left the party with Nolan that night when she had the chance. So much would have been different for them. Everything, maybe. She wouldn't have ended up in Patrick's car, for one thing, pissed off and still drunk and reeking of puke, and she wouldn't have taken that small white pill off the tip of his finger, and she wouldn't have done what she did after, to get his attention, to get his mind off Celeste and on to her. How easily her hand found its way to his crotch, how easy to rub him hard. He pulled over, told her to unzip his pants and finish him off, but when she tried to kiss him, he pushed her away, saying, "You smell disgusting." Which she did, but he could have at least given her this token, this one small thing. If she'd left the party with Nolan, none of that would have happened, and she would have been better off. Nolan, too, because if she had left with him, he wouldn't have still been there when the cops showed up. He would have never been arrested.

Detective Williams said, "Lucky for your brother, it was his first offense."

They'd released him into Sandra's custody with a warning.

Lucy was home in bed when they came through the front door a little after three in the morning. Sandra was crying and talking loudly about how damn lucky he was, how if she were that cop, she would have made him spend the night in a jail cell with the perverts and druggies, scare the idiot right out of him. Nolan mumbled something, then Sandra stomped down the hallway. A door slammed. Lucy flinched and pulled the pillow over her head, which was throbbing the beginnings of a bad hangover. She heard a click as her door opened. She lifted the pillow. Nolan stood in the doorway, peering in at her. After a few seconds, he whispered, "Lucy? Are you there?"

She whispered back, "I'm here."

"Good." He started to pull the door closed, then stopped and leaned his head through the crack again. "Ibuprofen, now, if you haven't already. And lots of water. I'll make you blueberry pancakes when you wake up."

She groaned, sick at the thought of putting anything in her stomach ever again, but it worked. She did what he said, ibuprofen and water, and when she woke up he had pancakes waiting and it was the most delicious food she'd ever eaten, and the hangover she'd been expecting never materialized. During her second helping of pancakes, she started to talk to him about the party, to apologize for being stupid and to tell him what Patrick had done, but something distracted him. He got up from the table and rushed to the phone, lifting it to his ear, before setting it down again, looking bewildered. He did this three times in a row before finally drifting off to his bedroom, Lucy and his own stack of pancakes completely forgotten.

"Those drugs weren't Nolan's," Lucy said to Detective Williams, suddenly feeling defensive.

His eyebrows arched high on his forehead. "I thought you were here to talk about his missing person's case."

"I am," she said. "I just, I think it needs to be said. Those drugs weren't his."

He offered her a stiff smile. "It doesn't really matter anymore, does it."

He opened a manila folder sitting on the desk in front of him and ran his eyes over the top sheet. "Detective Mueller seemed to be under the impression that your brother may have run away from home." His eyes snapped up to her again. "Do you have any reason to believe something else happened that night?"

The only thing she could manage to say was, "It's been ten years."

He stared at her, his expression unreadable, but even so making her nervous. She rubbed her thumbs together and reminded herself that she'd come voluntarily. She could walk out of here anytime she wanted. She wasn't a suspect. She'd done nothing wrong, despite the fact that Detective Williams was looking at her as though she had.

"You understand," he said, "that without any new leads, no new evidence, no suspects, not even a body . . . you understand, there's not much more we can do. Your brother's case is what we call 'cold.'"

"Which means what exactly?"

"That the evidence we have is slim to none. The leads have long dried up. So all we're left with are theories, possibilities, guesses. And, I'm sorry to say it, Lucy, I really am, but a case doesn't get very far on theories."

"I see."

Again that stiff, half smile.

"So his file," she said. "The evidence. It's just what? Collecting dust in the basement?"

He closed the manila folder and laid his hands on top of it. "Something like that, yes."

"Is that it?" Lucy leaned in for a closer look, reaching for the corner of the folder that was visible beneath his spread-wide fingers. "Is that Nolan's file? I'd like to see it. I'd like to know what steps were taken, who Detective Mueller talked to."

If she could just see the file all laid out in front of her, then maybe something would spark in her mind. She would remember something new about that night or see a connection everyone else had missed.

"I'm afraid it's not possible." Detective Williams moved the folder out of reach. "Letting you see the file would compromise the investigation. Such as it is."

"I don't understand."

He opened his desk drawer, slipped the folder inside, and then slammed the drawer closed again. "Lucy, I'm wondering, why the sudden interest in your brother's case?"

"I need a reason?"

"Seems odd, is all. The notes indicate you went to live with your father a few months after the case was opened and after that, silence. You've had ten years to come by, or call us up, to find out how things are going, but you didn't. So." He spread his hands open on the desk. "Why now?"

Lucy stared down at his palms, following his life line, or was that his love line, his skin creased with the passage of time, lines blurring until they disappeared. She asked, "Why not now?"

He was quiet for a long time, though the silence was not uncomfortable, and this, Lucy realized, was how he got people to talk. By lulling them into a state of calm, making them believe they could say anything, and he would listen without judgment, without shame.

"Was there something you remembered?" he asked. "Something that you wanted me to add to the file?"

She could tell him now. Come clean about the too-many hours from that night that were missing from her memory, tell about her bloodied knee and constant nagging guilt, about the alcohol and about Patrick. But then, what did she really know about any of it? Nothing, and so there was nothing to say, nothing to add to the file. Maybe when she remembered—if she ever did— maybe then, when she had no doubts, she would come back and tell him the whole thing from beginning to end.

Again her gaze caught on the missing children posters hanging across the room. She scanned their faces once more just to be certain.

"He would have called me," she said, more to herself than Detective Williams. "He would have written a letter, an email, at least."

Detective Williams nodded, but said nothing else.

Lucy stood. "Thank you for your time. I know how busy you are."

The phone on his desk flashed red, indicating he had new voice mails. Paperwork teetered in stacks and boxes around his feet. He shrugged without comment, and then walked with her to the station entrance where he handed her a business card with his cell phone number written on the back. "If you remember anything about that night, anything at all, whether or not you think it's relevant to the case, please call me immediately."

She stuck the card in her purse and left.

9

Stuart Tomlinson still lived on Skyline Road in the same house across the street from Lucy's childhood home. As a girl, she went to great lengths to avoid him, checking each time before she left the house to make sure he wasn't outside watering his zinnias or drinking tea on his front porch. If he did happen to catch her outside, she would walk quickly away from him with her head down, pretending she didn't see his arm noodling to get her attention, didn't hear him calling, "Hello, Lucy! Yoo-hoo! Hello!"

Sandra didn't like Stuart either. "What the hell is he doing over there?" she asked, whenever they saw him returning from one of his junkyard trips, his car laden with boxes of what, from a distance, appeared to be other people's garbage. Bits and bobs and knicks and knacks. Once he brought home a whole box of doll heads. No bodies, just heads. One of them fell out of the box and rolled into the gutter in front of the Durants' house. Nolan picked it up and added it to his collection of meteorites on top of his dresser.

"He's a creeper," Lucy told Nolan when he asked her once why she didn't like Stuart.

"But why?" Nolan pressed her. "Because he doesn't act the way you think he should act?"

She struggled then, as a child, to explain precisely what it was about Stuart that she didn't like. A middle-aged, single man, he mostly kept to himself, never had raucous parties, never even played loud music. He kept his house in good repair and even started mowing their aging neighbor's lawn after she broke her hip. He never said anything inappropriate to Lucy, never made any improper advances, unless she counted the time he told her he'd found a litter of kittens in his garage, and did she want to come and play with them? She'd declined, thinking it was some kind of ploy to get her alone, and hurried off to wherever she'd been going, but a few weeks later there was Stuart, going door to door with a box of kittens, trying to find them new homes.

Maybe it was the combed-over hair or his ferret teeth or his too-pale skin that was almost translucent, or his bulging fish eyes that came to rest on her far more often and far longer than was socially acceptable. Maybe it was that, like a vampire, he never seemed to sleep. Lucy could see his house from her bedroom window, and on several occasions she'd woken in the middle of the night to all his lights blazing. A few times she even saw him rocking in his front porch swing, well past midnight, his eyes fixed on their house, on her bedroom window it seemed, though she couldn't be certain. None of these things were proof of misbehavior. They added up to nothing, really, except an unsettled, nervous feeling in Lucy's stomach.

But even now, as an adult, she had to talk herself into getting out of the car and going up to his front door. She knocked and then glanced across the street at her old house. The new owners had removed every inch of grass in the front yard, replacing it with a landscape of river stones and small, decorative shrubs and grasses. Lucy was too distracted to notice this change the other night, but she guessed they'd done it because of the dead spot. A perfect circle right in the middle of the lawn that, despite extra water, fertilizer, and new seed, refused to grow. It appeared in the middle of the night shortly after their father moved to LA. A disturbing brown patch in the center of their once-perfect green, almost as if the grass had been singed by something. No amount of coaxing, pleading, or professional help managed to return it to its former glorious state, and after a while, Sandra gave up on it.

Lucy knocked on Stuart's door a second time and then rang the doorbell.

A few seconds later, that high-pitched voice from her memory, the one that made her skin shrink, called out, "Just a second!"

She suppressed the urge to run and instead followed Stuart's voice around the side of the house to a detached garage turned workshop. The hinged front door was open. Classical music drifted from somewhere inside. Stuart sat on a tall stool, hunched over a table that stretched across one wall of the shop. A swinging-arm lamp shone a bright beam over his work space, leaving the rest of the shop dim. Stuart's fingers worked delicately inside something that looked like a jewelry box. Near his elbow was a row of tiny plastic paint pots and every so often he swung his hand around, dipped a small brush into one of the pots, and then returned to the jewelry box. The workshop smelled of wood chips and glue and freshly mixed paint. Lucy stood outside the threshold, watching him a moment. Then she cleared her throat.

Stuart jumped and knocked a jar to the floor. It clattered and rolled, but didn't break. He blinked at her in confusion, his eyes huge and cartoonish behind a pair of magnifying lenses.

"I'm sorry. I didn't mean to startle you. I just . . ." She trailed off.

His expression changed then into one of recognition. He removed the lenses, set them on the workbench, and then slid off the stool, taking a step toward her, his lips spreading into a delighted smile. "It's you. Only you're so much older now. So much . . . bigger."

Lucy shifted under his gaze, which wandered lazily over her body, taking in all the ways she'd changed.

"I don't know if you remember me." She wasn't sure why she said this, when clearly he did. Nerves. She wanted him to stop looking at her like that, like she was something delicious, some sweet treat to devour.

His tongue darted over his lips, then finally, he lowered his gaze, bending to pick up the jar that had fallen on the floor. He set it on the workbench next to the glasses and reached for a rag, wiping his fingers one by one. "I was beginning to think I'd never see you again, Lucy."

She smiled, trying to be polite. "Well, here I am."

"Yes, here you certainly are." He walked to the wall of the garage and turned on the overhead lights.

He looked exactly the same as he had ten years ago, as if no time had passed at all for him. Same cornhusk hair slicked over his bald spot and pasted down with gel. Same pale, see-through skin. Same bulging eyes that kept shifting back to her, landing in different spots on her body, as if trying to memorize the place of everything, how she was put together. He was wearing stiff khakis and a pastel pink polo shirt, over which he'd tied a white linen apron. Paintbrushes and X-Acto knives poked up from the apron pocket. A small splattering of red paint the only blemish against the white.

"So," Stuart said. "To what do I owe this pleasure?"

She cut right to it, not bothering with small talk. "I was hoping you'd speak with me about the night my brother disappeared. About what you saw."

"Yes, of course." He didn't seem at all surprised that this was why she'd come.

He gestured with his arm, spreading it wide and inviting her inside the workshop, then went and grabbed a second stool from another part of the room, setting it down near the one he'd been using. Lucy perched herself on the edge of one stool, and Stuart settled comfortably back onto his. He laced his fingers together in his lap. His smile fixed, his shoulders stiff. She couldn't remember a time when she'd ever been this close to him, close enough to see the flecks of yellow in his brown eyes, and to smell the baby powder scent rising off his skin.

She looked away from him, trying to gather her racing thoughts and calm her quick-beating heart. She studied the room instead, taking in the small table saw, the stacks of uncut wood and nearby scrap piles, the paint cans and jars of glue, piles of cardboard and what looked like foam. Pages clipped from magazines and calendars, photographs of natural settings and abstract art covered the walls. Boxes on the floor overflowed with magazines as well as bits of paper and metal bobs, miniature dolls and furniture, old pillows and clothes, other things she couldn't decipher. Detritus, bits of other people's lives. A large oak wardrobe crouched in the far back corner of the garage, a handsome piece of furniture, intricately carved and polished to a shine. It looked out of place among the rest of it, a rich man squatting in a poor man's hovel.

Stuart noticed her looking at the wardrobe. "It was my great-grandfather's. Brought over from Germany before the war."

"It's beautiful," she said.

"Your brother used to come over and polish it for me."

Lucy didn't remember that.

"I paid him ten dollars." Stuart tapped his thumbs together. "He did other things for me, too. Raked leaves, washed windows. Stuff that I could have done myself, of course, but he was such a nice kid. I always liked him. And after your father left, well, he seemed so lonely. And sad. He liked the company, I think, more than the money I gave him."

After their dad left, Nolan changed. He became more and more withdrawn. He had nightmares. He'd walk through every room of the house with a bewildered look on his face, like he was trying to find some favorite, misplaced toy. He'd stopped eating for a while, too. Or rather, he'd eat, but then a few hours later, he'd be in the bathroom throwing up. She remembered he had to stay home from school for a few weeks, how jealous she was that he got to spend all day on the couch watching television, their mother waiting on him, worrying over him. The doctors couldn't find anything physically wrong. They said he just needed time to adjust, and they were right. After a while, Nolan started eating again. Then he went back to school and things went mostly back to normal for a while. Lucy had been upset about their dad leaving, too, but it wasn't like he was dead and they would never see him again. They would visit on holidays and sometimes during spring break, and they could call him on the phone whenever they wanted, even though most of the time he was too busy to talk for long. A lot of kids' parents were divorced, and no one made a big deal out of it. If anything, it was better because you got double the presents on your birthday and Christmas. Lucy tried to explain all this to Nolan once, but he just said, "I was an accident, you know. I'm not even supposed to be here." She'd been too young at the time to understand what he was talking about.

"Anyway," Stuart continued. "It's a shame what happened to him. A real shame. He was such a talented young man, naturally gifted. He could have made a name for himself one day." His thumbs stilled and he leaned slightly forward, his bug eyes growing even buggier. "Has there been any change in the case? Any new developments?"

"No," Lucy said. "That's why I'm here, actually. The police have been less than forthcoming, but I know you were a witness. You were the last one who saw him."

The corners of his mouth twisted, like they were sharing a secret.

"So, whatever you can tell me about that night," she added, "whatever you remember, I would be incredibly grateful."

The smile stayed twisted on his lips as he studied her face a moment, then he shifted on the stool, unlacing his hands and smoothing them over his thighs. When he started to talk, his lips made a popping sound, like a seal breaking open.

"It started with the lights, really," he said. "That's how it began for me anyway. To this day I don't know what they were or where they came from. For a while, I thought they were airplanes, certainly that must have been it, but having gone over it so many times, I realize now that they were just too bright, too low to the ground, and coming in too fast. Maybe it was kids driving their four-wheelers around in the boulder lands, but you know how those engines are . . . loud as hellcats . . . and these lights . . ." He shook his head. "They didn't make a sound."

Lucy stared at him. He had to be teasing her. He'd read the *Strange Quarterly* article, seen the pictures. He knew about Sandra and her baseless theories, and for whatever reason—maybe revenge for how Lucy treated him when she was younger, or maybe he'd seen her and Patrick flying the remote-control helicopter, or maybe simply because he was a sociopath—he had to be messing with her now.

Stuart must have recognized the incredulous look on her face because he held his hands in the air, shook his head, and said, "No, I know what you're thinking, and it's not like that. I don't have any reason to lie to you. I wouldn't do that. Not after everything you've been through. These lights were real, Lucy. I saw them as clear as I see you in front of me now. And I saw them more than once, too, more than just the night he went missing. That's why I was up so late. I'd seen the lights a few times in the weeks before and I was trying to catch them on video. That's why I was outside in the middle of the night. How I was able to see what I did."

He'd been sitting in the dark, in a folding chair in his back-yard with the video camera ready to go, waiting for the lights to come up over the horizon the way they had in nights past, when he heard shouting start up across the street. He snuck around to the front and watched Nolan shove someone into his pickup and drive away.

"You got it on video?" Lucy couldn't keep the hope from her voice.

"No. By the time I thought about it, he was long gone." He looked sorry to disappoint her and rushed on, saying, "I

called the police as soon as I heard about Nolan on the news."
He gave a sad little shake of his head. "I only wish I had called
sooner. That night. I should have called *that night*, right away,
as soon as I heard all that shouting, but I didn't think . . ." He
shook his head a second time with more ferocity. "He'd always
been such a good kid, never in any kind of trouble, a nice boy.
A *nice* boy."

"You couldn't have known." Lucy tried to sound reassuring. She knew what it felt like to live ten years carrying the
weight of one bad decision.

"Do you think it would have made a difference?" He
smoothed his comb-over. "If I had called that night instead of
waiting?"

Lucy shook her head. She truly didn't know.

Her gaze shifted to the jewelry box that Stuart had been
working on when she first got here. She stretched forward,
twisting for a closer look. It was some sort of diorama, a miniature world wrapped in velvet. A plastic doll, fashioned to look
like a little girl wearing a red polka-dot dress and black Mary
Janes, hung frozen in midair, her blond curls streaming behind
her, her legs kicked out as she pumped high on a tiny swing.
She was caught midlaugh, her mouth a perfect, upturned bow.
Tiny sparrows flew around her. Trees no bigger than a penny
crowded the edges of the box, a mysterious and beckoning
forest. The sky exploded, a gold and purple sunset that mim-
icked the end of the world. Or the beginning.

"Do you like it?" Stuart asked.

Lucy startled at his voice, not realizing how caught up she
was in the scene.

"It's remarkable," she said. "Everything's so small, and yet,
it looks almost real. It must take you forever. All those details."

Pink colored his cheeks. He smiled at his hands. "I have trouble sleeping sometimes, and I find the level of detail a piece like that requires to be especially soothing." He glanced at the diorama. "I call this one 'Misery in Gold.'"

She looked at it again, seeing things now that she hadn't before: a park bench hardly big enough for an ant, a merry-go-round made out of a button, the figure of a man hiding in the trees.

"How do you decide what to make?" Lucy asked.

"I look to the world. News articles, memories, scenes from my favorite books, sometimes even real-life experiences. I made this one two weeks ago after a particularly stimulating walk through the park." He reached to caress the box's velvet outside and then made a fine, nearly imperceptible adjustment to the little girl's skirt. "Her name is Molly. She has such a delightful laugh. Like a little bird."

He tapped one of the sparrows and all of them began to bounce. They appeared to be connected somehow and attached to some kind of spring, but to Lucy it seemed like magic.

Without taking his eyes from the diorama, he said, "I made a world for you and your brother once. What's that game you would always play? You'd run around in the front yard wearing those red and blue capes, pretending to be superheroes, I believe. Starman and Asteroid Girl, yes, that was it, now I remember."

He laughed, and the sound made her fingers curl tight around the edge of the stool.

"So clever, the two of you together," he said. "You reminded me so much of myself at that age. I had a sister, you know. We played together like you and your brother did, but she died when we were still young. Pneumonia, terrible thing.

Anyway, you and Nolan, the two of you were such an inspiration, and the world I made, oh, how divine. One of my best, if I'm allowed to say such a thing. Do you want to see it?" His eyes snapped to hers and there was an eagerness there, a hunger that scared her, but despite her fear, she nodded.

He leaped off the stool and crossed to the wardrobe, fumbling a moment with a clump of keys before finding the right one, inserting it into the lock, and opening the cupboard doors. He leaned in and began moving things around, muttering to himself.

As Lucy waited, she scolded herself for leaving her phone in the car. She hadn't told anyone she was coming here, and she had no idea what kind of man Stuart really was. She should have pushed harder to see the police report. Or she should have done what people did in movies and on television: create some kind of diversion and then steal the desired information. She could have at least tried. She could have asked Detective Williams for a cup of coffee or a Kleenex, something that would have required him to leave his desk for a few minutes, giving her the opportunity to slip Nolan's file out of the drawer and walk out with it tucked under her shirt. Which was probably a crime of some kind, obstruction of justice or tampering or some other legal term she didn't know, but at least she would have been better prepared than she was now. At least she would have known exactly what the police thought of Stuart after they questioned him, whether they considered him a suspect. She was a terrible detective. It hadn't occurred to her until this moment that she might be dealing with someone dangerous.

Stuart returned carrying something the size of a shoebox. The outside was black and speckled with tiny white stars. On the lid was a paper moon, moving through all its phases. Stuart sat back down on his stool, then offered the box to Lucy. "I made it after you moved away. It was just so quiet around here with you and your brother both gone. Too quiet."

She carefully opened the lid. It had a locking arm that held it upright so the underside of the lid became part of the inside scene. There was something familiar yet unsettling about the miniature world Stuart had made. In the foreground, a boy with a blue cape bent over a telescope that was pointed at a full and grinning moon glued to the underside of the lid. A girl with a red cape was frozen midstride, the cape fluttering out behind her, her arms bent at the elbow, one leg lifted, giving the impression that she was running circles around the boy. In the background was a rocket ship, spewing cottony smoke from its jet engines, red cellophane sparks lighting up the darkness. Lucy leaned closer. A face peered out a round window set into the rocket's tubular, metallic body. A pale-cheeked man forever watching the girl in the red cape.

Lucy started to close the box, but Stuart darted his hand inside, jabbing a finger at something that looked like a purple rock leaning up against a tree trunk.

"I never told anyone about it, you know," he said.

"About what?" Lucy squinted at the purple rock. Not a rock, a bag of some kind, a backpack maybe with black straps no wider than dental floss.

"The backpack." He took the diorama from her, fiddled with something inside, and then gently closed the lid. "I still have it."

A tingling sensation crept up the back of her neck, needle-like ant legs racing across her skull. She had no idea what he was talking about, and yet, some subconscious part of her was twisting, shriveling up in fear and dread, seeming to know something the rest of her didn't. Stuart returned the diorama to the wardrobe. When he came back, he carried a purple JanSport backpack, an exact color match to the miniature version. A fabric patch of the planet Saturn was stitched onto the front pocket, the silver threads starting to fray.

He stopped in front of her, holding the backpack by one strap, letting it dangle at his side. "I've been keeping it safe for you."

Lucy's mouth went dry. Pressure built in her head, a vise squeezing tighter and tighter. "Where did you get that?"

He gave her a questioning look. "You know where."

She shook her head. She reached for the bag, but he pulled it away.

"You hid it in the bushes outside my house," he said, as if she was the one not making sense. "The night Nolan went missing."

A buzzing in her ears, growing louder with each word. She was still shaking her head, couldn't seem to stop, as if the motion could protect her from what he was saying, his lies, because this couldn't possibly be true.

"After I saw Nolan drive away, I stayed out on the porch for another few hours," he said. "Waiting to see if he would come back. Waiting for the lights, too, I suppose. Just. Waiting. I was about to go inside when I saw you limping up the road. It surprised me, seeing you like that. You sort of appeared out of nowhere. And you were alone. It was so late. I called out to you, but you didn't hear me, I guess. You went halfway up the driveway and then you stopped and bent to pick something up. It was too dark for me to see what, but you carried it across the street and stuffed it under the bushes. Then went back to your house."

Lucy stared at the backpack. An image flashed through her mind of her almost tripping over the bag, stifling a scream because she'd thought it was a body. But she couldn't draw up any of the rest of what Stuart was telling her now, could only recall shivering hands, chattering teeth, the scrape of branches against her skin, the tangy scent of crushed spruce needles.

Stuart lowered his eyes to the backpack too. His voice grew quieter, like he was confessing. "I thought it was yours. I was going to give it back the next day, but in the morning I looked through it and there was some other girl's wallet inside, some other girl's clothes."

Lucy pressed her hand to her mouth.

"I waited to see if you would come looking for it, but you never did," he said. "And then the news came out about your brother and everyone was so busy over there. Cops in and out all the time. And then you moved away."

"Why didn't you give it to the police?" Her voice was hoarse and unfamiliar.

"Is that what you want me to do?" His eyelids fluttered in surprise. "I assumed you had a good reason for hiding it that night. I thought I was helping you."

"You did," she rushed to reassure him. "You are. Helping me. Thank you."

She reached for the backpack, but he pulled it away.

"What do I get in return?" His gaze settled on her mouth. "I took a big risk, after all, not telling the police *everything* I saw that night. I could have very easily told them about the backpack. I still could."

Lucy swallowed back a rising revulsion and moved closer to Stuart, pressing her body against his. His breathing accelerated. He smelled strongly of baby powder and something metallic.

With the back of her hand, Lucy stroked his cheek and smiled like she meant it. He shifted closer. His mouth puckered in and out like a fish sucking up food. Briefly, she wondered if Stuart had ever kissed anyone before. Then his free hand moved to encircle her waist. Before his fingers reached her hips, she snaked her arm out and grabbed the backpack. In his distraction, he loosened his hold, and it took Lucy little effort to tug the bag from his grasp. She ducked sideways out of his half embrace, then turned and ran.

Stuart started to chase after, but by the time he reached the bottom of the driveway, Lucy was already in her car, pulling away from the curb, the backpack slumped and brooding beside her in the passenger seat.

10

Lucy knew the backpack belonged to Celeste even before she laid out the contents across her motel room bed. She'd known as soon as Stuart took it out of the wardrobe. No one else had a Saturn patch like that one. Even so, Lucy needed to be certain. She needed more definitive proof, because what if her memory on this was wrong, too?

In the largest pocket she found a fringed leather vest and other clothes, a string of puka shells, a pair of slim, cheap rubber flip-flops, a constellation book, four chocolate chip granola bars, a reusable water bottle, a Greyhound bus schedule and a ticket to Santa Monica, and a well-worn map of California that had grown soft and thin from being folded and unfolded a hundred times. In the smaller front pocket was a red cloth wallet with a thick wad of cash, a Subway punch card, and a provisional driver's license issued by the state of Pennsylvania. Celeste's smiling face stared out at Lucy from behind the smudged plastic sleeve. She wiggled out the license for a closer look, and another card tucked behind it fell onto the bed. It was a business card, cheap, maybe even homemade.

**Wyatt Riggs. Field Investigator. UFO Encounters
For all your paranormal needs**

The phone number printed on the card was not the same phone number Wyatt used now, and when she tried calling it, she got an out-of-service message. She turned the card over. Scribbled on the back were the words: *If you ever need someone to talk to . . .*

The handwriting was familiar. She reached into her pants pocket and pulled out the list of names Wyatt gave her a few days ago, then held the list up next to the business card, comparing the two, finding them to be a near perfect match. She slipped both the business card and license back into the wallet, then returned everything to the backpack, trying her best to arrange it as close as possible to how it was before. Then she called Wyatt.

"I found something."

"Where are you?"

"At the motel."

"I'll be there in ten minutes."

While she waited, she listened to a voice mail Robert left earlier that afternoon when she was at Stuart's house. "I went by the new apartment, but you weren't there. I'll try again later." There was a long pause, and she thought that was it, he would hang up, there was nothing more to say, but then he inhaled sharply and gushed out a slew of words. "Look, Lucy, I know you might be upset with me for kicking you out and that's completely understandable, but I haven't heard from you in almost three days and that's just not like you. Even if you are mad, will you at least send me a text? An email or something? Let me know you're all right? I just . . .

Marnie's starting to get concerned. Okay, talk to you soon."
The message ended.

She sent Robert a quick text. Got your msg. Everything ok.
Will call soon.

He was on the list of people Wyatt wanted to talk to, but
Lucy didn't know what information he could provide that
would be even remotely useful. He'd been in LA the night
Nolan went missing, oblivious to any trouble his two children
might have been causing, and when the police did eventually
call, he didn't act the least bit surprised to hear his son was
missing. In fact, he was the first to suggest Nolan had run away,
said the only thing that surprised him was that Nolan hadn't
taken off sooner considering the kind of trouble he was getting into at home and at school. But it was possible the police
told him something in the early stages of the investigation that
could help her now, and he seemed to be trying to be a good
father, some kind of father anyway, more than he ever tried
when they were younger. Maybe he wanted to make it up to
her, and to Nolan. Maybe this was his chance.

First, though, she had to deal with this backpack.

Wyatt arrived at the motel a few minutes later. Lucy let him
inside and locked the door behind him.

"Well, what is it?" he asked.

"Stuart Tomlinson gave me something." She gestured to
the JanSport lying on the bed.

His expression was hard to read. At first he seemed confused,
but this quickly melted into something like inevitability, like
he'd been expecting this would happen someday. He released a
long, slow breath and rubbed his cheek. "Shit." He shook his
head and stretched his hand toward the backpack like he was

going to open it or pick it up, but at the last second he pulled his hand away again, curling his fingers at his side.

"She kept her whole life in there," he said quietly. "She would have never left it behind intentionally."

There were dirt stains and scuffs on the fabric, and the stitching on the front pocket was starting to unravel, but there were no rips or bloodstains, no obvious signs of a struggle. If Celeste had lost it in some kind of violent way, the evidence of that was not immediately apparent.

Wyatt collapsed into the only chair in the room. He was quiet for a moment, his gaze fixed on the backpack, concentrating. Then he asked, "He's had it this whole time?"

Lucy nodded.

"Why didn't he turn it over to the cops?" His eyes shifted to where Lucy stood by the window. "Do you think Stuart might have done something to Nolan or to Celeste? He could have made up that whole story about seeing Nolan fighting with someone. How did he seem to you? Does he seem like the kind of guy who's capable of something like that? Of violence?"

Lucy pictured Stuart, his pale and delicate fingers piecing together worlds in miniature. How much patience and time, how steady a hand and what an eye for detail one would need in order to create such works of art. Single, fleeting moments captured forever with bits of clay and cloth and wood, places he could return to again and again where, unlike real life, he had control. He was God. He could change the narrative, decide the colors, place himself at the center or at the edge. He could construct a whole new moment—one where he mattered. But she couldn't imagine him playing God like this in real life. She thought again of the box of kittens he carried around, how he made certain each of them found a good home. She thought, too, of how he talked about Nolan, the admiration in his voice.

"He was keeping it for me," Lucy admitted.

"What does that mean?"

"He saw me hide it in the bushes in front of his house," she started to explain.

Wyatt shook his head, not understanding.

"The night Nolan went missing," she continued, her stomach tying itself in knots. Saying the words out loud didn't make them ring any truer. She felt like an actress, playing some ridiculous part. "Stuart saw me come home a few hours after Nolan left. Celeste's backpack was in our driveway. I picked it up and chucked it in the bushes."

Wyatt stared at her. "Why would you . . . ? What were you doing out that late? You told the police you were at home sleeping." His eyes came to rest on the backpack again. He let out a slow breath. "What did you do, Lucy?"

She sank down on the edge of the bed and buried her face in her hands. "I don't know. I don't remember, I mean. Stuart says he saw me walking up the street in the middle of the night, after Nolan had already left. He says he tried talking to me, but I ignored him. He says he saw me pick up the backpack and stuff it into the bushes, but I have no memory of that. Of any of it."

"So he's lying," Wyatt said, with more confidence than Lucy deserved.

She raised her head again and, seeing the way he looked back at her, released the sob she'd been holding in since taking possession of the backpack. It was a single dry, rasping sound that could have been easily mistaken for a laugh, except for the tears gathered on her lashes. She wiped them away and shook her head, trying to shrug it off, not wanting to make a big deal of the panic burning in her chest. "That's the worst part. I don't think he is."

Wyatt seemed surprised to hear her say this. He started to get up from the chair, but then sank down again and spread his fingers over the tops of his knees, pressing into the flesh of his thighs. He seemed to be waiting for her to explain.

She took her time, fixing her gaze out the window, watching a motel employee scrape dead leaves from the surface of the pool with a long net.

"What I told the police," she said, "what I told Sandra, about where I was that night, it's not . . . I mean . . . some of it is . . . part of it is true. I was out with friends for a while. But we were drinking. A lot. And there's a big chunk of time missing. There are things I don't remember."

"Like . . . the backpack."

"Or how I got home. Or when. Or what I was doing in between."

"Do you remember seeing Nolan that night?" Wyatt asked. "Did you talk to him?"

Lucy started to shake her head, then stopped. She rubbed her temple. Her thoughts crowded together, pressing against her skull. A flash of light. A memory of someone grabbing her arm, spinning her around, but the face was obscured, the voice garbled and mechanical. Then Wyatt touched her shoulder. She snapped her head up, uncertain of how much time had passed since she closed her eyes.

"I'm trying to remember," she said, opening her hands in her lap, squeezing them shut. "But it's hard to explain. It's like I'm trapped in a fun house maze. I keep turning corners and running into dead ends. I keep seeing things out of the corners of my eyes that I think are real, but whenever I turn my head to look, they vanish. I chase a shadow into another room and find myself in front of a mirror that's all warped and distorted." She clenched her hands and shook her head. "I'm not making any sense, I know."

Wyatt sat on the bed next to her. "It sounds like maybe you saw something that night, but maybe whatever it was scared you so badly you suffered a kind of traumatic memory loss."

She brushed her fingers over her knees. She had scars there, faint striations that weren't obvious unless you knew what to look for.

"Think of it like selective amnesia," Wyatt continued, his voice gentle and reassuring. "If you saw something that disturbed you, if you saw something, say you saw what happened to Nolan, it's possible that your brain just wasn't equipped to handle whatever it was. Maybe it was so traumatic an event, your brain did the only thing it could to protect you by pushing the bad memories deep into your subconscious, allowing you to forget and carry on."

"So I'm repressing memories from that night?" Lucy stared at the backpack. "I know what happened to Nolan, but I'm just choosing not to remember? Is that what you're saying?"

"Don't think of it as a choice," Wyatt said. "It's not something you have very much control over. I mean, you were, what? Barely fourteen the night Nolan went missing? If you were a witness to something that happened out there in the desert, if it was something traumatic or even just something you'd never encountered before, then it's reasonable to assume you were too young to process it. Your psyche was too fragile."

"Too weak," Lucy muttered.

He touched her arm. "Too new."

She rose from the bed, went to the sink, and held a plastic cup under the faucet.

"You said you'd been drinking alcohol too?" Wyatt asked.

She nodded and took a sip of water.

"That would certainly have an effect on how your brain processed those memories," he said. "If you drank enough, you might have blacked out."

A flash of a memory: Lucy stretched out on her back, staring up at a starry night sky. This could have been from any number of moments in her childhood. Except, in this memory, the stars were spinning, a parade of lights dancing and twirling overhead, forming a pattern that bore remarkable resemblance to a flying saucer, only she didn't believe in flying saucers.

"Why don't you tell me what you *do* remember about that night," Wyatt said. "The truth, this time."

She set the empty cup back down on the counter. "I'm not going to read about this in the next issue of *Strange Quarterly*, am I?"

A smile tugged at his lips, and he shook his head. "Off the record. I promise."

"I left the house around seven, I think," she said. "It might have been a little earlier than that, shortly after Mom left for her shift at the hospital."

"Was Nolan there?"

"No, I hadn't seen him all day. Not since breakfast." They hadn't said a single word to each other. He'd been distant, distracted, acting like she wasn't even there.

"Patrick picked me up," she added.

"Patrick Tyndale," he said to clarify.

Lucy nodded and continued, "The part I told the police,

about how I was with Patrick, how we drove around for a while, listening to music, that part has always been true. So was the part about going to Burger Barn for milk shakes and fries. We did that. But we also picked up Adam Paulson."

"Who's that? His name didn't come up in the initial investigation. You didn't mention him in your statement."

"No, I left him out intentionally," she said. "He was a friend of Patrick's, not my favorite person in the world, but he was older, part of the cool crowd, and like I said, he was friends with Patrick. He was also the one who scored us drugs and booze and pot. Everyone knew that. If I had given his name to the police, they would have assumed, they would have been right, and I couldn't, I didn't want Mom finding out what I'd been doing. She was already going through so much."

"So you drank and smoked . . ." Wyatt prompted her to continue. "How much?"

"Too much." She remembered how easy it had been to slip into a nothing place—the beer making her whole body tingle, the pot making her float like a cloud—how badly she'd wanted to stay there, indifferent and numb.

"That's where things start to get blurry," she said. "All the details sort of bleed together, and I can't bring up any clear memory until the next morning when I woke up in my own bed hungover and wearing the same clothes as the night before."

She was surprised how good it felt to finally tell the truth and was going to keep going and tell Wyatt about the prank they'd pulled and what was really in those pictures, about what happened in the days following Nolan's disappearance, the promises she made to Patrick and to herself, but before she could say anything else, Wyatt jumped in. "So just to clarify.

You woke up in your bed with no memory of how you got there?"

"Yes, but if what Stuart says is true, it sounds like I may have walked home."

"But he said it was like you'd 'appeared out of nowhere.'"

"So?"

He rubbed his hands together, excited about something.

"Sometimes after an encounter . . ." he started. "Sometimes a contactee experiences what's referred to as 'missing time.' For instance, someone's driving down the highway and they look at the clock and see that it's a quarter to nine, then maybe they see a strange light in the sky or maybe they don't see anything at all, but the next thing they remember is looking at the clock again and seeing that three, four, sometimes five hours have passed and they're still driving, but they're on a different highway and they don't remember how they got there. It's like what happened to you."

"No. It's not . . ."

But Wyatt rattled on, paying her no attention. "This could be more proof of extraterrestrial activity. If you came into contact with the same craft that took Nolan, it could explain why you're having trouble remembering what happened that night. They don't want you to remember. Maybe They even left you with screen memories, which are different from missing time. They're fake memories, essentially, inserted into the subconscious minds of contactees who aren't ready to accept their new paradigm. It's a kindness, really. But if that were the case, you'd remember *something* happening that night. It wouldn't all just be a blank."

"Okay, look, Wyatt. Enough already," Lucy said.

Wyatt blinked at her, as if he'd forgotten she was even in the room.

"I appreciate that you're trying to help," she said. "And maybe you have a point about that selective amnesia thing or being so wasted I blacked out, but aliens coming down and wiping my memory? Or inserting false memories into my brain? No, I don't think so. That can't happen. It *didn't* happen."

"The evidence supports an extraterrestrial theory," Wyatt insisted. "Whether you believe or not."

"What 'evidence'?"

"The story you just told me," he said.

"Anecdotal."

"Fine, but what about the pictures your brother took the night before he went missing?" he insisted. "The orb that visited him at the house. If that's not solid, visual evidence, I don't know what is."

She opened her mouth to dispute him, but in the breath she took before speaking, she decided she couldn't, not yet. He needed to know that those pictures were fake, but Sandra needed to know first. Instead, she said, "You're seeing what you want to see. The evidence only seems to support your theory because you're forcing it in that direction."

"You're wrong," Wyatt said. "I'm looking at it objectively and this is the direction it's taking us."

"It's kind of hard to be objective when you're already so certain you have all the answers."

She expected him to puff out his chest and gnash his teeth, stand his ground against her. Instead, his shoulders sagged forward and his head drooped. He rubbed his eyes. "That's the thing, Lucy. I'm not certain. About any of it. If I was certain,

I wouldn't be chasing down leads and trying to get people to talk to me. I don't have the answers, so I'm out here looking for them." He fixed his gaze on her. "What about you? What have you been doing to help find him?"

"I found that backpack, didn't I?" She turned her attention to the window again. The motel employee was gone. The water turned glass in the late-afternoon sun.

"That's a start," he said. "But what about your memories?"

"What about them? If I can't remember, I can't remember."

"The memories are still there," he said. "We just have to draw them out of your subconscious mind and into your conscious one."

"And how do we do that?"

"Some people have luck with hypnosis," he suggested tentatively.

She shook her head. "No, absolutely not. What else?"

"Looking at old photographs or returning to the location where the traumatic event occurred can often bring memories to the surface again," he said.

"How reliable do you think that is?" she asked. "I mean, what are the odds that I look at an old picture of Nolan and suddenly remember everything? And then, I mean, we really can't overlook that one minor detail about me not knowing exactly where I was for most of the night."

"We can assume you were at the observatory."

"Can we?"

Wyatt sighed and ran his hand over his chin. "Okay, well, sometimes it just happens without any help at all. After a time, months or years, it's hard to say when or why, just one day you'll be walking down the street and suddenly you'll remember."

But she was done waiting. Besides, if the memories hadn't come on their own after all this time, what were the odds they ever would?

"There is one other thing you could try," he said, a cautiousness creeping into his voice.

"What?"

"Talk to Patrick."

CASEBOOK ENTRY #4

STRANGE HAPPENING:
Warnings

DATE: November 5, 1999

LONGITUDE/LATITUDE: 37.326494 W, 118.538113 N

SYNOPSIS: Since my false imprisonment, I have been receiving phone calls at the house. Whoever is calling speaks not a single word to me. The first time it happened was Oct 31, the day after the party. It rang four times before I answered. I heard a click. Then a dial tone. They have called twelve times in the past week at varying intervals. The only pattern I have discerned thus far is that there is no pattern. Sometimes I am alone in the house when they call. Sometimes Lucy and Mom are here. The only thing that is the same about each of the calls is this: whoever is on the other end either can't, or refuses to, speak.

OBJECT DESCRIPTION: NA

OTHER WITNESS STATEMENTS: When asked, Lucy and Mom both denied answering any hang-up calls this week. Lucy unhelpfully suggested I was hallucinating. However, I still must take her theory into consideration as a good investigator considers ALL theories possible unless and until they can be definitively proven false.

WEATHER INFORMATION: Half-moon waning to new; slightly warmer than average temperatures. No obvious weather phenomena to explain events.

LOCATION DESCRIPTION: Three-bedroom, single-story ranch house on Skyline Road within walking distance of Buttermilk Rocks. New development. Pacific Bell provides telephone service to this location. No caller ID service.

PHYSICAL EVIDENCE: Attempting to obtain phone records, which will serve two purposes: to trace the caller and to disprove the hallucination theory. Having difficulty getting phone company to comply with request.

CONCLUSION: I cannot be certain of the caller's objectives, but I believe it may be related to my arrest, some kind of government operation. A warning, a threat? Whatever their agenda, I know they are monitoring me now. They are watching closely to see what I will do. I must stay vigilant.

The camping trip was his mother's idea. Even though it was November and theoretically too cold to sleep outdoors. Even though Nolan was behind in school and on his homework, and scheduled for two shifts at the grocery store, she told him that fresh air and time away from the regular routine of life would do him good. But he could tell from the bags under her eyes and the extra glass of wine she drank every night since his arrest that she needed a break too. From him. Lucy wasn't invited on this trip. It was just Robert and Nolan. Quality time between father and son. Man and boy. Nolan wondered what his mother had said to get Robert to agree to it, what threat she held over his head.

The last time Nolan spent any stretch of time with his father was two years ago at Christmas. He and Lucy took the bus and then the train to Los Angeles to stay with Robert for the holiday. The trip started out well enough, in part because Robert was dating a woman who aspired to be Martha Stewart and kept everyone buzzed on sugar cookies, gingerbread, and fudge. They drank hot chocolate until their stomachs ached and played three rounds of Monopoly back to back and had a Christmas movie marathon. Nolan even started to think that maybe his father wasn't so terrible after all, and maybe he could figure out a way to get his parents to love each other again and put his family back together. But on the last night of their visit, he overheard Robert talking to his girlfriend about how his biggest regret in life was having children and that she should avoid kids at all costs. "They're not worth the effort," he'd said. "Ungrateful little bastards. All they do is eat your food and ask for money, steal your dreams and suck you dry." The Martha Stewart wannabe had laughed, "Oh, Robert, you don't mean that," and Nolan had waited for him to laugh and agree, to take back what he'd said, but Robert only grunted—a sound that revealed everything Nolan needed to know about his place in his father's world.

After that, anytime Sandra talked about sending them to LA for a visit, Nolan made up an excuse. He was sick. Or he had too much homework. It got easier when he started working at the grocery store—he couldn't get the time off, or he could have, but he never asked; the store was short-handed, or a coworker needed him to cover a shift; it was Thanksgiving or Christmas or Easter or Fourth of July, always some holiday he could work overtime; he had car payments to make, they needed the money. His mother never pushed the issue, and because of this, Lucy often ended up going to stay with Robert by herself.

He tried coming up with an excuse this time, too, but Sandra shook her head. "You can do your homework Sunday night when you get back. And I called your work and your manager said you could have the time off." She pressed her hand to his forehead. "You're not running a fever. You're going on this trip."

There was nothing else to do but say okay and pack his gear.

Saturday arrived and Robert with it, gunning up their driveway in his two-seater convertible. He honked the horn three times. Sandra yelled for Nolan to get his things, but he didn't move right away. He was lying in his bed, staring up at the ceiling, thinking of Celeste, wondering what she was doing this weekend, if she was worried about him.

He hadn't spoken to her since the party and his arrest. He was grounded, allowed to go to school and to work and then come straight back home, no detours. His mother timed the drive between each place and if he was more than three minutes late pulling into the driveway, she added another day to his sentence. He was late only once.

The Monday after his arrest, he'd driven to Gabriella's on his way home from work and when no one answered the door, drove all the way back to Jake's where he saw her through the front windows waiting on a family of four. She looked fine, unharmed. He watched her for a few minutes before driving home, where he walked through the door and got yet another lecture from his mother about responsibility and how much trouble he was in and not to press his luck and now he was grounded for eight days instead of seven and just keep pushing, mister, she'd make it nine. He made it home on time every day after that. He didn't like disappointing his mother, didn't want to make her life harder than it already was. Also, she was threatening to send him to military school—or worse, his father's house—if he screwed up again. So he didn't try to see Celeste again. He went to school and then to work and then back home where he watched TV and picked up the phone every time it rang, hoping it would be Celeste. It never was. Only silence on the other end, or sometimes a faint sound, like the ocean crashing against a rocky shore, or a murmuring crowd of people. Sometimes it was his mother, calling from the hospital to make sure he wasn't sneaking out, and he felt like a child again.

He wanted to hear Celeste's voice. He wanted to find out how she was doing, how she got home from the party, if she was really as safe as she seemed through the restaurant window. He tried calling Gabriella's house, sometimes three times a day and always when his mother wasn't home, but no matter what time he called, Celeste was never around. Gabriella told him she was passing his messages along, but Celeste had yet to call him back. Once he'd called Jake's and in a hurried whisper she'd said, "Now's not a good time. Can this wait?" He'd said yes, even though he meant no, and now a week had passed and she still hadn't called, and all he could think was that she'd heard about his arrest and knew he was being watched, that the government was suspicious and tracking his every move. Or worse, the government had found her despite his best efforts, had threatened her, and it was no longer safe for them to be in contact, and wouldn't be for a while. Still, he couldn't stop

himself from hoping every time the phone rang. Neither could
he stop thinking about her lips on his, the heat their bodies
made together. The night, the stars, the sweet taste of her.

Another honk sounded from the driveway.

"Nolan!" Sandra shouted. "Move it!"

He grabbed his sleeping bag, tent, and backpack stuffed with
a change of clothes and gear, then shuffled to the front door.

Sandra kissed his cheek. "Behave."

Robert drove over the speed limit and took the curves too
fast. With the convertible top down, conversation was impossible, which was just fine with Nolan. On the way up the
mountain, they passed a meadow that would have made the
perfect camping and stargazing spot, but Robert didn't even
slow down. "I reserved us a nice little spot by the creek," he
shouted, gunning around a tight corner. A claustrophobic al-
cove, crowded with trees whose branches knitted into a pine-
needle ceiling, blocking any view of the sky.

They unloaded the car in silence. Everything of Robert's
was still new in its packaging. He used a pocketknife to saw
through the plastic wrapping and cut off the price tags. Even
the hiking boots he wore had the clean, hard look of being
fresh out of the box. He spent twenty minutes reading the in-
structions on how to set up the tent, with all the parts spread
out in the dirt, before he finally threw up his hands. "You ever
set one of these things up before?"

Nolan put up the red, two-person dome with stakes in the
ground in less than five minutes, while Robert stood to one
side, taking swigs from a flask he carried in his jacket pocket.

"Well, it's certainly not the Ritz." Robert offered Nolan the
flask. "But I guess that's the point, isn't it?"

Nolan turned his back on the flask and began to set up the

tent he'd brought for himself, a lightweight, gray backpacking tent his mother gave him on his twelfth birthday. The top was full mesh, offering an open view of the sky whenever the rain fly was rolled up. Not that he'd be using that feature tonight. He stretched the rain fly over the top of the tent and staked down the corners.

Robert cleared his throat in the awkward way of someone who's about to speak, pausing a few seconds, dragging out the inevitable longer than necessary. Finally he said, "About those pills . . ." then let the silence balloon again between them.

"They weren't mine," Nolan said.

"Then whose were they?"

Nolan ignored the question. He didn't expect his father to believe him; no one else did. That was the genius of using cops to do your dirty work. In the general public's mind, police officers were the good guys. Officer Friendlies to be trusted and obeyed. To suggest that an officer charged to serve and protect had planted drugs in an innocent person's car was to suggest the system flawed, even dangerous. And no one wanted to believe that.

Nolan walked to the trunk of the convertible to unload what gear remained. Sleeping bags, firewood enough for two nights, a propane stove and lantern, a cooler of food and drinks, a hatchet with the protective plastic still covering the blade.

Robert took the hatchet from him and started splintering a chunk of wood into kindling. Between hits, he said, "You're lucky they didn't throw you in jail."

It wasn't luck. The government didn't want him locked up. They wanted to scare him, make sure he understood the extent of their reach and the kind of power they had, how easily they could wreck his life; but he was useless to them in jail. It came as no surprise to Nolan that Officer Williams released him into his mother's custody with no charges filed.

"That's it? He's free to go?" Sandra had been holding on to Nolan's arm, squeezing tight enough to hurt. "What about paperwork? A trial? Community service, at least? I'm sorry, I don't understand."

"I think your son learned his lesson here tonight." Officer Williams gave Nolan a knowing look. "Haven't you, Mr. Durant?"

And Nolan had nodded, going along with the charade. Anything to get out of that concrete bunker with its countless cameras blinking red, and doors that locked automatically.

Robert managed to get the fire going without too much trouble, thanks to a can of lighter fluid and a stack of wadded-up newspapers. He unfolded a camping chair in front of the twisting flames and sat down with a six-pack of beer cradled in his lap. "There's soda in the cooler if you want. Chips and hot dogs for dinner. No buns though. I left those on the counter. No mustard or ketchup. Forgot those too."

Nolan wasn't hungry. He sat in another camping chair opposite his father and tilted his head back, trying to glimpse the stars through a small hole where some of the branches didn't quite meet. The patch of sky wasn't big enough, the fire too bright. If he wanted to see the stars, he'd have to go someplace else. He pulled his down jacket tighter around his shoulders, stuffing his hands into his pockets and breathing hot air into the collar. Every so often, Robert cleared his throat like he was about to speak again, but then he'd crack a beer and tip it to his mouth for a swig, drowning whatever it was he was thinking about saying. His gaze stayed fixed on the flames, never once straying to his son.

Nolan played out imaginary conversations with his father. About school and college prep courses and SATs and what major he should choose: physics or planetary science. About Celeste and dating and what it felt like to be in love. About Lucy drinking and smoking and hanging around with the wrong crowd. In his head, he asked Robert for advice and Robert looked him in the eye and said, "Son, everything's going to work out just fine. Son, you're going to be okay." In his head, Robert said all the things a father should say, all the things Nolan needed to hear. In real life, he cracked another beer and went on saying nothing.

Robert had just opened the last can when a car drove up the gravel road, headlights swinging into their campsite. The car parked behind Robert's convertible. The engine shut off. The headlights went dark, then the driver's door opened and the dome light snapped on. A young woman, who looked closer to Nolan's age than his father's, fluffed her curly auburn hair in the rearview mirror and spread a layer of gloss across her pouting lips. She blew a kiss to herself and then got out of the car. Robert rose to meet her, smoothing his hair and tugging at the hem of his shirt to make sure it covered his small paunch. She trotted up to him smiling, her voice like a little girl's when she said, "Are there bears out here, Bobby?" He reassured her there weren't, but if there were, he'd protect her. Then he encircled his arms around her waist and lifted her a few inches off the ground. She squealed and kicked her stilettoed feet, then his mouth was on hers, devouring her, it seemed to Nolan. He turned away, stared into the trees instead.

A few minutes later, Robert led the woman to the fire pit.

"This is Melissa," he said to Nolan.

She smiled shyly at Nolan, who didn't smile back.

"Mind giving us a little privacy?" Robert gestured to the red dome tent. "An hour. No, two would be better." He winked and then pinched Melissa's butt.

"Bobby." She swatted his arm playfully. "He's just a kid."

Robert reached into his pocket, pulled a hundred-dollar bill from his wallet, and passed it to Nolan. "Don't tell your mother." He pulled Melissa giggling into the tent.

Sleeping bags rustled and swished. Robert's low voice rumbled in the dark. Melissa continued to giggle and squeak. Nolan crumpled up the hundred-dollar bill and tossed it into the flames. In seconds, the money became ash.

He stood and, without bothering to put out the fire or even find a flashlight, walked out of camp, a quarter mile back down the main road to the meadow they'd passed coming up. He pushed through waist-high grass to the very center, where no trees grew and nothing blocked his view. He tilted his head back, gulping in the juniper and late autumn air. The sky was a miracle of light and dark, and the stars were all there, and he wished he'd brought his telescope. There hadn't been room in his father's car, but he should have found the space. He wished Celeste was with him, too.

He sank into the grass and stretched out on his back. He didn't have to try hard to find the stars here. Wherever he fixed his gaze, there they were. Splashes of bright points as far and as deep as his eyes could see, and stars beyond those stars, too, hidden in darkness, too far away, millions and millions of light-years. Not enough time had passed for their light to reach Earth. He could lie here all night and still not drink his fill of the Milky Way poured out like cream across this black coffee sky.

He might do it, too, stay out here instead of returning to

camp. His down jacket was thick, the temperatures unseasonably warm for this time of year. There wasn't even any snow on the ground yet, though the air was edged with the familiar, metallic bite of winter's coming. He thought about his father's girlfriend, Melissa, a new one, not the Martha Stewart wannabe from two years ago. Then he didn't want to think about her anymore, and so he thought about bears instead, wondering if when they wandered late at night, they followed the silver path of the moon and used the stars to navigate home. He thought about bears and he thought about Celeste and he thought about the grass blades beneath his fingertips and the satellite arcing across the sky above him from left to right. He blinked, and the blink was slow, his eyes suddenly weighted, though he didn't feel tired. His whole body went heavy then, like his bones were made of hardening cement. The stars began to tremble. Funny—he could no longer lift his hands.

The next thing Nolan was consciously aware of was someone standing over him, shining a bright light into his face, shouting, "What the hell are you doing? Where are your clothes?" The voice raged loud and sounded like his father. "Get up! Get out of there! Goddamn it, Nolan! Jesus Christ!"

Firm hands gripped his arms, fingers pinching into his flesh, dragging him backwards, up and out of a cold creek. Water rushed over his legs. He'd been half-submerged, up to his waist in a babbling brook. He struggled to comprehend. He was drowsy, half-asleep, and numb from the waist down. He shook, teeth chattering.

A woman screamed, "Oh my God, oh my God, is he all right?!"

"Get his sleeping bag," Robert said.

A few seconds later Nolan was wrapped in something heavy and slick, and his father was rubbing his arms, his back, his legs, trying to get his blood flowing hot again. A lantern sat in the dirt beside them and cast unnatural blue light across the creek, making the running water crackle and spark.

"What the hell were you doing in there?" His father continued to press Nolan with questions he had no answers to. "Where are your clothes? Say something!"

The woman—what was her name again? Nolan couldn't remember, and he didn't care—hovered nearby. Her hair looked like flames, looked like the sun's corona. He closed his eyes a moment, shutting them out, his father, the woman, their nervous chattering. He tried not to think about the chill settling deep in his bones, and instead tried to think of the last thing he saw before he blacked out, the last thing he remembered. Lying on his back in a meadow, staring at a sky wild with stars. And then . . . and then a pinpoint of light becoming several small points of light, growing in size as they moved closer to him, forming a triangle right above him, hovering there, waiting for what? For him? He didn't remember what happened after that, or how he ended up in the creek.

He opened his eyes to find his father's face pressed close to his, a small flashlight swinging back and forth across his pupils.

"Did you see Them?" Nolan whispered, his voice hoarse and strange to his own ears.

"Get up." Robert clicked off the flashlight and returned it to his jacket pocket. "Get on your feet. Let's go."

He slipped his arm around Nolan's waist and guided him up the sloped bank and back to their campsite. Pine needles pricked the bottoms of his feet. Pebbles jabbed into his toes. The woman tripped after them, whimpering.

"Did you see Them?" Nolan asked again, forcing his voice louder.

"See who?" The woman sounded even more scared now.

"The Visitors," Nolan said. "Extraterrestrials."

Robert's grip tightened. He thrust Nolan to the edge of the fire, almost too hard, almost into the smoldering coals, almost. He tossed a handful of kindling and shredded newspaper onto the embers, and when a small flame appeared, he added a log and then another, turning the flame into a blaze.

"Bobby?" The woman stood on the other side of Nolan now, her cheeks orange from the firelight, her eyes startled and darting. "What is he talking about?"

Robert said nothing, just added another log to the fire.

"The meadow," Nolan explained. "After you told me to . . . after I left, I went to that clearing we passed coming up here. I wanted to see the stars. They were moving. There was one that came close, right over top of me and just stopped and . . ."

He could tell from the expression on his father's face that he wasn't explaining himself very well, that Robert did not believe him. Nolan needed something more than his inadequate words. He swung his gaze up to the sky, but it was hidden again by that thick layer of branches. Pinching the sleeping bag at his throat, so it stayed wrapped around his body, Nolan ducked away from his father and the woman, abandoning the fire's warmth for the cold, dark road.

Rocks and twigs stuck his skin, but the sting wasn't enough to slow him down. Robert barreled after him, lantern swinging at his side, shouting something about hypothermia, shouting for him to stop, but Nolan's sole focus was on getting to the meadow where everything would be made clear. There would be proof. Scorch marks in the grass. Broken limbs. Blown-over trees. Maybe the saucer itself would still be there, hovering above the clearing. He ran the whole way, retracing his tracks to the center of the meadow where he spun a slow circle, searching for evidence.

Robert appeared at his side, short of breath. A few minutes later the woman appeared too. The lantern threw blue light across the grass and that was the only reason Nolan saw them: his down jacket, his shirt, his pants, his socks and shoes. Everything he'd been wearing earlier, now stretched out in the exact spot where he'd been lying, looking at the stars. Everything perfectly placed as though something, or someone, had come and carefully lifted him out of his clothes. There might have been a body lying there, but for the flatness, the lack of a head, of limbs and breath.

Nolan ran to the empty clothes. "Look! This! My clothes are proof!"

Robert shone the lantern over them, looking for something he must not have found because his jaw tensed and he lifted the light to Nolan, inspecting him instead.

"Do you see?" Nolan demanded. "Do you understand? I was here. I was lying right here. Just like this. On my back." And then the light growing bright and brighter. "They came. They came for me. They took me away. They took me and left my clothes."

He knew he sounded crazy, his words tripping too fast from his tongue, but he couldn't seem to slow down. This was too important, too much of a miracle. He took a breath and, in the pause, tried to piece together an explanation of how abductions worked and the signs to look for. Blackouts, waking up naked in another location, seeing lights beforehand, a scar. He dropped the sleeping bag and felt his fingers over his skin, but found no unusual marks, nothing that hadn't been there before.

"Bobby, he's going to catch his death." The woman twittered like a baby bird.

Robert lunged, snatching the sleeping bag off the grass and throwing it over Nolan's shoulders again. "Goddamn it, Nolan. Enough."

"Did you hear Them?" He spun to look at the woman and then back to his father. "You must have heard Them. You weren't very far away." No more than a half mile. This level of activity would not have gone unnoticed.

"Nolan . . ." There was a wariness to his father's tone.

"What time is it? How long was I gone?" Nolan bent to inspect his clothes. He turned them over, looking for any kind of singe marks or tears, but they were unscathed. He pressed his face into the clothes and inhaled deeply. They smelled like pine dew and early morning and, there! He shoved the clothes at his father. "Smell that? It's musty, like damp cardboard. That's Them. That's the Visitors."

Robert reared back from the fabric bundle. "Are you on drugs right now?"

Nolan clutched his clothes to his chest and began to walk in ever-widening circles. He searched the ground for anything out of place, disheveled grass, burn marks, a landing strip.

"Stop this, Nolan. Look at me!" Robert grabbed his arm and shook him. He held the lantern up to his face, the light beaming straight into Nolan's eyes.

Nolan winced and looked away.

"What did you take?" Robert demanded. "Ecstasy? Is that it? PCP? What is it? What are you on?"

"Let me go." Nolan struggled against him. "Nothing. I didn't take anything. Let go."

He wrenched from his father's grasp and stumbled backward, falling into the grass where he lay for a moment, dazed, the sleeping bag slipping off his shoulders again, exposing his naked body to the cool night air. There was a dampness on his upper lip. He touched his finger to it and found something sticky dripping from his nose. When he looked at his finger again, it was dark with blood.

"Jesus."

"Oh God. Bobby. Do something." The woman squatted in the grass and held out a handkerchief that she seemed to have pulled from nowhere. "I think he's hurt. We should get help. Call 911."

"He's fine," Robert said. "He's high."

"I'm not." Nolan sat up. He pulled the sleeping bag tight around him and pinched the handkerchief to his nose.

"Well, let's drive him to the hospital at least," the woman insisted. "Get him checked out."

"I said, he's fine." Robert grabbed the woman's arm and jerked her to her feet again.

"You're hurting me, Bobby."

"Go home, Melissa."

That's right, Nolan remembered now. Melissa. That was the fire-haired woman's name. Melissa who was afraid of bears.

"But—"

"Go home."

"You know I don't like driving in the dark. And my stuff's already unpacked."

"Well, repack it then. Trip's over."

"What about you?" She looked at Nolan. "What about him?"

"He's none of your concern, all right?" Robert gave Melissa a little shove in the direction of the road. "Just go."

She sniffled and stumbled her way through the grass, cursing under her breath. When she was out of sight, Robert returned his attention to Nolan. He set the lantern in the grass and extended his hand.

Nolan stared at it, a pale starfish in the dark, then he grabbed hold and allowed himself to be lifted to his feet. He dressed slowly, struggling under the weight of exhaustion. What had They done to him? Why couldn't he remember? He wanted to, he tried, but the space of time between seeing that light and waking up in the creek stayed blank.

Nolan and Robert walked back to the campsite in silence. When they got there, Melissa was gone. Nolan started to unzip his tent, but Robert shook his head and pushed him toward the red dome, which smelled like sex and perfume inside, and Nolan backed away from it, but his father insisted. "I'm not letting you out of my sight again." Nolan relented, crawling into the red tent and zipping his sleeping bag closed around him. Robert turned off the lantern and a few seconds later, his breathing settled into the rhythm of deep sleep.

But Nolan couldn't sleep, his mind restless with questions, his body still shivering. Again he worked his hands over himself, feeling for bruises, tender places, notches in his skin, anything that hadn't been there before, but again he found nothing out of the ordinary. Why had They taken him? he wondered. Why now? Tonight of all nights. Maybe They were trying to warn him. But about what? Maybe They'd shown him something about Celeste, or given him a glimpse of the future, or the chemical formula for eternal life. If They had shown him something, he didn't remember it now. Maybe the why didn't matter, though, neither what They'd done or said. Maybe the thing that mattered was that he'd been taken. Finally, a universe so long hidden from him brought to light. In the blink of an eye, he had glimpsed the infinite and all he was capable of being and knowing and experiencing. He had crossed a threshold, moving from unknown to known, invisible to visible, separate to connected. A new reality revealed, and he was transcending, transformed, part of something miraculous now. They all were—his father, his mother, Lucy, Patrick, Wyatt, Celeste, even Melissa, every single person on this planet—whether they believed or not, they were all part of this miracle unfolding.

Nolan was still awake when morning slipped through the trees and washed the dome of the tent from black to red, when the first bird sang, when his father finally began to stir. The day after, and he was surprised at how normal he felt. On the surface, everything was the same as before, but at some subatomic level, he knew, everything was different.

After breakfast, Robert took down both tents, even though the plan had been to stay all day and another night. He gestured to Nolan's rolled-up sleeping bag and backpack heaped in a pile in the dirt. "Get your stuff. I'm taking you home."

Sandra wasn't happy to see them back early. She crossed her arms over her chest and glowered at them both. "Did something happen? Are you sick?" She reached with the back of her hand to feel Nolan's forehead.

He sidestepped away from her—"I'm fine"—and tossed his gear on the floor next to the couch. Then he flopped down, slouching deep into the cushions.

"Can we talk?" Robert asked Sandra, tipping his chin in the direction of the kitchen door. "Alone?"

"I'm about to leave for work." Her shift didn't start for another six hours; she wasn't even wearing her scrubs. "Why don't you call me tomorrow or something?"

"This is important, Sandy."

The nickname softened her. She led Robert through to the kitchen. They spoke in hushed voices, but Nolan could hear every word and he wondered if this was the gift the extraterrestrials had given him, this power of understanding.

"How long has he been like this?" Robert asked.

"Like what?"

"He went nuts up there," said Robert. "He was talking about the stars moving. About aliens taking him up in the air. He took off all his clothes—"

"He what?" Sandra interrupted.

"I woke up in the middle of the night and found him bucknaked in the creek, like he was trying to drown himself or something."

"Trying to drown himself?" Sandra sighed. "I doubt that very much."

"You weren't there, Sandy," Robert insisted. "You didn't see him. The way he was acting. The things he said. How he looked at me." He paused before continuing, "You're not seriously going to stand there and tell me you haven't noticed how strange his behavior has been lately. Isn't that the whole reason you asked me to take him on this stupid camping trip in the first place?"

"You're with him for less than twenty-four hours and suddenly you're an expert on our son's behavior?" Her words clipped short. "And where were you when all this was going on anyway? What were you doing that you didn't notice until *after* all his clothes were off?"

"Sandy, he's acting out. Probably because you're gone all the time—"

"Don't 'Sandy' me, Robert. And don't you dare start in on some lecture about my parenting skills. You don't get to do that. Not anymore."

Nolan pressed even deeper into the cushions and looked out the sliding glass door. A flock of starlings bobbed in the grass beneath a tree. He wished he was one of them. Not a care in the world, answering to no one. Movement in the hallway caught his attention. Lucy leaned against the wall, listening from the shadows.

"How long have you been standing there?" Nolan asked her.

"Long enough." She came and sat next to him. "So you're running naked through the woods now?"

He didn't respond.

"I guess that's one way to get attention."

"I'm not trying to get attention," he mumbled.

Her eyebrows arched. "Then what the hell are you doing?"

"Don't say hell."

"Don't tell me what to do."

They both fell silent again, listening to their parents fight.

"What is going on around here, Sandra?" Robert demanded. "I mean, really, do I need to be worried? First the pills. And now this claiming to be abducted bullshit. It's like Toby all over again."

"Don't," Sandra said. "Don't even. He's not Toby. He's just tired, that's all. Stressed out from school and work. Maybe he should cut back his hours at the store, or quit, or . . . I don't know. He's going through some stuff right now, the way all teenagers do, that's it. He's nothing like your brother. He's nothing like that."

Nolan squeezed his hands together in his lap.

"Who's Toby?" Lucy whispered.

Nolan shook his head, not knowing how to best explain what he didn't quite understand himself. Lucy was barely five when Uncle Toby left, too young to remember how he used to come over for dinner on Sundays, and too young to remember the stories he told about silver disks rising out of lakes, spiraling multicolored lights, Martian canals, and alien astronauts. Nolan remembered, though. He'd sit enthralled and wide-eyed, until halfway through a story, he would catch Uncle Toby winking at Robert and Sandra. Nolan was never sure what the wink meant, whether it was to indicate the stories were jokes and all in good fun, or that they were real and now he was in on the secret too.

Shortly after Nolan's seventh birthday, Uncle Toby started skipping Sunday dinners, and the times he did show up, his eyes darted, his hands shook, and he insisted that all the curtains be drawn and the doors locked. His stories changed, too, turning nightmarish and frantic. He said little gray beings with buggy black eyes were coming into his room while he slept and doing experiments on him, sticking things up his nose and into his privates. They talked to him through the lights.

He lost his job flying crop dusters. His longtime girlfriend broke up with him. The very last time Uncle Toby came to dinner he tried to cut a tracking device out of his neck with a kitchen knife. Nolan remembered the blood, remembered crying, hiding in the corner, and Robert shouting, grabbing his brother by the shoulders, shaking him hard. Sandra had dragged Lucy and Nolan into her bedroom, locked the door, and called 911.

After that, Uncle Toby didn't come around anymore, and anytime Nolan asked, his parents brushed away his questions. Uncle Toby was getting the help he needed, they said, and left it at that. For a while, Nolan thought his uncle was dead. Then on his tenth birthday, he'd received the alien books along with the strange note. Not dead then, just hiding in Alaska from the very same beings Nolan found fascinating, not fearful. Or maybe They weren't the same. The Encounters group had discussed before the probability of multiple and varying species of extraterrestrial visitors to planet Earth. Who's to say Uncle Toby hadn't encountered a hostile species, while Nolan was in contact with a more affable kind?

"You should have called me a long time ago." Robert's voice from the kitchen grew steadily louder. "You should have never let it get this bad."

Sandra forced a loud, sharp laugh. "Excuse me? *I* should have never let it get this bad? And where have you been all this time? Six years you want nothing to do with him. Six years acting like he doesn't even exist and now you come sweeping in here on your white steed, all knight in shining armor, shouting about what *I'm* doing wrong, how badly *I* fucked up. I don't think so. I don't fucking think so, Robert."

"You should have told me what was going on," he said. "I didn't know."

Her voice soft again, defeated. "You never asked."

There was a long crush of silence. Lucy curled herself into a ball, knees to chest, chin on knees, shoulders round. Nolan plucked at a thread coming loose from the arm of the couch. He wondered if he should apologize, but he didn't know to whom or for what. He'd done nothing wrong. It wasn't his fault the whole world was blind and deaf to what was really going on.

"I think I should take him in to talk to someone," Sandra said. "A psychiatrist or something. They might be able to help."

"The last thing we need is some overpaid quack picking through our lives, filling our son's head with even more bullshit, blaming all this on us, how we were mean to him when he was a baby, how he didn't get enough love. No, absolutely not."

"What do you suggest then, Robert?" Her voice thick with sarcasm. "Please, if you have a better idea, I'd love to hear it."

"He needs a swift kick in the ass, if you ask me."

"Excuse me?"

"You're too soft on him, Sandra. You need to lay down some rules, draw a line in the sand when it comes to this alien bullshit, and when he crosses it, don't give him any slack. Punish him."

The kitchen went quiet for a moment, then Sandra spoke again, her voice getting louder as she moved toward the door. "I think it's time for you to go now, Robert."

When she entered the living room, she seemed startled to see Nolan still sitting on the couch, with Lucy beside him now. Robert, trailing behind her, scowled at both of his children like they were bugs on his shoe, something to be scraped off and flicked away. Nolan glowered back at him. Robert's mouth opened like he was about to speak, but then he shook his head, his breath releasing in a sigh, abandoning whatever meaningless advice he'd wanted to impart.

He walked out of the house, paused on the front porch, and turned toward Sandra to say one final thing. "If you can't handle this, call me and I will."

She shut the door on him, then leaned against it, pressing her eyes shut and taking several deep breaths. When she turned toward Nolan and Lucy again, her lips were stretched tight across her teeth, her nostrils flared. She spoke to Lucy first. "I need to talk to your brother."

Lucy shrugged. "Okay." But she didn't move from the couch.

Sandra's nostrils flared wider. "Go wait in your room, please."

Lucy made a big deal out of unfolding herself from the couch, huffing and rolling her eyes, puffing out her cheeks, flinging her hands up, but eventually she was on her feet, stomping down the hallway to her bedroom. The door slammed shut. The picture frames hanging in the hallway rattled.

Sandra pinched the bridge of her nose and then smiled stiffly at Nolan. "You want some hot chocolate?" She moved toward the kitchen before he could answer. "I'll make us some hot chocolate."

Several minutes later, Sandra returned to the living room carrying two steaming mugs. She gave one to Nolan and then sat down in the armchair across from the couch where she could look at him directly without having to angle her head.

Nolan lifted the mug and breathed in the chocolate steam, but didn't drink. His stomach was still upset from the night before, and he didn't think he'd be able to keep down something so sweet. Sandra raised her cup to her lips and peered at him over the blue porcelain rim. She sipped slowly and then lowered the cup, still watching him, but saying nothing. He shifted beneath her gaze, not wanting to be the one to speak first, but after several stretched-out, silent minutes he couldn't take it anymore.

"I wasn't trying to drown myself," he said.

"I know you weren't."

He waited for her to say something else, but she stayed quiet, her gaze relentlessly fixed on him.

"They were really there," he said. "They came for me."

A flicker of alarm crossed her face. "Who came for you?"

"The Visitors."

"Aliens."

He nodded.

"From outer space."

He didn't like her tone. "It's not a joke."

"I never said it was." She placed her half-empty cup of hot chocolate on the coffee table.

"And I'm not making it up either," he said. "I'm not just telling stories to try and get attention."

"No?" Sandra leaned back in her chair. She spread her fingers over the armrests. "Then what are you doing, Nolan? I'm trying to understand here. I really am. But I need you to give me something to work with. I need you to talk to me."

He spun his cup in his hands, watching tiny chocolate waves ripple the surface. He asked, "Do you believe in God?"

She tilted her head. "Is that what these 'visitors' are to you?"

"No, not . . ." He tried again. "I guess I just mean, are you the kind of person who believes only in the material level of reality? Only what you can see with your eyes, touch with your hands? Or do you believe that there might be something more out there? Something . . . spiritual. Otherworldly. Something beyond all of this." He swept his hand in the air, gesturing to the pictures on the wall, the books on the shelves, the television, the carpet, the furniture, the mugs of hot chocolate, their own gravity-bound bodies.

Sandra thought for a minute and then said, "I think what you see is what you get."

"There's more, Mom." He locked eyes with her. "I've seen it. I've experienced it. There's so much more. Maybe the Visitors come from another planet, or maybe They stepped in from another dimension, I don't know yet. What's important is that They're *here*. On Earth. They exist. They've lived among us for a long time, and They communicate with us, or at least They try, and there's so much we could learn from Them, if only we started paying attention."

She made a face like he'd pinched her and then sat forward in her chair again, interlacing her fingers and studying him carefully. "You're looking a little thin. Have you been eating?"

The question surprised him. He didn't know how to answer.

"What about sleep?" She stretched out her hand, bridging the distance between them, and brushed a strand of hair off his forehead. "How have you been sleeping?"

He slouched away from her and mumbled, "Fine."

"Any nightmares?" When he didn't answer right away, she continued, "Insomnia? Night sweats? Have you been waking up with headaches?"

"Mom, stop," he said. "I'm not one of your patients."

"You're right," she said. "You're not."

She drummed her fingers on the arm of the chair. After a few seconds, she said, "I think we should make an appointment for you to see Dr. Alameda."

He was their family doctor, a man who had been taking care of them since Nolan and Lucy were babies. "But Dad said—"

"Your father is an idiot."

"I don't need to see a doctor," Nolan said. "I feel fine."

"You might feel fine, but I still think it would be good for you to talk to someone. A professional. Someone who isn't related to you." She smiled like she'd made a joke, but

Nolan didn't see anything funny. "Maybe he can run a few tests too."

"Tests." Nolan set his hot chocolate on the coffee table.

"Like an X-ray? An MRI, maybe? I don't know. That will be for the doctor to decide. He probably won't find anything, but it wouldn't hurt to look around a little. Just in case." She tried to keep her words light, easy, like what she was suggesting was no big deal. But her smile looked forced, chipped from stone, and it gave her away.

"You think there's something wrong with me." Nolan sat with his back straight, his whole body tensed. "Like I'm going crazy or something."

"I didn't say that."

"But that's what you're implying. That's what Dad thinks too. Like maybe I have a brain tumor or something, right? Some kind of physical ailment that's making me see things that aren't really there?"

She inhaled deeply and gripped the armrests.

"I'm not sick, Mom," he said. "There's nothing wrong with me. I don't need to see a doctor. I don't need tests. And I'm not crazy either. The things I've seen are as real as you sitting across from me now. Why would I lie to you? Why would I make something like this up?"

She sucked on her lower lip and her eyes narrowed. "I don't know why. I don't know. That's what I'm trying to figure out. I'm trying to understand how we got here. How my smart, imaginative, good boy turned into someone I hardly recognize."

"I'm still me," he said, but she was lost in her own thoughts, tracing the tips of her fingers down the side of her face, her eyes drifting toward the window for a moment before returning to him.

"Nolan . . ." She reached her hand through the space that separated them, but he didn't reach back. "I'm worried about you, okay? I'm worried about these stories you keep telling. These ideas you have."

"They're not stories."

"Ever since you started going to that UFO group, you haven't been yourself." It was a funny thing for her to say, since Nolan felt more like himself now than he ever had before. "What kind of things do you do there? What kind of things do you talk about? Are they putting these ideas into your head?"

"Mom . . ."

"Is that what's going on? You're trying to fit in with your new friends?"

He shook his head. She would never understand. Everything was black and white to her, everything that mattered was here on Earth.

"You know how much I love you, don't you?" A smile trembled on her lips, and he almost believed it. "You and your sister. I just want you both to be happy, healthy, and safe. Okay? That's not too much to ask, is it? At the very least, Dr. Alameda can give you something to help you sleep."

"No." He stood up, bumping the coffee table with his knee. Hot chocolate splashed over the side of his cup, saturating a pile of magazines. "No drugs. Absolutely not."

The government used drugs to control the masses, to keep people from seeing what was really going on and discovering the truth. Drugs were how they kept you numb and compliant.

"It would only be temporary," his mother said. "Until you started sleeping better."

"You're not listening," he protested. "I'm not dreaming or

daydreaming or hallucinating or whatever. The Visitors are real. I've seen Them. I've interacted with Them."

"Nolan, please," Sandra said. "Sit down. Let's talk this through. Let's really think about this. You remember your uncle Toby?"

Not even ten minutes ago, Nolan heard her tell Robert that he was nothing like Uncle Toby. Now he heard in her voice the implication that he was, in fact, exactly like Uncle Toby, or headed in that direction anyway. He didn't want to talk about any of this anymore with anyone. He wanted to be left alone. His head hurt, and even though he didn't want to admit it, he was tired from not sleeping. His brain seemed stuffed with cotton, everything thick and hard to sort through. He was tired, too, of trying to convince people to believe in something that to him was so completely obvious. It was like fighting with someone who kept insisting the world was flat.

"Why don't you believe me?" He sank onto the couch, overcome with an expanding loneliness that hollowed him out to his very core. "Why can't you just listen to what I'm telling you and then believe it's really happening?"

"I do believe you, Nolan."

He lifted his head, a sudden spark of hope.

"I believe that *you* believe what you're seeing is real."

He stood up again, finally understanding.

"Where are you going?"

"It's like you said. What you see is what you get." He smiled. "I get it now. You need proof. Something physical, something you can see and touch and manipulate. I'm going to get you proof."

She frowned. "That's not what I meant."

"Something undeniable." He leaned over and kissed the top of her head.

11

Monday morning dawned cool and foggy. Lucy didn't wait for the sun to rise above the mountains. In the chilled, gray light, she double-knotted her laces and jogged a slow half mile warm-up to Bishop Union High School. The track was open to the public, and within the next hour kids would be arriving for the first day of class after the winter break, but for the moment, Lucy was alone, racing herself. With each lap her pace quickened. She focused on her breath and her stride, trying to lose herself in the motion. Only this time, unlike all the times before, she wasn't running to forget. She hoped the familiarity of the track combined with the steady rhythm of her breath and body, the monotony of running in circles, might shake loose some, even one, small memory of the night Nolan disappeared.

Her mind was restless after finding the backpack. She felt like she was getting close to remembering something, but it was a dreamlike feeling, a déjà vu—whenever she tried to grasp hold of any kind of detail, it would slip away again, shifting into something else, camouflaging itself inside other, less important memories, and leave her frustrated and confused. It was something about Patrick, something he'd said or done or made her do. Or maybe it wasn't. Maybe she only thought it was because she hadn't been able to stop thinking about him since yesterday.

The cool air made her lungs ache, but it gave her something to focus on as she tried to slip into a relaxed state. Running was its own kind of hypnosis. Forget the world around you, focus on the body. Forget the responsibilities waiting for you in real life, focus on the breath. Don't think, don't stress, just run.

Lucy hadn't always loved running. When she first joined track and field, she was the slowest person on the team, and every practice, without fail, she wound up puking her guts out in the grass. But Patrick had encouraged her to stick with it. "Wait until you get your first runner's high," he said. "After that you won't be able to stop." He ran with her sometimes during practice, shouting encouragement, smacking her butt to go faster, and she did go faster eventually, and then faster still, until she was running near the front of the pack every time. Her body changed, too, becoming leaner and longer. Her first official race she came in second. Patrick brought her a dozen yellow roses and called her a natural.

After the party at Ship Rock, but before Nolan went missing, Lucy remembered being under the bleachers with Patrick, the very same bleachers she ran past now. She was missing Algebra, and he told her it didn't matter, that no one used math in real life. They sat close together. Her heart pounding triple speed. She didn't want to give him another hand job. What she wanted was for him to lean over, cup her face, and kiss her deeply, kiss her like he meant it. But he sat silent, smoking a joint and staring off in the distance. She moved her hand to his zipper because anything was better than being ignored, but he pushed her away.

"What's going on with your brother and Celeste?" he asked.

"Fuck if I know." She took the joint from him and sucked in hard, choking on the smoke.

"Are they hooking up or what?"

She thought about the party, the two of them dry-humping in the dark. "I guess."

Lucy didn't see what was so special about Celeste. She was a waiter at Jake's, so she was poor. She wasn't in school or taking classes at the community college, which meant she was stupid. And she wasn't very pretty either. There was something weird about her face and her eyes; the proportions were all wrong. Nolan never brought her over to the house. He hadn't even told Mom about her yet, but maybe it was good he hadn't if he really believed what he'd written in his casebook. Lucy hadn't been deliberately snooping around for that stupid book. Nolan had left it in his pickup, and one day before school—he was running late again and she was waiting for him in the pickup— the book just happened to be on the floor next to her feet. She'd seen him writing in it before. So, yeah, she was curious. She flipped through it and read enough to know that she didn't want to read any more.

"He thinks Celeste is an alien," Lucy said to Patrick, who whipped his head around to gawk at her. "He calls her Star Being."

"You're kidding me, right?"

She shook her head.

"He seriously thinks she's a . . . I mean, he can't, can he?" Patrick said. "It has to be one of his comic book stories or something."

Lucy shrugged. "It sounded pretty serious to me."

Patrick laughed and sucked down what was left of the joint. He stubbed the butt into the grass. "Oh, that's fucking rich. How do you know? He didn't just come out and tell you, did he? He can't be that far gone."

"He has this book. He writes down all his 'sightings' and shit."

"Of course he does. Of course he fucking does." He was still laughing. Then he leaned close to Lucy, his breath whispering across her cheek. "I could kiss you right now."

But he didn't. Not then, not yet.

Lucy lost count of how many laps around the track she'd run. She was drenched in sweat despite the cold. Her knees were starting to complain. That afternoon under the bleachers with Patrick wasn't a memory she'd forgotten, just one she hadn't thought about in a while. One she'd deliberately pushed aside. She ran four more times around and then walked another two, bringing her breath and heart rate back to normal.

She didn't know if she would ever be ready to talk to Patrick. About anything, but especially about the night Nolan vanished. When Wyatt first gave her his list of people to track down, she thought she would have found all her answers well before she reached Patrick's name.

She wondered what kind of man he was now. Some kind of big-shot attorney in Los Angeles, according to what Wyatt told her yesterday. Over the years, Lucy had imagined Patrick in so many places around the world—digging wells in Africa, researching a cure for AIDS in India, building orphanages in Brazil—and this whole time, he'd been living in the same city as her, maybe even just down the street. He could have found her if he wanted, if he had something to say.

Back at the motel, Lucy showered and changed into clean clothes. As she towel-dried her hair, a shadow passed in front of the window. Someone knocked. She squinted through the peephole in the door to see Wyatt on the other side with his hands stuffed in his pockets. He rocked back and forth on his heels, his gaze swinging up and down the length of the balcony. She let him in.

His eyes flickered to the closet and then back to her. "Did you get any sleep?"

"A little. Did you?"

He shook his head. The skin under his eyes was swollen and dark. Stubble shadowed his cheeks. He walked past Lucy to the closet and in the seconds before he opened it, she believed it would be empty, the backpack gone, never there to begin with. She had dreamed it all, and the guilt she felt was nothing more than the emotional scraps from her nightmares. But the backpack was there, sitting on the top shelf, exactly where she'd left it the night before.

They had both agreed to hold off on turning it over to the police. Lucy, for selfish reasons, because she wanted to know exactly how the rest of the night had unfolded first, and whether or not she would be considered a suspect. Wyatt because he didn't trust the sheriff's department. "Evidence goes missing all the time in police custody," he'd said, giving her the excuse she needed. "Fires, floods, rats, incompetent officers. Inyo County has already bungled Nolan's case more ways than I care to count. We don't want them screwing this up too."

Stuart kept the backpack secret for ten years. A few days more were nothing in comparison.

Wyatt closed the closet door and began to pace the small

motel room. "What was she doing with him? She wasn't even supposed to be in Bishop that night."

"How do you know?"

"She came to me, wanted me to help her leave town." Wyatt rubbed his cheek.

"You were friends?" Lucy asked, thinking of the business card in Celeste's wallet.

"We talked a few times. I knew her through Nolan."

Lucy waited, but he offered no further explanation.

In the days after Stuart Tomlinson's testimony to the police, there was a flurry of activity and media coverage as people tried to determine the identity of the person who had been with Nolan when he drove off that night in December, never to be seen again. Detective Mueller asked the public for help, again imploring people to come forward if they had any information, but as far as Lucy knew, nothing ever came of it. The identity of the other person in Nolan's pickup that night had remained a mystery until now.

"This doesn't have to be bad," Lucy said. "Maybe they ran away together."

"No." Wyatt shook his head. "No, no, I don't think so."

"It's possible—"

"She left her wallet? Her ID? All that money? No, something else happened. She wasn't planning on going anywhere with him that night."

"So, what, then? Nolan kidnapped her?" She wanted to laugh when she said it, and yet it wasn't completely out of the realm of possibility, no more so than Wyatt and her mother's alien abduction theory.

Wyatt scowled at the closet door and after a few seconds, asked, "Have you called Patrick?"

He'd given her the number to his office in LA as well as an email address and the address to his parents' house in Bishop.

"Not yet," she said.

He stuffed his hands into his pockets again, his shoulders slouching. "Anyway, the reason I came over here was to tell you that some of us are meeting at Jake's in twenty minutes and to find out if you wanted to come."

"Who's 'us'?"

"A few people from the UFO Encounters Group."

Lucy raised her eyebrows.

"Not everyone," Wyatt explained. "Just a handful who have been helping me and Sandra. They knew your brother from before, when he used to attend meetings." Then he added, "Sandra wanted me to invite you."

After the way they'd left things at the hangar the other day, Lucy was surprised Sandra had thought of her at all, let alone wanted to be in the same room as her again. But if this was a second chance, her mother's way of reaching out, then Lucy would reach back.

"Did you tell her about the backpack?" Lucy asked. "About Stuart seeing me that night?"

"I think that information should come from you," he said. "And the sooner the better."

"Let me get my wallet," Lucy said.

She and Wyatt were the first to arrive at the restaurant. They ordered coffee, and Lucy busied herself stirring in cream and sugar. After a few minutes, two women joined their table. Wyatt introduced the taller woman dressed in jeans and a leather jacket as Tilly and the shorter woman with smoky-white hair down to her waist as Gabriella.

Gabriella slid into the booth next to Lucy, offering her a warm smile and saying, "Peace and harmony be with you."

"Celeste lived with Gabriella for a while." Wyatt scooted over so Tilly could sit down too.

Gabriella pursed her lips, and her eyes kept darting to the ceiling like she expected something to fall down on them. She was dressed all in black, her long skirt billowing around calf-high boots that looked like they'd been around since the Victorian era, scuffed at the toes and with a million buttons running up the sides. Feathers dangled from her ears. Gold bangles chimed around her wrists. Every so often, she touched an onyx stone hanging around her neck. When the server came over, she ordered hot water with lemon and a side of dry toast. Tilly ordered a Bloody Mary and the pancake special.

There was an awkward moment where no one said anything and then Gabriella touched her onyx stone again and said, "You were right. Her energy is strong and curious, like her brother's." She spoke to Wyatt, but looked at Lucy who picked up her spoon and began stirring her coffee again.

Gabriella shifted on the bench, angling to face Lucy. "You want to ask me about her, don't you?"

Lucy glanced at Wyatt, who was caught up in his own, low-volume conversation with Tilly and not paying her any attention.

"You want to ask about Celeste," Gabriella clarified. She rested her arm on the table, her bracelets jingling, and leaned closer to Lucy. Then she tilted her head, smiling. "Did you know that often after an extraterrestrial encounter, humans will find they are suddenly able to read minds? Telepathy is the way our extraterrestrial brethren communicate. It's an elevated form of conversation. That's how I know you want me to tell you about Celeste."

Lucy tried to appear impressed, though she wasn't. Given how Wyatt had introduced them, it was no great leap for Gabriella to assume that Lucy was thinking about Celeste. Plus, he'd probably told the whole group the reason why Lucy was back in town, that there were things she wanted to know, questions for which she was trying to find answers.

"She wasn't what Nolan thought she was, you know." Gabriella spoke like she was confiding secrets. "She wasn't one of Them, though there was a time even I wondered if she might be. But no, she was flesh and bone, born of this planet like the rest of us miserable souls. Poor child had lost so much. I don't blame her for running away from that old life and chasing after a better one. I would have let her stay with me as long as she wanted, but things got complicated with your brother. We tried to tell him. We showed him the proof." She pressed her lips together and shook her head, like she was holding back strong emotions. The feather earrings fluttered against her hair.

"How long was she with you?" Lucy asked.

"About four months," she answered. "August through December. Your brother went missing the same day she left. A part of me has always wondered if he didn't try and go after her."

"Did you tell anyone that she was gone?" Lucy asked. "The police?"

"Why? She wasn't in any trouble. Wyatt came and picked her up from the house in the morning and drove her to Lancaster. She had a bus ticket to Santa Monica. She was almost eighteen, and she'd been taking care of herself for a long time before she came to live with me. This was her chance to make a new life for herself. Really make it stick this time. After the way your brother humiliated her, I thought she deserved a fresh start."

Lucy glanced at Wyatt again. He and Tilly were deep in conversation, but before she could get his attention, a man with a bushy white beard and wearing a cowboy hat sauntered up to the table. He introduced himself as Jim, nodding politely at Lucy before sitting down in the booth next to Wyatt.

Gabriella touched Lucy's elbow, drawing her attention again. "Celeste was a nice girl, and your brother, I think he really did love her in his own way, but he lost himself a little bit when he was around her. I only wish we had done more for him when we had the chance."

"Do you think he was abducted the way Sandra and Wyatt do?" Lucy asked.

Gabriella smiled. "My dear . . . stranger things have happened."

Sandra was last to arrive, bustling in ten minutes after everyone else, carrying a tote bag over one shoulder, and saying in a breathless rush, "So sorry I'm late. A signal came in."

Conversation stopped and they turned to her expectantly. She shook her head. "It was nothing, just some interference from an airplane."

Lucy had no idea what Sandra was talking about, but a consoling murmur rumbled through the rest of the group.

"Hope you all weren't waiting too long." Sandra smiled at each of them in turn. Her gaze lingered longest on Lucy, though her expression was harder to decipher. Some mix of relief and gratitude, but also trepidation.

They shifted to make room for her. She sat down across the table from Lucy, securing her tote bag on her lap. Once they were settled, Wyatt said, "Before we dig into the main business, any new experiences to share?"

Jim and Tilly exchanged a look and then, in turn, cast fleeting glances at Lucy. Sandra studied the menu like it was some kind of sacred text.

"She's safe," Wyatt said. "I can vouch for her."

Gabriella laid her hand on Lucy's arm. "Me too."

Lucy didn't blame them for being reluctant to share in front of her. She was a skeptic. She didn't deserve their trust, but Wyatt's words must have reassured them because they relaxed and began to talk. Gabriella went first. She told about a recurring dream she had about flying. She kept waking in the middle of the night to find herself standing on her balcony with her arms spread open, face tilted toward the stars. Jim told a story about strange lights following him home from work. They never got very close to his car, though. When it was Tilly's turn, she let her eyes sink half-closed, and her voice dropped into a dreamlike murmur, rising and falling like gentle waves. She was trying hypnotherapy again, she said.

"Cici took me all the way back to the summer of 1975. I was five, I think. That's when They first came to me. I was camping in the backyard with my two older brothers. We were sleeping in this tent . . . this all-blue tent . . . I remember how when the sun came through the fabric our skin turned blue too. Sometime around two or three in the morning, I woke up because I heard something. A loud thrumming sound, like an engine. Then I saw this light coming toward us. I thought it was a train, but that was impossible because we were nowhere near any tracks."

She paused to look around the table. Her cheeks flushed red, then she said, "They took me up into a bright room. Beings all around me, stroking my hair, my skin. They took off my clothes and told me not to be afraid. Then They sent me back home. That's it. That's all I remember. When I ask my brothers, they say there wasn't a light that night. That I walked out of the tent on my own. Like I was sleepwalking or something." She frowned at her hands. "I guess what I'm still struggling with is why They would take me so young. What could They possibly want with a five-year-old, you know?"

Jim suggested that in the same way humans study animals in all their life stages, so too would an extraterrestrial race study humanity. Gabriella added that though we did not always know why these things happened, we had to have faith in the Visitors as They had a greater understanding of the universe and our place in it. Wyatt and Sandra listened intently, but offered no reassurances or explanations of their own. Lucy kept her mouth shut. She was the outsider here and wanted to be respectful, so she said nothing. But silently she wondered if maybe Tilly wasn't making up this alien abduction story to cover up the real pain of an even more disturbing trauma. A stranger abduction, sexual or other physical abuse. Something happened. Whatever it was appeared to have left a terrible scar on her psyche, that was clear, but beings from another planet seemed a stretch.

"I'm going back to Cici next week," Tilly finished. "To see if she can draw out anything else."

Gabriella hummed in approval.

Then the group got quiet again. After a few seconds, Wyatt sat forward a little on the bench. "As you know, Sandra and I convened this special meeting to talk about the photographs Nolan took the night before he disappeared."

Sandra slipped the photographs out of her tote bag and passed them to Tilly.

"I know all of you saw them recently in the *Strange Quarterly* article," Wyatt continued. "And some of you have seen the originals before, too, but we want you to take another look. Tell us again your opinion, what it is you think we're dealing with here."

Lucy glanced across the table at her mother, who sat perfectly straight, her jaw jutting a little the way it did when she was feeling stubborn. It was the same expression Lucy remembered from childhood whenever she and her mother fought over one stupid thing or another. If the jaw tightened, it meant Sandra was starting to get upset. If it pushed out even a centimeter, the way it was now, then she was seconds away from sending Lucy to her room and winning the argument once and for all. Lucy understood then why she'd been invited to this meeting, why Sandra wanted her here. This wasn't a second chance. It was an "I told you so."

She watched as each person in the group flipped through the pictures in turn. They took their time, holding up this photograph or that photograph to the light, turning it at an angle, bringing it close for a better look, acting as if they had never seen them before. Jim looked through the stack twice and then said, "Night pictures like this are always such a challenge. We're sure this wasn't just a speck of dust on the lens?"

He rubbed his thumb over the glossy paper.

Lucy almost laughed with relief. Finally, someone talking sense. Maybe they would turn on Sandra and come to the right conclusion without Lucy having to say anything at all.

Sandra leaned across the table and wagged her finger in the

air, gesturing. "Look, see there near the bottom of the photograph?"

Jim squinted, then nodded enthusiastically. "Yes, I see it
now. Some sort of structure there, definitely."

He passed the photographs to Gabriella and then a few minutes later Lucy held them in her lap and the group watched,
waiting for her to agree with them, to say Sandra had been
right all along and Lucy wrong. She stared down at the top
photograph. Her vision blurred. The lights buzzed. The walls
of the restaurant pushed toward her. The smell of coffee and
frying bacon burned in her nose, made her stomach churn. She
was starting to feel claustrophobic. She dropped the pictures on
the table and pushed them back toward her mother.

There had been so many opportunities in the past for Lucy
to tell the truth, so many times she could have spoken up, but
she'd really believed the whole thing was too stupid to be taken
seriously. She never thought it would go this far. But it had, and
that was on Lucy. It was her fault this absurdity had gone on for
so long. She fixed her gaze on Sandra now, pleading with her
silently to try and understand, try and remember what it felt
like to be fourteen and in love with the wrong person.

"It was a stupid prank," Lucy said. "I'm sorry. I should have
told you sooner. But I didn't know how. We only meant it as
a joke. We wanted to scare Nolan, just freak him out a little."

"What are you talking about?" Sandra gathered the photographs off the table and clutched them to her chest as if they
were the only things left in this world that mattered.

"I tried to tell you before," Lucy said. "At the hangar the
other day. I tried to tell you it wasn't a UFO, but you wouldn't
listen to me."

She was listening now. They all were.

Lucy spread her fingers flat on the tabletop and stared down at her knuckle ridges as she continued, "He was always talking about those dumb aliens of his, the UFOs he claimed he'd seen. He was always trying to get attention and he was just . . . he was embarrassing me. And I . . . *we* thought it would be funny." She curled her fingers, pulled her hands under the table, and buried them between her knees. "We attached some parts to a remote control helicopter and added some lights. We built it in Patrick Tyndale's garage. I mean, the boys made it, really. They were the ones who put it together. I just told them what it should look like."

The table went silent. Jim and Tilly and Gabriella, Wyatt and her mother, all of them stared at her in disbelief and horror. Then Sandra flipped through the photographs again, quickly, her cheeks flushing red. She shook her head, as if she was unable to bridge the gap between what her eyes saw and what her ears heard.

Lucy rambled on, trying to justify and explain, anything to make them understand. "I didn't really think he'd believe it was a UFO. It was so clunky and obvious. For God's sake, we were standing right there at the bottom of the driveway steering the thing! Anyone else would have looked out the window and known right away it was a hoax. We didn't think he'd take it seriously. We didn't think he'd really fall for it. It was stupid. I know that now, but we were just kids. We were stupid kids doing stupid kid things. We didn't mean for it to go so far. We didn't mean for anyone to—"

"That's enough." Sandra dropped the photographs on the table.

Wyatt picked one up, eyes widening, finally seeing for the

first time, recognizing the blurred light for what it actually was. His grip on the picture tightened and when he spoke to her, his voice was stretched thin. "Why didn't you say something earlier?"

"I told you," Lucy said. "I tried anyway. At the hangar."

"No," Wyatt cut her off. "I mean, right after he went missing. When Sandra first found the pictures, when she was showing them to the police. Why didn't you say anything then?"

She thought Nolan had slept through the whole thing. She hadn't known the pictures even existed. No one showed her. No one told her anything. Lucy shook her head. Did her reasons even matter now?

"Did you at least tell Nolan what you'd done?" Wyatt pressed her. "Before he went missing, I mean?"

The morning after the helicopter prank, she and Nolan ate their cereal together in silence. She watched his face, looking for some kind of sign that he'd been awake the night before, that he knew what she'd done and was going to tattle to their mother, but he kept his head down, his thoughts to himself. He'd eaten quickly, anxious to leave the house, and Lucy let him go, believing she'd gotten away with it.

"We didn't think he even saw it," she said in answer to Wyatt.

"We've wasted so much time because of you. Because of these." He covered the pictures with his hand, and then a new thought came to him, something that made him wince and let out a labored sigh. "We're going to have to print a retraction."

Gabriella's fingers fluttered to her mouth. Tilly glared at Lucy.

"The debunkers are going to have a field day with this," Jim muttered. "They're going to rip us to shreds."

"I'm sorry," Lucy said, but they ignored her.

Sandra, who didn't seem to care anything at all about the backpedaling and explaining the group would have to do, suddenly demanded, "What else haven't you told me?"

Lucy flinched. She looked to Wyatt for help, but his jaw was set, his expression distant and disconnected. At some other table a fork clinked hard against a plate. The front door opened and a breeze blew through the restaurant, fluttering the napkins. At the cash register, a server counted out change.

"I wasn't home like I told you and the police." Lucy held her mother's gaze. "I wasn't home when Nolan left. I wasn't asleep."

Her mother inhaled sharply, but said nothing in response.

Lucy continued, "I was out with friends, that part was true, but I don't remember exactly what time they brought me home. All I know is that by the time I got there, Nolan was already gone."

"You don't remember. How can you not remember?" Sandra's voice trembled. Her hands shook.

"I was drinking," Lucy said. "That's why I lied, too. I didn't want to get in trouble. I didn't want you to be mad at me."

Sandra's eyebrows spiked high. She seemed about to say something else, only to purse her lips shut and quickly slide out of the booth, fleeing the restaurant through the front door.

"Mom, wait!" Lucy called out, rising to go after her, but Jim and Tilly were already up and pushing her out of the way.

"Don't." Wyatt grabbed Lucy's arm and pulled her back down. "You threw down a grenade. If she wants to run, let her run."

"I'm sorry," Lucy said, but he refused to look at her. "I should have told you sooner. I'm sorry about making the stupid thing in the first place, too, and about lying and about everything. I really am sorry. Wyatt, please."

He took money from his wallet and counted out enough to cover the check. "Stop apologizing and make it right."

He laid the bills down in the center of the table, then slid out of the booth and left.

Lucy cradled her head in her hands and choked back a sob. "That's not how it was supposed to go," she whispered, her breath ragged and damp.

Gabriella rubbed Lucy's back. "You have to try and understand, dear. All Sandra's had to hold on to for so long is her faith. She believes her boy is out there somewhere. Alive. She believes he might come back to her someday too. And that belief, that's what's keeping her from falling apart. She was in a dark place for a long time, Lucy, and it takes enormous strength for her not to go back there. You should be proud of her. Proud of how far she's come."

Lucy stared out the restaurant window. Jim and Tilly walked with Sandra between them; each had an arm around her, holding her upright, helping her back to her car where Kepler was waiting, his big black head sticking out the window, tongue dangling from his open mouth. Wyatt was a few steps behind, his head bent, talking into a cell phone.

"But she needs more than just faith," Gabriella continued. "She needs family. She needs you. She always has."

If that were true, if Sandra really needed Lucy, if she loved her daughter at all, she would have stopped drinking years ago. She would have worried more about Lucy skipping school, staying out past curfew, dying her hair pink. She would have acted more like a mother and less like an underpaid babysitter. And she never would have let Lucy leave Bishop; she would have fought for her to stay. It was true, Lucy had abandoned her mother at a fragile moment, but she'd been all of fourteen. She didn't know any better, and anyway, if they were keeping score, Sandra had abandoned Lucy first.

"I know it might not seem like it sometimes, but Sandra does love you, Lucy. She loves you very much, but she's afraid to get close to you, afraid of how much it will hurt if she loses you the way she's lost Nolan. But you can't abandon her now. Not again. You need her as much as she needs you. So you have to keep trying, Lucy, you have to find your way back to each other." Gabriella reached over and squeezed Lucy's hand.

Lucy stared, unable to speak, startled by the accuracy with which the older woman interpreted her private thoughts.

Gabriella laughed and shook her head. "Oh, child, your doubt is exhausting."

The man at the front desk, younger, with slender cheeks and a stylish fauxhawk, pointed Lucy to a chair in the waiting room and told her to have a seat. Then he dialed an extension and spoke into his phone, "Yes, there's a Lucy Durant here to see you?" A pause and then, "Yes, okay." He hung up and smiled stiffly at Lucy. "Mr. Tyndale is just finishing up a call. He'll be with you in a moment."

She didn't have an appointment. She'd driven four and a half hours straight from Jake's to Patrick's office in Los Angeles, a downtown high-rise near the Central Library. She had thought about calling first, but didn't want to give Patrick the opportunity to tell her no. She flipped through an *Architectural Digest* while she waited, but had trouble concentrating on any one page.

The last time Lucy saw Patrick was the day after Nolan's disappearance made newspaper headlines. He'd been missing for five days at that point, and Lucy's hands wouldn't stop shaking. She had been seeing shadows at night, darting in and out of her peripheral vision, and she was having trouble sleeping. When she did manage to fall asleep, she had nightmares where she was trying to run, but couldn't. Her legs were broken or full of sand or stitched on backwards. Also, she'd started hearing things outside her bedroom window late at night, or thought she was hearing things—whispers, revving engines, strange voices calling her name. No, the noises, the voices, they were all real. She definitely heard them. The other possibility, that she was losing touch with reality the exact same way Nolan had, was not one she was willing to accept. She was just overtired, nervous from all the people coming in and out of the house and from walking on eggshells around her mother. She was also, if she was honest with herself, feeling a little guilty about not being home the night Nolan went missing, about being drunk and not knowing for certain where she'd been and what she'd done. Then Detective Mueller came and asked her a bunch of questions she didn't have answers to, and she realized this was only the beginning, that her nightmares would get worse unless she filled in the blanks. After Mueller left the house and her mother locked herself in her room with a bottle of wine, Lucy called the one person she thought could help.

Patrick agreed to meet her at Juan's Taqueria, but when she got there he wasn't alone. Adam was there too, smirking and stuffing his face with chips and salsa. The three of them huddled together around a table at the back of the restaurant. An older woman with a slight accent took their order. Lucy had no appetite and asked for a Coke. Patrick and Adam, though, ordered enchiladas and four kinds of tacos and another basket of chips and salsa, enough food for a small army. Lucy told them about the detective coming to her house and asking her a bunch of questions about the night Nolan went missing, where she was, who she was with, what she was doing.

In a calm voice, Patrick asked, "So what did you tell him?"

"I told him we got burgers and drove around listening to music and then we went home."

Adam splintered a chip between his teeth. "You told him you were with us?"

"I told him I was with Patrick," she clarified, and then gave him a pleading look. "I was, wasn't I?"

"You don't remember?" Patrick asked.

Lucy massaged her temples. "I remember. I guess. I mean, I remember you came and picked me up and we drove around for a while. But I don't remember what we did exactly and I don't remember how I got home."

Adam snorted a laugh. "You *were* pretty drunk."

"So let me get this straight," Patrick said. "You told the cops you were with me, but you didn't say anything about Adam?"

She nodded.

"Fuck yeah, bitch." Adam slapped both hands on the table, rattling the glasses and silverware.

Lucy shrank under Patrick's hard stare. He dragged a chip through the salsa bowl and then crunched down on it. After swallowing, he shrugged. "Whatever. It's not like we did anything wrong."

"We were drinking," Lucy said quietly. "A lot. And driving."

Patrick shrugged again. "You didn't tell them that, though, did you? You didn't tell them we were drinking?"

"No, but—"

"Then I'd like to see them prove it."

He smiled at her, and her insides turned cold. "It's no big deal, really, Lucy. It's not. If they come talk to me, and they probably won't, but if they do, I'll tell them what you told them. We got burgers. We drove around listening to music. We went home. End of story."

But was it? Lucy wanted to know. Because she'd come home with cut-up knees and a faint memory of being somewhere she wasn't supposed to be, and no good explanation for either. "What about Nolan?" she asked. "Did we . . . ? I mean, was he . . . ?" She didn't know quite what she was trying to ask.

"We never saw him," Patrick said.

Then he made them both swear on their lives that whatever happened from this point forward, they would stick to the story they'd come up with today. "And," he said, taking a pocketknife from his jeans and nicking each of their thumbs enough to draw up a single drop of blood, "no one says anything about the fly-by either." He was talking about their stupid prank, but what that had to do with Nolan's disappearance, Lucy didn't know.

"We didn't do anything wrong," Patrick said. "Remember that."

He stuck up his thumb. A dark red bead quivered on the surface of his skin. Adam was quick to push his thumb to Patrick's, their blood smearing together in a macabre promise. The boys stared at her, waiting. Lucy looked down at her stinging thumb, at the blood bubbling from the place where Patrick's knife had pierced her skin. She had a sudden desire to run home, but there was no one there who could make her feel better, no one who could fix this. She'd pressed her thumb to Patrick's, her blood sealing the oath.

A door opened in the long hallway off the waiting room. Lucy put down the magazine.

She'd worn the nicest clothes she could find in the mess of boxes still piled in her car, but having Patrick in front of her now, dressed in an expensive three-piece suit, his Italian leather loafers polished to a shine, a diamond-encrusted watch glittering on his wrist, his smile just as brilliant and charming as ever—this, plus the way his eyes flicked over her like she was a painting and he was trying to figure out how he felt about the brushstrokes and colors, whether she was worth hanging on his wall or not—all culminated in her feeling completely inadequate, a third-rate slob. She tugged at the hem of her oversized black T-shirt and then wrapped her royal purple cardigan tight around her chest. For the first time she noticed the right cuff was starting to fray. Her designer jeans were faded. Dust coated and dulled her shoes, her stupid neon pink and green sneakers, like the kind a kid would wear.

For a second, neither of them spoke, and then Patrick said her name. "It's so good to see you." His voice was deeper than she remembered, but familiar still, and for a second, she felt fourteen again, all nervous energy and desperation, her heart leaping into her throat. He stepped forward and embraced her.

She had forgotten how good it felt to be held. By anyone, but especially by him. He smelled like clean laundry and some faint musky cologne. He'd grown into a strong man, bulkier in the arms and chest than when he was in high school. Clearly he spent more time lifting weights these days than running laps. He held her tight enough she could feel his heart beating, and she remembered how once, the same night as the helicopter prank, after they'd had sex for the first and only time, she'd tried to match her heartbeat to his, slowing her breath to synchronize the rhythm, but failing. His heart always at least a half beat ahead of hers, but she had believed that if she could do this one thing, get their hearts to sync up, that somehow this would make their love real. She remembered the possessive way his fingers had played with her hair, how they trailed greedily down her neck to her breasts. She remembered, too, the angry weight of him pressing down, almost suffocating her, the false promises he'd sighed into her ear, the way the stars looked upside down through fogged windows, the whole world upended.

Another beat and then Patrick released her and took a step back. "Let's talk in my office."

He led her down the hallway to a large, enclosed room with picture windows lining one wall and showcasing a billion-dollar skyline. The furniture was modern, clean lines and efficiency. He closed the door behind her and gestured to a minibar beside a steel-frame bookshelf loaded with law books and travel guides. "Something to drink?"

"No, thank you." She hated the stiffness in her voice, how clearly it betrayed her.

He invited her to sit on a contoured, gray plastic chair positioned at a slight angle in front of his desk. She sat. He stayed standing, leaning against his desk, crossing his legs at the ankle and his arms over his chest, peering down his nose, giving her that same once-over look he'd given her in the waiting room.

"Adam messaged me on Facebook," he said. "Told me he saw you hanging around Riley's, but I didn't believe him." He laughed a little, and Lucy's heart stuttered over the sound. Her stupid, useless heart. "Ten years, can you believe it? I'm sorry I haven't kept in better touch. I tried to find you on Facebook."

She hated herself for believing that he had actually tried. "I don't use Facebook."

"Well, that explains it." He smiled and then pushed off the desk and walked around to the opposite side where he lowered himself into a black leather office chair. "You're looking well, Lucy. Are you? Well, I mean? And happy?"

She ignored his questions and cut straight to the point. "We need to talk about the night Nolan went missing."

He frowned at a spot over her shoulder and then rocked back in his chair, lacing his fingers together above his chest. "What about it?"

His tone was all business now, curt and humorless.

"I want to know what happened," she said. "I'm trying to remember."

He tilted his head slightly. "Remember what?"

"What we did that night. What *I* did." She pressed a hand to her chest.

He sighed. "I'm sorry, Lucy, I'm having trouble understanding exactly what it is you think I can help you with."

"You were there."

"Where?"

She couldn't believe he was toying with her like this, making her beg.

"Please," she said. "Just tell me what happened that night. Tell me what we did."

A muscle in his jaw twitched and his eyes narrowed. "I picked you up. We went and got burgers. We drove around listening to music. Then I took you home." His voice was monotone. "End of story."

"But it's not, is it," she pressed. "There's more. There must be more. Patrick, please, I drove all this way—"

"No one asked you to."

"—just tell me the truth. What did we do? After the burgers, after we started drinking. What happened after that?"

He studied her a moment, and then with sympathy said,

"He was my friend once too, Lucy." When she started to protest, he held up one hand. "I know it's not the same. I can only begin to imagine how hard it's been for you. Growing up without your big brother, and all these years with no new developments in the case. All these years not knowing what the hell happened." He shook his head. "It's not right and I can imagine how all that wondering could start to wear on a person, but, Lucy . . ." He leaned forward again, placing his hands on the desk. "Believe me when I tell you that it's in your best interest to let this go."

"What do you mean?"

"You were drinking that night," he explained. "You remember that part at least, right?"

"You were too."

"Yes," he conceded with a nod of his head. "We were all drinking. But that's only part of the problem."

Patrick got up from his desk and went to the minibar where he poured himself a tumbler of bourbon over a single ice cube. He took a sip, then asked, "Are you sure you don't want anything?"

"If you know something," Lucy said, "if we went to the observatory that night, if we were there, you need to tell me. I need to know what happened to him. If we did something . . ." But the rest of the sentence got jammed in her throat and she couldn't finish.

"I don't know what happened to him." Patrick swirled the ice in the glass once, took another sip, and then carried the rest back to his desk. He sat down again, holding on to the tumbler with both hands. "You really don't remember anything at all?"

"Bits and pieces," she said. "But nothing feels real. It's all shadows and fuzz and most of it feels like a dream, you know, like I'm just imagining it."

"Okay," he said. "I'll tell you."

Her breath caught in her chest. All these years, and all she had to do was ask? It couldn't be this easy, this straightforward. Nothing was with Patrick.

He continued, a warning in his voice, "But, Lucy, I'm serious about letting this go. As a defense attorney, I deal with this kind of shit every day. We're always taking on clients who go around flapping their gums. Innocent people, witnesses, who tell the cops everything they saw and answer every question, thinking they're helping the investigation, only to find themselves marked as a person of interest. And once the cops have you marked, they tend not to look very hard in other directions. Do you understand what I'm saying?"

She did. She thought she did. "But if it's something that can reopen the investigation. If it could help bring Nolan home—"

"It won't." His words clipped short. "Trust me. The detective will twist it to fit his narrative, even if that narrative is wrong. I've seen more than one innocent person sent away for life because they were simply in the wrong place at the wrong time doing something stupid. But let me tell you right now. Stupidity is not a crime."

He reached across his desk and turned a frame toward her so she could see the picture behind the glass. The woman in the photo was model beautiful, with perfect bone structure and perfect straight teeth and long dark hair cascading in perfect soft curls around her shoulders. In her arms, she held a smiling baby with perfect dimples and a tuft of downy blond hair covering the top of its head. The ocean glittered diamonds in the distance behind them.

"My wife and daughter." Patrick turned the photograph to face him, his thumb running over the glass. "She'll be four months old tomorrow. Elizabeth. After my grandmother. We weren't planning on getting pregnant so soon, but . . ." He flashed Lucy a tight smile and returned the frame to its place near his computer. "These things happen." He folded his hands together on the desk, his thumbs working back and forth against each other nervously. "Lucy, you have to promise me that what I'm about to tell you won't leave this office."

She hesitated. "You know I can't do that."

His lips retreated into a thin line, pressed flat between his teeth. He seemed to be weighing his options, whether or not what he was about to tell her was worth the risk. He must have decided it was because he said, "We called Nolan that night. Do you remember that?"

"When?"

"Around midnight. A little before. We called from a phone booth outside of Liquor and Stuff. You pretended to be Celeste."

Lucy stared over his shoulder and out the window, trying to remember. Sandwiched between a knitting shop and a used bookstore, Liquor and Stuff was part liquor, part convenience store in a strip mall downtown. It was open twenty-four hours.

"We were trying to find someone to buy us beer," Lucy said, an image surfacing of the three of them—her and Patrick and Adam—pacing the sidewalk in front of the store, harassing an old man with an eye patch and a limp who just wanted to buy his forty and go. The manager of the place had come outside and said they had ten seconds to scram or he was calling the police. They'd gone, but only around the corner. The phone booth was covered in graffiti, the door missing.

In Patrick's office, Lucy covered her mouth and nose, remembering how rank the inside had smelled of stale piss and dog shit. Wyatt had been right. She didn't think it possible, but here it was, on her like the full force of a tidal wave. A memory resurfacing, and Patrick the one who triggered it.

The three of them crammed inside the phone booth. Lucy first, then Patrick and Adam, both of them pressing against her and she was too drunk to tell whose body belonged to whom, whose hands groped her ass. They were laughing. She laughed too. To cover up her excitement, her terror. The beer had gone to her head, her stomach, had taken over, making her legs and the place between hot and soft and trembling. As of last night she was no longer a virgin, a woman now, a woman madly in love and drunk, drunk in love, and as she stood stuffed inside that tiny phone booth it seemed anything was possible. Everything was. Patrick's hand, or Adam's, it didn't matter in that moment, a strong hand, a boy's hand, pressed against the small of her back. She leaned into it, wanting it to move up and down and all over her. She was alive with the electric night, her skin on fire with want and the thrill of being out past curfew, doing things no fourteen-year-old should be doing.

"Do it," Patrick had said, his breath hot on the back of her neck.

She fumbled with the receiver, dropped in dimes and quarters, listened as the phone rang and rang, as her brother picked up on the other end. She hung up that first time and the second time too, because she couldn't stop laughing. The third time she managed to say his name, but he thought she was someone else and that sent her into a panic. She didn't know what to do. She held the phone out to Patrick, who shook his head and then leaned in to whisper what she should say. She repeated everything exactly. Then, without warning, Adam grabbed her around the waist, his fingers digging into the soft flesh of her belly. She screamed and dropped the phone. Patrick picked it up and spoke into it in a gruff and menacing voice. "Come to the observatory," he'd said. "Wait for us there."

Lucy remembered how Patrick kissed her afterward, how he'd picked her up and swung her around like a fairytale princess. She remembered wanting that kiss to go on and on and on and here the memory cut off again. Here, another blank wall.

"And *after*?" she whispered, her mouth gone dry with fear that Patrick was going to reveal something even worse than the phone call. "What happened after we talked to him?"

Patrick spread his empty hands in the air. "I took you home."

She wanted to trust him, but people didn't change, not in the ways that mattered, and Patrick had betrayed her more than once, enough times for her to recognize when he wasn't telling the whole truth. A furrow formed between his eyebrows. He picked at his thumbnail and fixed his gaze a half inch above her head so he appeared to be looking straight at her, when in actuality he was staring at nothing. But whether he was lying about all of it or simply leaving parts out, she wasn't sure. What she did know was that he wanted her to believe he'd told her everything, and he was betting on her childhood infatuation with him and her faulty memory, on the amnesic effect of alcohol and time, that by giving her this sliver of truth, she wouldn't go looking for more.

"We didn't go out there to see if he'd show?" she asked.

"No." That same muscle in his jaw twitched again. "We didn't."

He held her gaze for a moment and then added, "Making that phone call was a stupid thing to do, I'll admit that. I've been living with my regret ever since, wondering if we hadn't called him, then maybe . . ." He shook his head, scowling at his hands, unable to finish his thought.

He didn't have to. Lucy was thinking the exact same thing: Nolan would have never left the house, would have never even been out in the desert that night if not for them. If not for her.

Patrick composed himself again and continued, "But last time I checked, making prank phone calls to your friends isn't illegal. However, any detective worth his salt could easily use this phone call to implicate us as suspects. We made that call, we were the reason Nolan was at the observatory in the first place, thusly we followed him out there and did something to harm him, or at the very least witnessed what happened. Either way, it doesn't look good. Because even if we could come up with airtight alibis and convince a jury that we were never in the desert that night, we still lied to the police. We hindered an investigation. Do you see now why it's better for us to stick with our original story?"

She found herself nodding in spite of her doubts. His voice was smooth and reassuring and what he said made sense in a way. He was the lawyer, after all. He would know better than anyone about these kinds of things, and there was something to be said about not muddying up the investigation with more leads that went nowhere, about not making themselves suspects if they'd done nothing wrong. Still, if it was like Patrick said and they didn't go to the observatory, then it was possible telling the truth about their activities that night might push the investigation in a better direction. The right one.

"Celeste went missing that night too," Lucy said. "Did you know that? She was with Nolan. A neighbor saw them leave together in his pickup."

Patrick raised his eyebrows, but otherwise his expression remained unchanged.

"Why would he have gone out to the observatory if he knew she was safe?" The thought only now forming in her mind, pounding at her temples. "If he knew it was a prank, why was he there?"

"I don't know, Lucy," Patrick said with a heavy sigh. "Maybe they were together when we called. Maybe he was pissed that we punked him again and he went out there to get revenge or something. I don't know what happened after they got to the observatory because I wasn't there. None of us were."

"Okay, but—"

"Look," he interrupted. "You came here wanting answers, and I've given you all I can. I wish there was more that I could do for you. I wish I could bring him back, I really do." He paused for a long time, almost long enough that Lucy thought she was being dismissed. Then he said, "Nolan pulled a knife on me, you know."

"What? When?" That didn't sound like her brother at all.

"A couple of weeks before he went missing," Patrick said. "At the grocery store. I went over there to try and apologize for what happened at the basketball game and he nicked me right here." He pointed at a place near his Adam's apple, but if there was a scar, it was too faint for Lucy to see.

"Why are you telling me this?"

"He's your brother, I get that, I do. But, Lucy, he wasn't an innocent. Whatever happened, he probably brought it on himself." He rose slowly from his desk and came around to her again. "But I think you knew that already."

He stared down at her with pity in his eyes, the same pity he'd had for her ten years ago in the parking lot of Juan's Taqueria when she'd tried to wrap her arms around him, when she'd buried her face in his shoulder and said, "I'm scared, Patrick. I'm really scared." She'd wanted him to whisper that he loved her and would never let anything bad happen to her. Instead, he'd sloughed her off like a tattered old rag. "I don't think we should see each other anymore." And when she'd started to cry, he looked embarrassed for her. "It's nothing personal," he'd said. "I just think you have the wrong idea about us, that's all, and I don't want to lead you on or anything. You're a good kid, Lucy." He'd left her standing alone in the parking lot, the smell of grilled meat, lard, and hot asphalt twisting her stomach, making her want to puke.

Patrick was her first—first love, first kiss, first time wanting, first time needing, first time losing herself in someone else, first shattered heart. He would always be her first, and though that meant something to her once, she owed him no loyalty now.

He twisted his wrist to look at his watch. "Is there anything else you need? I have some phone calls to make, and a client coming in soon."

Lucy stood and allowed Patrick to lead her to the door. "I appreciate you taking the time to talk with me. I know you didn't have to."

"Anything for an old friend," he said. "And, hey, maybe now you can finally start to put this all behind you."

"Yeah, maybe." She forced a smile.

"Take care of yourself, Lucy." He shut the door in her face.

13

Marnie answered the front door in loungewear and pink bunny slippers. Her hair was pulled into a loose bun at the nape of her neck. She blinked against the afternoon sun streaming through the doorway. "Lucy? What are you doing here? We weren't expecting you, were we?" She glanced behind her into the house. "Your father didn't say anything about—"

"Is he here?" Lucy interrupted, pushing her way inside.

"You might have called first." Marnie shut the door. "It's the polite thing to do, you know."

Lucy ignored her and walked down the long hall toward her father's office. Her sneakers were nearly silent on the travertine tile. Marnie's bunny slippers shushed quickly after her.

"He's on an important call," Marnie said. "You shouldn't go in there."

Lucy didn't bother knocking. Robert had his back to the door, his cell phone pressed to his ear. Upon hearing the door open, he swiveled slowly in his chair, a deep scowl creasing his face. "I'm sorry, Greg," he said into the phone. "Something's just come up. I'm going to have to call you back. Yes. Okay, great. Thank you."

He ended the call and set the phone down on his desk. "What is the meaning of this? Lucy, what are you doing here?"

He didn't sound pleased to see her.

Marnie pushed into the doorway behind Lucy and folded her hands primly at her waist. "I told her she should have called first."

"I was in the neighborhood," Lucy said, taking a seat in the high-backed chair. "I needed to see you. I needed to ask you about—"

"It couldn't wait?"

"—Nolan."

Robert's eyes narrowed, his lips pinched. Without turning his focus from Lucy, he said, "Be a love, Marn, and make us some coffee?"

Marnie made a sound in protest, but Robert shot her a hard look, and she sighed and shuffled out of the room, closing the door behind her. As soon as she was gone, Lucy took a breath to speak, but Robert was faster.

"What is going on with you lately?" he asked, laying his arms on the desk. "I've left several messages, which you've ignored. And now you show up here unannounced."

"I know. I'm sorry. I've been busy."

He perked up a little hearing that. "New job?"

"No, I . . . not yet . . . I've been . . ." She'd rehearsed what she wanted to say on the drive over from Patrick's office, and it had all been so detailed and rational and well-paced, but this was much harder to do in person. She took a breath and let the words tumble out whichever way they needed to. As long as she got them out, that was the important part, as long as she finally got her father to start talking about the one thing they should have never stopped talking about: the shadow in the shape of her brother who followed her from room to room, city to city, who was there even when she closed her eyes.

"I haven't picked up the keys to my apartment yet," she said.

"You what? Why would you—"

"The landlord's holding it for me until the fifteenth, but right now all my things are still packed up in the back of my car. Since I left here, I've been living in a motel," she said. "In Bishop."

He looked surprised. "Why the hell would you go back there?"

"I needed to try and talk to Mom. Those pictures she has, the ones she gave to *Strange Quarterly*, they're not of a UFO."

"Obviously."

"I had to tell her the truth."

"Lucy, I'm not sure I understand what you're saying."

She explained about the UFO she and Patrick built in his parents' garage. His eyes widened, and he sat back in his chair as if her words were physical shoves against his chest. She stopped short of telling him about the phone call she'd made luring Nolan to the observatory. She wasn't ready to share that information just yet. Not with him, not with anyone.

"How did she take it when you told her?" Robert asked.

"Not well," Lucy said, remembering the look of betrayal, how quickly Sandra fled the restaurant. "I'm not sure if she'll ever speak to me again."

"Yes, well, your mother . . ." But he didn't seem to know what to say next. He lifted his hands in a half shrug. "Did you get it out of your system, then? Do you feel better?"

The bald eagle statue on the corner of his desk was turned

at such an angle that it appeared to be staring straight at her, its eye narrowed into a thin, predatory slit.

"What do you think happened to him?" she asked.

Robert shifted in his chair. The leather squeaked. "Lucy, please, I don't want to—"

"I mean, everyone else seems to have their own theories. I want to know yours." She had never asked him before; she had never felt brave enough to hear his answer.

"To what end?"

She thought it might be a rhetorical question.

"You aren't the least bit curious?" she asked. "He was your son. Your *only* son. Don't you ever wonder? Don't you want to know where he is?"

"It wouldn't change anything." He spoke so quietly, Lucy wasn't sure she heard him right. She leaned forward in her chair as he continued, louder now, "The simple fact of the matter, Lucy, is that your brother lost hold of reality and couldn't figure out how to get back to us. Anything beyond that is guesswork."

Lucy slouched back, disappointed.

"And I don't think it's a good idea for you to start stirring things up like this," he added. "It's not healthy."

"I'm not a kid anymore," she said. "You can stop protecting me."

Robert tapped his fingers together and studied her a moment. She thought he was going to end the conversation and send her on her way. Instead he said, "I have a younger brother. Did you know that? Do you remember him?"

They never had big family dinners or holiday parties with extended relatives driving from all over the country like in the movies. Sandra was an only child, and Lucy always assumed her father was too. But she remembered a conversation between her parents a little while after Nolan was expelled from school, one she wasn't supposed to hear. They'd made a quick reference to a man named Uncle Toby, and she remembered asking Nolan about him, but getting no response. She also remembered a man with a booming laugh who would scoop her up in his arms, swing her above his head, and then tickle her with his shaggy beard, but the memory was from so long ago, so vague in her mind that she'd confused the man with her father, despite that in all the pictures of their family together her father was clean-shaven.

"Have I ever met him?" she asked.

Robert nodded. "When you were very young, but he went away before you really had a chance to get to know him."

"How come you haven't told me about him before?"

"It's not something I like to talk about," Robert said. "He's not well."

Lucy sat quietly, waiting for him to continue. When he did, his voice was distant and soft, so unlike the dynamic, controlling businessman she was used to.

"Both my parents died when I was nineteen," he said. "First, Mother from lung cancer. She loved her Virginia Slims. Then Father, shortly after, a single bullet to the head. His grief got the better of him, and he took the coward's way out."

Robert never talked much about his parents. Lucy knew they were dead, but he'd never told her how. There was a small framed black-and-white picture of the two of them on the mantelpiece in the living room, a photograph from their wedding day. Lucy never told anyone, but she always thought Nolan bore a striking resemblance to their grandfather. Same thin nose and kind eyes.

"Anyway . . ." Robert waved away some emotion threatening to well up and carried on with a stricter tone. "Toby, my brother, he was twelve when Father died. I did the best I could to finish raising him, but I was barely an adult myself, and Toby . . . he had his own ideas about things. We didn't always see eye to eye, but I took care of him. I made sure he had everything he needed. Food, a place to live, clean clothes. I made sure he did his homework. I made sure he graduated. And I found him a job." He clasped his fingers together, his jaw tightening. "A good job too. Selling men's shoes at a department store. But he said being inside all day like that, waiting hand and foot on rich men, he said it was making him crazy. He said he wanted to fly, be a pilot. Which he did. Somehow . . ." And here he laughed a little. "Somehow those idiots gave him a pilot's license."

He cleared his throat. "Anyway, after a while he was going off, doing his own thing, living his own life, and that was good. I had my life too. Your mother, my work, and later, you two kids. We would see each other sometimes, as often as we could, but we were both grown, both making our separate ways in the world, trying to figure it out. And I thought we had. Figured it out, I mean." He paused, the silence stretching long and thin, and then continued, "Toby was always a little different, head in the clouds, like your brother. I didn't really think anything of it until the day he tried to kill himself."

Lucy squeezed the armrests of her chair. The air in the room was suddenly too heavy, too hot. But she didn't dare move. Her father had always been such a private person, so completely unknowable, and now he couldn't seem to stop, the words his confession, an unburdening of guilt. And Lucy would listen because he needed her to, but also because she needed to know how it ended for Toby and Robert, how it might end for her too.

"He thought he was being tracked by the government and he took a knife . . ." Robert touched his neck and then shook his head, his hand dropping back to the desk. "Luckily we were there. Your mother and I. We were able to get him help, but things were never the same after that. He lost himself that day. He lost himself, and I lost my brother."

Robert frowned at the eagle statue before continuing, "The doctors diagnosed him as paranoid schizophrenic. He took medication for a while, but only when he was forced to, and then one day he just disappeared. Well, I guess 'disappeared' isn't quite the right word. He left. He moved to Alaska, to some cabin out in the middle of nowhere. He wasn't able to handle the reality of day-to-day life. He couldn't fit in with the rest of normal society, so he took himself to someplace where he could be alone. Where he felt safe."

Robert opened his hands over the desk and then clasped them together again, punctuating the end of his sentence. Lucy waited for him to continue, but he said nothing else and it seemed he'd said all he wanted to say, but she needed more.

"And that's what you think happened to Nolan too?" she asked. "He ran away to someplace where he felt safe?"

He winced a little and when he spoke again, his words were heavier than before, weighted with resignation or regret or both. "Your uncle sends me letters. The rest of the world can go to hell for all he cares, but he maintains contact with me. He sends me letters every month. Sometimes postcards. But every month without fail, he lets me know that he's still alive, still in Alaska, that he's okay and I shouldn't worry about him. I just got one in the mail yesterday."

He reached into the top drawer of his desk and pulled out a postcard. On the front was a picture of a dogsled team, chasing through a snowy, wooded wilderness. On the back were a few brief sentences.

Hi brother, Snow is up to my neck now. May have found work on a boat for next month. Nights last forever, but I've got enough wood and enough candles to keep me warm and bright through June. Love to your clan. —T

Lucy returned the postcard to her father. Her cheeks were beginning to tingle and go numb. "So you think Nolan's . . ." She struggled to say it out loud. "You're saying he's . . . dead?"

The word left a bitter, hot taste on her tongue.

"It's been ten years, Lucy," Robert said, and she hated the tone of his voice, how matter-of-fact he sounded, like he was trying to talk her into something. "Ten years and no one's heard from him."

Lucy swallowed a sob that was threatening to betray her. Of course she'd thought about this before, the possibility of Nolan being dead, but hearing her father say it, having the words thrust into the open, this was so much worse.

"So that's it, then?" Her voice was hoarse. "You're giving up on him?"

"No one's giving up, Lucy. I'm, just, I'm being realistic, that's all. And I urge you to do the same."

Lucy laughed, an angry sound. For all the ways her mother let her down, at least Sandra was trying to find answers. At least she was doing *something*.

"So, realistically then . . ." She did nothing to hide the fury in her voice. "How do you think it happened? How did he die?"

"The details aren't important."

"Yes, they are." The details were everything. They were the only way she could know for sure. "Suicide? Is that what you think? He went out in the desert that night to kill himself?"

Robert sighed impatiently. "He wasn't himself, Lucy. You have to remember that."

"How would you know what he was like? You weren't even there. You hardly ever talked to him. So how would you know *anything* about the kind of person Nolan was?"

"I saw enough, Lucy," Robert said. "I saw enough to know he was going through something much more complicated than a rebellious phase."

"And yet you did nothing to help him."

"That's not true," he argued. "I voiced my concerns to your mother. I told her to call me if things got out of hand."

"She did call you. She called and still you did nothing." She remembered when Sandra told her that Nolan was going to live with their father, how relieved Lucy was, how she thought things would start to get better.

"What was I supposed to do, Lucy?" Robert asked. "What would you have had me do?"

"You should have been there. You should have come right away. You should have stayed with us, I don't know, something, you should have done *something*." She wasn't sure Nolan would have even listened to anything their father said, but he could have at least tried.

"Nolan was changing," she continued. "He was acting so strange, and I was scared, and you and Mom, you were just pretending like nothing was happening, like if you ignored the problem long enough it would just go away. Guess what? It didn't go away. It got worse. *He* got worse."

"Your mother said she could handle it."

"Nolan was your son, too. If you saw how bad he was getting, if you saw and you understood, if you thought he was a danger to himself, then why didn't you try and help?"

"I did," he insisted. "I did try."

"Not hard enough." But the fight was leaving her now because she didn't know who she was really mad at: her parents or herself.

Any one of them could have stopped him, but no one had bothered. This happened because they let it happen. All of them were selfish, all of them at fault. Robert, who wasn't a bad parent but who wasn't a very good one either, who treated his children more like burdens, only doing the bare minimum—visits twice a year and only when pressed; child support checks; birthday and Christmas cards; the occasional phone calls filled with more silence than words—who seemed relieved after Nolan went missing, one less burden. One less nuisance taking up his time. And Sandra. Sandra, who filled her loneliness with long hours at work and extra glasses of wine, who let life's losses overwhelm her, who sometimes forgot she had children to take care of, or remembered, but still couldn't get up enough energy to care. Then Lucy, so self-absorbed in her own small life and petty problems—what shirt to wear; the cowlick in her bangs; how to get Patrick to kiss her—so focused on her own lonely heart, she failed to see how deeply immersed in fantasy Nolan had become, how dangerous the path he was headed down.

She'd been so embarrassed by him. Every word that came out of his mouth, every one of his stupid theories. The clothes he wore, how he cut his hair, the way he slouched down the halls at school muttering under his breath, the comics he drew, the way he scribbled in that stupid notebook of his. Everything about him humiliated her. Everything he did, she thought he did for attention. And back then, fourteen and so sure she knew what she wanted, back then Lucy would have given anything for Nolan to disappear. Now she would give anything to have him back.

Robert leaned slightly forward. The desk a dark continent between them. "Lucy, we all made mistakes. And we have to live with those. But he's gone, and we're still here. Do you understand what I'm saying?"

She brushed at tears welling in her eyes.

"When you called me to come get you," he said. "When you told me about the way your mother was behaving, how erratic and irrational she'd become, I knew I had to do it differently. I couldn't let you end up like your brother. So I came and I got you and I took you out of that shit show and I tried, Lucy. I tried my best to give you as normal of a life as possible."

She wished he'd tried like that for Nolan too.

"You should be thanking me," he said, bitterly. "If your mother'd had her way, who knows what kind of mess you'd be in today. Stuck in some psychiatric hospital knitting scarves most likely."

Lucy sat up straight and stiff. "What do you mean . . . ? If she'd 'had her way'?"

"She didn't want me to take you. She fought for custody." He laughed, a grim sound. "Of course, she didn't stand a chance after I told the judge about her drinking problem, how she got violent, how she lost her job at the hospital."

Lucy's stomach tightened. She couldn't reconcile her memories of her final days with Sandra with what Robert was telling her now. She was certain Sandra had been glad to see her go, had, in fact, pushed her out the front door.

"She fought for me?" Lucy's voice was barely a whisper.

"She wouldn't leave it be, either," he said. "Even after the judge ordered you into my custody. She kept calling. Every day at first, and then when I told her I was going to take her back to court, once a month."

"She called? To talk to me?"

"The first Sunday of the month. Without fail. Until your eighteenth birthday. She stopped after that, good riddance."

"Why didn't you tell me?" Lucy dug her nails so hard into her palms the skin started to burn. "Why didn't you let me talk to her?"

"It was for your own good, Lucy," he said. "She was an emotional train wreck. And you needed stability."

She stood quickly, pushing the chair backward a few centimeters.

"Where are you going?" Robert stood too.

"Back to Bishop," she said.

"There's nothing for you there."

Only now she knew there was. She moved toward the door.

"You have to move on with your life at some point, Lucy." He followed her into the entryway. "You can't keep chasing fantasies. You're better than that."

Marnie came from the kitchen carrying a tray with a pot of freshly brewed coffee, cups, sugar, and cream. She stopped in the doorway as Lucy brushed past her.

"Lucy, please wait." Robert chased after her. He grabbed her elbow as she reached the front door. "Traffic's terrible right now, and it's going to get dark soon. Stay the night. We'll get the guest room ready for you, and we can order Chinese food from that place down the street you like. Okay? Just, sleep on it for now, and if you still want to go in the morning, fine, but at least give yourself some time to think about what you're doing."

The past ten years she'd done nothing but think. She jerked her arm free. "I know what I'm doing."

Robert pinched the bridge of his nose and then sighed and dug into his pocket. He pulled several twenty-dollar bills from his wallet. "Take this."

She hesitated, no longer wanting anything from him, especially his charity. But he pressed the bills into her hand anyway, saying, "I'm trying to help."

She took the money and stuffed it into her purse.

"Call if you need more," Robert said.

Walking back to her car, hands shaking, Lucy texted Wyatt. I need to talk to my mother. ASAP.

A few minutes later he texted back. She's at Paiute Palace until midnight.

CASEBOOK ENTRY #5

STRANGE HAPPENING:
Shadows

DATE: November 9, 1999

LONGITUDE/LATITUDE: 37.3635 W, 118.3951 N

SYNOPSIS: I'm being followed. Most likely government agents, the Department of Defense, military—some covert, black-ops, leave-no-paper-trail kind of group. Maybe the same ones who have been calling the house and hanging up. I noticed it first on the way back from camping. An SUV tailed us the whole way down the mountain and all the way to Skyline Road. Later that night, I saw a black sedan parked outside the house, engine running, someone sitting inside. I went out to confront them, but they drove off as soon as they saw me.

OBJECT DESCRIPTION: Black vehicles with tinted windows. So far I have seen an SUV and a sedan, but make and model of both were impossible to determine, and there may be others I have not seen. No license plates visible.

OTHER WITNESS STATEMENTS: I asked Lucy if she saw the black sedan parked outside the house; she said she did, and then asked if it was the FBI coming to take me away. She was mocking me, not understanding the seriousness of the situation, but I am certain now that at least this was not a hallucination.

WEATHER INFORMATION: Dry roads. No wind. Clear skies.

LOCATION DESCRIPTION: Skyline Road is a residential cul-de-sac. All houses have driveways. It is unusual to see cars parked along the curb unless one of the neighbors is having a party, and based on the intel I've gathered, none of my neighbors had parties this weekend. Streetlamps provide ample illumination to distinguish shapes in the dark.

PHYSICAL EVIDENCE: Cigarette butts discarded at the bottom of my driveway. Have secured evidence in plastic bags for possible DNA or fingerprint tests.

CONCLUSION: I need to speak to Star Being. If she's being followed too, then it may already be too late for us.

Technically, Nolan was grounded until midnight on Tuesday, but he managed to convince his mom to shorten his sentence by a few hours so he could attend the Bishop Union versus Kern Valley basketball game. She seemed relieved that he was showing interest in something other than aliens, and gave him twenty dollars for the concession stand. "Why don't you see if your sister wants to go with you?" she suggested, and Nolan smiled and said he would. But Lucy wasn't home. He had no idea where she was, and he wasn't going to look for her. As soon as Sandra left for work, Nolan put on his shoes, grabbed a jacket and keys, and drove to Gabriella's house where he was surprised to find Wyatt's car parked alongside the curb. He parked directly behind it and stared at the vanity license plate: STRGZR. Wyatt had returned—yesterday, today, Nolan didn't know when—but he'd come here first, to Celeste instead of Nolan.

The front door opened, and Wyatt stepped onto the front porch. Celeste stood in the doorway behind him. She didn't look happy at all. Her eyes were red like she'd been crying, and she had both arms wrapped around her middle, like she was trying to keep herself from falling apart. Wyatt said something to her, and she shook her head forcefully.

"I'm not ever going back," she said, her voice loud enough to be heard through the pickup's closed windows.

She stepped back into the house, then, and shut the door in Wyatt's face. Wyatt hesitated on the porch. He made as if to knock again, but then changed his mind and turned away from the door. In one hand he clutched a large manila envelope that appeared to be stuffed full with papers. The other hand he lifted to shade his eyes from the sun sinking low to the horizon. His expression did not change when he saw Nolan getting out of the pickup. He lowered his arm and walked down the driveway to meet him.

"What are you doing here?" Wyatt asked.

"I could ask you the same question." Nolan folded his arms across his chest, trying to look more confident than he actually felt.

Wyatt glanced over his shoulder at the closed front door. "I had to talk to Celeste. There were some loose ends that needed tying up."

"And?" His insides were trembling, anxious to get this over with and go comfort Celeste, wanting to hear what Wyatt had discovered, and yet afraid of the answers, too, afraid they would conflict with what he'd come to believe so absolutely over the past few days.

"Maybe we should go somewhere else to talk about this?" Wyatt kept sneaking glances at the house.

"This is fine." Nolan didn't like the idea of leaving Celeste alone and unguarded, not until he figured out exactly what Wyatt had been doing these past two months. "What took you so long?" he asked. "Where have you been?"

"It was all quite a bit more complicated than I expected," he said. "On account of her being a minor and a ward of the state. I had to pull a few strings, call in a few favors. I found most of what I needed in Pennsylvania, but ended up taking a few detours as well, just to double-check everything. Florida, New York. It's all right here, though." He tapped the manila folder. "Birth certificate, school records, family history, news articles, court records, foster care information."

"Wait, slow down." Nolan was having trouble following him. "Is she? Or isn't she?"

Wyatt smiled patiently and then shook his head. "It was a good theory, Nolan. An interesting one to say the least, but I'm afraid it didn't pan out. She's no more alien life-form than you or I."

"She's terrestrial," Nolan said, just to be clear.

"As human as they come."

A curtain inside Gabriella's house fluttered. A hand retreated.

"How can you be so sure?" Nolan asked.

Wyatt held out the envelope. "Look for yourself."

Nolan took it, but didn't remove any of the papers. "What did they promise you in exchange?" he asked. "Money? Power? What is she worth to them?"

"What are you talking about?" He seemed genuinely confused, but Nolan knew a liar when he saw one.

He'd never seen Wyatt wearing such nice clothes before. A collared shirt, khaki pants, leather shoes freshly shined, expensive cuff links winking in the sunlight.

"When did you start working for them?" Nolan asked. "Are they holding something over your head? Is that it? Threatening you?"

"I'm not working for anyone." He tugged on his shirt.

"Are they listening to us right now?" Nolan leaned closer, trying to catch a glimpse of the wire he was most certainly wearing.

"Who?" Wyatt took a step back. "Who is it you think I'm working for, exactly?"

"The government," Nolan said. "The Department of Defense. The FBI. The Air Force. Whoever's in charge of extraterrestrial operations."

"No one's in charge . . ." Wyatt shook his head. "That's not even a thing, you know that. The US government stopped investigating UFOs and shut down all their programs years ago. The only aliens our government cares about these days are the ones coming across the border from Mexico."

"That's what they want us to believe anyway. What they told you to tell me." The realizations came fast now, torpedoing from his mouth in a rapid-fire fury, "You're trying to convince me that she's not special, and then when I'm not paying attention, when my guard's down, you'll swoop in and take her to some underground bunker where she'll be locked in a windowless room and experimented on, dissected, torn to pieces."

"Nolan, please." Wyatt's voice was firm, steady.

"And then what? What happens after? They won't let you live knowing what you know. No matter what they promised, you know that once they're finished with her, they'll be finished with you." Then he had another, more terrifying thought. "Did you tell them about me?"

He knew the answer already. Even now a black car drifted past Gabriella's house, trying its best to look inconspicuous, turning right when it reached the stop sign, and disappearing.

"Nolan, come on!" Wyatt sounded exasperated. "You can't be serious about any of this. I mean, look, I get it. I was hoping things would turn out differently, too, but the proof is pretty clear." He reached for the envelope, taking it from Nolan's hand. "Let me show you."

He slid a thick stack of papers from inside and flipped through them, holding the important ones out for Nolan to see. "Here's her birth certificate. See right there . . ." He jabbed his finger at one of the filled-in boxes. "Born at 8:52 P.M. on Saturday, April 6, 1982, in Tallahassee Memorial Hospital, Tallahassee, Florida. I even managed to get ahold of her parents' birth certificates, too, and ancestry information tracing her lineage all the way back to the Spanish-American War just in case you tried to argue that the alien genes came from her great-great-grandfather or something."

He pulled out another page, some blurry, photocopied newsprint. "This is the article about the car accident. She wasn't very old, four, still in a car seat. That's what saved her. The police weren't sure what happened. Single car accident. No witnesses. They were coming back late from someplace. It was dark, but the roads were dry. Her father was driving. Her mother was in the front passenger seat. He lost control somehow, went off the road into a tree. Her mother died instantly at the scene. Her father sustained critical injuries and died on the way to the hospital."

The letters on the page began to wobble and blur, running in inky black drips off the bottoms of the pages. Wyatt's voice, too, was becoming garbled and distant. Nolan struggled to pay attention.

"Not a scratch on her . . . no living relatives . . . orphaned . . . in and out of foster homes . . . runaway . . . pretty clear to me . . . all the evidence indicates she originated from planet Earth."

Nolan shook his head. "I don't . . . I can't believe it. I know her. I know everything about her." He pushed the documents away. "These are fakes. Good ones, great ones, even, I'll give you that, but still fakes."

"They're not fakes, I assure you. I can show you my itinerary, my correspondence, my receipts. You can see exactly where I was and what I was doing and who I was with. You can talk to my contacts, if that's what you need." Wyatt slid the papers back into the envelope. "Or maybe you should just ask Celeste."

Nolan glanced at the house. He couldn't tell for sure, but thought he saw her shadow in the front window.

"She confirmed that everything I found out about her was, in fact, the truth," Wyatt continued. "She certainly wasn't happy I'd been snooping around in her past, but she didn't deny anything. Quite the opposite, actually."

"You're lying."

"I know it's not what you want to hear." He reached to place a hand on Nolan's arm. "Trust me. I was as disappointed as you are, but there will be other opportunities, more strange happenings to investigate. We were wrong about Celeste this time, but that doesn't mean we're wrong about everything else."

It occurred to Nolan that Wyatt might have been in league with the government for a very long time before this, might even be using the Encounters group as a cover. Perhaps he was not a forward-thinking man investigating paranormal events at all, but rather a government agent sent to spy and spread disinformation, to destroy the group's efforts from the inside. He thought of all the times Wyatt had told a group member to wait before going public with something or to hold back information completely, how he was always the one talking to the press, never anyone else from the group. And what about all those times he disappeared? Gone for weeks, making no contact with anyone, and returning with only a flimsy explanation of needing to research "a top-secret project." What was he really doing? Reporting to his superiors, feeding them information, betraying his so-called friends.

"Gabriella mentioned you got into some trouble while I was gone," Wyatt said. "Is that what has you all stirred up?"

Nolan shrugged out from under Wyatt's heavy hand. "I think you should go."

Wyatt massaged his palm against his forehead. "You're in pretty deep with this stuff, aren't you?"

It was a stupid question. Nolan didn't respond.

"So . . . what?" Wyatt asked. "Let's think this through. Say you're right. Say I'm lying. I'm working for the government or whoever and she really is some kind of extraterrestrial being. Then what? Why is she here? Why was she sent to you? Are you supposed to help her get back home or something?"

"I don't know why she's here," Nolan said. "Even if I did, I wouldn't tell you."

Wyatt sighed. "Okay, look. Let's back up a little. Has she said or done *anything* that would qualify as proof of her extraterrestrial nature? Telepathy? Levitation? Telekinesis? Astral projection, even?"

Nolan thought about the kiss, the electricity that sparked between them when they touched. He thought about the encounter he'd had in the mountains, the time lost, about how every night since, she'd visited his dreams. Proof enough for him, but Wyatt would demand more, was always demanding more and more, and now Nolan knew why. To distract, to divide, to plant the seed of doubt so nothing meaningful was ever accomplished.

"Nolan," Wyatt said, trying to sound patient. "She looks nothing like what we've always assumed extraterrestrials would look like."

"You know as well as I do that the world's not ready for this shift in paradigm," Nolan countered, unable to control this need to defend himself and his beliefs, however strange and impossible. "If the Visitors were walking around in Their true form, imagine the witch hunts, the experiments. We'd destroy Them before They even had a chance to tell us why They're here. It's safer for Them to look like us and blend in."

He pressed his lips together, silently berating himself for doing it again, letting Wyatt draw him in, revealing too much. This was why Celeste was in danger in the first place. Because of his big flapping mouth.

"You do realize how ridiculous you're acting right now, don't you? How crazy you sound?" As Wyatt spoke, he became increasingly agitated. "Is it drugs? Is that what's going on? Some kids offer you some shit at school and you try it and just start freaking the fuck out on me?"

Nolan clenched his jaw tight enough to make his molars ache.

"The worst thing you could do right now is to go around claiming these theories are true, when we have significant proof of the exact opposite." He rattled the envelope. "I have a reputation to protect, you know," Wyatt added. "And what about everyone else in the Encounters group? This affects them too."

When Nolan still didn't say anything, Wyatt reached into his pocket and pulled out his wallet. "Maybe you should talk to someone. I know this drug and alcohol addiction counselor. She's great."

He tried to pass along her business card, but Nolan refused to take it.

Wyatt held it out for another beat and then tucked it back into his wallet. "You're really starting to scare me here, Nolan. I mean, I'm starting to think you might be dealing with something more serious than a simple case of mistaken identity. Let me drive you home. We can talk about this some more, talk to your parents."

Nolan pretended Wyatt wasn't there. His voice a buzzing bumblebee. His words bits of dust drifting. They stood in silence for a few minutes. A car pulled into the neighbor's driveway. Doors slammed. A few seconds later a plane passed overhead, engines thrumming, a white contrail feathering the deepening twilight sky.

"You can't stay here forever, Nolan," Wyatt said.

The sun was almost gone. Venus was rising.

Nolan said, "I'm not leaving until you do."

Wyatt sighed and shook his head. "Well, take these at least. Look through them again." He shoved the envelope against Nolan's chest, forcing him to take it.

Nolan didn't relax until Wyatt drove out of sight around a corner. He waited a few minutes to see if he would double back, but the road stayed empty. Holding the envelope at arm's length, like it was contaminated, Nolan carried this so-called evidence to the trash can next to the garage and tossed the whole package inside, slamming the lid shut and clapping his hands clean. Then he went to get Celeste.

W e should just go," Celeste said. "Just keep driving."

The highway unfurled a dark ribbon in front of them, a dark ribbon behind. Light streaked past their windows, setting off small explosions in the corner of Nolan's eyes. She sat with her feet propped up on the dashboard, the right one wiggling relentlessly. She chewed her fingernails and stared at the road, the road that could take them anywhere.

"For how long?" Nolan asked.

"Until it ends."

"And then what?"

"We take another road," she said. "And another one after that until we reach the ocean."

"And then what?"

She shrugged one shoulder. "Whatever we want."

They passed the Burger Barn, then a bar and, after that, a Mexican restaurant.

Celeste ran her hand through Nolan's hair. "That's the whole point. We don't have to decide until we get there, wherever *there* is. No plans, no obligations, no one telling us what we can or can't do, we just go. We just do. We just live."

He liked the simplicity of it, wished life could be so easy. But it wasn't. Life was complicated, increasingly so because of her.

After Wyatt had left Gabriella's house, Nolan had gone up to the front door. He knocked, and when no one answered, he knocked again. "Celeste? I know you're in there. It's me. It's Nolan."

A few seconds passed and then the door cracked open. She peered out at him. "Nolan? Oh thank God. I thought it was . . . come in."

She stepped back and let him inside, then closed and locked the door. He followed her to the guest room where all her things were laid out on the bed, the backpack lying empty on the pillow.

"What's going on?" he asked.

"I can't stay here anymore."

"Did something happen?" he asked, even though he already knew.

Instead of answering, she began to shove her belongings into her backpack, struggling to fit everything. Nolan touched her hand, and she froze. Tears trembled on her lashes. There was so much he wanted to say to her, but he didn't trust this house anymore. It had probably been bugged from the beginning. He tried to offer her reassurance with his gaze, hoped she recognized his comprehension of the situation, the silent promises he was making. Her expression softened when she looked at him. She relaxed a little under his touch.

"Let's go to the basketball game," he said.

"What?" She started to withdraw her hand, but he held it tight, pleading with her to trust him.

"It'll be good to get out of the house."

She looked confused, but nodded, abandoning her frantic packing and allowing herself to be led by the hand out the front door.

He drove toward the school, forming a plan as he did. For the first time since the party at Ship Rock, his head felt clear again. He felt focused, fully alive and alert, tuned to every slight movement and subtle sound. It was like that when he

was with Celeste. She enabled him to think more clearly, to
see better, sense more, understand things he'd never before
understood. Nothing made sense when they were apart, but
together, everything fell into perfect place. She was the most
important thing that had ever happened to him, and he wanted
to shrink her down, wrap his hands around all of her, cup her
in his palms and protect her from all the sharp and painful
parts of life on Earth, allow her only the beautiful and lovely.
But first he had to figure out what to do about Wyatt. And the
government agents that could ruin everything.

"I'm sorry, by the way," Celeste said. "For ditching you the
way I did at the party. That was a really awful thing for me to
do, I know, and I'm sorry. I just freaked out. It's hard to explain, but I—"

"You don't have to explain anything to me," he interrupted.
"Ever."

"Patrick said you were arrested."

He glanced at her, the side of her face speckled with orange
and red lights. "When did you talk to Patrick?"

"He comes into the restaurant a lot."

Nolan returned his attention to the road. "The cop let me
go with a warning."

"Good," she said. "That's good."

He turned into the parking lot of the school, and Celeste
sighed. When she spoke, her voice was quiet, her words slow
and pensive. "I meant what I said about leaving."

He parked and turned off the engine, then reached across
the seat and took her hand in his. Dim light from a nearby
streetlamp enfolded them both in a pale orange haze.

"I thought I could fit in here," she continued. "I wanted to.
I tried, but it's not working. Not anymore. What happened at

the party, the police showing up like that, it scared me, Nolan. It really scared me. I can't go back there. I just can't."

He didn't ask her where "there" was. It didn't matter. "There" was apart from him, and that was all he cared about.

"I can keep you safe," he said.

"I don't know if you can."

"Let me try."

"You don't understand." Her voice dropped even lower, her eyes darting around the parking lot where cars were circling, finding spots, people emerging dressed in blue and silver, walking toward the gymnasium. "Someone's been calling Gabriella's and hanging up. It's happened a couple times in the past few days. The phone rings and when Gabriella answers it, no one's there. It's really starting to freak her out. She asked if I'd given anyone at work the number to the house, but I haven't. I don't know who it is."

"Maybe someone just keeps dialing the wrong number," he said, not wanting to scare her more by telling her he'd been getting the same calls. He needed her to stay calm until he could make a decision about what to do next.

"It's more than that. I don't know. Maybe I'm being paranoid." She flinched a little when she said this, but then continued, "Sometimes at work, I see the same car parked in front of the store for my whole shift. There's someone inside, but they never get out or go anywhere. And Gabriella's seen it too, parked outside of the house. Like someone's following me."

"Did you get a license plate number?"

"Of course we did. Gabriella called in a favor from a friend who works at the DMV. All they could tell us was that it was a government vehicle of some kind. The county or cops or something like that. And today this guy showed up on my doorstep." She shivered and drew closer to Nolan, sliding across the seat until their bodies were pressed together. "He knew things about me, Nolan. Things he shouldn't have known."

His jaw tensed. "Like what?"

"It doesn't matter. What matters is that he could make things difficult for me."

He didn't know what to say. It was his own damn fault that they were in this mess, his fault Celeste was scared and wanting to run.

She interpreted his silence as something else, though, pulling away from him again, saying, "I'm sorry, this isn't your problem. I shouldn't have even asked you. You have a life here, school, family, people who love you. Of course you can't just leave. I'm sorry. Forget I said anything."

She laughed awkwardly and started to open the pickup door. Nolan grabbed her hand. She looked over her shoulder at him.

"I love *you*," he said.

Her eyes widened a little in surprise. He saw for the first time how the flecks of gold were arranged like planets, orbiting through copper space around the dark sun of her pupil.

"Wherever *you* are," he said, "that's where I want to be, too."

She leaned over and kissed him, and even though she didn't say the words out loud, he knew she loved him too.

When she pulled away, she was smiling again. She said, "We can talk about this later. Let's just go and enjoy the game, okay?" She got out. "You coming?"

"Yeah, one second." He leaned over and rummaged in the narrow space behind the front seat. He'd tossed his backpack there after school the way he always did. As he sifted through the contents, his books and binders, pencils, a ruler, he felt a dread creeping up through his chest into his throat. It couldn't be. He sifted faster, finally turning his backpack over and dumping everything onto the floor of his pickup. It wasn't possible. He'd had it this morning.

"Nolan?" Celeste peered through the window at him. "Are you okay?"

He opened the glove box, scattering papers and napkins and empty CD cases everywhere. Then he leaned over and checked under both seats, finding only an empty French fry container, two pennies, and a dime. He sat up again, closing his eyes against a rising wave of nausea.

"Did you lose something?" Her voice was muffled by the window and the sound of his heart beating in terror.

Everyone knew that the fastest way to get picked up, bound, blindfolded, and tossed into the trunk of a black Cadillac with tinted windows and no license plate was to tell the world your secrets, and his casebook was full of those. People with lesser knowledge and lesser proof had disappeared for lesser mistakes than this one.

He groaned again and squeezed the steering wheel. *Calm down, calm down. It's probably at home on your desk underneath that pile of overdue homework assignments you can't seem to finish. Or it's in your locker.*

Only, he remembered having it with him during last period, remembered writing down his plans to bring Celeste to his house and finally introduce her to his mother as proof that he wasn't crazy and aliens did exist, were living among us on Earth. He remembered putting it in his backpack when the bell rang and then putting his backpack right here, behind the front seat.

He checked again. If his casebook had been in his backpack

earlier this afternoon—and he was certain it had been—it was gone now.

The buzzer rang, signaling the start of halftime. Nolan jumped a little in his seat, and Celeste squeezed his hand, giving him that same look she'd been giving since they'd walked into the gymnasium. She wanted to know what was wrong, what he'd been searching for so frantically, what he hadn't found. He couldn't tell her. Not until he checked his locker and scoured his bedroom. Not until he confronted Wyatt, who knew about the casebook, who knew Nolan kept it close at hand, and who could have easily driven back to Gabriella's, broken into the pickup, and taken it, all while Nolan was inside the house with Celeste.

He told her it was nothing, a missing assignment. He didn't want her to panic. He'd used a code name whenever he wrote about her, but there were enough details in there, enough clues that her identity would be obvious to anyone who had two eyes and half a brain. If she knew such a sensitive document was floating around, if she knew what this mistake might cost them . . . he didn't want to think about the consequences.

The first half of the game lasted almost forty-five minutes, though it felt like a thousand more than that to Nolan. Bishop Union was up by ten points, a small enough spread to make the crowd twitch nervously. People were standing, stretching, wandering down to the concession stand set up across the hallway from the gym. Every time someone bumped against Nolan accidentally, he flinched. His head ached, and not just his head, his whole body too. Every muscle a stiff knot. His breathing was shallow, panicked, he couldn't get enough air, there was never enough air.

A girl holding a clarinet brushed against his knees. He leaped to his feet, startling her.

"Sorry," she mumbled and kept walking.

"I'm going to the concession stand," he said to Celeste before she could ask him for the millionth time what was wrong. "Want anything?"

She hesitated, then said, "Skittles. If they have any."

He left her and scrambled down the bleachers to the exit. As he went, kids he recognized, but had never been friends with, reached out and slapped his back or offered high fives. Since his arrest, this had been going on. Kids at school treating him differently, high-fiving him in the halls, saving seats for him at lunch, inviting him to parties he had no interest in attending. He'd gone from loser to legend in the space of twenty-four hours, and for something so stupid, a crime he didn't even commit. He ignored them, walking with his head down, scowling at scuff marks streaked across the linoleum floor.

The line for the concession stand stretched halfway down the hall. Nolan joined at the end and stood waiting. The line crept forward, stopped again. People were staring at him. Not in the same way as earlier, with admiration and a touch of envy, not even the same way as before his arrest, with disdain and disinterest. This was different, something was happening. He felt the shift in the air, heard paper rustling, the sound of a many-winged monster taking flight.

A girl, the same one who had bumped into him with the clarinet, pointed in his direction, and then leaned in to whisper to her friends. They clutched something in their hands. Papers. A book, maybe. Not a book. Individual sheets that they passed around to one another. The girl grabbed a boy in passing and shoved a stack of pages into his hands. He stopped to read them, and then he laughed, and then he turned, found Nolan standing in line, and laughed again. He ran off with the papers, flagging down another boy farther down the hallway.

The pages were passed along like this, from hand to hand, and as they spread, Nolan heard his name repeated, a murmur beneath the loud chatter coming from the gymnasium, the flutter and snap of so many crisp edges. It seemed everyone was holding a small stack of papers now. Everyone was reading.

Nolan gave up his place in line. He approached the girl with the clarinet and snatched the papers from her hands.

"Hey!" But she didn't try to grab them back.

He turned his back to her, and everyone else who was staring, turned instead to face one of the many lockers stretching the length of the hallway. Before he even started reading, he knew. He recognized his handwriting. His stomach went cold and then hot again. The whispers turned to a roar. Paper whispers, human whispers, susurrations, the sound of his own panic—all of it getting louder and louder until his head felt like it was going to explode. He swallowed hard. Swallowed again.

He flipped through each page, not really reading, not needing to, but growing sick even so at the sight of too many familiar words. Words not meant for public consumption. Words he'd written thinking no one but him would ever read. Things that had no place in a serious scientific endeavor, but that he'd written down anyway because they had been burning hot in his brain and the only way to be rid of them was to put them on paper. Things he should have kept to himself.

Where is she from? Andromeda?

Is she a shape-shifter? Or is it a space suit made to look like a human body? Perhaps she is manipulating our perception of her through telepathy.

Sexual intercourse—is this even a possibility? Does she even have sex organs? The right kind of genitalia? Would our two species find pleasure together? Would it be like slipping into another dimension? I want to find out; I am too afraid to ask.

The crowd in the hallway was growing, getting louder as they combed through his private thoughts. Their minds were too simple, closed to the possibility that any of this could be real. Even if he tried to explain it, they would never understand, never see beyond their own dull, snub noses. He knew what they were thinking, what they would say later: a boy lost in his weird obsessions, caught up in his own fucked-up imagination, couldn't tell real from pretend. Crazy, they would say, the straitjacket kind of crazy. He wasn't.

He *wasn't.*

The last paper in his stack was an entry he'd written shortly after he met Celeste. Down to the very minutest of details, he had described her eyes, her hair, her clothes, the Saturn patch on her backpack. He'd transcribed as much of their conversation as he had remembered and, at the end, theorized that she was no ordinary girl, but an extraterrestrial, his Star Being, arrived here from outer space with a message for him and all of planet Earth. He never used her name, but it didn't matter. He had drawn her on that white page in black letters as clearly as if he had taken her picture. He crumpled the paper into a ball, squeezing it in his fist as tight as he could, not tight enough to make it disappear. Then he turned and began snatching pages from people standing nearby.

He didn't bother to read any of it; he remembered very well

what he'd written. Each entry a description of the fantastic things he'd witnessed, the Buttermilk Rock Lights, the craft that had touched down at the observatory, the stars dancing into a clear triangle formation before he blacked out high up in the Sierras. He grabbed handfuls of pages, grabbed and grabbed, but they only seemed to duplicate, another stack always just out of reach, spreading like an infection. His arms were full and still there were more. He couldn't stop it; there were too many copies and too many people, and now those people were making their way back into the gymnasium, climbing into the bleachers, stretching white from one side to the other.

Nolan followed the paper trail into the gymnasium, stopped just inside the doorway, and scanned the bleachers until he found his seat. Celeste was still there, and for a moment, he thought he could fix this. He would run to her, push people out of the way if he had to, take her by the hand and drag her away from all of this. They would get in his pickup and drive. It didn't matter where. As far from here as they could get and then a thousand light-years more. They would go and just live and everything would be okay.

Someone shoved a stack of papers into her hands. She looked around at everyone reading, at the people turning to stare at her now, too. She lowered her head over the paper, and Nolan's whole body turned to stone and all he could do was watch as she read first one entry, then another and another, as her eyes grew wider, as her mouth fell open and her cheeks flushed violet. She looked up, frantic, scanning the crowded bleachers.

She was looking for him, he knew, and when her eyes found him there in the doorway, they flashed lightning hot and he could see everything she was thinking, her emotions moving like thunderclouds over her face: confusion, horror, betrayal.

His thoughts and explanations, his intentions, his connection to her—all of it unspooling too quickly for him to gather it up again. He opened his mouth, but no words came out.

Slowly, she rose to her feet, crushing the pages against her chest like they were precious. The people sitting closest to her went silent, their eyes following her gaze and finding Nolan, settling on him like so many heavy stones around his neck. She raised her eyebrows, asking Nolan a silent question for which he had no answers. Then she opened her arms. The papers spilled and tumbled, drifting in white heaps, slipping through the cracks in the bleachers, disappearing. Then she turned and stumbled down the bleacher steps—shoving her way through the gawking freshmen and slack-jawed sophomores, the juniors who shook their heads, the seniors who thought they had seen everything, the parents who had no idea what was going on—shoving toward the opposite side of the gymnasium as him, toward a door that opened on to the parking lot. Only then did Nolan find his voice.

"Celeste, wait!"

Her name echoed through the gym, but she didn't stop, or even slow down. She slammed through the door and stepped into the night. Nolan stood rooted, watching her go, wanting to move, to chase after her, but finding even the smallest step impossible, his breath hitching, his vision ringed and spotted with shadows. The buzzer sounded. The two teams sprang onto the court for the second time that night. Basketballs pounded the wood floor. The crowd began to clap and cheer. Upbeat pop music crackled through the loudspeaker. Above it all came a familiar laugh, like a slap. Nolan turned to look behind him.

Patrick and his clones were clumped together in front of a vending machine opposite the gymnasium door. Adam leaned against a locker, one foot resting on the metal door, his arms crossed over his chest. He smirked at Nolan and shook his head. Grant leaned on the locker next to Adam. His teeth tore into a stick of red licorice. But it was Patrick who had Nolan's full attention. Patrick who stood in the middle of the hallway with a grin on his face so wide Nolan could count all his perfect white, sparkling teeth. He lifted a black composition book over his head and waved it back and forth, saying, "Hey, Spaceman! Not so badass now, are you?"

Nolan rushed him, grabbing for the casebook, but Patrick pulled it out of reach.

"How did you get that?" Nolan demanded. "Where?"

"Found it lying around." Patrick thumbed through the pages, laughing and shaking his head. "You've got some really strange ideas about things, don't you, buddy? Do you really still believe in all of this shit? I mean, I knew you were a little eccentric, but this . . ." He snapped the casebook closed again. "This is batshit certified."

Nolan clenched his fists at his side. He was struck with a sudden memory of the summer before eighth grade. Patrick's twelfth birthday party. He'd invited a bunch of his friends, including Nolan, to spend the night at his family's lake house. Despite the fact that Nolan had been too scared to swim with the other boys, he remembered it being a good weekend until Patrick pushed him off the dock into the glassy, black water.

When the other boys had asked Nolan why he wasn't swimming, he told them the stories his uncle used to tell about secret alien bases built underwater and flying saucers rising from the murky depths. Instead of making fun of him, the boys took it upon themselves to turn Nolan's fear into a game. They pretended they were on a different planet and took turns diving as

deep as they could into the middle of the lake, returning with
ever more elaborate reports about their findings. Nolan was
their team leader, coordinating the dives as he stood on the
dock taking notes on an imaginary computer and reporting
back to their ship's commander. Patrick thought the game was
stupid and juvenile and tried to get them to do something else.
He brought out his sailboat, and some water guns, and when
that didn't work, he got into his father's liquor cabinet and offered up shots of expensive scotch, but no one paid him any
attention. They kept swimming, kept diving, kept bringing up
new information for Nolan to interpret.

Nolan didn't see Patrick come up behind him. One second
he was standing at the edge of the dock, dragging a branch
through the water to make ripples, shouting at one of the boys
to take a reading of the vibrations, and the next he felt a shove
against his back and then he was tumbling headfirst into the
black water, sinking deeper into the darkness, choking on
something bright and cold. He might have drowned if someone hadn't jumped in after him and pulled him ashore. Nolan
remembered the horrified way the other boys had stared at him
while he crouched in the sand crying and coughing, trying to
catch his breath. He remembered how Patrick crouched beside
him, patting his back, smiling, saying, "You okay, buddy? You
almost died, you know. Lucky for you I was close by." Water
dripped from his hair. His clothes dripped too.

No one else saw it happen. They thought Nolan was just
clumsy and a bad swimmer. And when Patrick came in after
Nolan and pulled him to safety, everyone called him a hero,
so Nolan didn't dispute it because maybe it was an accident, a
mistimed nudge, nothing more sinister than a foot or an elbow
in the wrong place at the wrong time. They were boys, things

like this happened all the time. Up until this very moment, Nolan had gone on believing the push he'd felt was accidental. Patrick would have never done something like that intentionally. Yet here he was, with the very same smile on his face as he had that day, the smile of a kid with a secret. The kind of smile a winner bestows upon a loser not because he's kind, but because he likes the way an ant feels crushed under his thumb.

Nolan dropped the papers he was holding. They exploded in a flurry around his feet. He slammed Patrick against the lockers, pressing his forearm against his throat, forcing his chin and his head up. Patrick choked on a breath. His eyes were wide and wild with panic, but his fingers still gripped the casebook, refusing to let go.

"Lighten up, Nolan." Patrick somehow managing to push the words through his clenched teeth. "We're just kidding around a little. It's a joke. You know what a joke is, right? Come on, buddy."

Nolan hated when Patrick called him that. He pressed his arm harder against Patrick's windpipe, forcing him silent. His face turned bright red, and he started to cough. Spit flew from his mouth and gathered in white clumps on his lips.

A crowd of high schoolers gathered, circling like so many vultures, hissing them on. Most of the adults had returned to the gymnasium to watch the game. The noise from inside drowning out the scuffles in the hallway. Every other adult who passed hurried on without stopping, not wanting to get involved.

Suddenly Nolan was wrenched backward. He fought against Grant and Adam, but their fingers clamped around his arms, two against one, and they were stronger, stretching him out like a rubber band until it felt like his shoulders were going to pop.

Patrick brushed off the front of his shirt, taking his time. He smiled at Nolan, a closed-lipped impatient smile, and said, "When this is over, don't forget, you started it." Then he hammered his fist into Nolan's chest. The force, and a crack of pain in his sternum, bent Nolan double. No air. No sound, no sight. He floated in a void, hearing only a distant buzzing sound. The sound grew louder, then a rush of exploding colors and noise and hurt.

The black dots in his vision cleared just as Patrick lined up a punch to the face. Nolan ducked at the last second, but Patrick's fist kept going and landed hard on Grant's jaw. Grant cried out, releasing Nolan. He cradled his head and laid down a string of curses.

"Shit!" Adam let go of Nolan's other arm to check on his friend. "You all right?"

Patrick shook his hand in the air, clenching and unclenching his fingers. All eyes were on Grant now, who was bent over, still holding his face and blubbering. Strings of thick, red drool dangled from his lips. The crowd shifted their feet, murmuring, glancing over their shoulders to see if any adults would step in now that punches had been thrown, blood spilled. None did.

In this quiet pause, Nolan gathered his breath. His ears rang. He tasted blood in his mouth, his own, very human blood. The pain in his chest flared hotter the longer he stood doing nothing. Patrick still gripped the casebook in one hand. The black and white blobs on the cover melted to a gray blur as Nolan replayed the horrified look on Celeste's face as she read the photocopied pages, as she turned her back on him and fled.

She was gone because of Patrick. Her true identity exposed because of Patrick. Ruined because of Patrick. All of this because of Patrick.

In a single, swift motion, Nolan raised his fist and hammered it straight into Patrick's nose. The bones beneath splintered. Patrick grunted and fell back against the lockers. He raised his hands to his face, dropping the casebook on the floor. Nolan swooped and grabbed it. Blood dripped through Patrick's fingers, splashing bright red onto the beige linoleum.

"Jesus fuck." His voice muffled and strange. "What the hell is wrong with you?"

Nolan slammed his fist into the locker near Patrick's head, making him cower.

"You piece of shit!" Nolan didn't recognize his voice, the violence of it. "Do you know what you've done? Do you even fucking realize the magnitude of this situation? They're going to make her disappear now. They're going to make it seem like she never existed. Is this what you wanted? Is it?"

He couldn't get his rage under control. Some small whisper inside him knew it was useless, that he should be spending this energy tracking down Celeste instead, figuring out a way to get her out of Bishop alive, but that whisper was fast drowned out by a roaring sound coursing through his blood into his ears, taking over his brain. He was anger, he was vengeance, he was supernova. He slammed his fist into the locker a second time, hard enough to make a shallow dent. Patrick didn't cower this time. He lowered his arms to his side and stood up straight, squaring his shoulders, lifting his chin high. His eyes were already bruised a deep purple. Blood poured from his nose, but he didn't wipe it away. He grinned, displaying sharp, glistening red teeth. Then he spat in Nolan's face.

Nolan stepped back, wiping at his cheeks and lips. It was all the space Patrick needed. He lunged and tackled Nolan to the floor. They rolled, clawing and gnashing, fists flailing. Blood and spit and sweat smearing everywhere. Then Patrick was on top of him, pummeling with both fists. Nolan raised his arms, but punches got through and each blow was fresh pain, and he began to drift and lose a part of himself, and in the back of his mind he started to think that maybe he deserved this.

Then Patrick was wrenched up and back, and more hands were reaching, grabbing, lifting Nolan to his feet too. A swirl of bodies, of voices. The PE teacher, who was also the track and field coach, shoved his face into Patrick's, shouting. Patrick hung his head, pinching his nostrils shut, but still the blood dripped. Miss Simpson, the school librarian, was there too, appearing out of thin air and storming, breaking up the crowd of onlookers, nudging students in opposite directions, telling everyone the show was over, get back inside the gymnasium or go home, but don't just stand here staring or they'd all find themselves in detention tomorrow.

Nolan sagged back against whoever was holding him up. It hurt to breathe. It hurt to blink. Every part of him cracked open with pain. He recognized his chemistry teacher's voice loud in his ear, asking, "What happened, Nolan? What were you thinking?"

He had no answers, only aching bones and ringing ears, bruises everywhere and empty hands. When Patrick tackled him, he lost hold of his casebook. He scanned the floor for it now, but it wasn't there. Then he saw Lucy hovering at the edge of the dispersing crowd. He hadn't even known she was at the game until this moment. Her back and shoulders were rigid. The expression on her face unreadable. Her fingers pinched around the spine of his casebook and she held it slightly out in front of her so he would see. When they made eye contact, she slipped the casebook into her backpack, then turned and disappeared in a crush of students fleeing Miss Simpson's wrath.

The crowd gone, Miss Simpson snapped her attention to Patrick and Nolan. The muscles in her neck were clenched tight. Red spots glowed high on her puffy cheeks. She could muster no words of reprimand, simply jabbed her finger toward the front of the school and both boys shuffled alongside their escorts to the principal's office.

14

The sun slipped behind the Sierra Nevada mountains, turning the sky the color of a new bruise. Lucy turned into the Paiute Palace Casino's parking lot a few minutes before nine o'clock. Traffic had been slow leaving Los Angeles and didn't clear until she was through Santa Clarita, but the rest of the way she practically had the road to herself. She was glad for the drive. It gave her a chance to walk back through her conversations with Patrick and her father, digest the information she'd received in smaller, more manageable bites. By the time she reached Bishop, she was breathing normally again, no longer on the verge of crying. She could handle this. She'd made more poor choices in the past when she hadn't known any better, but she had no excuses now. She had to make right what she could, while there was still time.

She entered the casino, pausing a moment to let her eyes adjust to the dimly lit room and the frenzied flash of slot machines. Music pumped through speakers in the ceiling. The whole place smelled of carpet cleaner and old cigarettes. A man in a cowboy hat sat alone at a slot machine near the door, sipping a beer and smoking a cigar, his shoulders hunched forward, his hand trembling as he played. When Lucy walked in, his head turned and his eyes moved up and down her body, inspecting her. He winked. She ignored him and scanned the rest of the single-floor casino until she spotted her mother behind the bar, making change for a customer.

Sandra stopped fussing with the cash register when Lucy walked over. "Who let you in here?"

"I came to apologize."

Sandra slapped a few bills and loose change into the customer's hand, then walked to the opposite end of the bar, ignoring Lucy completely. Lucy slid onto a stool and propped her elbows up on the counter. After a few minutes, Sandra returned, swiping a rag in front of Lucy and setting down a cardboard coaster with warped corners. "Are you going to order something or make me call security on you for loitering?"

Lucy ordered a Coke. Sandra took her time bringing it and then she turned her attention to another customer who had come in and then another one after that, and Lucy was half-finished with her soda before Sandra came over to check on her again.

"What I did," Lucy said. "The helicopter prank. I know it was wrong. And I know I made it worse by not telling you sooner what was really in those photographs."

Sandra stiffened. Her lips pressed razor thin.

"I didn't think he would take it seriously," Lucy continued. "I didn't think *anyone* would take it seriously."

"No, you didn't think, did you?" Sandra twisted the rag in her hand. "Do you know how much time we wasted with those photographs? How much energy and . . . and hope?" Her voice cracked, but she kept going. "And then to find out it was just a hoax? That we'd all been duped?"

"I know." Lucy hung her head. "And I am sorry. I really am. It was a shitty prank to play on him. We shouldn't have done it. And I'm sorry you got wrapped up in it too. I know how this is going to reflect on your UFO group. But maybe that's not a bad thing, you know?"

Sandra's eyebrows shot up.

"I mean, maybe now with the UFO stuff out of the way," Lucy tried to explain, "maybe now you can start considering more realistic possibilities, and we can make some actual progress in finding Nolan."

A man sitting at the opposite end of the bar looked at them with open curiosity. He leaned in their direction, making no effort to hide his eavesdropping.

Sandra pursed her lips and then shook her head. "Let's talk outside." She called back to someone in the kitchen. "Luis? I'm taking my break."

A man grumbled in response, then Sandra removed her apron and came out from behind the bar. She gestured for Lucy to follow her out the back door of the casino into the parking lot. They walked first to Sandra's car where Kepler waited in the backseat. He leaped to his feet, happy to see them, his whole body wagging. Sandra clipped a leash to his collar, and then the three of them walked toward a picnic table chained to a fence that separated the casino parking lot from an expanse of empty land.

The sun was completely gone now, disappeared behind the mountains, and the pale gray twilight was fast collapsing midnight blue to black. A few streetlamps scattered throughout the parking lot flickered on. Kepler sniffed at tufts of grass along the fence. Sandra walked with him a few feet until he lifted his leg to pee on a post, then she pulled him back to the picnic table and sat down. Lucy sat beside her. Kepler positioned his body to lean against both of their legs.

Sandra scratched his ears. "Kepler was Wyatt's idea. He said a dog was a better alarm system than anything else on the market. They're loyal and never run out of batteries."

"He's a good dog," Lucy said, stumbling over the stilted way her voice sounded. Now that they were alone, her words failed her.

A car started up and drove out of the parking lot, the headlights sweeping across them for one bright second before retreating to darkness.

Sandra tilted her head back, her gaze swinging across the dome of the sky. "It's strange, isn't it? How we say 'the stars appear'? As if they go somewhere during the day only to return to us at night." She was quiet a moment, then added, "But they don't go anywhere at all, do they? We're the wandering ones."

Every second, twilight vanished, and the stars grew ever brighter. The moon bared half its face tonight, peeking from the horizon like a bashful child. Lucy scanned the darkening expanse, but nothing above them moved. It was a still life, a painted glass dome, and they were trapped beneath.

"You used to believe, you know," Sandra said. "You and Nolan would play out in the yard for hours searching the skies for UFOs. Once you even came running inside saying you'd seen one, that the little green men had come down from a silver ship and told you secrets. You told me I didn't have to worry, that they weren't going to hurt us. They were our friends."

Lucy remembered. How much easier it had been to see the

universe the same as her brother then, how wild to believe in worlds beyond Earth, imagining far-off civilizations casting messages into a sea of stars, then imagining those messages traveling here through all those many, many miles, somehow finding their way to her and Nolan. It made her feel important, believing in something like that, even if it wasn't true.

"I was a kid," Lucy said quietly, keeping her eyes on the multiplying stars. "Kids believe in a lot of things that aren't real. They make stuff up, too."

Sandra ran her hand down Kepler's neck, digging her fingers deep into his fur. "Do you remember that dead patch we had in the front yard? That circle where we couldn't get any grass to grow no matter how hard we tried?"

Lucy nodded.

"I thought your brother had done it on purpose," Sandra said. "I thought he came out with a blowtorch one night and set the grass on fire. Or used bleach or something. He swore up and down it wasn't him, but I didn't believe it. I even called in one of those lawn experts? Those landscaping guys? Paid him way too much money to come out and tell me he had no idea why the grass wasn't growing back." She laughed and then said, "Nolan claimed it was a UFO landing site."

"Someone probably just parked a car there for too long and it leaked oil into the ground," Lucy suggested.

Sandra was quiet for a long time, then she said, "This isn't all there is, Lucy. This physical realm, this material world . . . There's more. So much more."

"You sound sure about that."

"I am," she said. "They showed me."

"They."

"Yes, the Ones who took Nolan."

"The aliens."

"Don't say it like that."

"Like what?"

"Like you're talking to a child." At the sharpness in Sandra's voice, Kepler tilted his head, moving his ears forward and then flattening them back. "Like you think I've gone off the deep end."

"But seriously? I mean, think about what you're saying—"

"I have thought about it," Sandra interrupted. "I've thought about it at great length. I've gone over it so many times, trying to talk myself out of it, trying to come up with another explanation, but I've seen things, Lucy. I've experienced things that defy rationality. And some people might think I'm crazy or making it up or suffering some grief delusions, but I can assure you, what I've seen, what I experienced, it was real as you and me sitting right here, right now talking under the stars. It was as real as this . . ." She pressed her fingertips against the side of Lucy's face. "You feel that, don't you? If someone asked you about it later, you'd say this really happened, wouldn't you? You'd say what you felt, the warmth of my touch, the pressure against your skin, you'd say that it was real."

She took her hand away and cold air rushed in. Lucy raised her hand to her cheek, touching the place where Sandra's fingers had been, feeling the echo of her there, thinking how strange it was for a daughter to go so long without a mother and not realize what she's missing.

"I saw Dad today," Lucy said.

Sandra looked surprised, but sat quietly, waiting for her to continue.

"Is it true?" she asked. "Did you really call every month until I turned eighteen?"

A pained expression trembled on Sandra's face, then she brushed a loose strand of hair behind her ear and bent to pet Kepler again. "Yes, well . . . I needed to know you were all right."

"Why did you stop?" Lucy asked. "Calling, I mean."

"You made it pretty clear you had nothing to say to me." There was an edge to her voice that made Lucy want to shrink into stardust and drift away. "Every month for four years. A mother can take only so much rejection."

"I didn't know." Lucy's voice was choked with some raw mix of anger and grief. "He never told me."

Sandra met Lucy's gaze. The light from the casino sign glinted in her eyes.

"I didn't know about the phone calls until today," Lucy repeated. "If I had, I would have . . . I didn't know about any of it, that you fought for custody, that you wanted me to stay. I thought . . . I thought you stopped loving me. That you didn't want me anymore."

"Oh, Lucy, no. I would never . . ." She touched the side of Lucy's face again, this time letting her fingers rest there as she continued speaking. "Of course I wanted you to stay. You're my daughter. My only daughter." She laughed a little and then settled both hands in her lap. "You know, when I found out I was pregnant with you, I cried for two days straight. Not because I was sad, though, don't get the wrong idea. I was just . . . I was so, so happy. A daughter. I'd dreamed of having a daughter my entire life. I'd dreamed of you and then there you were, pink-faced and squalling and so delicate, so new. The day you were born, I promised myself I'd do everything I could to keep you safe. Of course, I broke that promise the second I took you out of that hospital."

"Mom, no."

Sandra hushed her. "Being human hurts. So much sometimes it's easy to get lost in that pain. I couldn't cope. I didn't know how. No one ever taught me. Your grandmother. She is, well, let's just say her way of coping is similar to mine. It runs in the family, I guess."

Lucy remembered the three of them driving to Carson City, Nevada, one Christmas. Nolan sat in the front. Lucy had the whole backseat to herself. They listened to Christmas carols and when they tired of that, David Bowie albums. They played "I Spy," and Nolan started off, "I spy something silver." "A guardrail," Sandra had guessed. "A car," said Lucy. He laughed. "You'll never guess, never," and he was right.

In Carson City, Lucy and Nolan met their grandmother for the first time. She smelled like cough syrup and mildewed socks and several of her teeth were missing, but they had to hug her anyway. While they waited for dinner to be ready, Lucy and Nolan tried to play Mouse Trap in the living room, but the game was missing most of its pieces. They watched a boring football game on television instead and listened to their mother and grandmother fight in the kitchen. Dinner was terrible. The ham still frozen in the middle. The Jell-O salad runny like snot. The mashed potatoes lumpy and dry. They picked at their food and their grandmother drank brandy and snipped at their mother. "What's wrong with your children? Spoiled little brats is what they are." On the drive home, their mother had said, "There. That's done. I did my duty as a mother, I introduced you to your grandmother, and now we never have to see her ever again if we don't want to. Who wants hamburgers?" Lucy told herself that when she got older, she'd be friends with her mother. They'd have Christmas together as a family every year no matter where they were living or what they were doing, they'd spend Christmas together and the ham would be perfectly cooked.

"When things got hard," Sandra continued quietly, "when life overwhelmed me, I drank. I drank, and I let you and Nolan both down."

"It's okay," Lucy said, surprised to discover she meant it.

"It's not. As a mother, I failed pretty spectacularly." Sandra stared down at her hands for a few seconds and then smiled tentatively up at Lucy. "But I'm trying to forgive myself. What matters is that you're here now. You came back and you told the truth about the pictures and, yes, I was upset at first, but I'm not anymore. Because you were right, Lucy. I let myself see what I wanted to see. I should have questioned. I should have known it wouldn't be that simple to find him. Nothing in life ever is."

"So what now?" Lucy asked.

"Keep looking." Her voice was strong with conviction. "The pictures led nowhere. Okay, we know that now, but that doesn't mean we stop trying."

"But the alien thing," Lucy said. "I mean, it's pretty obvious now that we should be looking in other, more realistic directions, right?"

Sandra drew back slightly. "You can do whatever you want. The pictures were only one piece of a very complicated puzzle that I'm not ready to give up on yet. I know that's hard for you to understand."

"Tell me, then." Lucy grabbed her mother's hand. "Tell me what you saw to make you believe."

She took her time telling Lucy the story. It was like the ones Nolan used to tell, full of things that couldn't possibly be true and yet the details were so startlingly clear, her voice so steady and weighted with conviction. It wasn't possible, but then again, people used to believe the world was flat and if you took a boat to the horizon you would sail right off the edge into a pit of hungry dragons.

The night Nolan went missing, Sandra took her break around one thirty in the morning. On normal nights, she would go to the cafeteria, grab a cup of coffee and an apple, and read a magazine or chat with the other nurses, but that night something was different. Something felt off. Her stomach was upset. She was nervous, pacing. She couldn't sit still for more than a minute before she was on her feet again, checking someone's chart or filing paperwork. When her break started, instead of taking the elevator to the cafeteria, she pressed the button to the top floor. Then she took the stairs to the roof. Even though technically the staff wasn't supposed to go up there, the door was always unlocked. Doctors, nurses, radiology techs, sometimes even patients came out to get fresh air or have a smoke. Sometimes to cry.

There was no one else around. Sandra walked to the east side of the hospital where she could look toward the White Mountains and south toward Big Pine. It was a pretty good view that high up, with much of Owens Valley visible as a patchwork of bright lights and shadows. Her focus kept turning east toward the observatory. Something was out there, something was coming. She didn't know what, but she felt it, somehow knew that now was not the time to look away. A churning started in her gut, twisted her heart to knots, and she watched for what felt like hours, growing steadily more afraid. Though of what, she wasn't sure. Then she saw it. A light, a bright glowing orb hovering far in the distance, out over the desert.

Her first thought was plane, or a helicopter. Then she thought comet or meteor or satellite. Any of those things would have been preferable to the truth. But the light had moved too erratically, too quickly, unlike any celestial object she'd ever seen before. It defied the rules of physics and challenged everything she'd once believed possible, her very existence on this planet. And there was something else that happened, too, something far more revealing than the light. As she watched the orb move back and forth across the desert, she experienced a kind of paralysis. Her limbs turned to stone. She couldn't lift her arms or take a step forward or back. Her heartbeat and breathing slowed. She couldn't even open her mouth to shout for help.

She tried to move, she did, but whatever force kept her still was much stronger than her. She could do nothing but stand and watch the light, and the longer she watched, the more overwhelmed with panic she became because she kept seeing Nolan's face in her mind, scared and calling out to her. That's when she knew he was in trouble, that something horrible had happened. But she was useless to help him, could only stand and silently scream his name as the light grew dimmer and dimmer and then disappeared.

Lucy listened in silence until Sandra finished her story. Then, she asked, "Did you tell the police any of this?"

"I didn't realize what had even happened to me until it was too late."

"What do you mean?"

"I had to recover the memory," she explained. "It sank too deep into my subconscious for me to bring it up on my own. Cici thinks They may have replaced the true memory with a screen memory to keep me from remembering, but I think I just wasn't ready to accept the impossible reality of what had happened to me."

"Cici?" Lucy recognized the name from the UFO meeting. "The hypnotist?"

"She's not a hypnotist. She's a hypnotherapist."

"Is there a difference?" Lucy felt Sandra tense up again and she rushed into another apology. "Please, I'm just trying to understand."

Sandra said, "I was a wreck for a long time after your brother was taken. And for nearly all of that time I had no idea why. Of course, there was the obvious struggle over the loss of my son, of not knowing where he'd gone, but there seemed to be something more, too. Something dark and disruptive bubbling beneath the surface. I started having nightmares, terrible, terrible nightmares. They were so bad some nights I was too afraid to even close my eyes. Then there were the panic attacks. I'd be walking down the street or just sitting in a coffee shop and suddenly I was certain the world was going to end, right then and there. I didn't understand. I couldn't explain what was happening to me. I drank to try and drown it all out and when that didn't work, I tried seeing a regular therapist, but his answer was to put me on medication and then I just started mixing the pills with the booze, which made everything so much worse. But I didn't care. I was lost. I was confused. I was in constant pain. I'd lost my son, I'd lost you. The two of you, you were my whole life, and after you were gone there was nothing left but shame and doubt. My whole life was falling to pieces. It was a long, slow descent into madness. And then I met Wyatt."

A group of people burst out of the casino, laughing and lighting up cigarettes, blowing smoke at the stars.

"When he asked me about where I was the night Nolan

was taken, I couldn't remember." Sandra's gaze lingered on the group huddled by the casino doors. "And that's what got me thinking, what made me wonder. Because I knew I was at the hospital. There was a record of me signing in to my shift. And I remembered going in and out of patient rooms and looking through charts, but I couldn't remember any specific details and faces. That's when Wyatt suggested the possibility of a screen memory. And that's when he introduced me to Cici."

The group finished their cigarettes and reentered the casino. When the door swung open, a blast of country music rushed out. The door slammed shut. Silence descended over the parking lot again.

Sandra inhaled deeply before saying, "The first session I didn't really remember anything. I was so scared. I kept waking up. The memory was buried too deep. I had to go back three times before I was finally able to relax enough. When the reality of what happened to me that night surfaced, I wasn't surprised or in denial or even very angry. More than anything, I was relieved. I had answers now. They weren't what I was expecting, sure, but finally things started to make sense."

Lucy hesitated, then asked, "But couldn't some of what you remember, some of the feelings, be more related to the hypnotic trance you were under and not something that actually happened?"

"It happened," Sandra said fiercely. "It all happened."

"I know it feels like it did." Lucy tucked her fingers into the sleeves of her sweatshirt. "But how do you know you weren't just making it up after the fact?"

"Are you saying I'm lying?"

"No," Lucy rushed to say. "No, that's not what I'm saying

at all. I'm just saying how can you trust what you remembered if you remembered it so long after the fact? I mean, by the time you remembered this event, something bad *had* happened to Nolan, right? So it makes sense that while you were under hypnosis, you would be afraid for him, and that you might project your present fear on a past memory. Or even sketch in a brand-new memory that was never there in the first place."

"That's not how it works." And she sounded so certain, Lucy wasn't sure what to say in response.

"I know you think it's impossible," Sandra added. "I would too if I hadn't experienced it myself. But I know what I saw. I know what I felt."

"People misremember events," Lucy said quietly. "It happens all the time. You can understand, can't you, why I'm skeptical? Why I'd rather see some kind of evidence?"

"You sound like your father," Sandra said, bitterness creeping into her voice. "Always demanding evidence, but then when evidence is presented, shrugging it off, saying it's not good enough. Saying it's not the *right* kind of evidence. Trust me, Lucy, you are not the first person to try and talk 'sense' into me." She made quotation marks in the air with her fingers.

Lucy sighed and spread her hands flat against her knees. "I just want you to consider all possible angles."

"And I want you to stop trying to rationalize everything and explain it away," Sandra said. "I know what I saw. I know what I felt. There was an extraterrestrial aircraft in the desert the night Nolan went missing. I saw it and I know it was there for him. I may not understand *why* any of this has happened. Why Nolan? Why *my* son? Maybe I'll never have answers to those questions, but maybe I'm not meant to. Maybe it's enough to know that he's still out there. Somewhere. Maybe it's enough to believe he's alive. Can you understand *that*, Lucy? Can you try?"

Sandra got up from the table and brushed her hands on her pants. She started to walk Kepler back to the car, but stopped after a few steps. A spray of blue from a nearby streetlamp made her hair glow like stardust.

"I think you should talk to Cici," she said.

Lucy curled her fingers around the edge of the bench. "Why?"

"I know you feel Them, Lucy. I've seen it in your eyes. The fear. The uncertainty." Lucy started to protest, but Sandra spoke over her. "Have you ever felt a whisper across the back of your neck at night? A rumbling of a memory wanting to rise up from some deep place in your mind? Haven't there been times when you hear footsteps coming up fast behind you, but then you turn and no one's there? Seen things out of the corners of your eyes? Shapes that dart away before you can really get a good look? That's Them, Lucy. They're here whether you believe in Them or not."

Sandra tilted her face to the stars. "It's incredible, isn't it?"

Lucy looked up. The sky was awash, each star more brilliant than the next. The Milky Way was a pink-hued brushstroke following the curve of the mountains. As if the whole of the universe was making itself known to her, slipping out from behind the dark curtain of night to glimmer and shine with such brilliance, making it impossible for her to look away.

"How long has it been since you've seen the sky like this?" Sandra asked.

"Too long," Lucy answered.

After a moment of silence, Sandra spoke again. "He's out there, Lucy. Imagine what would happen if we went looking. Imagine what we might find."

15

"You are relaxed." Cici made each word buzz a low hum. "You are sinking deeper. You are feeling yourself start to drift. Your arms are weightless. Your legs are weightless. There's nothing here that can hurt you. You are fully relaxed."

Lucy had agreed to one session with the hypnotherapist. Though she doubted anything useful would come from it, she didn't see the harm in trying, especially since it made her mother happy. When they'd arrived at the office, which was little more than a room above a garage, Sandra and Cici embraced like old friends. Then Cici turned to Lucy with a warm smile and clasped her hand, saying how much she looked forward to getting to know her better, Sandra had told her so many wonderful things.

Cici was an older woman, heavyset, with chestnut hair hacked short about the ears. The black slacks and matching jacket she wore over a dark purple silk blouse suggested a professionalism that Lucy hadn't been expecting, and after the initial introductions, she was indeed all business, gesturing much like any other talk therapist for Lucy to have a seat on the couch in the center of the room. Then she took her own seat in an adjacent arm-chair and smiled at Lucy. "Are you comfortable there?"

Lucy nodded.

"Good. And your mother?" Cici asked. "You want her to stay for the session, correct?"

Lucy nodded again. Sandra had taken another armchair off to one side, out of Lucy's direct line of vision.

Cici crossed her legs and shifted her weight to rest on one arm of the chair. "Before we get started, do you have any questions for me?"

Lucy stared at the rug for a moment, following the swirling floral pattern until she lost the path. She looked up at Cici again and asked, "What exactly should I expect here? You're going to do what? Put me to sleep and then . . . ? Tell me to dance in circles or quack like a duck or something?"

Cici didn't laugh. "That's a different kind of hypnosis. A parlor trick. That's not what I do. You see, Lucy." She leaned forward in the chair. "Sometimes after a particularly frighten-ing or traumatic experience, our minds will do whatever they can to protect us. Memories get lost, buried, forgotten. Our mind might deliberately cover them up with some other false memory, what we call a screen memory. We can experience many various types and levels of amnesia. Think of it as a sur-vival mechanism, a way our brains keep us calm and happy and able to carry on with the business of living."

Lucy folded her hands and rubbed the pads of her thumbs together. She was having a hard time looking at Cici without breaking into nervous laughter so she focused on the brooch pinned to the lapel of her jacket instead. White gold curled in on itself like the flowers of a petal with a dazzling emerald at its center.

"Hypnosis is a tool we use to relax the mind and bring our buried memories up to the surface in a nonthreatening way," Cici continued. "The subject . . . in this case, you . . . is put into a relaxed state of consciousness at which time I ask a series of questions that will begin to draw these memories out of your subconscious mind and into your conscious mind. You will start to remember things that you may have forgotten. But at all times you maintain control. I cannot compel you to say things you do not want to say. I cannot force you to tell us anything you don't want to. You are in charge of this session."

Lucy had her doubts about that, but she stayed quiet, only glancing at her mother, who smiled encouragingly.

"Hypnosis is not mind control, it's not ventriloquism. And you're not asleep, either," Cici added. "You talk when you want to talk. You stay silent when you want to stay silent. You can come out of it anytime you need to."

She paused with her eyebrows raised and, when Lucy asked no further questions, reached for a notebook that had been sitting on the table beside her chair. "So let's get started, shall we? First, while you're still fully aware, I'm going to ask you some introductory questions. Try to stay relaxed and calm during this part. This isn't a test. There aren't wrong or right answers. I'm asking these questions to get a better idea of the areas that need drawing out."

She opened the notebook on her lap and used it to jot down Lucy's answers. How long had she been back in Bishop? How long had she been away? Did she have any medical conditions? Was she working? Did she have a boyfriend? Lucy wasn't sure how any of this related to the reason she was here today, but she promised Sandra she'd try, so she answered every question honestly. Then the questions started to get a little more complicated. What was her very first clear memory? The last time she was happy? The last time she cried? With each answer, the questions became even more specific, and more focused on Nolan. What's a good memory you have of your brother? What's a bad memory? What do you remember about the night he disappeared? Lucy felt herself starting to tense up. She stumbled over her answers, fumbling to find the right words.

Cici noticed her discomfort. "I think that's good for now."

She rose from her chair and moved around the room, closing the curtains, dimming the lights, and lighting a candle that sat on the small table next to her chair. After she sat down again, she told Lucy to lie back and get as comfortable as possible, to soften her gaze and clear her mind.

"Try to relax," she said.

And Lucy was trying, but the whole thing was too silly. The candle reminded her of the games she'd played at sleepovers when she was a girl. Fingers on Ouija boards, calling out the spirits of the dead. Spinning around in front of a mirror, saying Bloody Mary three times in a row. Lying on your back with your eyes closed, girls around you whispering, light as a feather, stiff as a board. None of it real, except in your mind. She jiggled her feet, and Cici told her to relax, let her thoughts come and go, whatever she was feeling, let those feelings pass through her. After a while her shoulders began to loosen and her eyes grew heavy, but then she snapped to attention again, her whole body flinching, leaving her with a panicked fluttering at the back of her throat. Then Cici again told her to try and relax, and her voice was like warm water lapping at her feet. More than once, Lucy had to fight back laughter. This was ridiculous. How had she let herself get talked into this? Hypnotism didn't work. Then for what felt like the millionth time, she was relaxing, growing calmer, looser. She was slipping under and it felt so nice she didn't fight it. Her eyelids grew heavy. She let them close. It wasn't like being asleep at all. It was like floating in a pool, like sinking into a warm bath, like lying in a bright spot of sun and feeling completely void of fear. She sighed. Cici continued to talk. She began to ask more questions, her voice slow and even, more hum than words.

I want you to go back to the night Nolan disappeared. Tell me what you remember.

It's late. And dark. I don't think that I can tell you anything else.

It's okay, Lucy. You don't have to be afraid now. There's nothing here that can hurt you.

I'm not afraid.

Good, that's good. Tell me about that night.

I'm in my room. Sleeping. But Nolan isn't here anymore.

Relax, Lucy. Take a deep breath. You are sinking deeper. You are fully relaxed. There you go. What scared you just now?

Nothing. Nothing scared me.

Were you afraid of something you saw that night?

No. It . . . I don't know. Nothing. There's nothing. Nothing happened. I just want to stay in my room.

Okay, you're safe in your room.

Yes. There are walls and a roof and a door. They can't get me in here, can they?

Who?

I don't know. No one.

You are safe, Lucy. They can't get you here. Whoever they are, they're gone now. They can't hurt you anymore.

I . . . I . . . know, but . . . I . . . I don't know where I am.

It's okay. Nice, calm breaths. Look around you. What do you see?

Shadows. It's dark.

And what else?

Big white things. The telescopes. Oh! What am I doing here? I don't want to be here. I shouldn't be . . .

Lucy, I'm right here with you. We're at the telescopes together and you're safe here. Do you see anything else?

Yes. Something's moving down there.

Down where?

In the desert by those cars.

Can you go any closer?

No. No. No. I can't.

Okay, that's okay. Let's back up a bit. How did you get to the telescopes? Do you remember what you were doing before?

We're driving.

Who's with you?

Patrick. Patrick and . . . and he's holding my hand . . . and Adam. I like when he holds my hand. I wish Adam wasn't here. He smells funny and I don't like the way he's looking at my boobs.

Is there anyone else with you now?

No. I don't think so. Patrick wants to go get someone else. No, let's not. I just want to drive around and listen to music, okay?

I want you to go back to the desert now for me. I want you to visualize yourself seeing the telescopes again. Is Patrick with you?

. . .

Is Adam with you?

. . .

What about Nolan? Do you see Nolan, Lucy? Do you see your brother anywhere?

God, it's fucking cold out here. Where's my jacket? I don't

remember what I did with it. I don't . . . it's not . . . Jesus! What was that? What—? Did you hear that? It was like a . . . it was loud, like a—oh my God, oh my God, oh my God.

Lucy . . . Lucy, you are fully relaxed. Count backwards from ten. You are even more relaxed. You are falling into a deeper state. There you go. There you go. Tell me, what did you hear just now?

There's a light down there. It's kind of pretty, but I don't like it.

What don't you like about it?

It's not safe. No! Nolan!

Lucy, what's happening now? Where's Nolan?

Running. I can't find him. There was the light and then an explosion, like thunder, like . . . Nolan! Shit! Oh, shit!

Slow down, Lucy. Tell me what's happening. Talk me through it. Tell me what you see.

Blood.

Is someone hurt? Did someone get hurt just now?

Blood on my knee. There's something . . . I fell down. I'm sitting on the ground. It stings and it's bleeding everywhere and I want to go home. I don't want to be here anymore. I should have gone home. I should have never come . . .

Lucy, I want you to go back to the desert, to the telescopes. I want you to tell me about the light. I want you to tell me about Nolan. What did you see at the telescopes? Was it Them? Was it aliens?

He's not here anymore.

Where did he go? Did you see where he went?

There's blood on my knee. Why is there blood? Did I fall? I don't . . . what am I doing here?

Lucy, what are you seeing now?

The light. It was so bright.

Okay, we're going to try and go back and go through this slowly and you must remember that you're safe. That nothing in this room can harm you. You're on the outside, you're apart from it, you're just the watcher, you're just telling us a story. Tell me more about the light, Lucy. What color is it?

I don't know.

Was there one light or many?

I don't know.

Was the light anywhere near Nolan?

The moon. What time is it? How long have I been out here? God, Mom's going to kill me. What's that? What is that? Oh, ha, a lizard . . . I thought . . . no, there's just a lizard sunning itself on a rock. God, isn't that funny.

What's funny?

That lizard. Brown with gray stripes down its back. It's sunning itself in the moonlight.

Lucy—?

I'm ready to wake up now, okay?

Okay. You are starting to come awake, you are starting to rise.

There's nothing out there.

You are lifting into the present. You are feeling your fingers and toes come alive.

Nothing happened.

Your breathing is returning to normal.

I want to stay in my room.

When I count to three you will be fully awake. One . . .

Where they can't . . .

Two . . .

I think I'm going to be sick . . .

Three.

Lucy opened her eyes. The ceiling whirled above her. She sat up and immediately clamped a hand to her mouth. Cici pointed to a door in the corner. Her lips moved, but Lucy couldn't hear a word over the sonic boom of blood pulsing in her ears. The room tilted, swinging out from under her feet. She stumbled into the bathroom and dropped to her knees in front of the toilet. Her small breakfast of toast and orange juice rocketed from her stomach. She hugged the toilet, waiting for the nausea to pass, then slowly rose to her feet and went to the sink. The cool stream of water did little to quench her thirst. She splashed her face and stared at her reflection in the mirror, pressing her fingers to her cheekbones, pushing at the skin around her eyes and mouth. She looked exactly the same on the outside and yet it felt like she'd been cracked open like an egg. A migraine beat steel fists against the inside of her skull. She splashed more water on her face and took another long drink.

Someone knocked on the bathroom door. "Lucy, are you all right?"

She opened it to find both Cici and Sandra standing there, staring expectantly, with eyes too wide and bottomless black. She pushed past them and hurried across the room.

"Come and lie down again," Cici said. "We can talk about what happened. About what you remembered."

The curtains were open again and sunlight scorched the room, bleaching it of all its colors. The edges of the world blurred and then grew too sharp. She needed to get out of here, as far away from this place as possible. The candle gave off a chemical scent, turning her stomach again.

"Lucy . . . wait."

But she was already at the door, grabbing her purse on the way out, ignoring Cici and her mother's pleas to stay.

16

Lucy didn't care where she ended up, as long as that place was far away from Bishop. She stopped by the motel after leaving Cici's, gathered her belongings and Celeste's backpack, paid the outstanding bill with the cash her father had given her, then got in her car and drove north on Highway 395. The narrow, two-lane road curved through several small mountain communities that, in summer and again during Christmas and New Year's vacations, were vibrant and bustling with families and tourists, but for the moment appeared deserted.

The road was vaguely familiar to her from the rare family trip they'd taken to hike or swim or ski. Familiar, too, because Patrick's parents had a cabin up here somewhere. She'd been inside it only once. A few days before the basketball game that ended in expulsions for both Nolan and Patrick. It was a small party, if it could even be called a party. Just her, Patrick, Adam, Natasha, and Megan. They sat around for a while drinking and smoking and eating potato chips and gummy bears. Talking about Y2K and the impending apocalypse, talking about nothing. Natasha and Megan painted each other's fingernails.

Lucy chugged two whole cans of beer before she felt brave enough to bring out Nolan's casebook. After Patrick learned of its existence—after she'd *told* him—he asked her to bring it to him. "I just want to look at it," he'd said. "I swear. I'll give it right back to you. He won't even know it's gone."

They passed the notebook around. Everyone but Lucy took turns reading from it out loud. The more they read, the angrier she became. With the others for laughing so hard beer sprayed out of their noses, and with herself for bringing the stupid thing in the first place. Nolan's ideas were bizarre, but he didn't deserve this. She tried to take the notebook from Adam, but he shoved her back. "Whoa, missy, we're just getting started. Sit the fuck down. Relax. Have another beer."

Patrick touched her hand. He gestured to the stairs leading to the second-floor bedrooms. "Want to ditch these losers?"

Adam and the other two girls started smooching and moaning and making sex sounds. Lucy's cheeks flamed, but she went with Patrick, allowing him to lead her to his bedroom where he shut and locked the door. Downstairs, the laughter continued.

Patrick sat on the bed and patted the space beside him. She sat down next to him, her head spinning from the beer and the possibility of what she and Patrick were about to do. She wished she'd worn cuter underwear, a simple black pair instead of the ones she was wearing now, childish ones covered in rainbows and unicorns. She wished she could brush her teeth first too. Or go back downstairs and ask Natasha and Megan what she was supposed to do, what it felt like, if she would like it, if she would feel different after and how? She wished she had more time to think and decide if she was really ready for this. But Patrick didn't have sex in mind right then. Instead he reached over and pulled something out of the drawer of his nightstand.

Lucy had never seen a gun before. She backed away from it, but Patrick said, "It's all right. It's not loaded. Want to hold it?"

She took it from him and held it like it was a baby bird, something fragile and easy to hurt. She hated the weight of it, the coldness of the metal against her skin. She passed it back to him after a few seconds and he laughed, pointing the gun at the wall across from them, his finger slipping over the trigger. "You're cute," he said. And then, "Bang, bang."

Lucy jumped and felt immediately stupid for doing so, but Patrick didn't seem to notice. He lowered the gun and set it on the nightstand, not in the drawer like before, but on top where Lucy could still see it, a menacing shape in the dark. Then he reached for her, reached and pulled her down onto the bed. "Is this okay?"

She nodded.

"Thanks for being so cool about everything," he said, tracing his finger across her cheek. "It means something to me that you did what I asked. Loyalty's important, you know?"

She stiffened under him. She could still hear Adam and Natasha and Megan downstairs reading through Nolan's casebook, unable to control their laughter. She wanted to stop, or slow down at least, but Patrick's lips were already pressed to hers, his tongue finding its way into her mouth, choking her a little. His hands grabbed parts of her she didn't want grabbed, his fingers pressed into places she realized too late she wasn't ready to share with him. She didn't fight, though. She liked him. He was cute and lots of girls would be happy to trade places with her, and besides she'd already told him it was okay, so she tried to relax and enjoy herself, despite his impatient hands. Despite the gun on the nightstand gleaming in the moonlight. It was over before it really began. One second he was pulling off her shirt, unbuttoning her jeans, and the next he leaped to his feet, angling his body away from her. "Fuck," he said.

"What happened?" Lucy fumbled her shirt back over her head, hugging her arms around her body to keep herself from shivering. "Did I do something wrong?"

"No," Patrick said, but his tone made it sound like she had. "Just. Just go downstairs and get us some more beers, okay?"

She did as she was told, but before she could bring the beers to him, he came back downstairs, fully dressed and avoiding her questioning gaze. He ignored her the rest of the night. She'd been so upset and confused and buzzing from too much sugar and beer that she forgot to ask for the casebook back, didn't even think about it until Natasha was dropping her off at her house and by then it was too late.

Lucy tightened her grip on the steering wheel. She'd been driving for over an hour, gaining elevation, leaving behind the low sagebrush and spindly juniper trees for taller, denser pines that sucked up what little daylight remained and turned the road into a gray and endless tunnel.

The memory of that night at Patrick's cabin wasn't one that Cici had called up during the hypnotherapy session. It had always been part of Lucy's history, simmering at the surface of her thoughts, filling her with shame. She was old enough now, years enough removed, to know that Patrick had manipulated and used her, but she still had some responsibility. He hadn't forced her to do anything.

But the memories that *had* manifested during the hypnotherapy session, she wondered now how much was real and how much imagined. Because what had she seen exactly? Not much. The telescopes. A lot of shadows moving around in the distance, none of them very clear. A flash of light. A sky blanketed by roiling thunderclouds, the stars obliterated. And it was all jumbled together, too, snapshots moving through her mind too quickly for her to really examine. For all she knew, they might have been memories of a different night, a different year. Or they might have been made up, fully born of her imagination.

Cici had drawn Lucy into a very vulnerable place, a dream-like state, where her mind could be easily manipulated and suggestions could take hold and begin to feel real. That was all, wasn't it? Lucy distinctly remembered Cici asking leading questions, saying the word "alien," wanting to know if that's what Lucy had seen, if she had seen "Them." It seemed that would be opening enough for her mind to wander down a fictitious path, weaving a story about the night Nolan disappeared and making her believe she'd been there and seen things she couldn't have possibly seen. Because she wasn't at the observatory that night. Patrick told her he'd taken her home after the prank phone call. Patrick told her none of them were at the observatory. So why then was she picturing him, standing with Nolan, the telescopes towering over them, making them seem like ants? Quite reasonably, most of what she remembered during the session had happened at some point or another in her life and so, by that logic, could be actual memories of her own very real experiences, but whether they all happened on the same night—on *that* night—and whether they had anything to do with Nolan's disappearance was something else entirely.

The raging headache plaguing her since the hypnotherapy session was finally quieting to a dull hum. Her eyelids felt swollen and weighted. Her brain crowded and slow, unable to tell the difference between real and not real, fact and fabrication. Is this how Nolan had felt then, his grasp on reality slowly slipping? Had he been as alone, as afraid as Lucy felt now?

She was having trouble keeping her eyes open. It wasn't that late, but whatever Cici had done to her during the session had drained her energy. The car's gas tank was a little less than half-full. Hopefully it would be enough to get her to the next town. She turned on the radio to keep herself awake. The only station that came through the static played oldies music. The Beatles, the Temptations, pop music from the '50s and '60s, disco from the '70s. She drove with the window cracked open, a cool breeze shuttling in, smelling of dry grass and fresh pine, and tried not to replay the images Cici had dragged from the deep wells of her mind, tried not to follow her thoughts down that path where she was, in fact, at the observatory the night Nolan went missing. She couldn't believe it. If she did, then she'd have to admit the hypnosis worked and her mother was right, and if her mother was right about that, then what else might she be right about?

The mountain road Lucy was following suddenly narrowed to one lane and then a quarter mile later turned to gravel, and she realized that somewhere along the way she'd made a wrong turn. She turned her car around and headed in the opposite direction, but by now the sun had set completely and darkness was settling in, thick and impenetrable. The world shrank to the size of her headlight beams. Where the light ended, the road disappeared and it seemed like any second she would drive straight off a cliff. She thought she saw a light up ahead, another pair of headlights, another car, or a house through the trees maybe, but then the road curved and the light winked out, if it was ever there at all. The music on the radio crackled in and out of range.

Lucy drove over a narrow bridge she didn't remember driving over before. She stopped the car on the shoulder and took her cell phone from her purse. No service. She held it up to the windshield, but it didn't make a difference. With the car still running, the headlights cutting through the dark, Lucy got out of the car and walked back and forth along the shoulder, stretching her phone in the air, trying to find a signal. After a few minutes, she gave up and returned to her car, where she rummaged through Celeste's backpack for the California road map. She unfolded it across the steering wheel and ran her finger along the ridge of the Sierra Nevada mountains until she found Bishop, a green spec in a vast beige sea. As she traced her finger along Highway 395, the dome light flickered. She glanced up. The car engine sputtered and then died. The dome light went dark. The headlights blinked out. The music stopped. Lucy sat in the sudden silence and darkness for a few seconds, blinking, bewildered.

She shoved the map onto the passenger seat, reached for her keys, and cranked them hard in the ignition, but the car did nothing. She turned the ignition all the way off and then on again. Still nothing. She flipped the headlights off and on too, pushed the buttons on the radio, opened the door and closed it again. The silence and darkness remained.

Her car was dead. She didn't know why. There'd been enough gas in the tank for at least another hundred miles. She took her cell phone out of her pocket. Emergency services were sometimes still available, even if she was out of her service area, but the cell was as dead as the car. She held down the power button for a long time, even shook the phone a little. The screen stayed dark.

"Shit," Lucy said under her breath. Empty road stretched

in front of her and behind. Trees lurked, crowding both sides. The hairs on her arms and the back of her neck stood on end. The air coming through her cracked open window smelled electric.

She reached under the dashboard and popped the hood, then went around to the front of the car and squinted down at the tangle of wires and batteries, engine, carburetor, valves, all things that made a car run and theoretically could be fixed by someone who knew what the hell they were doing. If it wasn't black as ink out here and they could see what needed fixing in the first place. Lucy shut the hood and leaned against it, staring down the road where the shadows seemed to expand toward her, like a thick, curdling smoke. She shuddered and hugged her arms tight around her body.

In the distance, thunder rumbled. Clouds skipped across the narrow gap of sky overhead, playing hide-and-seek with the stars. Lucy turned to get back inside the car and caught sight of another flare of light through the trees on the opposite side of the road. It was dim at first, pale orange like a porch light in the distance, but then it began to grow brighter and change color, stretching like a slow-motion explosion, a tentacled star, orange to red to white to red to orange again, retreating as it returned to its original color, dim and dimmer until it was a pinpoint, barely visible in the choking darkness. Then the cycle started over again, reminding Lucy of the swing of a light-house beam or cars passing on the freeway, light gathering in a single bright beam and then spilling away, mesmerizing her.

There was something familiar about it. The color, the same rhythmic brightness fading and returning, the strange tingling under her skin and pressure against her chest. It was similar to the light she'd recalled under hypnosis, that brief flash near the telescopes the night Nolan disappeared. She wondered if this light she was seeing now was somehow related to her session, if maybe she wasn't still half in a trance and hallucinating, projecting her fear into the dark.

Another loud clap of thunder, this time right above her. Lucy flinched and ducked her head. The light flared bright, and then a twig snapped in the trees behind her. She twisted toward the sound, but no shapes emerged from the dark.

"Hello?" she whispered, but got no response.

She turned back to the light, but it was gone, and the tree trunks, once sharply defined, were now little more than a thick black smudge. Anything could be out there. Anything could be watching from the shadows, and Lucy would never know. She rubbed her hands together for warmth. The thunderstorm was moving to the northeast now, away from her, the low rumbles growing quieter and quieter. She stared at the place where the light had been, soothing her tired and skittish mind with the reasonable explanation that what she'd seen had been some form of lightning. Raging currents of static electricity. Surges of electrons flowing from cloud to ground. A bright flash lighting up the night, gone as fast as it had arrived.

She reached for the car door handle, but the sound of a running engine coming up the road made her pause. Headlights swept over the trees, illuminating the forest for a brief second before reaching her in an explosion of white. The pickup truck traveled in the opposite direction as her, headed up the mountain and making good time. She stepped into the road and waved her arms over her head.

The pickup pulled alongside her car, and the driver, a young man with a thick beard and curly hair, rolled down his window. "Tire blown?"

"I don't know. I might have run out of gas or something with the spark plugs?"

The man pulled forward a few feet and parked on the shoulder, leaving the engine running, the high beams illuminating Lucy's broken-down car. She explained how she'd gotten turned around and was trying to figure out how to get to the main road when the car shut down without warning. The man made a complete circle around her car, then opened the driver's door. The dome light flared.

Lucy inhaled sharply. The man glanced at her, then sank down into the driver's seat and turned the key. The radio blasted to life, blaring a David Bowie song. Lucy jumped back, startled by the noise. The man turned the headlights on and off and then on again. Both beams worked fine. He pressed a little on the gas, revving the engine, then he climbed back out of her car, hooked his thumbs into his belt loops, and rocked on his heels.

"Can't say I know what happened, but it seems to be working all right now. Bad place to have a breakdown, you ask me. Strange things happen on this road at night." He swung his gaze along the trees edging the road, then turned and gave Lucy a tight-lipped smile. "Good news is, you've got plenty enough gas to make it to the station down on Boulder Drive about ten miles from here. I know the owner, Matt. He can take a look under the hood for you, if you want. See if there's any spark plugs loose or cables missing or something so this doesn't happen to you again."

Lucy nodded. "Yeah, okay. Boulder Drive?"

"I can lead you back that way. Make sure you get there safe." He went to his pickup.

Lucy got into her own car, turned off the radio, and buckled her seat belt. She stuck close to the pickup, following the twin red lights around sharp corners and wide bends. Every few minutes she glanced in her rearview mirror. The road behind her collapsed in total darkness.

A reasonable explanation for everything, Lucy repeated to herself the whole way to the gas station.

The driver of the pickup was already talking to Matt when Lucy pulled up alongside a pump. He waved her forward toward an open garage door, then motioned for her to stop, and came around to the driver's window.

"Heard you had a little trouble on the hill?" He spoke with a slow drawl and an easy smile. "Want me to have a look?"

She explained again what happened. He told her to leave the engine running and then held open the door for her as she got out. "There's a fresh pot of coffee in the office. Go on in and make yourself comfortable."

She thanked him, and the pickup driver too, who gave her a two-finger salute and said Matt would take good care of her. Then he wished her better luck on the rest of her trip and left.

The gas station office was small and cramped, with a large metal desk and swiveling chair, file cabinets, and stacks of car magazines. Lucy poured herself a cup of coffee and stirred in a good amount of sugar and cream. Just holding it, warming her fingers around the cup, was a comfort. This day had stretched on too long; this night even longer. Her cell phone beeped inside her purse. She took it out, surprised to see it had somehow turned itself back on. She had two voice mails. She listened to the first one.

"Lucy? It's your mo . . . It's Sandra. Wyatt gave me your number. Listen, the way you ran out of Cici's . . . I just . . . I think we need to talk about what happened. Wyatt said he

went by your motel, but you weren't there? We're both worried about you." There was a long, crackling pause and then
she said, "*I'm* worried. Lucy . . . I need to know if you're
okay. Please . . . call me . . . call *one* of us . . . as soon as you
get this."

The second one was from her father. "I just got off the
phone with your mother? She said you bolted out of a *hypnotherapy session* and they don't know where you went and now
no one can get in touch with you? Lucy, what the hell is going
on? Do I need to come out there?" The only time she'd ever
heard him this riled up was over a business deal that wasn't going his way.

She texted Robert first. Don't come. I'm fine. Please, just
trust me.

Almost immediately he responded. If you need anything . . .

I know, she wrote back.

Before she could reply to her mother, Matt sauntered into
the office, wiping his fingers on a greasy rag. "You said it just
shut down on you? The engine? The lights? The radio? All
of it?"

"Yes." She slipped her phone back into her purse. "It sort of
hiccupped and then nothing."

He frowned at the wall for a few seconds and then shook his
head. "Well, I took a close look at the spark plugs and the fuel
line, but all that looked good. I checked the battery to make
sure it was holding a charge, and it was. I checked your fluids.
That's all good. As near as I can tell, your car's in great condi-
tion. I didn't find anything that would explain it just shutting
down on you like that."

"Nothing at all?"

Matt wiped the rag across the back of his neck. "I guess it

could be something with the computer chip. Everything's run by computers these days," he said with some disdain. "But I don't have the equipment to test for that." He leaned forward and shuffled through a pile of papers on his desk. "I know a guy in Bishop could take a look at it for you."

She took a business card from him and asked how much she owed.

He waved the question away with the rag. "Fill up your tank, we'll call it even."

Boulder Drive reconnected with the highway one mile south of the gas station. To the south was a violent glow, lights sparking on the horizon, a road that led her straight back to the one place she'd been trying her whole life to leave behind. To the north, mountains crowded the road, but beyond them were endless possibilities, new places, whole towns, entire cities of people who didn't know her name, had no idea who she was or where she'd come from or what she'd done. Lucy idled at the intersection, torn for a moment about which direction to take.

She didn't want the memories she recalled under hypnosis to be true. The implications terrified her—what she might have done, what she didn't do. More than that, she didn't trust them. But if they were accurate, if what she'd recalled under Cici's guidance actually happened, then Celeste and Nolan weren't the only two people at the observatory that night. And after what just happened on that dark forest road, she needed to be certain. If there was a reasonable explanation for what happened the night Nolan went missing, she needed to find it. Lucy eased her car onto the highway heading south and back to Bishop.

CASEBOOK ENTRY #6

SIGHTING:
Mountain Lights

DATE: November 13–22, 1999

LONGITUDE/LATITUDE: All over Eastern Sierras and White Mountains

SYNOPSIS: Sudden and significant increase in UFO activity. Numerous sightings are being reported online by residents from Bishop all the way to Olancha. Reports even coming in from Mammoth and June Lakes in Mono County. Locally, Channel 9 news and the Bishop Register have filed three separate reports (see attached documents).

OBJECT DESCRIPTION: Though there are some outliers, descriptions of UFOs appear to be consistent. Orange, green, and sometimes blue orbs hover for several minutes, then make a sharp counterclockwise circle and shoot straight up into the air before vanishing.

OTHER WITNESS STATEMENTS: I have followed up with four witnesses who submitted a report. Three refused to talk to me, saying they changed their minds, it was probably just an airplane or lightning. One woman pretended not to be home.

WEATHER INFORMATION: Some cloud buildup over White Mountains with reports of thunder. Otherwise no significant weather patterns. No meteorological phenomena would explain this many multiple and separate reports of lights behaving erratically over such a large area.

LOCATION DESCRIPTION: Inyo means "dwelling place of the great spirit." I do not think it is coincidence that our area is experiencing such miraculous events. For reasons unknown to us, They have chosen this place and this narrow moment in time to make Themselves known. They have chosen me.

PHYSICAL EVIDENCE: One of the witnesses initially reported capturing the lights on video, but later said the tape was destroyed in an electrical fire. Also, according to an article in the Bishop Register, Inyo County deputies went to the area where a craft was recently spotted and claimed to have found nothing unusual. Typical. Even if they had found something, they would never tell us. I would have gone out there myself, but if there was evidence, the government has it now.

CONCLUSION: This is the largest documented cluster of UFO activity in the history of this region. While not all accounts can be confirmed, there is enough evidence here for me to state with absolute certainty that a paradigm shift is coming.

Nolan knew he shouldn't be writing any of this down. It was too dangerous now to keep a written record of his encounters, and yet he couldn't stop himself. He found his casebook on his bed the day after his expulsion. Lucy must have left it there for him. Other than a bent corner and a few rumpled pages, the casebook was unscathed, all of his notes intact. He was tempted to tear it to pieces right then or set it on fire, this thing that had caused him so much trouble, but there was so much of Celeste in these pages—to destroy these memories of her would be heartbreak. So he tucked the book in his bottom desk drawer, which had a lock, and tried to forget about it, only to take it out again a few days later when the news started reporting strange lights in the sky, sightings happening all over the valley. It was dangerous, yes, but the work he was doing was important, the events worthy of documentation. If he didn't record the truth, who would? He would be more careful this time, though. He would make no mention of Celeste, not even in code, and when he wasn't writing in it, the casebook would stay locked in his desk.

Nolan only left the house for work now. For ten minutes in the parking lot after his mother had been called down to the school, she'd wept into a ratty old tissue pulled from the bottom of her purse. "I raised you to make better decisions than this." She'd sobbed. "I raised you to be a better person. I don't understand what's going on inside your head? Fighting? Nolan, look at me. What do you have to say for yourself?"

He didn't know what to tell her that hadn't already been said. No one seemed to care that the whole thing had been Patrick's fault, that the fight would have never happened if he hadn't stolen Nolan's casebook, copied the pages, and passed them around to his classmates. No one seemed to care, either, that Patrick had—technically—thrown the first punch. Both boys were expelled, but only Nolan's mother was given a brochure about mental illness from the school guidance counselor. To her credit, she'd balled up the glossy bullshit and tossed it in the garbage on the way out of the principal's office. He thought that would be the end of it, but last night he overheard her talking on the phone, her voice drunk and loud enough to float through walls. "I don't see any other choice, Robert. I can't afford the private schools around here and Bishop won't let him come back until next school year. If he stays, he'll be a year behind, if he manages to graduate at all." She was talking about sending him to live with his father. He was running out of time.

The day after the basketball game, he'd driven to Gabriella's on his way home from work hoping to talk to Celeste, to try and explain. Gabriella had answered the door, but refused to let him inside. "She doesn't want to see you right now, Nolan."

He'd called a few hours later and when Gabriella told him Celeste wasn't there, he called the restaurant, but the woman who answered said she wasn't scheduled to work that night, and so he tried the house again, but could only bring himself to dial the first three numbers before hanging up. The things he needed to say to her needed to be said in person. He was going to try and wait her out—eventually she'd have to let her guard down—but his mother sounded resolute, and if they wanted to escape this place, slip away unnoticed and drop off the grid, make new lives for themselves someplace else, then they had to move fast. Nolan needed to figure out a way to make Celeste understand what was at stake. Somehow he needed to regain her trust.

He drove by Gabriella's and by Jake's on the way to work and on the way home from work for five days straight. He saw her sometimes through the window or walking down the driveway to get the mail, but she never smiled at him, never waved, never waited when he called her name. She ignored him, turning and going back into the house, pretending he didn't exist.

Finally, three days before Thanksgiving, she came to him. He found her waiting by his pickup the way she had the night of their first kiss. Only this time there was no picnic basket and she didn't look at all happy to see him. Nolan spoke first.

"Have you seen the lights?" he asked. "They've been all over the news this week. Dozens of sightings up and down the valley and even at some of the mountain resorts."

"Nolan . . ." She sounded tired.

"I think They're here for you."

"I need you to stop following me," she said. "You humiliated me. And I'm trying to let it go, I'm trying to forget, but you're making it impossible."

"We have to talk about this." He tried to get close to her, but she backed away.

"I don't have anything to say to you." She started to walk away from him.

"Then just listen."

She stopped with her back to him, but she stopped, and that had to mean something.

"Look," he said. "I know you're upset."

She laughed, a fragile, cruel sound. "That's the understatement of the year."

"I screwed up, okay? I screwed up big-time, but you have to try and understand—"

"All those things you wrote about me?" She spun around to face him. "Is that what you really believe? What you think I am? A Star Being?" She stumbled over the words, a look of confusion passing over her face. "Because I'm not. I'm definitely not from anywhere up there." She pointed one finger to the sky.

Nolan took a step toward her. "You don't have to do that. You don't have to pretend. Not with me."

She hugged her arms around her chest and shivered.

"I know you're scared," he continued, speaking slowly, quietly, like he was trying to calm a spooked horse. "But you don't have to hide from me. I'm on your side. I want to help you."

Nolan moved to comfort her, reaching his arms for an embrace. She pushed him away.

"Don't touch me." Her voice like ice. "Don't come any closer. I'm not what you think I am. I'm not *that*, okay? I'm not. I was born in Florida."

She was trying to protect him by lying, but he didn't need her to do that. He could take care of himself; he could take care of both of them. All they needed to do was leave Bishop, under the cover of night preferably, find a new town, give themselves new names, blend in, and if the government tracked them down in this new town, they'd move on again, to another new town, and another, as many as it took. There were millions of towns on this planet, a million places to hide, and he didn't care where they were as long as they were together.

Celeste was still talking, saying something about a group home in Philadelphia. Why was she talking about Philadelphia? What did that have to do with anything? Was this where she wanted to go next? Nolan struggled to get his brain to catch up to her mouth. Sound floated around him, but he couldn't quite capture the words. He focused on her lips until she started to make sense, the individual sounds syncing up in his brain to form coherent sentences again.

"I stayed in Bishop because of you," she said. "And I'll always be grateful for what we had. I mean, you made me feel like I was someone important, someone special, but I just, I have to go now, okay? We have to move on."

"Yes, that's exactly what I've been trying to tell you," he said, glad she was finally understanding. "It's not safe here anymore. We have to leave."

She looked annoyed, confused. She shook her head. "Not *us*, Nolan. Just me. I'm leaving."

"I'm coming with you," he insisted. "What did you say the other night? We just go? We just get in the car and start driving?"

Her expression softened. "No, Nolan, not anymore. That was before. I can't go anywhere with you now. Not after what happened."

"It was an accident." Panic flared white-hot behind his eyes. "It won't happen again. I won't write about you anymore. I won't write down any of it, if that's what you want. I know better now. I learned my lesson. I would never let anything happen to you. I'd die before I let them take you."

"Nolan, slow down, you're not making any sense. No one's dying here. No one's 'taking' me. I'm just, I'm going, that's all. I'm leaving Bishop."

"You have to take me with you."

"And why would I have to do that?"

"Because . . ." He grasped for a reason that wasn't foolish. She didn't need him. She'd be better off without him and his bumbling human mind, and yet, he was better with her.

"Because you love me," he said.

In her eyes, heartbreak and regret, and he hated that he'd been the one to cause this, that she was suffering because of his failings. He yearned for her to look at him the way she'd looked at him the first day they met, like she saw into the very core of him and their shared future beyond. He yearned to press his lips to hers, one final time, to hear the stars sing her name. He yearned for so much, even as he felt it slipping away.

He reached into his pocket and took out a folded slip of paper. He handed it to her, and she unfolded it. "Is this supposed to be me?"

"No," he said, and then, "yes."

She sighed impatiently.

"I drew this before I met you," he tried to explain. "She's a warrior princess from the planet Aurelia, which is made up, by the way, at least as far as I know. Maybe it exists somewhere. Humans just haven't found it yet."

Celeste handed the paper back to him. "That's nice." Her voice flat.

"Don't you see? She's you. Or you're her. Or . . . you get it, right? It can't just be a coincidence that I drew her a few months before you showed up. That I drew her and she looks exactly like you."

"It's a drawing, Nolan. And she doesn't look exactly like me. Her hair's longer."

"Yeah, but—"

"And the nose is all wrong," she continued. "And her hips are wider. And the freckles." She held up her hand, showing off her constellation. "Where are her freckles, Nolan?"

Nolan squinted at the drawing, certain he would see them, a tiny *W* at the base of her thumb, but there was nothing there.

He hesitated and into his silence, she spoke.

"I'm sorry, really, I am. I wish . . ." She shook her head. "I wish things could be different, but please, try and understand.

I'm not that girl. I *can't* be her even if I wanted to. I'm me, Nolan. What you see is what you get and, for whatever reason, that's not enough for you. Please don't make this any harder than it has to be, okay? It'll be easier on both of us if I just go. So just tell me good-bye. Tell me good-bye and let me leave."

She waited another minute, but he couldn't say the words she wanted to hear. Some part of him thought maybe if he didn't, she would stay. She gave a small shrug, said, "Good-bye, Nolan," then turned and walked into the dark, disappearing down the very same alleyway she'd materialized from three short months ago.

Nolan barely made it to work on time the next day. He was scheduled for a three-to-close shift and didn't think he'd need to set his alarm, but he hadn't been able to fall asleep until four in the morning—his brain was on a never-ending loop, replaying every conversation he and Celeste ever had, every glance, every touch, every shared moment, every betrayal— and when he woke again, it was a quarter to three. He sprang from bed, pulled on the same clothes he'd been wearing the day before, and drove to the grocery store, clocking in at 3:01, technically late, but not enough that his manager noticed.

His brain was a fog, still half-asleep. He didn't want to think of Celeste leaving him behind, but this was all he could think about. The image of her walking away sucked him into a slow-motion vortex, turned his thoughts to a dull, but constant roar.

He walked out of the break room and somehow made it to aisle four where a pallet of generic cereals waited beneath blinding fluorescents. He took a box cutter from his apron pocket and set to work, finding the repetitive actions of drag-ging a sharp blade through tape and shrink wrap, grabbing bags of Crispy Rice and slapping them down on the shelves, oddly comforting. The rhythm of it soothed him, and for a few minutes at least, he didn't think about Celeste. Or the strange lights people were seeing and then denying they'd seen. He didn't think about Patrick or the fight or his still-aching ribs or the many, many ways he'd fucked up every good thing in his life. He didn't think about anything at all except the movement of his arms, the twisting of his body, the brightly colored bags of cereal. He was a cog in a machine. A robot made of metal parts that never got old and never broke down, never wept, never got rusty. A soulless machine who didn't know the meaning of lonely.

Halfway through emptying the pallet, he registered movement, a vague shadow in his peripheral vision. He plastered a polite smile on his face, the smile he used for customers. But when he lifted his head, his smile slipped.

It had been nearly two weeks since the fight, and though the swelling had gone down, the bruises around Patrick's eyes were still deep purple. Gone were his easy swagger and wide smile, too. Now he walked with head lowered, his hands shoved deep into his pockets. He stopped a few feet from Nolan. "I didn't come here to start anything."

Nolan tightened his grip on the box cutter. "Let me guess . . . you just needed some Coco Roos?" He grabbed a bag off the shelf and tossed it at Patrick's chest.

Patrick caught the bag and held it at his side. "I wanted to apologize."

Nolan laughed and went back to unloading the pallet.

"No, really." Patrick took a shuffling step closer. "What we did to you was shit, man. I mean it." He dropped the bag of Coco Roos onto its proper shelf. "Friends?"

"Fuck off." Nolan stabbed the box cutter through a piece of tape and slit open the last box of cereal he needed to unpack.

"Don't be like that, Nolan."

"You ruined my life." Nolan threw the bags of cereal onto the shelf, no longer caring about getting them straight or whether he was crushing the cereal inside.

"I ruined *your* life?" Patrick's hands curled at his side. "What about me? I was having a fucking stellar year. Straight As. Running my fastest times on the track. College scouts were starting to notice me. And then you had to go and fucking lose your shit over some stupid prank. You had to turn it into this big fucking deal and throw punches and get me kicked out of school. Now I'm stuck at some dumb-ass boy's academy with a bunch of dumb-ass losers and no track team and I'll probably end up at some fucking suck-ass state school. Because of what? Because of some stupid diary. You're a real piece of work, you know that, Nolan? A real fucking piece of work."

Nolan swallowed back all the words he wanted to say in his defense. He knew better now. Patrick didn't care about anyone but Patrick. "Why did you do it?"

He shrugged. "Why not? Why'd you even write all that shit down anyway? I mean, you were kind of asking for it, you know."

It wasn't a good enough answer. Nolan took a long step toward Patrick. His foot knocked into the box he'd been unloading, turning it over and spilling bags across the linoleum floor. Patrick backed away from him, but Nolan crowded him up against a shelf and pressed the box cutter to his throat. Cereal boxes collapsed around them, bursting open, scattering puffed rice cereal in all directions. Patrick held up both hands near his head, fingers splayed. His Adam's apple bobbed terrifyingly close to the sharp blade. He looked scared now, smaller and younger somehow. Nolan had never noticed before the black ring circling Patrick's irises. Like a fence, a boundary, keeping the blue ink from spilling into the white.

Patrick reared his head back as far as it could go, trying to escape the blade. "It was Lucy's idea."

"Yeah right." Nolan pushed the blade closer.

"I didn't even know anything about your casebook until she told me about it." Patrick spoke quickly, a whine edging his words. "She stole it from your truck and asked me to make a bunch of photocopies and pass them around at the game, so I did."

For a second, Nolan's fury wavered. "She wouldn't do that."

"She did, I swear to God. She was jealous that you were spending so much time with Celeste. She thought if she could break the two of you up—"

Hearing Celeste's name from Patrick's lips was like a cracking bone, shattering glass, the force of a meteorite exploding through the atmosphere. Nolan forced his shoulders and arms forward, shoving Patrick as hard as he could, pressing the blade to his skin, drawing a thin line of blood. The shelf swayed. More boxes crashed down around them, cereal spilling everywhere.

"Think about it," Patrick pleaded. "No one else would have been able to take that stupid book without you noticing. No one else even knew about it. Ask her, fucking ask her!"

Nolan kept Patrick trapped for another beat, their eyes locked, their chests heaving in unison, the blade trembling, blood beading a red smear against pale flesh, the air around them filled with fine powder, drifting, smelling of cinnamon, sugar, and oats. Then Nolan lowered the blade and took a step back, releasing Patrick. His heart slammed, he couldn't catch his breath. Bright crystals sparkled at the edge of his vision. He didn't know who he was anymore, when he'd become the kind of person who held a blade to someone else's throat, the kind of person who lashed out like this, so violently, so primitively.

Patrick smoothed his hands down his shirt and brushed his fingers through his hair. He pressed his thumb over the small nick the blade had made on his neck and pulled it away again. He looked shocked to see blood there. Color drained from his cheeks. Before either boy could say or do anything else, Carol, the store manager, rounded the corner. She stopped and stared at the mess of boxes and crunched-up cereals, the two boys: one with blood dripping down his neck, the other holding a knife.

"What is going on here?" Carol wrenched the box cutter from Nolan's hand.

Her eyes darted between them, demanding an explanation. Nolan hung his head. Sugar crystals shimmered on his shoe-laces.

"Nothing." Patrick began to slide sideways, maneuvering around the debris and pressing his fingers to his neck to cover the blood. "It was an accident." He ducked around the end of the aisle and disappeared before Carol could question him further.

Carol focused her attention on Nolan. She glared at the box cutter, the blade now retracted, safe in its case, then at Nolan, and then she said, "I think it's best if you clock out early to-night."

Nolan took off his apron.

"Oh, and don't bother coming in tomorrow," Carol added. "We'll mail you your final paycheck." She unclipped a radio from her belt and spoke into it, calling another employee to bring a broom. There was a cleanup needed in aisle four.

When Nolan got home, he went straight to Lucy's room and barged through the door without knocking. She was lying on her stomach in bed, reading a book, legs kicking the air. She had headphones on, bobbing to the beat of whatever song was playing. She didn't look up when he came in. Her head still bobbing, she said, "Get out of my room, freak face."

He marched over to her and yanked off the headphones.

"Hey!" She leaped to her knees and tried to grab them back.

He held them out of reach. "Did you take my casebook?"

"Give them back." Her hand swiped the air.

"Did you take my casebook?" Nolan repeated, louder, still holding the headphones above his head.

"I gave it back to you," she said. "I don't know where the fuck it is now."

"Watch your language."

She rolled her eyes and made a final lunge, snatching the headphones from Nolan's grasp. She slid them back on her head and lay down again, returning her attention to her book. "Get out of my room. Or I'm telling Mom."

Nolan stood in front of her bed with his arms crossed over his chest. Lucy glared at him and took a breath, like she was about to yell.

"Call her," Nolan said. "I'm sure she'd be very interested in hearing what part you played in getting me expelled."

She clamped her lips together. Her cheeks puffed out, then she released her breath all at once in a loud, rushing sigh. She removed her headphones and rolled over, sitting up again and kicking her feet over the edge of the bed. "What are you talking about?"

"Like you don't know."

"I didn't have anything to do with that stupid fight. That was all you." She stood and brushed past him to her dresser where she pawed through a collection of nail polish for a few seconds, before finally settling on a sparkling blue color. She returned to the bed and propped one foot on the edge, spreading her toes.

"Patrick came to the store." Nolan tried to hang on to the anger he'd felt driving home, the righteous rage he had when he first burst into her room, but it was hard when she refused to look at him, when her head hung down over her knees, her hand carefully brushing sparkling blue confetti onto her big toe.

"He told me what you did," Nolan continued. "He told me you stole my casebook and asked him to make photocopies to pass around school. He said it was your idea."

Lucy lifted her eyes to his. "He told you that?" She looked hurt.

Nolan nodded.

She dropped the small nail brush back into the bottle, leaving half her toes unpainted. She stared out the window for a few seconds, as if trying to work out something in her head. When she returned her attention to Nolan, her eyes were swirling tempests. "He's a liar."

"You didn't take it?"

She pushed her jaw forward and went back to painting her nails, with more violence this time. "I did take it," she admitted. "But it wasn't my idea. It was Patrick's."

Nolan sank onto the bed beside her, all the fight leaving him in a single breath. "Why?"

She shrugged. "He asked me to." Then quickly added, "He didn't tell me what he was going to do with it, he just asked if I could bring him your casebook. If I'd known he was going to show everyone . . ." She jammed the brush back in the bottle and twisted it hard. "I had nothing to do with that part."

She waved her hands above her toes to help dry them. They were tiny blue crystals now, glittering sapphire toes.

"Anyway," she said. "You totally overreacted."

Nolan sprang from the bed and began pacing her room. "The things I wrote in there were private! You had no right—"

"You freaked out over nothing."

"It's not nothing," Nolan said. "You know it's not nothing."

She tipped her head, watching him closely. "Just because you write something down doesn't make it true. You know that, right?"

He stopped pacing.

"I mean, you can't really believe any of that stuff actually happened." Lucy said. "You don't really think Celeste is a . . . what did you call her? Star Being? You can't possibly think she's actually from outer space. You know how crazy that is, right?"

"What Celeste may or may not be is none of your business."

Lucy's expression hardened again. "You weren't this bad before she came around. You were actually, you know, kind of normal. You were fun. People liked hanging out with you. *I* liked hanging out with you. But then Celeste shows up." She said the name with a sneer. "And it's like she's got some kind of power over you or something, I don't know, you just . . . you're just different." She shrugged again and lowered her feet to the floor. "You know, I'm actually glad it happened this way.

Maybe now you'll start thinking straight again. Maybe I'll finally get my brother back."

The whole time she'd been talking, Nolan's fingers had been curling tighter, his nails digging into the palms of his hands, his knuckles tingling.

"I'm not crazy," he said quietly, and then pleading with her to remember, "you've seen as much as I have."

"No, I haven't," and she sounded sad about that.

"What about the lights we saw as kids?" Nolan insisted. "Remember? Right after Dad left? We were in the backyard and you said they looked like yo-yos? Or . . . or . . . what about over the summer? At our stargazing rock? You and Patrick were both there when that craft appeared."

She scowled at her lap, her shoulders curling forward as if she was trying to disappear.

"You used to hunt for them with me!" His voice grew steadily louder and more frustrated. "You had your own pair of binoculars. You said you saw them. I remember." He rubbed his temples, trying to think of a specific time when Lucy had been the one to see the UFO first, when it had been her pointing it out to him instead of always the other way around.

"I remember playing with you in the backyard when we were kids," she said. "I remember you pointing up at the sky and saying, 'Look, Lucy! A UFO! Do you see it?'" She imitated his squeaking, cracking little boy voice. "And I said I did because you're my big brother and I wanted you to keep playing with me. I didn't want you to tell me to leave you alone, so I pretended to see whatever you wanted me to see. But there was nothing up there, Nolan. There never is. I don't see any UFOs, because UFOs don't exist. And these Visitors, little green men, Star Beings, whatever you want to call them, they don't exist either. Not actually. All of the things you claim to see are just figments of your freak imagination. It's not real except in your own twisted brain."

"Don't say that," he said. "You're just having trouble wrapping your mind around something as big as this, that's all. And it's all right. That's completely normal. Someday you'll be ready to accept the truth and you'll remember what you saw, you'll remember everything."

"No, I won't, because there's nothing to remember. There is no 'this' to wrap my mind around. Don't you get that? There isn't anything bigger." She flapped her hands in the air, gesturing at nothing. "We're it. You and me and Mom and all the other stupid, ugly people on this planet. That's all there is. We're all there is."

Her words pricked his skin. "No," he said. "There's more. I've seen it."

"Everyone thinks you're a lunatic," Lucy said. "You know that, right? Mom thinks you have a brain tumor. And the kids at school think you've gone full Mad Hatter. The whole school is treating me like a pariah because they think whatever you have is contagious, like crazy runs in the family and if they get near me they'll catch crazy, too."

"I don't care what anyone else thinks."

Lucy spread her arms out at her sides. "What about me? Do you care what I think? Do you care at all what happens to me?"

He reached to comfort her, but she recoiled. "Of course I care," he said. "It's just, this is bigger than me, than you, than any of us. Can't you try and understand that?"

She squeezed her eyes shut and shook her head. "Just get out of my room and leave me alone, okay?"

"Our current paradigm is shifting, whether you believe in it or not," Nolan said. "You're still a part of Their plan. Eventually you're going to have to—"

A frustrated scream blasted through her clenched teeth. "God, Nolan! Shut up! Just shut up with your stupid theories and go back to whatever stupid planet you came from, okay? No one likes you. No one believes you. No one wants you around. No one fucking cares!"

As she raged, she shoved him toward her bedroom door. He was surprised at how strong she was, how efficiently her toothpick arms rushed him across the threshold. Though, to be fair, he didn't put up much of a fight.

She slammed the door in his face so hard it rattled the walls, sending a hanging framed photograph crashing to the floor. Nolan picked it up. Their mother had taken the photo six years ago. Lucy and Nolan stood together at the foot of one of the giant telescopes at the observatory, their arms slung around each other's shoulders, grinning madly.

Sandra appeared at the end of the hall then, pinning Nolan with her gaze. "Come into the kitchen, please. I need to talk to you."

He hung the picture back on the wall and followed Sandra to the other side of the house. She stopped beside the kitchen table, on top of which were two plastic bags. Zipped inside each one was a frozen, dark mass surrounded by crackling ice crystals.

"Do you know anything about this?" She waved her hand over the bags.

They were labeled with a date, time, and location, the handwriting distinctively Nolan's. Without moving closer, he knew they contained the birds he'd found dead in his truck bed.

"They were in the deep freezer with the turkey . . . ?" Sandra coaxed.

The turkey sat in the sink, still wrapped in its blue and orange Butterball packaging.

"Nolan," she said. "Talk to me."

He went to the table and picked up one of the freezer bags. The bird's eyes were open, glassy now with a cobweb of ice across the lens. Its feathers were stiff, the edges white where freezer burn was starting to set in. He carefully set the bag back down on the table. "The county health inspector won't return my calls."

Sandra shook her head, clearly not understanding.

"I want to know how they died," he tried to explain.

"Why would you want to know that?" Fear edged her words.

"Sometimes when a UFO passes overhead, there will be an electromagnetic pulse that disrupts the atmosphere, temporarily shuts down the power grid, and . . ." He gestured to the birds. "Knocks birds out cold. I wanted County Health to determine if that was the case with these birds because if it was, then that's proof. Actual physical proof."

"Of UFOs," she said.

He nodded.

She stared at the birds again and her eyes flared with panic. Before Nolan could stop her, she scooped up both bags and carried them through the door off the kitchen that led to the garage. He followed her outside to the garbage can.

"Mom, wait, I need those—" They made a solid-sounding *thunk* when they hit the bottom of the can.

Nolan tried to reach around her and salvage the birds before they melted to useless, rotten flesh puddles, but she placed herself between him and the garbage can. When he didn't back down, she said, "That's enough, Nolan," and then repeating herself, shouting loud enough to finally startle him motionless. "I said, that's enough!"

"I need those," he said again. "They're evidence."

"I'm not doing this with you anymore." She untied the apron she was wearing and balled it up in her hand. "I can't . . . I just can't. I'm tired, Nolan, do you understand? I'm tired and I don't know who you are anymore and I've tried, but you're not getting any better. And I just, I don't know how to fix this. I don't know how to fix you."

He didn't need fixing. He needed those birds.

"I'm sending you to live with your father." Her words knifed through his thoughts.

Even though he already knew this was coming, he was still surprised. She wouldn't look him in the eyes as she continued, "You'll spend Christmas here with us. That will give you some time to pack. But you'll be starting at a new school in January. You'll be finishing up your junior year in Los Angeles."

"Mom, no," he stammered. "Please, don't make me live with him. I can't. He hates me."

"He doesn't hate you, Nolan. And really, you haven't given us much of a choice here." She tried to smile, to soften the blow, but her expression looked painful and stitched on. "Maybe you can come back to Bishop after that, for senior year, depending on how everything goes. But maybe you won't even want to. Maybe you'll like it better out there. There'll be more activities and clubs for you to participate in, new people to meet. Not as much free time. Maybe you'll want to stay, and if you do, that's okay." She laid her hand on his cheek. "I just want you to be happy again. I just want my Nolan back."

I'm right here, he would have said, except she wasn't listening. Except it wouldn't have changed her mind.

"This is for the best, okay? Trust me." She had a strange look in her eyes, and that's when Nolan began to notice all the places where someone could hide a camera or a microphone.

Under the eaves, inside the trash can, under a rock, on the other side of the fence, in the bushes along the driveway. So many places. Even his mother could be bugged, a wire strung up the back of her shirt, hooked to her bra. The government, the people Wyatt was working for, they'd gotten to Sandra somehow, too, and now they were using her to find out what he knew, how much information and evidence he had stored away. Worse, they were making her send him away so he could no longer interfere with whatever they were planning next. He backed away from her.

"Nolan, wait." She came after him. "Talk to me. Say something."

He ignored her and fumbled his way back inside the house. She stayed on his heels, demanding he talk to her, though there was nothing more to say. When Nolan reached his bedroom, he closed the door in her face, then leaned against it, trying to sort through his racing thoughts, only managing to work himself into even deeper confusion. His mother? His own mother? How did they get to her? What did they threaten her with that she would turn her back on her own son?

"Nolan?" Sandra tapped on the door. "Can I come in? We're not done talking about this. I need to know that you understand what's happening. Nolan? Say something. I know you can hear me."

"I just want to be alone right now," he said. "Please."

He could hear her breathing through the door.

He told her to go, but he didn't mean it. What he really wanted, what he could barely even admit to himself was this: he wanted her to force her way inside this room, look him in the eyes the way she used to, and say, "I believe you, Nolan. I believe in you." Then they would sit together and she would listen to everything he had to tell her, without judgment, and when he finished, she would tell him he could stay. She wouldn't send him away to Los Angeles, to his father's. They would figure out what to do together. He listened to her quiet breathing and counted off each passing second.

A whole minute went by and he knew that any second—the next one even—he would feel the knob turn against his back and he would step away and let her through. She was going to come through that door any second now. Any second. Another minute passed, then Nolan heard the creak of a floorboard. She was backing away. She was leaving him.

He listened to the soft shuffle of her socks against the wood floor, the quiet thump of a cabinet door closing, a clinking of glasses, the pop of a cork. Then her footsteps again as she retreated into her bedroom with her wine and shut the door. He slid to a heap on the carpet, curled his legs to his chest, and pressed his knees into his eye sockets. It was the only way he knew how to make the whole world disappear.

17

Lucy dreamed of flashing lights and flying saucers. She dreamed Nolan was walking toward a shadowy cave, and when she tried to run after him, her legs melted to sand. She screamed for him to stop, but her words turned to grasshoppers leaping from her wide-open mouth. She woke in a panic, panting and drenched in sweat, trying to separate real from imaginary. She didn't recognize the room she was in. The furniture was sleek and black. The sheets pinstriped blue. She pressed her fingers into the soft gray comforter she'd been sleeping under, trying to recall how she'd come to be tucked beneath it. Then she remembered: getting lost on a dark mountain road, her car breaking down, the drive back to Bishop, all the motels with No Vacancy signs lit.

With nowhere else to go, Lucy drove to Wyatt's. He'd come out of the double-wide before she even had a chance to exit her car. Sandra and Kepler joined him soon after and stood silently, watching her, the relief on her mother's face unmistakable. It was almost one in the morning, and Lucy was exhausted, but she could see they had questions. She started to explain, but

Sandra waved her off, saying they could talk in the morning, they were just glad she was safe. She took Kepler with her to the hangar, and Wyatt led Lucy into the double-wide. He gave up his bed for her, said he'd be fine sleeping on the couch, and then left her alone. She was asleep as soon as her head hit the pillow.

Now she rolled out of bed and wandered into the living room. The couch was unoccupied. A blanket lay in a heap on the floor. Lucy picked it up, folded it, and draped it over the couch arm. Light streamed through the kitchen window. She could see the hangar through it, the door slid half-open. She put on her shoes and went outside. Kepler met her in the yard, a flurry of excited circles, half jumps, and tail wags. She scratched his head. He stayed glued to her side until she entered the hangar and then he trotted to where Sandra was working at her desk in the corner.

Sandra smiled shyly at Lucy. "Wyatt went for coffee." Then she got up, grabbed a folding chair from another part of the room, and brought it over to the desk. "Come see what I'm working on."

The back half of the hangar was a mess of printer-paper boxes, magazines, phone books, and newspapers teetering and sliding in jumbled piles. Some of the boxes had lids, but others were open, papers spilling out, newspaper and magazine clippings, brochures, letters, articles printed off the Internet, typed pages with red notes in the margins. Several of the clippings along with blurry photographs of flying saucers had been tacked to the wall above the computer.

Lucy plucked a piece of paper from one of the open file boxes. It was a page torn from the *National Enquirer*. The headline read in bold: ALIEN SKULLS FOUND ON MARS. In the picture underneath, two oblong skull-like objects lay together on the dusty ground. Rocks or plaster casts, whatever they were made of, to Lucy they were clearly fakes.

Lucy returned the paper to its box and moved to examine a star map hanging on the wall. A circle was drawn around the Andromeda Galaxy, the pencil marks dark and severe. Beside this was a topographical map of Owens Valley, stabbed through with dozens of multicolored thumbtacks in no obvious pattern, crisscrossing from north to south and east to west and back again, a cluttered mess.

"Whenever someone reports strange lights or UFO activity, we mark it on the map," Sandra explained. "See how the most activity seems to be clustered here?" She pointed at a section of the map jammed with pins. "That's the observatory."

Lucy shifted her gaze to a sketch pinned beside the map. It was familiar to her, one of Nolan's comics. She couldn't remember when he'd drawn it or which storyline it followed. It was a single panel with no words. A boy that could have been Nolan stood in the middle of an empty desert in a beam of white light that emanated from a large disc hovering near the top of the page. The boy's right hand was raised, but whether in greeting or fear it was hard to tell.

Sandra seemed about to speak again, but Lucy didn't want to talk about the picture, didn't want to hear how Nolan had left this clue for them, his art turned premonition or whatever it was. She pointed at a CB radio that took up one end of the desk. "Does this thing still work?"

It had once belonged to Robert, but he'd left it behind after the divorce and she and Nolan had claimed it as their own. They didn't know how to use it, but they played with it anyway, turning the knob, scanning the stations but finding only static, pretending the noise came from the stars. Sandra leaned over and flipped the switch. The lights flickered on.

"Who do you talk to?" Lucy asked.

"No one. I just listen." She unplugged a pair of headphones that had been sitting off to one side. Crackling static filled the hangar. Kepler tilted his head and perked his ears toward the sound. They listened for a few minutes to the rising, falling hiss, then Sandra turned the radio off again.

"If your brother's out there, he might be trying to communicate or get a message to us."

"What do you listen for exactly?" Lucy asked.

"Signals. Patterns. Something that doesn't fit with the natural world. Something that doesn't have a rational explanation." She paused. "His voice."

Sandra wasn't the first person to point an antenna toward the stars. SETI researchers had been hunting for abnormal signals and patterns for over fifty years. As a little girl, Lucy imagined herself growing up to be one of them, like Jodi Foster in *Contact*, and she had imagined Nolan with her, the two of them teaming up to search the depths of the universe for signs of intelligent life. A steady pulse on a specific frequency, something clear and straight and meaningful. Something that would stand out from the regular chaos and noise of the universe, something impossibly alien. She told Nolan about her plan once and he laughed at her, saying it was a waste of time and money. Why bother searching the universe when extraterrestrials had already arrived on Earth, had been with us since the beginning? She kept her daydreams to herself after that.

There was a big difference between her mother and SETI, though. SETI had radio telescopes the size of football fields. They could pick up hundreds of channels at once. They had

funding and resources and science behind their projects. With
her minimal equipment and minimal resources, Sandra would
only be able to search a dozen stars, maybe two dozen. Two
dozen out of billions upon billions, and some so far from Earth
that even if there was a signal to be heard, it would never reach
her in time. It was an impossible project sustained by impossible hope.

"I know what you're thinking," Sandra said. "This is crazy.
It's a waste of time. The odds of receiving a message from him
are so improbable, why even bother?" She laid one hand on
top of the radio, protectively. "I'm just not ready to give up on
him."

While Lucy tried to think of something to say in response,
she scanned the rest of the hangar and noticed for the first
time a telescope propped up in the corner. She went over to
it and ran her hands over the shimmering blue shell, touching
her fingers to a large scrape down the side where Nolan had
dropped it once when they were out in the desert.

"You kept it," she said to Sandra, and then bent to look
through the lens. There was nothing to see except a dark blur
of the ceiling.

"You should take it out sometime," Sandra said. "I think
Nolan would be happy knowing it was still getting some use,
that there are still people looking up at the stars. That *you* are
still looking."

Lucy straightened and looked at her mother. "What if you're
wrong? About the . . . the aliens . . . taking Nolan." She felt
weird saying it, but there really was no other way.

"So what if I am?" she said. "Wouldn't it be worse to learn,
after it's too late, that all these years he was alive, waiting for
us to find him?"

Lucy ran her hands over a stack of closed boxes. "But what if you never find him?"

"At least I can take some comfort in the fact that I never stopped trying." After a few seconds of silence, Sandra said, "I never thought I'd see you again and yet here you are. So that means something. To me it does."

Lucy let her gaze again roam over the stacks of papers, the photographs of UFOs, the map on the wall, the unexplained mysteries of the universe.

"Do you want to talk about it?" Sandra asked.

"About what?"

"What happened at Cici's. The things you remembered."

Lucy returned to the desk and sat down in the folding chair next to her mother. She rubbed her thumb across a water stain marring the surface of the wood and avoided Sandra's gaze. "I read somewhere that almost every person alive today can be induced to remember an abduction or UFO experience, whether they've actually had one or not."

Sandra said nothing so Lucy continued, "The tropes are so prevalent in our culture. Aliens are everywhere. In our books, our movies, in advertising. It's so deeply embedded in our subconscious mind that all Cici has to do is ask the right questions, and a 'memory' of an extraterrestrial encounter will surface. It doesn't mean the memories are of a real event though."

"I was there, Lucy," Sandra said. "I heard the things you said to Cici, the way you reacted when you were talking about the light you saw. How can you say that what happened to you wasn't real? It seemed real to me, watching you relive it. Far too real."

"It felt like a bad dream. Only I was awake."

"That's how it was for me too," Sandra said.

"But I can't trust it. I can't know for sure." Lucy glanced at the comic of the boy and the spaceship again, feeling a flutter of panic in her throat. She looked back at her mother before continuing, "Even Cici said that our minds can create false memories, and they'd probably feel just as real and have the same strong emotional response as something that really happened."

Sandra's chair creaked. Under the desk, Kepler sighed.

"Or what about this?" Lucy continued, the words coming slowly as she tried to piece together her scattered thoughts. "What about our subconscious desires for this abduction theory to be reality? We want this to be what happened. We want the alien theory to be right because it's easier for our brains to accept that Nolan is alive in a spaceship somewhere, touring other galaxies with an advanced race of beings. As crazy as that theory is, we like it better than the one that's probably true."

"Which is?"

Lucy stared at the lines crisscrossing her palms. "That something terrible happened out there. That he's gone and not ever coming back. That he, that he died, that he's dead."

Sandra pushed away from the desk, her chair screeching across the concrete floor. Kepler got to his feet too. She went to a tall filing cabinet, opened the top drawer, and began rifling its contents.

"We might always disagree on this, you know," Lucy said. "You and I, we might never be on the same page when it comes to extraterrestrial life, but we are on the same page when it comes to Nolan."

Sandra stopped rummaging.

"We both want to know what happened to him."

Sandra slammed the filing cabinet shut and returned to the desk. She slapped a stack of papers down next to her and moved the mouse, waking the computer screen from sleep. "Does that mean you're going to have another session with Cici?"

"What? No." Lucy focused her attention on the screen, surprised to see a picture she recognized accompanying a new article posted on *Strange Quarterly*.

The picture used to hang on the wall outside her bedroom door. In it she looked to be about seven or eight years old. They'd taken a trip together as a family to the observatory and her mother had made her and Nolan stand together at the base of one of the telescopes. They had their arms around each other. Their grins huge and silly. Her hair was flying off to one side. It had been so windy that day. Sand caught in her hair, her eyes, her teeth. She raised her fingers to her hair now, feeling for something that was no longer there.

Next to this picture was another photo of the fake blue orb. The headline read: UFO PHOTOGRAPH HOAX, BUT MISSING BOY'S FAMILY STILL BELIEVES.

Lucy's throat went suddenly dry. She had to swallow several times before she could finally ask, "What is that?"

"I wanted to tell you about it earlier, but Wyatt said to wait." Sandra scrolled slowly through the rest of the article. "We didn't use your name."

Lucy curled her fingers in her lap, squeezing tight. "Why are you letting him publish this stuff?"

"People deserve to know the truth," Sandra said. "The articles are just the beginning. When the book is finished—"

"Book?" Lucy stared at her in disbelief. "What book? About Nolan? You're writing a book about Nolan?"

Sandra nodded.

"You can't possibly think this is a good idea."

"Wyatt says that a book is the best way to reach more people," Sandra said matter-of-factly. "He says by sharing Nolan's story with the world, we'll be paving the way to a new paradigm. We'll be helping a lot of people who are struggling to make sense of the experiences they've had. People who are struggling the way I struggled. The way you're struggling. You were at the observatory the night he went missing, Lucy. You can't deny that anymore. Now you have to come to terms with what you saw. That's what we're trying to do with this book. We want to help people like you recognize and accept what's really happening."

She reached for Lucy's arm, but Lucy stood and backed away from her. Kepler padded over and pressed his nose into her hand. She pushed him away too.

"I can't believe you're even considering this," she said. "This is a family matter. It's nobody else's business. And these ideas you're spreading, they're worse than useless, they're dangerous."

Sandra's jaw tightened. "The more people who know about Nolan, the more eyes we have on the sky. The more people listening. The more people looking. And maybe someone somewhere will find him."

"Why do you even want this to be real?" Lucy asked, anger rising in her voice. "How could it possibly be any better for him to be abducted? If it is true, who knows what They're doing to him. He might be hurt. At the very least, he's scared."

"Nolan was never scared of Them, so I won't be either." Sandra opened a drawer in her desk and pulled out a stack of papers that Lucy recognized as pages photocopied from Nolan's casebook. The police had kept the original. "He welcomed Them into his life. He wanted this. I have to believe They're benevolent, that They're keeping him safe."

"But what could They possibly still want with him after all this time?" In all the other alien abduction stories Lucy had heard over the years, the ones she sought out and the ones foisted upon her by strangers who thought she cared, every abductee was returned to Earth within hours of their abduction. At most, a few days. "Why haven't They brought him back?"

"What happened to your brother, what's happening even still, it's revolutionary." Sandra spread her fingers across the casebook pages. "It changes everything. Our entire way of thinking about the universe and of being human. I don't know why They're choosing to keep him from us, but I believe it's because he's special in some way, that he is of use to Them. It might be forever beyond our comprehension, but that doesn't mean we have to be afraid. We can embrace this change the way Nolan did. This is how I'm choosing to do that." She gestured to the computer screen. "By moving forward and accepting our new reality. And by sharing my truth with others."

"Wyatt's helping you write it?" Lucy asked.

"It was his idea."

"Of course it was. And I bet he's taking half of whatever you make from this book, too, isn't he?"

"It's not about the money," Sandra said. "We have let fear and uncertainty rule our lives for too long and fooled ourselves into believing that the reality of life on Earth is all there is. But there is more, Lucy. So much more. Your brother understood that. He tried to get us to understand too. Wherever the Visitors are from originally, They are here now, in this space and time. They have chosen to interact with us and you can bury your head in the sand and cover your ears and pretend it's not happening, but that won't change the fact that it *is* happening. They are a part of our reality now."

As Sandra spoke, her voice rose and fell in waves, in a way that reminded Lucy of the street preacher she encountered last year, and of Nolan before he went missing. It was a strange way of talking, marked by passionate devotion and hinting at violence, and it was obvious that nothing Lucy said would change her mother's mind.

"I need some air," she said and walked out of the hangar.

She stood next to the satellite dish and looked up at the milky blue. Dark clouds gathered far off in the distance, but directly above her the sky was clear. The sun warmed her chilled bones. A gentle breeze tugged her hair. On the wind, the scent of rain.

As she stood squinting at nothing, a car pulled into the driveway. A door slammed, footsteps scratched the dirt, the hangar door slid open and shut. Silent again, but for a lonely bird whistling a lonely song. A few more minutes passed, and the hangar door opened again. Wyatt appeared at her elbow holding two cups of coffee and a brown paper bag stained with grease. "Sleep okay?"

"Fine."

"Got you a coffee, black . . ." He handed her one of the cups. "And a ham and cheese croissant."

"I'm a vegetarian." But she took the bag anyway and started walking to her car.

He called after her, "I'm sorry! I should have told you about the book a long time ago."

She stopped, but didn't turn around.

"You deserved to know sooner, and you should have heard it from me. But I'm not sorry for trying to get Nolan's story out there. People need to hear it, Lucy. They need to know they're not alone, that the things they are experiencing have an explanation. They need reassurance that they're not losing their minds."

But what if they were? What if the whole world, all of humanity, every single person, was slowly descending into one grand delusion? Lucy tightened her grip on the paper bag.

"Nolan would want this," Wyatt said. "You know he would."

Finally, she turned to face him. "Why was your business card in Celeste's wallet?"

He looked shocked by the question, and his gaze dropped to the ground, searching the sand for answers.

"Why didn't you go to the police and report her missing too?" Lucy took a step toward him. "Why is no one looking for her?"

He lifted his eyes to hers, his expression shattered. "I fucked up."

"That's it? That's all you have to say about it?"

"I didn't know she was missing, not really," he said. "Not until you found her backpack. This whole time I let myself believe she had made it out, that she was in Hollywood chasing her dreams. I mean, a small a part of me wondered, but . . ." He shook his head. "I took her to the Greyhound station in Lancaster the same day Nolan went missing. She told me she was going to buy a ticket to Santa Monica, that she was going to start over. I have no idea how she got back to town, why she was at your house that night, what she was doing with Nolan. I have no idea. She needed help. I tried to help her."

"And Nolan? Did you try to help him?"

"Of course I did," he said. "That afternoon he came here, to the hangar, ranting all kinds of crazy, and I tried to get him to calm down. I even texted Gabriella and told her to send the police out here to help me. I thought he was going to hurt someone, himself maybe. I thought we could get him into a hospital or something, I don't know. He was pretty far gone, ranting about Celeste and wanting to know what I'd done with her. I should have listened more closely to him. I wish I had. Clearly something more was going on—"

"What time did he leave?" she interrupted.

"What?"

"Your hangar. What time was he here? What time did he leave?"

Wyatt looked confused. "I don't know. Early. It was around noon, I guess. Or a little after. It was still light out. Why?"

"What were you doing later that night?" she asked. "Where were *you* when he went missing?"

As he realized what she was implying, his cheeks paled. "I cared about your brother, Lucy. I still do."

"Because it seems to me like this whole alien abduction theory is a great cover story," she said, hating herself for it even as the words kept coming. "It's awfully convenient, isn't it? And now you've got my mom believing in it too. It's the perfect distraction."

Wyatt shook his head fiercely. "Stop it, Lucy. You know I would never . . . Is this about the book? Because I'm not doing it for the money. I don't care about the money. If we make any, it's all yours. Yours and Sandra's. For bills, living expenses, school, whatever you want to use it for. Pay for a private investigator, I don't care. But know this. I did not hurt Nolan. I was nowhere near the observatory that night and if I was, I would have been there fighting on his side."

He stepped toward her, reaching to cradle her elbow. "Your

brother was extraordinary. He looked at the world, at the universe, and saw limitless possibilities. He saw so much that's invisible to the rest of us and he had so much conviction about it, too. Even as we were telling him over and over that he was wrong, he never backed down from his beliefs. And maybe he took it all too far, or maybe . . . maybe he understood things that none of the rest of us ever will." He let go of her elbow and opened his hands in a half shrug. "Regardless of what happened that night, we all let him down. You, me, your mother. Every one of us did wrong by not believing in him."

The wind picked up. The light shifted, turning gray and then purple as clouds bunched into thick piles overhead, blotting out the sun. Thunder cracked, making Lucy flinch. Lightning flickered. She pressed her fingers to the tattoo on Wyatt's wrist, tracing the outline of the alien's bulging head. She pressed her thumb against its eyes. What was it about these creatures that made her so afraid? This silly little freak of nature. This thing that could not possibly exist. She let her fingers linger, feeling the faint, steady beat of Wyatt's heart thrumming beneath his skin.

"What I don't understand," Lucy said in a low voice, "I mean, if aliens *do* exist. What possible use could we be to them? What wisdom could an infinitely more advanced race of intelligent beings draw from an inferior species with substandard technology who spends their time warring and killing each other over petty differences? Why waste any of their precious time and resources on a race like ours?"

They both stared down at her fingers pressed to his skin, at the alien staring back at them, and then Wyatt said, "We have something They're missing, I suppose."

"Like what? Water? Food? Fossil fuels?"

"Solar energy, maybe. Or maybe it's something more cerebral. Maybe They're trying to understand art and beauty, or the reasons why we love."

Lucy let go of his wrist, and there was another moment of strained silence with the wind gusting small dust devils around their feet.

"I can't stop looking for him." Her voice sounded unfamiliar to her, thick with grief she hadn't allowed herself to feel in so long. "When I moved away from here, it was easy to separate myself and my life from his. I have no memories of the two of us in any other place in the world except this one. And it was just like I went away on this dull adventure and when I returned he'd be here waiting for me. But he's not here. He's nowhere. And logically, I know he's not supposed to be here. I'm not going to turn the corner and see him standing there waiting for me, but I still catch myself looking, holding my breath and crossing my fingers." She was quiet a moment, her gaze flitting over Wyatt's shoulder, watching the storm approach. "Isn't that ridiculous?"

"Not at all." Wyatt took his time, choosing his words carefully. "Maybe somewhere deep in your subconscious mind lies a truth you're not prepared to bring to the surface yet. That feeling you have? Thinking he's going to come around the corner at any moment? Maybe it's there because you know on some instinctual level that Nolan is still alive."

"Zipping around the Andromeda Galaxy with his alien friends?"

"Something like that." Wyatt laughed. "Think about the size of the universe," he said. "Think about the billions upon billions of stars out there. In our galaxy alone there's something like three hundred billion stars. And that's just our galaxy." The excitement began to build in his voice, like a child describing his favorite toy. "There's something like two hundred billion galaxies in the universe and that's just a best guess. We haven't reached the edges of the universe yet. Not even close. It's all still unfolding. So I mean, if you think about it, really think about it . . ." He lifted his free hand and with the tip of a finger, began circling patches of sky at random. "There are all of these unexplored places, so many billions of galaxies, so many billions of stars with orbiting planets, so many billions we have yet to discover. It's hard not to believe there's intelligent life out there. Somewhere."

She asked, "What about the Fermi Paradox?"

He said nothing.

"If intelligent life does exist on other planets, they have had plenty of time to explore and colonize our galaxy and we should see them everywhere," she said, feeling the hard and soft edges of every letter. "But we don't. We don't see them anywhere. So what do you think that means?"

Wyatt smiled. "Have you ever seen a giant squid?".

"Not up close and personal."

"So . . . if you've never seen one, how do you know they exist?"

She rolled her eyes. "Other people have seen them. They've washed up on beaches and scientists have taken samples and run tests. There are pictures and videos and proof . . ."

His expression stopped her.

"No." She shook her head. "No, it's not the same thing."

A timpani drumroll trembled the air. A raindrop struck her cheek. Wyatt hurried to take cover beneath the hangar eaves. When he saw Lucy hadn't followed, he called out, but she stayed where she was with her head tilted back and her eyes open wide.

A black and churning thundercloud unlike anything she'd ever seen before swallowed up every last inch of the blue day sky. It stayed in constant motion, doubling over and then exploding, roiling and angry and looming closer, making it seem like the world was imploding, folding in on itself, like the universe collapsing. Purple lightning flickered in its center. Then the cloud ripped open, drenching her with rain.

18

The three of them came up with the plan together. They all agreed Lucy needed to talk to Patrick again as soon as possible, but it was Wyatt's idea to have them meet at the observatory. "Familiar surroundings can trigger memories," he reminded her. "It's the only thing you haven't tried. And now that we know you were there that night, returning might be exactly what you need to remember the rest of it."

"We don't *know* I was at the observatory," she argued. "We're making an educated guess."

"It seems more likely than not," Wyatt said.

She'd told them about the phone call she made to Nolan pretending to be Celeste, how Patrick confirmed her memory, but then swore vehemently that they'd gone home after, that none of them went to the observatory. But there was also Celeste's backpack to consider and Stuart's conflicting testimony that Lucy came home much too late for Patrick's version of events to be true.

Sandra listened to Lucy's confessions with a pained expression on her face. Afterward, choking back strong emotions, she said, "Oh, Lucy, I should have been there for you. I should have—I'm so sorry." She grabbed Lucy's hand and held on tight.

Wyatt wanted to go with her to the observatory, but Lucy knew that his presence would only send Patrick running in the other direction. If she had any hope of getting him to tell the truth, she needed to go alone.

"Take Kepler, then," Sandra said. The dog's ears perked up, hearing his name. "I don't know how useful he'll be, but it will make me feel better knowing you're not completely on your own out there."

Lucy agreed to take the dog, if only for his good company.

She called Patrick's office, but was told he was unavailable. So she left a message. When after a day he still hadn't returned her call, she sent an email, which he also ignored. She sent a second email, this time threatening to go to the police about the prank phone call and Patrick's involvement unless he agreed to meet her at the observatory to talk. His reply came a few minutes later: Friday, 10pm.

Lucy arrived a half hour before their appointed meeting time and parked her car several yards from the entrance and the giant telescopes rising white and huge and silent behind a sagging barbed-wire fence. An outbuilding hunkered nearly invisible in shadows but for a single lamppost illuminating the front door. A half-moon cast weak light across the desert, giving definition to the shapes of things, but keeping details hidden.

She'd been hesitant about meeting so late, but now she was glad for the dark. It gave her better perspective, a closer connection to the night Nolan went missing than would have been possible in daylight. She parked as close as possible to the exact spot where Nolan's pickup was found. She closed her eyes and tried to imagine him here waiting, what he must have been thinking, how he must have been feeling. A dull ache throbbed the base of her skull.

During the early days of the investigation, Lucy had joined the police, her mother, and a small group of volunteers to search the area surrounding the observatory for clues. It was after they found Nolan's pickup abandoned, after the detective showed them the last entry in his casebook. They formed groups and searched in a grid pattern for any sign of him, but only twenty minutes in Lucy had a migraine so bad her mother drove her to the ER for an MRI. The imaging didn't turn up anything worrisome. Probably just the heat, the doctor had said. Drink plenty of water, rest, and stay out of the sun for a while.

She rubbed the back of her neck, trying to stave off the migraine she knew was coming now. Being in this place brought it on. Partly, she knew it had something to do with her guilty conscience, ten years spent stuffing down the truth. But it felt like something else, too, something specific to this area making her sick. Electromagnetic waves coming off the telescopes, or toxic waste improperly buried in the ground, or maybe she'd simply stumbled upon another Bermuda Fucking Triangle.

Kepler watched her from the passenger seat. His ears were twin telescopes turned in her direction, waiting, listening. His dark brown eyes were alert and soulful. She dug her fingers into the thick fur around his neck. "What do you think, Kep?"

His tail thumped and he spread his lips in a sloppy, sharp-toothed grin. She opened the door and got out of the car. Kepler leaped after her and began making circles in the scrub, nose to the ground, sniffing out jackrabbits.

Lucy stretched her arms over her head and then checked the time on her cell phone. Almost ten o'clock. The road Patrick would take to get here was a long scratch in the sand, disappearing into a black-hole darkness with no edges, no horizon, no dividing line between earth and sky. Death Valley stretched out to forever, and she was balanced there, on the edge of the universe, with all the things known and unknown and yet to know.

Several minutes passed and then headlights appeared in the distance. Tires rumbled over packed dirt. A dark-colored Expedition pulled to a stop behind her car. Patrick didn't get out right away. He sat for another minute, engine running, headlights blinding. Finally, the lights snapped off, the engine shuddered to silence. The driver's door popped open. Patrick stepped out and came toward Lucy. A second later, the passenger door opened and Adam unfolded himself from the cab. He was dressed all in black and positioned himself a few steps behind Patrick, crossing his arms over his puffed-out chest, mimicking a bouncer's stance.

"What's he doing here?" Lucy asked.

"This affects him too," Patrick answered.

Kepler appeared at her side then, leaning his full weight into her legs. His muscles were taut, the fur on his neck raised. A low growl emanated from deep in his throat. Lucy grabbed hold of his collar and the growling ceased.

"What are we doing here, Lucy?" Patrick glared at the dog.

"I remember now," she said, trying to sound confident. "What we did after we called Nolan."

Adam shifted his feet. Patrick arched his eyebrows. "Oh yeah?"

"You lied," she said. "You didn't go home. You came out here. You came to meet him."

"Who told you that?" He shot a cold look toward Adam, who gave a quick shake of his head and tightened his arms around his chest, his biceps popping larger.

Lucy almost laughed. This whole time she'd been doubting what she recalled under hypnosis, but if Adam's reaction was any indication, her memories of that night were very real. Once that sunk in, she wanted to curl into a ball in the dirt and cry.

"No one told me," she said quietly. "I remembered."

Adam snorted a laugh.

"It's true," Lucy insisted.

"Tell us what you remember then," Patrick said.

"It's hard to give specifics," she said. "It keeps coming in bits and flashes, and not all of it, not everything."

They were looking at her with bemused contempt.

"But I remember being here. Over there somewhere." She pointed west, in the direction of the highway at a small rise overlooking the observatory. "And looking down at Nolan, who was here, by the telescopes. And you," she said to Patrick. "You were with him. You both were. You were arguing about something."

"And this memory, it just, what?" Patrick said. "Came to you in a dream or something?"

"No, I was hypnotized." She realized her mistake as soon as the words left her mouth, but she pressed on anyway, driven by a need to make herself understood. "I didn't believe in hypnotherapy before either. I thought it was just some dumb parlor trick, and nothing real could ever surface, but it's not that. It's not like how it is in the movies or in magic shows. The therapist simply brings you to a deeper state of consciousness, a relaxed state, which allows you to remember things that have been locked away in your subconscious because of fear or trauma. And it works. I'm telling you it does. Because I remember that night. I remember what we did."

Patrick's mouth twisted into an ugly smirk, and then he laughed. Looking at Adam, he jerked his thumb toward Lucy. "Can you believe this?"

Adam turned and spat into the sand. "Bitch is crazy. Like her brother."

"Tell me, Lucy." Patrick tilted his head to one side. "What else do you remember from that night now? A bright light? Little green men? A flying saucer coming to take you away?"

Adam made a whistling noise and flitted his hand in the air above his head.

"I didn't think it was possible," Patrick continued. "But Adam's right, you're just as cracked as your brother was."

The knot twisting in Lucy's stomach cinched tighter. She thought about releasing Kepler's collar and letting him fly at Patrick's unprotected throat, but the time to defend Nolan was long past. If she'd wanted to be his hero, she should have done it ten years ago.

"So what if we came out here that night?" Patrick asked. "Now, I'm not admitting to anything. I'm not saying yes, we were here, but for the sake of this conversation, let's say we were. So what?"

"You can tell me what happened to him."

"But you just said you were here that night, too. You're so certain you saw us. So . . ." He spread his arms out in front of him. "Why don't you tell *us* what happened?"

She hadn't been standing close enough to see much or hear what words were exchanged, and then there was a moment of confusion, and then she was running down the opposite side of the small hill she'd been standing on, running away from the observatory, and away from Nolan, but she couldn't remember exactly why.

"Earth to Lucy." Patrick snapped his fingers in her face.

"I don't know what happened," she whispered, defeated. The dull ache at the base of her skull had turned into a crackling fire.

"I know you don't," Patrick said in a soothing tone. "We wouldn't be out here if you did."

He reached out to pat her shoulder. Kepler snarled, and he pulled his hand back.

"Look, Lucy," he said. "We all want to know what happened, but I can't tell you what I don't know."

"You were here," she protested.

He shrugged. "So you say." Then he sighed and rubbed his hand across the back of his neck. "You told me the other day that Celeste was with Nolan that night, so I don't know, maybe they ran away together. They were young and in love, right? So maybe they started new lives in Chicago, changed their names and lived happily ever after."

"But his pickup," Lucy said.

"They left it behind as a decoy so no one would come after them. Or maybe," he continued, "maybe they tried to run away together, but they got caught in a flash flood. There was a big storm that night, remember? A deluge. Record-breaking rainfall. There are a lot of washes around here. It would be easy enough for someone to stumble into one without realizing it. And you know as well as I do how difficult it is to escape a flash flood. By the time you hear the roar, it's too late. The water is already on top of you."

Each new scenario was worse than the last. Each like a knife to the heart, but she let Patrick keep going because some part of her needed to hear them all. She had this idea now that she would know the truth when she heard it. Like the final turn of a safe unlocking, it would all click into place. She would feel it as an electric jolt to her brain. She would just know.

"There are coyotes out here," Patrick said. "Bears. Mountain lions."

"Crazy motherfuckers with guns," Adam added.

Patrick gave him an encouraging look and then said, "Maybe they were hitchhiking. Maybe they got into some psycho's truck and he killed them and tossed their bodies over a cliff. You see how hard it is, Lucy? Without witnesses, without proof, without even a body, it's impossible to say with any kind of certainty what actually happened that night. There are just too many ways for a person to die, and that's assuming he's dead. Because maybe he's not. Maybe he just doesn't want to be found."

Then he got quiet. He stared at the telescopes over her shoulder for a minute. When he looked at her again his eyes were cold obsidian, and she couldn't remember what it was about him that she had once loved so much, what had made her sacrifice everything.

"Or maybe you're right." His voice was low now, a knife at her throat, a gun to her head. "Maybe I *was* here that night. And maybe I beat up Nolan and his stupid bitch and then tied them to a tree and let the buzzards pick their brains. Or maybe I shot them. Bang, bang, one to the back of the head, then buried them somewhere in the desert. Good luck finding their graves."

Lucy trembled. Kepler whined.

A slow smile spread across Patrick's face. "Or maybe it was you."

Her headache was red-hot now. The night smelled like burning hair.

"Maybe you're not the good and loving little sister you thought you were. You were pretty jealous about all the attention he was getting. I mean, that's the way I remember it anyway. And you never did like Celeste very much." He leaned closer to her. "Tell me, Lucy, are those the memories you're having trouble with? The ones you've so conveniently 'blocked'? Was it the trauma of seeing your hand wrapped around a tire iron, your brother's blood all over your clothes, that made you forget? It would make a good defense. You drank a lot, blacked out. You weren't in your right mind. You could plead insanity."

For all the ways Nolan had pissed Lucy off, how easily he got under her skin, he was still her big brother. She still loved him. She would have never hurt him, not like that, not with such calculated intent. And yet, the memory still wouldn't surface. And Patrick was right that she *had* been drinking. And so, maybe . . . She bit down on the inside of her cheek, tasted copper pennies. No, she would never believe that of herself, never.

Patrick gave an exaggerated shrug. "Then again, maybe your mother's right and Nolan was abducted by aliens. Maybe they're experimenting on him as we speak."

He and Adam exchanged a glance, and then he said, "Which story do you like best, Lucy? Because the truth is, whatever we say happened that night is what happened that night. Nolan's not here to tell the real story, neither is Celeste, and you clearly don't remember much. Even if you did, no one would take you seriously once they found out you remembered only after hypnosis."

Kepler began to bark then. Lucy tried to quiet him by tugging on his collar, but he wouldn't stop.

Patrick raised his voice to be heard, "We agreed to say we weren't in the desert that night. We got burgers, we drove around listening to music, and then we went home. That's the story we agreed to, and that's the story I'm going to keep telling. If you suddenly feel the need to tell a different story, be my guest. Just try and remember one thing, okay? Adam and I? We're your alibis. If we go down, so do you."

He seemed on the verge of saying something else, but then he shook his head and gestured to Adam. "Let's get out of here."

Lucy made no effort to stop them. Something to the east had caught her attention. It started as a glint hovering low against the sloped mountain ridge, and at first she thought it was the moon, but the moon was behind her and then the light moved a little closer, growing to the size of a tennis ball and then a basketball, expanding and contracting, growing bright and fading dim, exactly like the light she saw the night her car broke down in the forest. Only there was no thunder tonight, no electrical storm to blame. Then maybe a plane or helicopter. She listened for the sound of a droning engine, but heard only Patrick and Adam walking away from her. Doors slammed. The Expedition revved and peeled out, pulling a sharp U-turn and racing into the dark.

The light grew bigger, brighter, and right above her, a white-hot halo, trapping her in its singular glare. Her head pounded from the intensity of it, yet she could not look away. Kepler barked furiously. She could still feel him at her side, a heavy, warm presence leaning against her knee. Each time he barked, his chest heaved, rocking her a little, and yet his barks were faint, like he was miles away. She flexed her fingers, adjusting her grip on his collar as the light drew even closer, and in that moment the dog bucked, wrenched from her grasp, and sprinted away from her.

She opened her mouth to call him back, but her voice died before it reached her lips. She wanted to run after him, run as fast and as far as she could from this place, but she couldn't move. And it made no sense. She'd had terrible migraines before, ones that made her throw up, ones that made her see double, ones that made her lie in bed for days and groan, but she'd always been able to control her arms and legs. She'd always been able to move, even if it was just to roll over and grab the vomit bucket off the floor.

A vibration trembled the earth, pulsing like she was standing near a bass speaker, feeling music course through her. Only there was no music and no speakers. The light flickered sparks of orange and yellow. She felt it in her chest, her brain, beneath her skin. Sparks of pain. This was the worst migraine of her whole life, and she had a fleeting thought that when it passed— because it would pass, they always did—she must remember to call her doctor. Then another thought, that what was happening was not a migraine at all, but an extraterrestrial encounter and that would explain the strange lethargy she felt, the heaviness in all her limbs, but no, that was impossible, she knew it was, and yet—something moved beyond the light, a figure coming toward her. A thrumming, a thrumming through the earth. Rising, rising into the soles of her feet and trembling her bones. And her head—God, it felt like she was going to split in two from the pain. She tried again to move. Her hand, this time, lifting. Her fingers outstretched. Such a brilliant kaleidoscope of colors. A prism so magnificent she didn't dare blink, didn't dare breathe, for fear of missing all the infinite possibilities cracking open, the universe expanding into eternity.

CASEBOOK ENTRY #7

SIGHTING:
Skyline Road Orb

DATE: December 3–4, 1999

LONGITUDE/LATITUDE: 37.326494 W, 118.538113 N

SYNOPSIS: At 00:00 I woke to a popping, hissing sound which continued without cessation for the duration of the sighting, a total of 12 minutes, 00:01 to 00:12. The craft maneuvered in several ways. Four times it rose to the top of a nearby lamppost, approximately 25 feet off the ground, and hovered a few seconds before descending to approximately 2 feet off the ground. It also moved side to side on three occasions, but appeared to be less stable with this motion. No clear message or pattern detected. No physical or telepathic contact made. At 00:12 the orb went dark. I waited another ten minutes, but it did not reappear.

OBJECT DESCRIPTION: The craft was approximately 3 feet in diameter, slightly larger than our mailbox, smaller than any other craft I've sighted. It emitted a flickering blue light that was very bright, almost white, in the center, but decreased in brightness moving to the outer edges. I was unable to discern any structural elements of the ship due to the lights.

OTHER WITNESS STATEMENTS: No other known witnesses.

WEATHER INFORMATION: 35°F; wind from NNW 11mph; clear; waning crescent moon

LOCATION DESCRIPTION: Orb visible from my bedroom window which faces Skyline Road. Orb hovered at the bottom of our driveway, an estimated 20 yards from the house.

PHYSICAL EVIDENCE: Photographs taken. Film to be developed ASAP.

CONCLUSION: Once the skeptics see these photos they will no longer be able to deny what's happening. They'll see I've been right all along.

Nolan took the 35mm film case from the camera, slipped it into the envelope, and handed it to the girl working at the Walgreens Photo Center. She told him to come back in an hour and disappeared through a door into some back room where he assumed the film would be processed, the photos he'd taken the night before blown up and printed on glossy paper. He was nervous leaving them alone with her, but he didn't know how to develop film or even have the necessary equipment and chemicals to try. He paced in front of the counter and then looked through a spinning rack of greeting cards trying to distract himself. What was taking so long? There were no windows looking into the back room so he couldn't see what the girl was doing. He returned his attention to the greeting cards, straightening them and returning misplaced cards to their original slots.

Last night, when he'd pulled back the curtain, his first

thought was *I wish Lucy and Mom were awake to see this.* But he hadn't gone to wake them, too afraid that the orb would vanish the second he turned his back. Then he remembered his mother's old Nikon. He still had it in his top desk drawer. He moved slowly, not wanting to scare the orb away, opening the drawer, fumbling for the camera, sliding it out of the desk, lifting it to the glass. He took shot after shot, trying to get as many angles as possible. Even after the orb disappeared, he kept taking pictures until the button wouldn't depress anymore and he was certain the roll was finished.

He didn't know if any of the pictures would turn out clear, if they'd show something more than a blurry bit of light, something obviously not of this world, but if they did, he'd finally have something to show them. *See?* he'd say to his mother, his sister, anyone who would listen. *See, I'm not crazy. Something* is *happening to me, to all of us. It's not just in my head.* What had Lucy said? Figments of his freak imagination. *No, Lucy,* he thought. *It's so much more than that.*

He glanced at the clock behind the counter. Only ten minutes had passed.

The man standing in front of the beer case was making Nolan nervous. Everything about him was too clean, too professional. His tie too straight. His suit too black. His hair too slick. His shoes too shiny. His shoulders too straight. His hands too stiff. Men like him with expensive suits and haircuts didn't linger in Bishop, rarely ever came here in the first place. He'd been standing at the beer case for as long as Nolan had been at the photo counter as if he was having trouble deciding. But it was nine o'clock in the morning. Who bought beer at nine o'clock in the morning? Not men who dressed like this one.

The man noticed Nolan noticing him and raised his hand to his ear.

Nolan glanced at the door through which the photo girl had disappeared. A sense of unease crept along his spine. He looked back to the beer case, but the man in the black suit was gone. He rang the bell attached to the counter, but the girl didn't come out. He rang it two more times and stretched his torso over the countertop. "Hello? Excuse me?"

Shadows moved in his peripheral vision. There were two of them now and they looked identical to each other. Same height, same body shape, with matching suits and shoes and slicked-back, walnut-brown hair. Their eyes hidden by dark sunglasses. They moved in unison, their strides the same length, covering the same amount of distance, circling him.

Nolan pushed away from the counter and bolted toward the front door. The men in suits reached for him. A hand caught the back of his shirt. He wrenched from their grasp and kept running, barreling into a woman carrying an armload of socks to the front registers.

"Hey!" she shouted.

The socks tumbled to the floor. Nolan skipped over them.

He glanced over his shoulder. The two men strode after him, covering ground in a way that seemed to defy the laws of physics. No one else in the store paid any attention to the two men. Customers scowled at Nolan as he darted past, and a Walgreens employee came out from behind her register, waving for him to stop, but the two men slipped through the crowd unnoticed.

Nolan burst through the front doors and ran into someone standing on the sidewalk.

"Whoa, there!" The man grabbed him by the shoulders. "Nolan? Is everything all right?"

Nolan blinked up at the man, panic blurring his vision for an instant before he realized it was one of his teachers, his chemistry teacher, Mr. Burdoch. "You have to help me! They're right behind me!"

"Slow down, Nolan. What are you talking about? Who's behind you?"

"The men." He turned his head around, squinting to see into the store. Two tall silhouettes peered at him through the murky glass. "Them, right there! Those two men! They're with the government. They're going to lock me up so I can't tell the world what I know."

"Nolan? What men?" He was staring at the doors, staring right at them. "Why don't you sit down on that bench and catch your breath, okay? We'll call your mother, have her come get you."

Nolan broke free of Mr. Burdoch and sprinted across the parking lot to his pickup. This whole town was against him. Somehow the government had gotten to every single person he knew; there were no safe places anymore. Not here, anyway, not in Bishop. As he climbed into the cab and started the engine, he looked back toward the store. Sunlight reflected off the window glass, making it hard to see clearly, but he was certain something was moving inside that brilliant glare. Two shadow figures shimmering like optical illusions, growing larger as they hurried toward him. His tires squealed as he peeled out of the parking lot.

He drove in circles for an hour, eyes roaming, scanning the road ahead and behind and every side road, too, for a suspicious

car. It would be black or silver. It would have tinted windows
and either a government-issued license plate or no license plate
at all. It would creep around corners. It would stick close to his
bumper. It would try to corral him onto a dead-end street or
run him off the road. He could never go back for those pictures. That girl behind the counter must have been working
with the two men from the beginning. She probably called
them as soon as Nolan walked into the store. Those photos, his
proof—lost to him forever.

Then it happened. Just like he thought it would.

As he passed Bishop's Grocery, a black sedan pulled out from
the parking lot and followed him for about a quarter of a mile.
When he sped up, the black sedan did too. He turned right
onto a side street. So did the black sedan. He blew through two
stop signs and then made a left and then another left and when
he looked in the rearview mirror, the black sedan was nowhere
to be seen. He'd lost them—for now—but he knew that, as
long as he stayed in this town, he could never really be safe.

Nolan pounded his fists on the door for what felt like forever before Gabriella finally answered. She sighed when
she saw him and invited him inside. He raced past her through
the front of the house toward the guest room. Gabriella followed, her steps heavy across the carpet.

"She's gone, dear." There was a hint of sadness to her words;
she had lost someone too.

He had to be sure. He had to know absolutely. He flung
open the guest-room door without knocking. Until this moment when he saw the mattress stripped bare, he'd hoped to
find her here. He went around the room twice, checking the

closet and corners, under the bed, checking every drawer, but nothing here belonged to Celeste. There was no sign she'd been here at all, that she'd even existed.

Nolan stood in the middle of the room and stared up at the ceiling, looking for a crack that hadn't been there before, a stain, a pattern in the spackling, some kind of arrow pointing the way, something for him to follow. The ceiling blurred. A whisper at the back of his mind, growing louder, louder, taking over, but none of the words made sense.

A hand clasped onto his arm. He jumped, winging his elbow and knocking Gabriella in the side of the face. She cried out in surprise and stumbled back from him.

"I'm sorry!" Nolan moved to help her. "I thought you were someone else. I didn't mean to . . ."

Gabriella waved away his apology. The bracelets on her wrist clanged together. She worked her jaw back and forth a few times. "I think I'll be all right. Nothing broken anyway."

"When?" Nolan asked, gesturing to the empty room.

"This morning."

"Did she say anything? Leave a note at least?"

Gabriella offered him a strained smile. "She told me what happened, Nolan. She told me about the casebook going around school, and what you wrote about her."

He didn't want to talk about that again. It had happened. It was over. He couldn't go back in time and change anything. "Did she tell you where she was going?"

Gabriella pinched her lips together. He didn't like the way she was looking at him, like he was the bad guy in this scenario, like he was the one to fear.

"This is important," he pressed. "I have to know she's safe. I have to know she got out and she wasn't just . . ." He couldn't finish, couldn't stand the thought that the men in the dark suits had gotten here before him, that they'd tied her up and stuffed her in an unmarked car and driven her to some secret location, not marked on any map, and then erased all signs of her.

"Just . . . what, Nolan?" Gabriella asked. "What do you think will happen to her?"

Her voice was stiff, and she didn't blink, and he didn't like the way her head was cocked to one side, how her bracelets kept jangling. She always wore so much jewelry. A large medallion around her neck, turquoise earrings in the shape of horseshoes, half her arm covered in gold bangles. So many places to hide a tiny microphone or even a video camera, and with all that jewelry, no one would ever notice.

"Where is she?" Nolan demanded, stepping close to Gabriella.

Even though he towered over her, she didn't back away. She met his gaze and said, "I don't know."

"I think you do." He grabbed her wrists, felt the brittleness of her bones.

Her eyes widened, but she didn't fight him. "Nolan, let me go. You're not yourself right now. You're not thinking straight."

"I'm thinking fine." He loosened his grip, and Gabriella jerked away from him.

She rubbed her wrists. "Wyatt said he talked to you about Celeste. He said he showed you all the paperwork, the proof that she's not a Visitor."

"You talked to Wyatt?"

"We care about you, Nolan. And we want to help you figure this out, but you have to slow down and listen to what we're saying. You have to *let* us help you."

He grabbed her by the shoulders, trying this time to be gentle. "Gabriella, please, when did you talk to Wyatt?"

"This morning," she said, like it wasn't a big deal.

"Before or after Celeste left?"

"Nolan . . ."

"Before or after?" He shook her.

"He came and picked her up."

It was the worst possible scenario he could have imagined. Celeste hadn't just left him, she'd been taken, and not by her own kind, but by the government, whatever entity Wyatt worked for, and hours had passed between then and now and who knew what was happening, where they'd taken her, what they were doing. Nolan barreled past Gabriella toward the front door.

"Nolan, wait!" She chased after him. "It's not like that! It's not what you think!"

He didn't stop to listen. He ran down the porch and jumped into his pickup. As he drove away, he saw Gabriella in his rearview mirror standing in the middle of the driveway, a cell phone pressed to her ear. Her arm stirred the air with urgency, and he knew she was talking to the men in dark suits. They would come for him eventually, and he didn't want to be anywhere near here when they did.

Wyatt was bent over the engine compartment of an ATV, tinkering with something inside, when Nolan barged into the hangar. "Where is she? Where are you hiding her?"

Startled by the disruption, Wyatt grabbed a wrench off the floor and held it over his head, ready to swing, but he lowered it again upon seeing Nolan tearing through the hangar, turning over boxes and kicking aside piles of junk.

"What did you do with her?" A box of discarded machine parts clattered across the floor.

"Nolan, calm down." Wyatt moved toward him, with empty hands outstretched. "What happened? What's wrong?"

"Celeste. You took her." Nolan kicked a pile of grease rags.

"She needed a ride to the bus station in Lancaster."

"Bullshit!"

"She's halfway to Santa Monica by now."

"You're lying! You brought her here and then what?" He scanned the hangar, but there was nowhere she could be hiding. "Then your goons came and got her and took her where?"

"My goons?" Wyatt shook his head. "I have no idea what you're talking about."

Nolan charged Wyatt, grabbed his shirt, and shook him. "I want to know where she is. You tell me where she is."

Wyatt shoved him away. "What the fuck is wrong with you?"

Nolan rushed Wyatt again, who easily sidestepped out of his way this time. Nolan crashed into a metal filing cabinet. The impact was enough to diminish his rage.

He closed his eyes for a second, trying to piece it together, all the things that were coming loose around him. It didn't make sense. She should have been here, but she wasn't, and he didn't know where to look for her next. He fluttered his eyes open. Movement out the open hangar door drew his attention, but it was just a cloud shadow skimming blue across the cracked, taupe-colored earth.

"Listen, Nolan." Wyatt spoke softly. "Celeste told me how upset you were when you found out she was leaving. She asked me to check up on you. I know it's a lot, it sucks. I know you cared about her. But you have to stop thinking that everyone is out to get you." He spread his hands wide in a gesture of peace. "I'm not your enemy."

When Nolan didn't respond, he walked across the hangar to the minifridge. "Want something to drink? Water or soda or something?"

He opened the door and rummaged around inside, pretending to look for drinks, pretending because Nolan could see the cell phone in Wyatt's hand, his thumb moving quickly over the keypad. When he turned around again, though, the cell phone was gone, stuffed back in the fridge behind a carton of milk or something, and the only things in his hands were a soda can and a bottle of water.

"The best thing you can do for yourself right now is forget about her," Wyatt said. "Move on and let her move on too. Let her get on with her own life and you get on with yours."

Nolan refused the drinks that Wyatt offered. He sidestepped toward the hangar door. "I'll find her, you know. Wherever she is, you won't be able to keep her from me."

"You know, Nolan, not everything is a conspiracy. Not every shadow you see is a bad guy coming to get you." Wyatt set both the soda can and water on top of the fridge.

Through the hangar door, a dust cloud rolled on the horizon.

"Some things in life are simple," Wyatt continued. "This is one of those things. I'm not working for any kind of secret government agency. And Celeste is human. I swear to you, on my mother's life. There's nothing, there's *no one*, you need to protect her from. Do you understand what I'm saying, Nolan? Nolan, look at me."

The dust cloud rolled closer. Something flashed in its center, the sun reflecting off glass or some smooth, bright metal. Finally Nolan looked at Wyatt, who smiled as though nothing was wrong.

He never should have come here. Nolan ran out of the hangar.

Wyatt followed him. "What are you going to do?"

Nolan slammed his door closed and started the engine. Wyatt's lips moved, but Nolan couldn't hear what he said through the glass. He stepped on the gas. The pickup lurched forward. He cranked the wheel hard to the left, pulling a tight U-turn. Wyatt waved at him to stop, even stepped in front of the pickup a second before leaping away again when he realized Nolan wasn't stopping.

Whoever was coming up the driveway was halfway to the hangar now. A smudge of black was visible through the dust, a flash of light reflected off a metal grill. Nolan pointed his pickup directly at the approaching car and increased his speed. Twenty miles an hour, twenty-five, thirty, thirty-five. The sedan was all he could see in his windshield now. A black beast with gnashing teeth and wicked red eyes. Nolan would not be the one to slow down, he would not pull over. His pickup was bigger. At the last second, the sedan jerked to the right, bumping off the road, spinning out over the flat plain alongside the driveway. A horn blared. Rocks scattered and pinged against the side of Nolan's pickup.

He kept going, increasing the distance between the two vehicles. For a moment there was nothing but dust, then the cloud cleared and in his rearview mirror he saw brake lights glaring red. He leaned over his steering wheel and pressed the gas pedal to the floor. Behind him, the sedan grew smaller and smaller, becoming little more than a black dot on the horizon before vanishing completely. Even then, Nolan did not slow down.

✦ 19 ✦

Someone shook Lucy's shoulder. A woman asked if she was okay. "Should I call an ambulance?"

Lucy blinked away grit. She was on her back, the stars above partially blocked by whoever was crouched over her. Her tongue felt like sandpaper, her throat as dry and cracked as the earth beneath her. She shivered and tried to sit up, but the woman pushed her back down.

"Lie still. You might have hit your head."

"I think maybe I passed out," Lucy said, though she wasn't sure exactly what had happened.

She moved to sit up again, and the woman sighed, relenting. Hands on her arms, slipping under her back, helping her fight against the heavy weight of gravity. The stars tilted and dropped behind the mountains. Lucy closed her eyes, waiting for the world to stop spinning; it would never stop spinning. She inhaled long, deep breaths. She inhaled and pushed away panic.

"Here." The woman pressed a plastic bottle to her lips. "It's water."

It was like swallowing rocks, but it dampened her mouth

and helped clear the fuzz from her brain. She looked to the east. A land swallowed up in darkness.

"Did you see that light?" she asked.

The woman followed Lucy's gaze. "What light?"

"It came from over there somewhere."

"Sometimes kids drive their ATVs out here."

Lucy remembered only one beam, not two, not headlights, and no engine sounds or tires hushing through the sand. A remnant of pain lingered behind her eyes. She rubbed at a newer, sharper pain in her shoulder. Most likely an injury from falling. She wondered what she would tell her mother and Wyatt when she saw them again, if she would tell them about the light, if she would admit that for a brief moment during the episode she believed Nolan's aliens had returned for her even though she was certain now that what she had seen was nothing more than a migraine-induced hallucination. An aura, a visual disturbance, whatever she called it, the light had come from someplace inside her. The light *was* her.

The woman still had her hands on Lucy's arms. Her fingers were delicate, her touch light. "Are you hurt anywhere? Bleeding? Anything broken?"

"I don't think so," Lucy said, feeling her own hands over her body, touching her face, her head, her neck, and then carefully down her ribs, which were a little sore too.

The woman sat back on her heels. "What are you doing out here anyway?"

Lucy shook her head. She wasn't sure anymore. She'd come out here looking for answers, though more and more she was beginning to think there were none to be found.

"Can I call someone for you?" the woman asked. "I don't think you should be driving anywhere right now."

The woman retrieved Lucy's cell phone from her car and called Wyatt.

"He's on his way," the woman said, handing the phone to Lucy. "Why don't we wait for him in the office where it's warm."

With the woman's help, Lucy got to her feet. She swayed. The woman tightened her arm around Lucy's waist, keeping her upright. The earth heaved and swelled beneath her, breathing and shifting, like time was speeding up, and she could feel it all, the trembling, melting hot core, the anger of the world, the way nothing ever stayed in one place. They were always moving—the plates beneath them shifting farther apart, the earth spinning in its orbit, the galaxy spinning too, and the universe expanding, stretching itself too thin.

Together they walked to a car parked on the side of the road with its engine running. The woman helped Lucy into the passenger seat and shut the door. She steered the car through the gate to the observatory outbuilding. The woman had flowing, dark brown hair to her waist, streaked through with gold. Her skin was dark. Her eyes like agates. She had a soft smile and a keen gaze. She said her name was Allison and she was a research scientist at OVRO, studying the formation of galaxies.

The observatory building was split into several sections. They entered a classroom first, set up with tables and chairs and chalkboards. Then they went through a computer room with blinking lights and wires and too many machines to count. They ended up on the other side of the building in a small break room. Bookshelves lined one wall. Allison guided Lucy to a sagging couch and then disappeared into another room for a few minutes, returning with a fleece blanket.

"So you think you might have passed out?" She wrapped the blanket around Lucy's shoulders.

Lucy pulled the blanket tight. "I don't know. Sometimes I get these bad migraines." She touched her fingers to her temple.

"Epilepsy?" Allison asked, her tone authoritative, yet comforting.

Lucy shook her head. "Not that I know of."

"You'd know," Allison said, the corners of her mouth tugging down. "Make sure you see a doctor as soon as possible, okay? Migraines, fainting, seeing lights . . . you want to get that kind of thing checked out."

Lucy nodded. "Yeah, thanks." And then after a while, "What time is it?"

"Almost midnight."

Lucy hid her surprise. She had talked to Patrick and Adam for twenty minutes maybe. A half hour at the most. Then the light came. Then Allison was waking her up. That space of time between a blank. She shivered again, though she wasn't cold anymore. Then, remembering Kepler, she jolted upright. "There was a dog. I had a dog with me. A big black German shepherd. Did you see him?"

Allison looked concerned. "No, I didn't, I'm sorry."

Lucy felt sick thinking about Kepler out there all alone. She didn't know if he was the kind of dog that could find his way home. She hoped so because she didn't think she could tell her mother that her dog was gone now too. Another thing she loved vanished because of Lucy.

"I'm sure he'll turn up," Allison said reassuringly. She sat on the other end of the couch at a slight angle so she was facing Lucy. "You gave me quite a scare, you know. I was working up on the mountain all day today, at the Cedar Flat site. Finally decided to call it a night around eleven thirty. Then I'm pulling up to the gate and I see your car parked there and I start to freak out. 'Oh God,' I'm thinking. 'Not another one.'" She smiled. "You have no idea how happy I was to see you lying in the middle of the road like that."

"Another one?"

"A few years ago," she started and then squinted off into the middle distance, like she was calculating. "Well, I guess it was more than that. Ten years ago now. I was working out here when a local boy went missing. He parked outside the gate and no one knows what happened to him after that. He just vanished."

Lucy shifted on the couch, sitting forward, slightly closer to Allison.

Noticing her interest, Allison asked, "Do you live around here? Do you remember hearing about that boy? You might have been too young."

"He was my brother."

"God, oh I'm so sorry. I didn't know. Oh . . ." She trailed off, lost in thought.

Somewhere in the room a clock ticked.

When Allison spoke again, her voice was intense, but quiet. "I was here the night he went missing. I wasn't supposed to be. No one was. We were shut down for the winter break, but I was finishing up some last-minute things. What can I say? I'm a workaholic." She laughed a little, though there was a sadness to it. "I've always felt so guilty. I've always wondered if I could have done something. I mean, I was right here."

"You didn't see anything?" Lucy asked. "Hear anything?"

Allison frowned at the floor. "No . . . well, yes, maybe. Some people shouting. Engines revving. A car backfiring. But people come out here all the time. Tourists, hunters, drunks, four-wheelers, bored kids. The desert has a funny way of stretching sound, too. Noise echoes off the mountains. It's not unusual to hear things happening outside. We don't have time to check on every bump and sigh. And like I said, that night, I wasn't even supposed to be here. I was in a hurry and I was . . . the telescopes were acting strange."

She bolted from the couch and disappeared into the computer room, returning a few minutes later with a stack of papers, printouts filled with graphs and numbers and dots and lines and things that made no sense to Lucy. She sat back down and shuffled through them until she found the page she wanted.

"We picked up a pretty interesting signal that night." She jabbed her finger at the paper. "See here, where these numbers switch to letters? There was a surge in signal strength unlike anything we'd ever seen before, and much stronger than any natural radio source we would expect from the section of the sky we were pointed at. I thought the telescopes were malfunctioning, at first, but according to all the diagnostics I ran, everything was working as it should. The signal faded a few seconds later, here." She pointed to where the letters returned to numbers.

"What do you think it was?" Lucy asked.

"It's hard to say. Most likely interference from a satellite or some unidentified military craft or maybe a local transmitter we were unaware of before. We scanned the same patch of sky for a few nights after that, just in case, but never picked up the signal again. So whatever this was, it was a one-time thing. An anomaly."

The date across the top of the paper was December 5, 1999, the day Nolan went missing. The time stamped 12:01 A.M.

Lucy knew what her brother would say if he were here. There is no such thing as coincidence. Everything, every person and event, small or big, every planet, star, and galaxy, every creature, every gust of wind or falling raindrop, all of it, he would say, is interconnected. We may not see or understand the many different ways the threads tangle, but they do. Nothing and no one exists in isolation. The whole universe weaving, conspiring, moving us all toward some grand and meaningful end. Pull on one thread and another one tightens and another one breaks and a new one appears and on and on to infinity. A beautiful serendipity and everyone has a destiny to fulfill and every event is leading up to something else, but Lucy had never been able to fully embrace this notion, however appealing it might be, and she did not imagine herself doing so now. Not even after all that happened. Events took place every day on this planet that appeared to be connected, choreographed by some omniscient life force or creator, but they weren't. It was only our brains making links, tying it all together.

This was what she believed. This was what she would always believe. We are wired to connect the dots, to see patterns. We want all of this—the chaos, the pain, the triumphs, the losses and aches—to be connected. We need it to be. We cannot bear the thought that we are really and truly alone, that none of this means anything. We cannot live inside our own insignificance. So we make connections where none exist. We fill in the blanks with threads of our own making. We believe in impossible things and give shape to the emptiness. We struggle and fight and pray that one day it will all make sense to us. We struggle and fight and pray in vain. The universe has no meaning except for the stories we tell.

"Hey." Allison touched Lucy's knee. "Are you okay?"

"I will be," she said, then handed back the paper, the anomaly, the signal that explained everything and nothing at all.

20

On the drive back to the hangar, Lucy traced her gaze along the shadowed ridge of the mountains. Wyatt snuck glances at her out of the corner of his eye, but said nothing. When they pulled into the driveway, Sandra came running out to meet them. Kepler was close behind, his mouth open in a stupid grin, his tags jingling.

"You're here!" Lucy crouched and buried her face in his soft scruff for a moment before looking up at her mother. "He pulled away from me before I could—" But Sandra shook her head and lifted Lucy to her feet, gathering her up in her arms, squeezing so it hurt to breathe, but Lucy didn't mind. It felt good to be held so tight, anchored to Earth once again.

The four of them went inside the double-wide. They kept all the lights off except the one directly above the kitchen table, a bare bulb spotlight drowning them in sour yellow. Kepler settled himself beneath the table, lying across Lucy's feet like a rug. According to Wyatt, he'd shown up at the hangar door around midnight, scratching to be let inside. Burs tangled his fur and there was a shallow cut on his nose, but otherwise he was unharmed.

"We were worried something terrible had happened to you." Sandra's voice trembled.

"Then Allison called a few minutes later," Wyatt said.

"What happened out there?" Sandra asked.

It was the same question Lucy had been trying to answer for herself ever since Wyatt picked her up from the observatory.

She told them what she remembered, even the parts they already knew and the parts she had never forgotten, starting from that day in July when it all started to fall apart. How worried she had been about Nolan's sudden strange and volatile behavior, how much she missed the old Nolan, but how she was too afraid to say anything. She told them, too, about Patrick, how her crush spiraled too fast into something dark and terrible over which she lost control, how scared she was of losing the only boy she'd ever loved. Even more terrifying, though, was how quickly she lost herself. She told them about stealing the casebook for Patrick, but said that if she'd known he was going to plaster it around the whole school, she would have never done it. She wanted to believe she wouldn't have anyway. She stole the casebook, then it all went to hell.

Nolan exploded in a way that was so out of character. He broke Patrick's nose and got them both expelled, and all the kids at school started teasing her and, worse, ignoring her, and she wanted Nolan to stop obsessing about all his stupid alien stuff and be her brother again. She just wanted him to see how absurd it was, so when Patrick suggested making a fake UFO, she didn't see the harm in it. Only it didn't work the way they thought it would. Nolan didn't even see it, or they thought he didn't. Patrick was disappointed, said he wanted to try something else. Lucy told him how Nolan thought government spies or the FBI or someone was calling the house and hanging up, and after that Patrick kissed her and said he loved her, but he was drunk and didn't mean it, even though at the time she thought he did.

They waited until dark. All of them were drunk, and there was a touch of unreality to the night, everything blurry, every hard edge soft, the air tasted sweet like plums. Lucy did exactly what Patrick told her to do, said exactly what he wanted her to say, and tried not to laugh. If she laughed, she would blow their cover. Somehow Nolan bought it, even though her voice sounded nothing like Celeste's. She could hear how freaked out he was, and for a second she felt bad, but then Patrick was lifting her off her feet, laughing, swinging her around, telling her what a great job she'd done. He pulled her in for a kiss, erasing whatever doubts she had.

She thought that would be it, that the phone call would be enough. They'd drive around, listen to music, maybe she and Patrick could ditch Adam and go somewhere alone. By morning, the phone call would be a distant memory, a funny story to tell at school, maybe she would even tease Nolan about it when they were older and he was himself again. Then Patrick and Adam started talking about actually going out to the observatory to see if Nolan would show up. She tried to talk them out of it. She told them it was a waste of time. Nolan was smarter than that. But they insisted on going, and so she asked them to drop her off at Bishop's Grocery. She would walk home—fuck those guys—but as she stood on the sidewalk watching their taillights shrink and disappear, she started to get an ache in the pit of her stomach remembering the fight at school. The power of Nolan's fists, the blood, the look in Patrick's eyes,

how quickly a friendship disintegrated, how it seemed they
wanted to kill each other that day, how they might have if no
one had stepped in to pull them apart.

Lucy trotted along the side of the highway in the direction
of the observatory. Thunderclouds gathered in the distance.
It was four miles, a little more, long enough for her feet to
start hurting and her T-shirt to be drenched in sweat, before
the telescopes finally came into view. She veered off the pavement and cut through an empty stretch of scrubland until she
reached a small rise where a single tree grew. The only tree
visible for miles. From here, she looked down and saw Nolan's
pickup parked near the gate. Patrick's car was there too. Figures moved in the headlights. Patrick and Adam shoulder to
shoulder facing down Nolan and another person, a girl. Celeste.
Celeste was here. This was all wrong. Nolan knew Celeste was
fine, that she wasn't in trouble or kidnapped by the government, yet he had still come.

At first Lucy didn't get it. Why was he here? Why come
all this way for no reason? Then it was like a hand wrapping
around her throat, all the air squeezed from her at once.

She was the reason.

Nolan was here because he thought Lucy, not Celeste, was
the one in trouble, his sister the one who needed saving.

The three boys were arguing, flinging hands, posturing,
and Celeste tugged on Nolan, trying to pull him away, and
maybe she was saying something too, but Lucy couldn't hear
any words, only faint mutterings across the desert, sound rising
and falling. She raised her arms over her head and waved, but
it was too dark for him to see her from this distance. She tried
to shout his name, but her voice came out strangled and soft.
Patrick and Nolan inched closer to each other and Lucy didn't

like the look of their shoulders, the way their fists were raised. She had to get down there so Nolan would know she was fine. She had to get down there before something bad happened.

She started down the sand dune, struggling to keep her balance, her head spinning and her stomach cramping. If she hadn't had so much to drink earlier, maybe she would have been faster, maybe she wouldn't have stumbled, fallen to her hands and knees. Her eyes were off her brother for less than a minute. Her temples began to throb. She was close to throwing up. Then the light appeared. A flash so bright it lit up the sand around Lucy. Pale fingers gripping pale earth, the whole world reduced to monochrome and fine particles. A flash of light and then a crack shattered the air. Too sharp to be thunder, too loud for a door slamming, it reminded her of Fourth of July fireworks, of a car backfiring, a supersonic jet splitting the sky, and then it was silent again, and dark, and her hands were blurred shapes she hardly recognized. Up on her feet and running again, only somehow she'd gotten turned around and was running up the sand dune now, not down it, away from Nolan, not toward. Running from an inexplicable terror she couldn't name. All she knew, all she remembered, was a feeling of fear, of knowing that the light had something to do with Nolan, that it was dangerous and if he knew she was here, he would tell her to run, run and don't stop running until she was as far away from the observatory as possible.

Her knees burned. Blood dripped into her sock. Tears poured down her cheeks. Eight miles home, the longest she'd ever run in her young life—a distance she didn't even know she was capable of and probably had more to do with adrenaline than skill—eight miles never once looking back. When she found Celeste's backpack in the driveway, terror gripped her again. She didn't want anyone to know where she'd been, what she'd done, what she'd failed to do. She didn't want to be responsible. She hid the backpack in the bushes across the street. But inside the house, she was overcome with guilt for leaving him.

She called the hospital, but the person who answered said Sandra was unavailable, possibly on break or with a patient. *Do you want to leave a message, hon?* No, Lucy said, no, it's okay. She didn't want her mother to worry over nothing. She thought about calling her father, but what could he do from so far away? And the police. She shuddered at the thought of having to explain her drinking to them, to anyone, for that matter. And what would she report anyway? What was the emergency? An ill-planned prank, boys being boys. Already her mind was beginning to seal the events of this night behind thick walls, sweeping them under heavy rugs, pushing them into dark corners without her permission. Already she was starting to forget.

Nolan could take care of himself. He'd be fine. He'd be home soon. She walked in circles around the living room for a while, and then she sat on the couch and tried to watch television, but she couldn't concentrate. Her ears straining for the sound of Nolan's pickup pulling into the driveway, her eyes darting to the front door. Any minute now it would swing open. Any minute he would come inside and scold her for staying up so late. Any minute.

"I fell asleep on the couch waiting for him." Lucy spread her hands across the table. "But when I got up the next morning, I was in my bed. I don't know how I got there, but I was wearing the same clothes from the night before. Only they were torn and bloodied, and my knees were scabbed. I couldn't remember what happened. I couldn't remember anything except

I'd been out drinking with Patrick and Adam. I was so scared about getting in trouble, about getting *Patrick* in trouble. And then when I realized Nolan wasn't home . . ." She shook her head, disappointed at her younger self, sickened by her misplaced loyalties. "I was afraid of being blamed. I was afraid you would never speak to me again."

Sandra cried silently, wiping her tears with the back of her hand. Wyatt left the table and returned with a box of tissues, which he set in front of Sandra. He squeezed her shoulder before sitting back down in his chair.

"I know this probably isn't what you were hoping to hear," Lucy said. "I know it doesn't really explain anything or get us any closer to bringing Nolan home, but it's all I can remember."

But even now, she doubted herself. She knew how unreliable memories could be. Our brains never recording and then replaying our pasts frame by frame. Instead, memories were torn down and rebuilt with each retelling, our histories forever reinvented. And Sandra wasn't helping, reaching across the table, timidly suggesting that maybe it was a screen memory, that maybe if she went back to Cici they might be able to uncover the rest, they might find Nolan somewhere inside the light, but Lucy shook her head. She wanted so much to write her mother a happy ending and fix her broken heart, but she did not have faith enough for that.

"What about this Patrick kid?" Wyatt asked. "Do you think he could have done something to Nolan?"

"No, absolutely not," Sandra answered before Lucy had a chance. "I mean, he and Nolan, they were best friends." But there was doubt in her voice.

"If he did, we have no way of proving it," Lucy said. "Unless Adam comes forward as a witness against Patrick, but even then . . ." She bit down on her lip, not wanting to say what she was thinking in front of her mother. That it would be Adam's word against Patrick's. That without a body, it would be hard to prove a crime had even been committed. Justice demands proof, and they had none.

Wyatt nodded like he understood exactly. "So what now?"

"I have to retract my statement, give the police a new one," Lucy said.

Sandra and Wyatt exchanged a glance.

"It's late." Sandra reached across the table to cover Lucy's hand with her own. "And I think you've had a long enough night already. We can talk about this again in the morning."

"A few more hours won't make much of a difference at this point," Wyatt added.

She didn't fight them. Eventually she would have to call Detective Williams and tell him what she'd done. She'd have to turn over Celeste's backpack and retrace the events of that night, leaving nothing out this time. She didn't know how much trouble she would be in after that, but whatever the consequences, she would accept them. Because Patrick was wrong—what they did that night mattered. They hadn't just been in the wrong place at the wrong time doing something stupid. They'd planned it. They set the whole thing in motion. Nolan was at the observatory because they told him to be there. Whatever happened to Nolan that night, the parts she remembered and the things she never would, she and Patrick and Adam, indirectly or directly, they were the ones responsible. The least Lucy could do for her brother now was tell the whole story, the true story as far as she understood it. Though she doubted it would ever be enough to bring him home.

Lucy got up from the table first, but Sandra refused to let go of her hand. She said, "Whatever happens, Lucy, whatever you decide to do, I'll be there with you. We both will."

Wyatt nodded.

Then Sandra brought Lucy's hand to her lips, a promise sealed.

They went their separate ways after that. Sandra and Kepler to the hangar, Wyatt to the couch again, and Lucy to his bedroom where she lay down on top of the blankets without getting undressed. Her head no longer hurt. There wasn't even a remnant of pain. But she would call the doctor tomorrow and make an appointment just in case. She stared at the ceiling, waiting for sleep she knew would never come. After twenty minutes, she got up and tiptoed to the front door. She waited until she was outside to put on her shoes.

It was a fifteen-minute drive to the Buttermilks, and another fifteen-minute hike to the rock she and Nolan played on as children. It would have taken only five minutes coming from the house on Skyline Road, but that way was barred to her now. She brought along Nolan's telescope and a flashlight, which she didn't turn on, choosing instead to stumble along in the dark until her eyes adjusted. All around boulders lurked like monsters. Lizards or mice or snakes, creatures she couldn't see, skittered away from her feet. Each step taking her deeper into the shadows, farther from the safety of her car.

The path they used as kids was gone now, rubbed out by wind and rain and time, but her feet remembered the way. She picked her way up a hill to the wide, flat rock where she and Nolan once spent hours waiting for UFOs, filling the time by pretending they were traveling through space, saving the universe from black holes and corrupt politicians, zipping through other dimensions and alternate realities. A calm settled over her when she reached the rock and laid her hand flat against its smooth surface. She remembered this place well, and her love for it, too. She unfolded the tripod legs of the telescope and balanced it on top of the rock, then climbed up beside it and pointed the lens at the stars.

It had been a while since she used one, but it didn't take long for her to figure out which knobs focused the lens. She studied the craters of the moon first, marveling at how close it seemed, close enough to brush her fingers through the silver dust. She found Saturn next, its rings little more than thin, bright scratches against the vast darkness, small but visible still, protruding like tiny ears from either side. That was the extent of her sky knowledge. Without Nolan here to point the telescope for her, she had no idea what to look at next. She spent a few minutes swinging the lens back and forth, focusing on faraway pinpoints of light, bringing them an inch closer, making them only slightly brighter. After a while, she sat down on the rock next to the telescope and looked out across the valley instead.

To the south, someone set off fireworks. Bottle rockets streaked in the air and then exploded in a fury of green and gold sizzles and pops. They set off ground fireworks too, barely visible but for the flicker of light against the dark, the thin trail of smoke rising to the stars, the crackle and spark. The fireworks continued for a long time, so long Lucy started to see patterns, imagining the explosions as messages flying through the dark. The fireworks went up and up, and if Nolan were here, he would have built a story for her about a brother and sister elsewhere in the universe, on some distant planet from Earth, another pair looking up at a different night sky and looking down on Earth, seeing the pop and spark of fireworks, even though their weak light couldn't possibly reach that far, couldn't even be seen from the International Space Station, but still Nolan would say that the brother and sister saw the fireworks and for the first time realized they were not and had never been alone.

When the fireworks stopped, Lucy stretched out on her back and stared at the spreading dome of stars above her. The billions upon billions of faraway places. She willed something to happen—for a disc-shaped mass to materialize above her; for whatever craft Nolan claimed to see out here that summer ten years ago to appear now; for the light from the observatory to reveal itself again; for Nolan himself to come walking through the dark and climb onto the rock beside her. Nothing happened.

She opened her eyes as wide as they could go, filling her vision with light. It occurred to her that some of the stars she was looking at now had burned out long before she was even born. They had collapsed, returned to dust, and she was looking upon their ghosts. She blinked. The stars reeled and then returned to their place in the heavens, exactly where they'd been all along, exactly where they would stay long after she was gone.

She remembered something Nolan told her once, how the ancient Greeks made the night sky an immortal resting place for their gods and goddesses, how instead of dying, they lived forever in the stars. She took the flashlight from her pocket and pointed it overhead at an impossibly distant spot in the sky. The faint, white beam was barely strong enough to reach the top of a nearby juniper tree, but Lucy waved it at the stars anyway, in an arc overhead like she was trying to get someone's attention. There was no response.

It bothered her that what happened to Nolan was still a mystery, that there were still so many questions unanswered. There were events she hadn't been a party to, conversations she hadn't heard, missed connections, broken pieces that she would never be able to recover because she'd never had them in the first place. That his story might never have an ending was hardest to accept. Lucy wished for her mother's certainty, or Wyatt's conviction, or even her father's willful ignorance, but all she had was doubt. Yet somehow she had to carry on in spite of this. She had to figure out a way to live inside the not knowing.

Still holding the flashlight high above her, as far as her arm could reach, Lucy turned off the beam and then turned it on again. A burst of bright white, and then dark. Again and again, on and off, alternating between short and long, radiant streams, though there was no pattern to it, the message decipherable only to her: *Greetings from planet Earth. Is anyone out there?*

The stars looked on in silence.

CASEBOOK ENTRY #8

DATE: December 5, 1999

LONGITUDE/LATITUDE: 37.231453 W, 118.282702 N

SYNOPSIS: Midnight and this carefully stitched up reality is coming undone. I don't know what's true anymore, if anything ever was.

OBJECT DESCRIPTION: I believe the things I saw were real, even if no one else does. They are real. For what is reality but a construct of our own minds? Is yours the same as mine the same as Theirs? And must we agree for a thing to be true?

OTHER WITNESS STATEMENTS: Uncle Toby was right: Trust no one.

WEATHER INFORMATION: Thunderheads gathering in the distance. A storm approaches.

LOCATION DESCRIPTION: Back where it all began.

PHYSICAL EVIDENCE: We can spend our whole lives looking and finding and presenting what we've found, and still it won't matter. There will never be proof enough to satisfy the skeptics.

CONCLUSION: This world is too small, the people too weak. I do not belong here, not anymore, not after everything that's happened. I want more from this life; I know there is more.

I'm sorry.

Nolan thought he might like to say good-bye, write his mother and Lucy a note telling them not to worry, but so much time had been wasted already.

He packed only necessities. A change of clothes, a tooth-brush, an unopened box of Wheat Thins, the last two apples in the fridge, his wallet, his casebook, a compass, a map, his tape recorder and the Nikon, and the wad of emergency money his mom kept in a coffee can in the pantry. Two hundred sixty dollars and change plus the five hundred he'd withdrawn from his bank account after leaving Wyatt's—it wasn't much, but it was enough to get him far away from Bishop. He checked the time again. A quarter to eleven.

He pushed aside the front window curtain and looked out onto the street. There were no strange cars parked along the curb, and no one he could see that was watching the house. He kept expecting Lucy to suddenly appear and walk through the front door, ruining everything, but the driveway stayed empty. He glanced at the clock on the wall for what felt like the thousandth time that night. 11:10 P.M. Precious minutes wasted, miles and miles lost.

He didn't know why he kept stalling. Some part of him hoped that if he waited just a little longer Celeste would give him a sign. Lights would appear in the yard, or a beam would come through the ceiling and lift him through the rafters into a shining silver spaceship. He had no idea where Celeste was, but if he was going to do this, if he was going to leave Bishop, the only home he'd ever known, and crisscross the world to find her, then he needed to leave now. Before his mother came home and tried to talk him out of it. Before the men in dark suits showed up on his doorstep and dragged him away.

He grabbed his backpack and headed for the door, but a few steps short, the phone rang. The sudden, harsh clatter made him jump and spin. He dropped his backpack on the floor and answered, "Hello?" But there was only silence on the other end, stretching into eternity. Then a soft click and the rapid beeping of a call disconnected.

He hung up the phone and grabbed his backpack again. The phone rang a second time. He pounced on the receiver. "Hello? Who's there? Hello?" But again, only silence. Again, the call disconnected with a soft click.

Heart pounding, he moved toward the door. He knew what they were trying to do, and he would ignore it when the phone rang a third time. And it did, just as he was reaching for the doorknob, and he let it ring once, twice, three times, then he ran back to the kitchen and lifted the receiver to his ear. He didn't speak. Someone was there, breathing, a quick and panicked sound. He stayed quiet, waiting. A dim glow from streetlamps filtered through the kitchen window. It was never dark anymore at night, not really. People were too afraid of what they could not see. The clock above the stove ticked off the seconds, moving the minute hand closer to midnight. Everything in shades of gray and grayer. Another minute passed and then a voice came through the line, thin and shaking and barely audible, like she was a million miles away, but he knew it was her, knew it the same way he'd known the first night they'd met that she was something more, that their destinies were intertwined.

"Nolan . . . Is that you?"

"Celeste." Saying her name was like releasing a breath he'd been holding for weeks. "Where are you?" She didn't answer right away and he thought he'd lost her again. "Celeste? Are you still there? Celeste!"

He heard whispering in the background, but maybe it was nothing, the rustling of his shirt against the receiver, and then, her voice again, so small and far from him. "Nolan. I'm scared."

"What's going on? Where are you?"

"I don't . . . I . . . I don't know. It's so dark."

He could barely hear her. He pressed the phone harder to his ear.

"These men," she continued, her words coming slow and a little slurred like she'd been drugged with something. "I was walking home and they pulled up next to me in this van and they grabbed me. Tied my hands. Covered my eyes. Gagged me." She let out a sob and it was like a knife twisting in Nolan's chest.

Her voice trembled. "Nolan, please. You have to help me. I think they're going to do something to me. Something terrible. I think they're going to—"

There was a scuffling sound in the background, a muffled scream and then something that sounded like laughter. Then voices talking over one another, hurried words Nolan couldn't understand. He shouted for her, but he couldn't help her, not here, not like this. He heard doors slamming. He had no idea if anyone was listening, but he shouted anyway, "Please, don't hurt her! I'll do anything. What do you want? Please!"

The sounds stopped and then a deep voice spoke into his ear, clear and calm and detached, turning his veins to ice. "Come to the observatory. Wait for us there."

"What do you want?" Nolan repeated. "Why are you doing this?"

Then Celeste was on the phone again and it sounded like she was crying, "Please, Nolan. I'm so afraid. Please. Hurry!"

Another scuffle, then a click and that horrible dial tone, mocking him. Nolan slammed the receiver down and raced out the front door. He tossed his backpack in the truck bed and was going to unlock the driver's door when he saw movement in the shadows at the end of the driveway. Someone stood by the mailbox. The person took a few steps closer, moving into the pale yellow circle cast by the porch light.

Nolan's first thought was that she was an apparition, an astral projection, her spirit come to guide him safely to her. She seemed to be floating, her legs hardly moving, her hair flowing over her shoulders and spreading behind her. Her hiking boots made no sound as she moved toward him. Then she reached his side and he was close enough to smell her coconut shampoo and see the glint of copper in her eyes. Close enough that a piece of her hair fluttered across his arm. She was real. He felt the heat of her breath on his face.

"You're here!" He grabbed her because he still couldn't believe it. Even touching her felt like a dream, like any second she would dissipate, slip through his fingers like fog.

Celeste shifted uncomfortably. "You're hurting me."

He loosened his grip. "I can't believe it. How did you . . . ?

What . . . ?" He was having trouble getting the words to come out right.

"I've been out here for an hour trying to decide whether or not to knock on your door," she said.

"An hour?" He glanced at the street, seeing all the deep pockets of black, all the places a person could hide.

"I didn't want to wake you." She pressed her lips together and took a breath before continuing. "I made it all the way to the Lancaster bus station before I turned around and hitched back here. I thought I could just go, but I can't. Not with how we left things before. I don't want that to be our ending. I can't go until I know you're okay. I needed to see if you were okay." She glanced at his pickup, at the backpack in the bed, the keys in his hand. "Are you going somewhere?"

He leaned close, running his fingers over her face, her arms, checking for cuts and bruises. "I was coming to save you."

"Nolan?" She touched his arm. "Are you okay? What's going on?"

He rubbed his forehead, trying to push away the clouded thoughts, the confusion taking hold. "How did you get away? Did they change their minds? Let you go?"

"Who? What are you talking about?"

"The men who kidnapped you," he said. "They put you in a van. The government. They took you away. You were crying. You were, you were . . ."

"Nolan . . ." She shook her head. Her fingers were still pressed to his arm, like she was trying to draw him back from some far-off place. She looked over his shoulder at the house. "I think maybe we should go inside. I'll wait with you, make some tea. Do you want me to call someone? Your mom? Is Lucy home?"

Something wasn't right. He felt it prickling against the surface of his skin. His toes and fingertips were going numb. He
couldn't catch his breath. He leaned against the hood, the
world spinning too fast under his feet. He tried to fit the pieces
together, but it all kept slipping his grasp.

Without looking up, he said, "That wasn't you on the phone
just now?"

"I don't know what you're talking about," she said. "I already told you, I've been pacing for like an hour trying to
decide whether to come up and knock on the door or not."

He lifted his eyes to hers and knew she was telling the truth.

"Nolan, please, you're scaring me. What's going on?" She
took his hand. "I didn't mean to surprise you like this, it's just
I was thinking about us and how we clicked so perfectly and
the ways you were there for me when no one else was, and how
maybe now it's my turn to be there for you. I shouldn't have
run, but I was afraid. I didn't know if I could handle—"

"Shut up." He jerked his hand from hers.

"Nolan, I'm sorry. But I'm here now and—"

"Shut up!" He pressed his fingers to his temples again. "Just
shut up and let me think for a second."

He'd made a mistake, that much was clear. He'd wanted it to
be Celeste on the phone and so it was Celeste's voice he heard.
He'd been so caught up thinking about her, so concerned about
her well-being, that he'd never asked for proof, and going
over the conversation again, he realized the truth with growing horror. He stared over his shoulder at the dark and empty
house, sick with shame over his carelessness and inattention. It
wasn't Celeste on the phone. The men hadn't known where she
was. This whole time, she'd been safe in Lancaster, on her way
to someplace else, somewhere she couldn't be found, but she'd

come back for him, and he wished she hadn't, wished she'd never walked out of that alley with her stupid map and starlight eyes, wished he'd never met her. Then he wouldn't be in this mess. None of them would.

"Get in the truck." He grabbed Celeste and dragged her to the passenger side.

"What are you doing? Let me go." She fought against him, slapping at his chest and shoulders, trying to wrench from his grasp. "Nolan, stop! Tell me what's going on!"

"I'm sorry, Celeste. I'm sorry. It's Lucy. They have Lucy."

Her voice on the phone so small and far away and he should have known it was her. If he'd been paying any attention at all, if he hadn't been so caught up in his own ego, thinking he was part of some Grand Destiny, that the stars had plans for him. The stars were indifferent. Destiny was a winding path built on your own small choices.

"Who has Lucy?" Celeste continued to struggle. "Should we call the police?"

"Just get in the truck, Celeste."

But she wouldn't. She beat her fist against him until he twisted her arm behind her back. She froze. Her shouts turned to whimpers.

"I don't want to hurt you," he said, pressing his mouth close to her ear. "But they've given me no other choice, do you understand?"

Celeste nodded and climbed in. He shut the door and climbed in on the driver's side. He felt her staring at him, felt her trembling. He stuck the keys in the ignition and revved the engine.

"Nolan, please."

He wanted to reassure her, but there was nothing to say. He

had turned betrayer, and it didn't matter what she said now or how many tears she cried, he wouldn't change his mind. He backed out of the driveway, tires squealing, and tore off toward the highway.

"Buckle your seat belt," he said.

"Where are we going?" Celeste whispered. "Why are you doing this? Nolan, talk to me."

She started to cry and apologize. For what he didn't know. She'd done nothing wrong except be herself. She'd done nothing but be exceptional. He hoped that when the men in dark suits took her, they recognized her true worth. He hoped that, whatever they did, she wouldn't be in pain for too long.

"I won't call the police or anything," she said. "Just stop the truck and let me out right here. Just let me go, Nolan, okay? I won't tell anyone."

He drove faster, blowing through stop signs and red lights when the intersections were clear. He'd been stupid, thinking Lucy was safe. The government wanted Celeste, and would use any means to get to her. He should have seen this coming.

Lightning split the sky to the east and Celeste flinched at the bright flash. Tears streaked her face and for a second he saw his own terror reflected there, his failures, his missteps, all the ways he'd let this go too far, all the ways he could have stopped it from ever happening. There were so many obvious signs, but he'd been blind to them. Worse, for a second, he thought maybe he had gotten it all wrong. There were no men in dark suits, no UFOs, no extraterrestrials, and Wyatt was right, Celeste was not his Star Being, but a normal human, and whatever that phone call had been, it was nothing, Lucy was fine and would be home soon and there was still time. He could turn around, retrace his steps back to the beginning, fix the mess he'd made. But then the cab descended into shadow again, and he remembered how scared Lucy sounded on the phone, the way she screamed. He thought about the men at Walgreens, how quickly they moved, with panther-like stealth. They were smarter than him, stronger, better prepared, and given the chance, they could take away everything and everyone he'd ever loved. He pressed down on the gas pedal, urging his pickup faster. Celeste let slip a single, damp sob, and then clamped her hand over her mouth. Maybe, if he had just a little more time, he could think of a way to save them both.

Storm clouds chased them, roiling and churning overhead, smothering the stars. Thunder cracked. Through the partially open windows came the peppery tang of sage, the scent of coming rain. Then and suddenly, the telescopes appeared on the horizon, rising ever taller, gleaming white giants, beckoning, showing him the way, guiding him through the dark.

When Lucy was eight and Nolan ten, they got a set of walkie-talkies for Christmas. They tore into the packaging and immediately took them outside, even though there were other presents waiting to be opened. Their mother shouted at them to bring their coats, but they ignored her. Nolan went to the backyard, Lucy to the front.

"We're on different planets." Nolan's voice crackled through the walkie-talkie speaker. "I'm on planet Magellan and you're on planet Degas."

Made-up planets with made-up names, planets that had yet to be discovered.

A light dusting of snow had fallen overnight. The driveway and street were white and shining. The whole outside world unfamiliar and new. The light, too, had changed. Everything etched in silver. Lucy shivered in the frozen grass, her breath rising in white ribbons. She had left Earth. She was the first girl—the first human—to set foot on this strange new planet where anything was possible.

Nolan's voice crackled again as he began to describe the

planet he was on. "Everything's backwards. The sky is green. The grass is blue. The cats bark. The dogs meow."

Lucy laughed, but she hadn't pushed the walkie-talkie button, and Nolan didn't hear her. She was adrift, floating through space, light-years away from him.

"What's it like where you're at, Asteroid Girl? Any signs of life?"

She pressed the button this time, but waited a few seconds before talking, letting the silence expand and fill her chest with want. Then she held the walkie-talkie to her mouth and whispered, "I'm all alone out here, Starman."

She released the button. Static hissed and it seemed forever before there was a click and Nolan's voice reached her. "I'm entering your coordinates into my navigation system. Hang tight, Asteroid Girl. I'm coming to get you."

A few seconds later, he came around the corner of the house and chucked a pitiful snowball at her back. She squealed as a cold blast of ice spilled down her shirt, then bent and scooped up a handful of snow, but it was too soft and wouldn't hold its shape. She threw it anyway, silver flakes spraying, twinkling on their descent back to Earth.

This is the illusion of time, and the heartbreak: that an event occurring over seventeen years ago can feel so much like yesterday, that a decade can pass within the span of a single breath, another year gone in the blink of an eye. Eleven years and three months missing and if anyone were to ask, Lucy would say she doesn't think Nolan is coming back. No one asks.

She is enrolled at UC Berkeley now. Her father pays her tuition. He may not understand her sudden interest in stars and space and the complexities of the universe, but to him a planetary science degree is better than living out of her car, wiping down tables at a café, taking breakfast orders, chasing down her mother's crazy fantasies. Better than mooching off him for the rest of her life. And this is something he can tell his friends over dinner—my daughter, the scientist—something he can say with pride.

She isn't a scientist quite yet, but she's getting there. Slowly. She's spent most of the last year catching up on general education classes. Math and science, all the things she only half-paid attention to in high school. Most of the time she feels like she's barely keeping up, but when grades come in, she gets Bs and As and this is good enough for a summer internship at the SETI Institute working with researchers at the Allen Telescope Array.

Most of the students in her classes are younger, fresh out of high school, and most have no idea what they want to do with the rest of their lives, let alone what they want their majors to be. But Lucy applied to Berkeley specifically for the astronomy program and a chance to work with Dr. Brandon Shipley, a leading researcher in the search for extraterrestrial intelligence. She found his office on the first day of class and introduced herself. He asked her about her interest in SETI. "Why not some other field? Something a little less disappointing?"

She countered with a question of her own. "Do you believe there's intelligent life out there somewhere trying to communicate with us?"

He thought about it a moment before answering, "I don't think it matters whether I believe or not. There either is or there isn't. We'll either find them or we won't. It's the search that's interesting. What about you, Lucy Durant? What do you believe?"

"We're alone in the universe. Very much alone." Then she

added, "But if I'm wrong, if there is something else out there, someone else, I want to be the first to know."

He shook her hand and invited her for a tour of the Hat Creek Observatory, which was where she learned about the internship and what her plans for the summer would be. By some stroke of luck, they approved her application, and now she's here, working with some of the best planetary scientists and astrobiologists in the country, in the world even. She spends her days and nights alongside them, hunting the stars for a miracle.

A total of forty-two radio telescopes make up the array. They are much smaller than the ones in Owens Valley, but can be paired up, or all linked together to mimic a single giant telescope with a narrowly focused beam and better resolution. Every evening after dinner, Lucy goes for a run, circling the perimeter of campus and finishing in the very center of the array, where she waits for the stars to appear. The telescopes operate all day and will continue into the night. Unlike optical telescopes, they do not need the dark to see. They make a low humming sound as they make small adjustments, correcting for Earth's continuous orbit.

Sometimes they point toward planets discovered by the Kepler space telescope. Other times they listen to "hab stars," stellar systems less than 1,000 light-years from Earth that show characteristics of being suitable for life. Tonight they are tilted at a sharp angle observing a small region near the center of the Milky Way. At all times they collect data, looking for signals, specifically artificial ones that can only be coming from an extraterrestrial, intelligent life-form. So far nothing conclusive has been found, but the search continues, and now Lucy is an active part of it.

The day after meeting Patrick at the observatory, seeing the strange light, and remembering all she was going to remember about the night Nolan went missing, Lucy went to the sheriff's office. Sandra came with her. Breaking her blood oath to Patrick and Adam, Lucy told Detective Williams about the phone call and what she'd seen at the observatory, what she'd heard, and how scared she'd been, how she'd fled, how the last time she saw Nolan, he was still very much alive, but now she couldn't be sure. She turned over Celeste's backpack, too. It belonged to the person Stuart Tomlinson had seen with Nolan, to a girl who went missing that night, too. A girl who was more than a girl in Nolan's mind. Detective Williams was less than pleased it took Lucy this long to come forward, but he let her go with a warning in exchange for her full cooperation on the case. Whatever he wants, she'll do it—wear a wire, identify a body, testify against a boy she once loved— whatever it takes to bring Nolan home. So far he hasn't asked her to do anything, but when the day comes, if it ever does, she'll be ready.

Patrick sent Lucy several emails shortly after she told Detective Williams the truth. He raged, he pleaded, he threatened, he wrote: I can't believe you betrayed me like this. I thought you cared about me, I thought we were friends. I will make your life a living hell. She wrote back only once: If you didn't do anything wrong, then you have nothing to worry about. Now anything that comes from him she sends straight to the trash folder without reading.

She returned to Los Angeles before the fifteenth and her landlord grudgingly handed over the studio apartment keys where she lived out her six-month lease, working full-time for one of her father's business associates and taking general education classes at the community college while applying for and then waiting to hear back from Berkeley. Once accepted, she packed her things again and moved north to be near the university. Even though she hasn't had any migraines since leaving Bishop, she followed up with her doctor who took her blood and ordered an MRI and ultimately found nothing. On paper she is a healthy twenty-four-year-old woman and the only conclusion her doctor can offer is that the migraines were stress-induced.

She lies awake some nights thinking of all the things she would do differently if she could go back to the year Nolan went missing. She would have never gotten involved with Patrick in the first place. And she would have paid more attention to Nolan before things got so out of control; listened, really listened; accepted him for who he was; she would have loved him more, loved him better; she would have tried to believe—maybe that would have been enough, but maybe not. Maybe nothing on this Earth could have kept him here.

She calls Detective Williams once a month to find out if there have been any new developments and to make sure her brother's case stays a priority. She loves her mother, but she will never believe as Sandra does, and will continue to look for answers elsewhere. It would be easier to believe. In Sandra's mind, Nolan is still alive and there is comfort in that, and Lucy has seen her fair share of high strangeness, events that—for the moment—defy rational explanation, but as long as other, more terrestrial, possibilities exist, she will forever remain a skeptic.

Tomorrow Lucy will see her mother and Wyatt for the first time in almost six months. The two of them are attending a UFO festival in San Francisco this weekend, but first want to come by and take a tour of the observatory. She's nervous about seeing them both and about introducing them to her colleagues and peers. *This is my mother*, she imagines herself saying. *This is my mother who believes.*

She spent the winter break in Bishop trying to piece together a relationship with Sandra from the shards of what they had before, but nothing fit. Too much has gone missing. So they are starting over from scratch and discovering they have very little in common, but Sandra is trying and that means something to Lucy. They are both trying. They talk on the phone once or twice a week, about what Lucy's studying in school and about sightings people have reported to Sandra and Wyatt. They circle around each other, careful with their still-tender scars, and they try. Sometimes Sandra emails Lucy articles that she or Wyatt has written and Lucy offers her feedback, ways this idea or that sentence could be improved, but even though it's been suggested dozens of times, she refuses to have her name added to the byline. No one in the scientific community will take her seriously if they think she's mixed up in ufology, and she wants to be taken seriously.

Sandra and Wyatt both agree that Lucy's experiences at the observatory are hers to share if she so chooses, not theirs. They write now about the things Sandra witnessed, the general high strangeness surrounding Nolan's vanishing, and the things he wrote about in his casebook. They speculate theories and press the government for answers. Strangers write letters, sometimes angry, sometimes kind, but they comb through every one, looking for anyone who may have seen Nolan in the past eleven years and three months, either here on Earth or in some cylindrical space room with flashing lights, curved walls, and zero gravity. Everywhere they go, they search for definitive proof, they collect stories, build their case, and offer comfort to those who need it.

Lucy thinks they're wasting their time, but then she steps out into a night like this one, the sky shimmering like so much broken glass. Nights like this, the space above so dark and clear and drenched in stars, nights like this that make her wonder. From where she stands now only a small fraction of the universe is visible; from anywhere on Earth this is true. The universe is so much bigger than anyone can ever hope to see in their lifetime, let alone begin to understand. Even with the powerful telescopes SETI uses, the many frequencies they are optimized to search, they are only listening to a small fraction of what's actually there, only seeing a brief and eclipsing moment.

A pinprick of light appears above her and begins a slow arc across the sky. It grows bright and brighter, then flashes and goes dark. It continues this same pattern of bright to brighter to dark, moving toward the eastern horizon. It's only a satellite, but alone out here, surrounded by all this space, so huge and incomprehensible, Lucy understands how a person can believe it's something else entirely, something not of this world.

She watches the satellite disappear behind a ridge. Behind her, the telescopes whirr and begin to shift, moving like synchronized dancers, a few inches to the left and then back to their original positions, making small adjustments, fine-tuning themselves to better capture the universe's extraordinary secrets.

They are listening all the time. Every minute, every hour, but even with a million of these telescopes, they would never be powerful enough to reveal all the hidden places of the universe. Deep space and dark matter, all the stars and planets and galaxies, light-years upon light-years away, too far for us to detect, all of it spinning past unnoticed. Yet as futile as it seems, new discoveries are made every day and humanity's understanding of space and life grows exponentially with each find, and given enough time, Lucy thinks, maybe the impossible will happen. The night sky is vast, the stars infinite, and so, too, her hope.

Acknowledgments

This book was a challenge to write. I wanted to quit on it more than once. More than once, I almost did. My thanks to the following people who wouldn't let me:

Julia Kenny, whose enthusiasm for my spark of an idea got me started and kept me going.

Caroline Starr Rose, dear and patient friend, who always knows exactly what to say.

Alisa Callos and Alicia Atalla-Mei, earliest readers who encouraged me to keep digging for the real story.

Ryan Geary, without whom I would have fallen to pieces. Love to infinity.

Thanks are also owed to those who helped with research. Deputy Coroner Investigator Adrianna Butler, who was not afraid to discuss dead bodies with me and proved to be an excellent resource on missing persons. Keith Rowell and Oregon MUFON, for welcoming a skeptic into your group and letting me ask as many questions as I wanted. The research scientists and grad students working at the now-decommissioned CARMA Observatory, who were kind enough to give me a tour and chat at length about the stars. Any errors of fact are completely my own. The Owens Valley Radio Observatory in this book is loosely based on a real place that does real scientific research and offers tours to the curious public on the first Monday of every month.

Finally, and with wild enthusiasm, I must thank the fantastic team at William Morrow, hardworking people who have again taken my jumble of words and turned it into this beautiful thing called a book to be delivered into the hands of wonderfully voracious readers. Special thanks and a shooting star to Emily Krump, for jumping in with both feet and helping me wrangle this strange collection of pages into a book that I am finally proud of. I feel incredibly fortunate to be surrounded and supported by so many people who love books as much as I do. Thank you to the moon and back!

About the author

About the book

Read on . . .

Insights,
Interviews
& More . . .

Meet Valerie Geary

Caitlin A. Doughty

VALERIE GEARY is the author of *Crooked River*, a finalist for the Ken Kesey Award. Her short stories have been published in The Rumpus and *Day One*. She lives in Portland, Oregon, with her family. ✑

The Story Behind
Everything We Lost

I am a skeptic in a family of believers. My paternal grandparents were Evangelical missionaries in Senegal, my grandfather a reverend. My maternal grandfather was also a reverend. Go even further back in my family tree and you'll find more clergy, more believers. I was raised by conservative Evangelical parents, regularly attended a conservative Baptist church, studied at a Pentecostal university. I grew up believing in angels and demons, in heaven and hell, in a man who was also God, who was born of a virgin and performed miracles, who died for my sins and was resurrected and carried up to heaven to sit at the right hand of the Father. I grew up believing I was *in* this world, but not *of.* I was separate, I was saved. I was meant for greater things.

I didn't set out to write a book about belief. When I started *Everything We Lost*, I was just coming off an *X-Files* binge. I wanted to write a book about aliens, but the words I set down on the page were emotionless and disconnected, and the characters sounded plain crazy. I couldn't get the plot right either. So I began to research ufology, which is the study of UFO-related phenomena. I talked to people who believed they'd been abducted. I read books written by ufologists and debunkers alike. I ▸

The Story Behind *Everything We Lost*
(*continued*)

listened with an open mind, and what surprised me was how familiar it all sounded. Faith is faith, however unique the tenets. That's when I realized just how deeply personal this book was going to be, and that's when I almost set it aside. I didn't think I was ready to take on something that, for me, has always been incredibly complicated and fraught with difficult emotions.

The religion I grew up with taught me that nonbelievers are sinners, souls that need saving. At a very young age, I was tasked with bringing my friends to Jesus. I invited them to church. I told them about heaven and how if they didn't pray a certain prayer, they were most definitely going to hell. I believed with my whole being that my purpose on this planet was to be a solider for Christ, to save as many lost souls as possible. I trained, I prayed, I wrapped myself up in these beliefs. I lost myself in them. They became everything. They defined me. My friends stopped hanging out with me; I pushed them away. I told myself I didn't need anyone but Jesus. Isolation as penance, a burden to bear, the price of heaven. Like Nolan, I chose to be outside the mainstream, outside normal. And like Nolan, my beliefs came with a cost.

When I was in my early twenties, my faith was radically shaken after my mom died unexpectedly from a pulmonary embolism. Overwhelmed by grief, I began questioning every belief to which

I once clung so tightly. The power of prayer, absolute truth, the idea that God had some great Plan for my life, that everything happens for a reason. None of that made sense anymore. Life began to feel more like chaos and chance and collisions. It was then that I stepped out of my religious garb and donned the clothes of an agnostic. I stopped pretending to know everything and accepted the simple fact that I knew nothing. I spread my arms wide to the world and found it more strange and more beautiful than I ever thought it could be. Like Lucy, I questioned everything and embraced mystery. But this too comes with a cost.

This is hard for me to write about. Faith and belief—it's so personal. There are people in my life who still believe, who are saddened by my disbelief. On some level, I wrote *Everything We Lost* for them. But I also wrote this book for myself, and others like me, who are trying to figure out how to navigate life with one foot in both worlds: as believers, as skeptics. Is it possible to be both? I honestly don't know. Not every question has an answer. But that doesn't mean we should stop searching. ◠

Questions for Discussion

1. We are presented with two alternating narratives: Lucy, in the present, and Nolan, in the past. What impact does this dual narration have on the story?

2. Nolan's point of view always begins with an entry from his personal journal, documenting his sightings of extraterrestrial activity. How do these entries illuminate Nolan's character? Do they affect your interpretation of any of the events in the novel?

3. In flashbacks, we see Nolan and Lucy's relationship change over time. How does their dynamic shift? How much of a role do their friends play in their relationship? To what extent, is this true of all relationships?

4. Think about the character of Celeste. How does your impression of her change throughout the book?

5. We see Lucy and Nolan's mother, Sandra, in flashbacks and in the present. How has Sandra changed after the disappearance of her son? Why has she reacted in this way?

6. Think about Lucy's relationships with each of her parents. How do Sandra and Robert express their love for their children? Do you empathize with one parent's approach more than the other's? Why or why not?

7. Lucy lived for many years with the secret that she had played a hoax on her brother. Why did she wait so long to tell the truth about what she'd done? If she had confessed earlier, would anything have changed?

8. What was your impression of Wyatt in the beginning of the novel, and at the end? What do you think his motivations were for his involvement in the Durants' lives?

9. At the end of the novel, Lucy has made peace with her family's claims about extraterrestrial life. Were you surprised by the way Lucy comes to terms with what happened that night? Do you think she is a believer now?

10. Every character has their own answer to what happened the night of Nolan's disappearance. Who do you think was telling the truth? Why?

11. Do you consider Lucy and Nolan to be unreliable narrators? How much of their point of view do you believe? How did this change throughout the story? ᴄᴡ

More from Valerie Geary

CROOKED RIVER

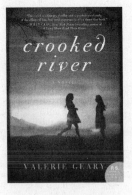

With the inventiveness and emotional power of *Promise Not to Tell*, *The Death of Bees*, and *After Her*, a powerful literary debut about family and friendship, good and evil, grief and forgiveness

He is not evil. I am not good.

We are the same: broken and put back together again.

Still grieving the sudden death of their mother, Sam McAlister and her younger sister, Ollie, move from the comforts of Eugene to rural Oregon to live in a meadow in a teepee under the stars with Bear, their beekeeper father. But soon after they arrive, a young woman is found dead floating in Crooked River, and the police arrest their eccentric father for the murder.

Fifteen-year-old Sam knows that Bear is not a killer, even though the evidence points to his guilt. Unwilling to accept that her father could have hurt anyone, Sam embarks on a desperate hunt to save him and keep her damaged family together.

I see things no one else does.

I see them there and wish I didn't. I want to tell and can't.

Ollie, too, knows that Bear is innocent. The Shimmering have told her so. One followed her home from her mom's funeral and refuses to leave. Now, another is following Sam. Both spirits warn Ollie: the real killer is out there, closer and more dangerous than either girl can imagine.

Told in Sam's and Ollie's vibrant voices, *Crooked River* is a family story, a coming-of-age story, a ghost story, and a psychological mystery that will touch readers' hearts and keep them gripped until the final thrilling page. ▶

More from Valerie Geary *(continued)*

Praise for *Crooked River*

"*Crooked River* is an ambitious debut with a beautiful soul. Geary's dark pen is lyrical and tender, boasting clever dialogue and provocative prose."
—Lisa O'Donnell, bestselling author of *The Death of Bees*

"An absorbing mystery." —*Library Journal*

"A swift and beguiling read. . . . [Sam] is finely drawn, an update on Harper Lee's Scout." —*BookPage*

"[Valerie Geary] captures her readers at once and doesn't let them go."
—Oklahoma City *Oklahoman*